Serpent Moon

C. T. ADAMS
and CATHY CLAMP

TOR®

paranormal romance

A TOM DOHERTY ASSOCIATES BOOK
NEW YORK

This is a work of fiction. All of the characters, organizations, and events portrayed in this novel are either products of the authors' imaginations, or are used fictitiously.

SERPENT MOON

A Tor Book
Published by Tom Doherty Associates, LLC
175 Fifth Avenue
New York, NY 10010

www.tor-forge.com

Tor® is a registered trademark of Tom Doherty Associates, LLC.

ISBN 978-0-7653-6425-8

First Edition: March 2010

Printed in the United States of America

0 9 8 7 6 5 4 3 2 1

DEDICATION and ACKNOWLEDGMENTS

First and always, we would like to thank Cathy's husband, Don, and Cie's son, James, for unstinting support and for believing in us. Also to our wonderful agent, Merrilee Heifetz, her able assistant, our terrific editor(s), and the throng of other folks who help bring a book from the idea stage to actual written words on the page. Special thanks to our friends and family, and the other writers who offer understanding when we need it.

Last, but not least, thanks to you, the readers, for coming along for the ride. We hope you enjoy reading these books as much as we enjoy writing them.

TO OUR READERS

Many readers have requested that we tell the story of particular secondary characters. Holly Sanchez, the best friend of Catherine Turner, is one who has received a lot of votes. Holly has had a hard life, much of which was detailed in *Howling Moon*.

Eric Thompson will be brand-new to readers. While in our minds, there was always a Canadian wolf pack (just as there is an Alaskan pack) it's never really been featured in the books. We hope you like what we've done with that pack because there will be more about them in future Sazi episodes.

Finally, this book completes the world arc about She/Marduc. So much of the events of prior books lead up to this that it's hard to do it all justice. But you'll notice there is a bunch of stuff that ties in to former books—finally revealed in full. A lot of it will be a surprise because there were plots within plots (as all worlds have.)

This book was an amazing thrill ride to write and we're confident you're going to LOVE it! Thanks so much for going on this particular journey with us. We look forward to lots more Sazi adventures, in whatever form they appear. You guys are the best!

C. T. Adams and Cathy Clamp

Fan Information

Fans who wish to sign up for our newsletter can contact us as catadamsfans@gmail.com. Our website is www.ciecatrunpubs.com.

Serpent
Moon

Chapter One

THE COLD AIR cut like daggers as Eric painfully pulled in another deep breath. *God, not again. Please not again.* Then the howl came, riding on a magic so powerful he couldn't resist it. He raised his muzzle to the sky and rent the air with a deep, mournful sound that caused the deer ahead to scatter into the trees.

Except there were no deer . . . and no trees.

A part of his brain remembered that he was actually in the basement of a low-slung concrete building in the desert, running on a treadmill with electrodes pasted on skin shaved bare of fur. But it seemed so *real*. The forest with pines sparkling in the snow as they passed, the sensation of ice under his feet, and the scent of blood and fur and fear. A pack surrounding him, huffing and panting and racing forward after the game like birds in flight.

Another howl, accompanied by raking magic from the most powerful alpha wolf to ever be born to the Sazi, and Eric felt his mouth forced open to answer. Would it never stop? His lungs burned from the cold—or maybe it was just exhaustion. How long had he been running, been howling so they could gather their data?

And how many people had died as a result?

"Have to . . . stop. Can't . . . breathe." His voice sounded hoarse even to his own ears and the cough that followed felt like he was expelling his lungs.

Just a few more times. You have to call the pack. They can't find their way without you. You have to protect them, came the response in his mind, words that weren't sounds his ears would recognize. He felt adrenaline rush into his muscles and he surged forward into the snow.

Yes. The pack. Have to protect—

Another burst of magic and this time Eric felt his chest expand, felt his throat open, and the sound that erupted reached out, and out. It sliced through the snow and the weighty canopy of trees, pushing past the pressure of the air itself to find his people. Tiny obstacles pressed back but they fell too as the howl reached farther. Another object pressed in, slicing and cutting at his howl. It felt familiar . . . too familiar.

Eric tried to focus, fought against the need . . . and his instincts, to remember, even as the knives tried to cut his howl to pieces.

Knives. Slicing. Chopping.

Chopper. The word screamed into his mind and

he could sense it then. It was a small helicopter, not one of the big military ones, and it was falling. The sound wave was making it bob in the sky like a toy balloon. He could feel the turbine that drove the blades struggle against the pressure. More, he could feel the pilot and the two passengers inside begin to panic. Could smell their fear.

They promised. They swore there would be no flights out here. And they apparently didn't know, because the magic continued to rake over him, tried to pull more sound from his chest. He pulled back the howl, but it was like trying to turn the sea. All he could think to do was stop it cold and hope the chopper could recover.

"No!" He screamed the word, or at least hoped he did, and slammed shut his muzzle. He felt his head thrash from side to side as the wave of power tried to unlock his jaws. But still he could feel the machine in the sky falter, the wave of sound beat at it as the last remnants pushed into the sky. Eric's legs wobbled and he fell forward. The part of his brain that remembered where he was panicked as he felt the electrodes rip from his skin as his lower jaw smacked against the still-moving treadmill. His feet braced against the nearest support so he didn't go flying backward. Yet he still saw a woodland scene in his mind, and the sensations of metal and rubber didn't match the image of fluffy snow.

"Shut it down!" He heard a tinny voice crackle in the distance. "We've got a chopper in trouble! Stop him!"

The magic stopped then, cut off like a switch was thrown, so suddenly he felt like he'd slammed into a wall. Then Eric recognized the voice of Lucas Santiago, the alpha wolf who'd been supplying the magic. "I think he stopped *himself*. Ten-four. We've cut power. Talk to me, David. What's happening out there? There aren't supposed to be any aircraft out here tonight."

"It looks like a life-flight chopper, probably on the way to the hospital in Cortez. I think it's okay now. The prop seems to have stabilized and they're moving past ground zero. But wait until you see the video I just took. The pilot hit the wave and it went straight up and then dropped . . . damn, must have been fifty feet. It's one thing to talk about this in theory, but another to see it."

There was a small growl from Lucas. Eric wished he could stop seeing the movie running in a loop in his brain. Even though his body had stopped, he was still seeing snow and trees and running game.

"Tatya, turn that police scanner up to full volume, just to make sure they arrive safely. We might have to help out if their prop was too damaged to finish the trip." Lucas paused and let out a frustrated breath. Something made a chirping sound. Probably the walkie-talkie phone. "Okay, everybody, come on in or e-mail your reports. It's been a long night. We'll correlate what data we can. Maybe it'll be enough for the council to make their decision."

His vision of trees and snow was replaced by painted concrete and half-finished drywall so abruptly it made

Eric's head ache. He blinked and even that small movement was painful, as though his eyes had been wide open for too long in the wind. He had to shake his head once, then twice, before the sounds and sights around him made sense.

"Are we done?" He asked the question even though he knew the answer. No, they weren't done. They'd never be *done* with him.

"For now." Lucas was back in human form—had he ever actually shifted? Eric winced as he peeled the remaining electrode patches from his ears, face, and chest. "Quick thinking on your part, Thompson. We'd probably be picking up the pieces of that chopper if not for you. But it also means you weren't completely in a trance. Your mind just can't focus. We might have to put you on the Wolven obstacle course and throw the works at you to pull out a true calling howl."

Eric sighed. "Fiona tried that. I told you—it has to be the right combination of circumstances. I have to be in charge, there has to be a threat so great that I *need* help, and the pack has to be in danger. There's no way to duplicate it with a simple vision or course, because I just can't make myself believe the threat is big enough. No, I'm not willing to risk it, Chief. Not again. It'd just be better if the council put me back where they found me and find someone else to lead this pack. I didn't bother a soul in the Outback." With all the electrodes finally off, he backed carefully off the treadmill and padded to where his clothes were waiting. The four other people in the room didn't even glance his way when he shifted to naked human form. He'd always been rather private about nudity, but there was no way to remain modest as a shifter. Tatya Santiago stopped him before he could even pull on his underwear and started to perform an exam on him right there. He sighed. It would do no good to argue. "Did you get any readings that will help?"

"Another deep breath," Lucas's wife said as she held both a stethoscope and her flattened palm to his chest and then closed her eyes to listen and . . . well, *feel* was the best he could figure. Being both an M.D. and a magical healer gave her an edge in treating shifters that no one else could match.

He complied as Ivan Kruskenik spun on a padded stool across the room, took off his headphones, and spoke in his usual deep baritone. A tall, husky bald man, he was a Siberian bear in animal form, and he carried that same power to his human side. "Of course, my friend. *We* have been working hard while *you've* been playing in the snow." He said it completely deadpan, and when the sharply citrus scent of humor floated across the room, it only made Eric grin.

He couldn't help but laugh at his former partner. It was a real honor for an ordinary Wolven agent to get tapped to work a special project with the head of the Chief Justice's guard. But working with Ivan had been a privilege of its own. Eric *liked* the big bear, so he found himself grinning even as he rubbed his aching throat. "Oh, yeah. *Loads* of fun playing today. So what did you find?" Of course, rubbing his throat brought it to Tatya's attention and she immediately had him open his jaw so she could stare into his mouth with a light, and laid her fingers on his neck until he could feel heat and soothing magic ease the stinging.

"We confirmed what we already knew—that your howl has physical properties beyond simple sound. Some of the agents we have stationed around the area haven't checked in yet because of the disruption of the air waves. As soon as they do, we'll know more." Ivan looked at the man across the room watching a graph scroll across a computer screen. "Since you arrived just before we started, you didn't get to hear about the full array of tests we've been running. Tony, could you bring Eric up to speed?"

"Tony" was a Wolven agent Eric had only met a few hours ago. While his real name was Joe Giambrocco, everyone seemed to call him Tony. With his medium build and ordinary features he wasn't particularly noticeable, nor did he seem very powerful magically. But there was *something* about him . . .

"Sure. It was a bitch to set up and has been confusing to correlate, but it's really interesting." Tony rolled his stool to the side with a quick flick of his feet, and pointed at the screen. "We had three tests running at this location—seismic activity from six points around the building, sonar buoys at two points in the river about a mile from here, and a variety of security sensors in a sealed, locked room on the other side of the building that respond to heat, motion, and noise. Raven's been stationed at Denver International Airport in the control tower, watching for radar anomalies. Bobby is in Pueblo, which is a lot closer, watching for the same thing, and several hawk shifters are flying near NORAD in Colorado Springs, watching for any military activity out of the ordinary. We also have agents trained in meteorology watching the NEXRAD Doppler at the local TV station for echo intensity. We did our best to soundproof this room using various acoustic materials, so that—" The phone rang just then, interrupting him. Tony glanced at the display and put the call on speaker.

"Hey, Bobby. How are things looking in the friendly skies?"

There was a lot of background noise and static on the line, and Eric had to struggle to make out the words as he began pulling on his clothes. "Not so friendly. There were pilots all around the city reporting clear air turbulence."

"Any reports of equipment malfunctions?" Eric hopped on one foot trying to get a sock on while staring at the speakerphone with the same intensity as he felt.

Bobby paused, and only the background noise let them know he was still there. "A Cessna disappeared from radar. They're looking for it now." He hurried to add, "But I don't know if we can attribute it to this experiment, so don't get too excited. It'll depend on the time. There may have been issues with some part of the autopilot. I'll have to find a way to take a look at some Doppler LIDAR records and compare them to your test times to know for sure. I'm going to hang around here until I know more. I'll be in touch."

Bile rose into Eric's throat and the room swam

enough that Tatya grabbed his arm to keep him from falling.

All he had left to put on were his shoes. He spotted an empty chair and was headed toward it when Tatya surprised him by saying, "You can put those on in the car. We're going to be late if we don't get moving."

Eric's brow furrowed. Nobody had told him he was supposed to be traveling tonight. "Where are we going?" The hint of a growl voiced his suspicions better than words could.

Tatya gestured imperiously, as if to say *Don't question your superiors, child.* He felt the flesh on his back raise where his hackles would be in wolf form. He didn't lower his gaze. If the council decided this was going to be his territory, he had every right to question a healer, no matter how powerful.

The radio on Lucas's hip squawked again. He picked it up, turning away as Eric and Tatya continued challenging each other with their eyes.

"Go ahead."

"This is David. I'm on my way back and found something weird. I'm bringing it in."

From the corner of his eye, Eric saw Lucas move his eyes from his wife to the other men in the room. He let out a deep sigh that could mean a lot of things and shook his head. Eric caught the wet scent of sadness from him, which was surprising. But Lucas recovered quickly and answered David with authority. "Stay where you are. I'll come to you."

Ivan gave a small dip of his head which seemed to Eric to be an odd thing to do—almost as if he was giving Lucas *permission*. Lucas sighed and walked out of the room without a word.

Tatya was gathering her purse and clipboard in a hurried fashion and didn't seem to notice anything odd about what was going on. Ivan leaned back against the wall and regarded her for a long moment. Finally, when it seemed she was ready to leave, he spoke.

"Vere exactly are you taking our new Alpha, Tatya?"

Eric winced inwardly. Ivan's voice was taking on a Russian accent. That was *never* a good sign. If Tatya noticed, she didn't show it. She was patting her pockets, apparently looking for something, and didn't even bother to turn his way. She tucked her hand into her purse and extracted a cell phone. "I've arranged for a mobile MRI trailer in Cortez to save me the last spot on their schedule. But we have to leave now to make it before they go. It'll take at least an hour to get there."

It took another long silence before it finally occurred to Tatya that something was amiss. Maybe it was the growing wave of power flowing from Ivan that stung skin. Eric hadn't seen him raise power like that in a very long time. Of course, he was always *capable* of it. You don't rise through the Wolven ranks and then get to be the personal guard of the Chief Justice if you can't fight off even the toughest opponents. But Ivan was remarkably even tempered. Normally he didn't raise much of a fuss about anything. Now, however, Tony backed his stool a little and winced, then scratched at his bare arm, likely to relieve the same biting ants sensation Eric was experiencing.

A deep, resonant growl rumbled from the great bear's huge chest. "And how exactly did you plan to hide the evidence *this time*, Tatya? You are, according to your own words, *on the schedule*. There will be lists and reports and data—*photographs*—in a computer. You vill be having human technicians looking at scans of, one would presume, a supernatural throat and chest that have stumped our best people. Ve have no idea vat they'll find. Super capacity lungs? An abnormal voice box? Are you going to ask Wolven to clean up your mess again? Vill we have to threaten them, pay them off, or even *kill* them? Vat could you possibly imagine you'll find that vould be worth that sort of trouble?"

There was a long pause, and while Tatya seemed at a loss for words, her underlying scent wasn't confusion or fear. It was anger. "I've already worked out the details, Ivan. It'll be in my report to the council, and is none of your concern."

Ivan's eyes narrowed dangerously. "Doctor Santiago, the council has given you a great deal of leniency due to its affection for you and your husband and things you've done in the past for the Sazi. But you've already proven your inability to *vork out the details*. You're barely off probation for the fiasco in Boulder." He raised one hand in a frustrated gesture that matched the scent now roiling off him. "After all of Wolven's efforts, in conjunction with the council, the healers, and the seers, to keep the testing of Mr. Thompson a complete secret, why would you make plans, to satisfy your own personal curiosity, that could ruin everything?"

She gritted her teeth, obviously unaccustomed to being spoken to in such a manner. Her scent was strong enough to choke on, peppery and thick with anger and embarrassment. "I am not *ruining* anything. I simply thought of the MRI at the last minute. I have contacts with the company we used to use in Boulder. They're discreet and allow me to handle the equipment personally while they go out to dinner. I've been trained and have my certifications. There's no more danger in this situation than there was when I was the healer in Boulder and had someone's knee scanned. As soon as I explain the situation to the council, they won't have a problem with it."

Ivan's eyes narrowed even further. He had small eyes anyway, but when they narrowed, they nearly disappeared from his face. "Then pray proceed. *Explain* the situation."

She stood in an odd attempt to look down on him. That was impossible, of course. Even sitting, he was taller than the tiny blonde. She raised power in a hot wash that let them know she wasn't one to be trifled with. Yet Ivan simply stared at her until she was forced to speak. Her words dripped honey, and her scent was sweet and cloying, betraying the dark glee that lurked underneath. "If there was a council member here, I would."

"There is, so please proceed." *Uh-oh. He's using*

that *voice. That's never good.* Eric moved back from what was about to become a battle zone and made several sharp jabs with his thumb so Tony could see it behind Tatya's back. The other man casually stretched and stood, moving with Eric toward the rear of the room, near the emergency door.

Eric didn't sit down until he was right next to the door and immediately began pulling on his shoes. He needed to be ready in case he'd be running through the cactus in a few minutes to escape the explosion.

The healer let out a small laugh, either not knowing, or uncaring of the great bear's anger. "*You're* not a council member, Ivan. I *know* all the council members."

Ivan stood slowly, stepping closer to her, keeping the same level of power as he approached. She let out a little shudder, but didn't otherwise acknowledge the magic. "Perhaps you did at one time, but you've been out of favor for some time now. You're neither an Alpha, nor the wife of a councilman. I was voted the council representative of the bears at the last quarterly meeting."

She stiffened. "Lucas didn't tell me that."

Ivan tightened his power around her. Tatya's purse dropped from her shoulder and she didn't move to pick it up. She didn't have the ability to do *anything.* Ivan had frozen her in place. "Lucas was *advised* to keep a tighter grip on his tongue as you've proven you're incapable of keeping secrets. With the addition of the Hayalet and the volatile situation in Bosnia, the council decided that a new seat was needed. I was elected unanimously."

It must have taken a tremendous amount of willpower to speak, but somehow she managed it. The words were mumbled, making it sound like she had cotton in her cheeks. "What new member? What situation? I've only been out of contact for a few months. That much can't have hap—"

Ivan increased his power just enough that she froze completely. "And yet, that much *has* happened. The ghost tiger, Rabi Kuric, was nominated for a full council seat as the representative of the Hayalet Kabile, in order to secure safe passage through his territory to keep watch on our enemies. With Antoine Monier as his new brother-in-law, Angelique's raptors unrepresented until she recovers from her injuries, and the additional support of Ahmad for the snakes, Charles had little choice but to approve the nomination. As for the situation in Bosnia, that is none of your concern. It's a Wolven matter and, as I said, I doubt Lucas will have much to say to you about it." He raised his eyebrows and crossed his massive arms over his chest. Then he released the woman so abruptly that she stumbled and wound up on her knees. "So, explain to *me* your reasoning for this test."

Ivan mentioned enemies, which was confusing. To the best of Eric's knowledge, the Sazi had no enemies, just lawbreakers. If that had changed, he needed to know before he took over a pack that might have to be protected. It might not be a bad idea to spend some more time with Ivan . . . perhaps when Tatya was talking with the technicians.

Before the doctor could get to her feet, Eric raised his hand to catch Ivan's attention. "You know what, Ivan? Let's just go ahead and do it. I've always been kind of curious, and the scan's already on the schedule. I know you have good aversion magic. If Healer Santiago can handle the equipment, we can be in and out of there before the technicians even know what happened. And once we get a healer posted down here, maybe we can try the tests again."

Ivan's sigh spoke volumes and Eric felt himself tense. "I wish we had one available, my friend. There simply aren't that many."

He felt his head shake even before he could think of the words to say. "I don't like that. We're too far from a decent hospital, particularly with the Boulder pack splitting up. I'm going to be the only Alpha, and if anyone gets seriously injured in a dominance fight or hunt, we're in real trouble. Could we at least get a *piece* of one? Someone who comes around every few weeks or so on rotation?"

This time it was Tatya who shook her head. "There truly is nobody. Right now there are only five true healers in the world. Me, in Paris; Amber, who splits her time between Germany and Washington; Raven, who's second in command of Wolven, and he already has five packs to keep track of. Betty's in Albuquerque, but that's too far to travel here that often—"

Eric felt a growing unease. "Patrice, the healer in the Canada pack, recently died, and they haven't found a replacement for her either."

"Oh!" Tatya looked stricken, turning to him abruptly. She actually smelled wet with sorrow, which threw him off guard. "I hadn't heard about Patrice's death. I'm so sorry. Please offer your mother my sympathy. Well then, I guess there are only four of us. There are a few with minor healing abilities, like Raven's father, Raphael, and Duchess Olga in Chicago, but they lead their own packs. They can't just leave to visit yours at the drop of a hat."

Eric mentally tallied in his head once more. "What about Holly Sanchez?"

Ivan's brows raised just as Tatya's lowered. "Who?"

"Holly. The woman Lucas sent to Australia to deliver the council's request for me to take over this pack. She's out of the Boulder pack."

Tatya let out an odd chuckle. "She's not part of that pack anymore. She *resigned*, as I heard it. She's the daughter of the pack omega and a *human*. If she has any healing ability at all, it won't be enough to be any good to anyone."

Once again, Eric felt his hackles rise. "I beg to differ. She's actually an exceptional healer. Before I came into contact with her in the Outback, she stopped at Crocodile Annie's place outside Tarcoola. The old woman was nearly dead after a snake bit her, and Holly healed her right up."

Ivan blinked in surprise. "How did you come to find this out?"

Eric shrugged. "Annie's a friend. We'd meet up nearly every Saturday at the local pub to raise a pint, and when she didn't show, I went to go find her. She was just getting on her feet again and raved about the young doctor who'd healed her. Holly also fixed up

Jake, Annie's old dingo mix with hip displasia, who, I might add, hadn't walked properly in nearly five years. Annie called it a miracle and insisted I stay to meet her when she got back from getting supplies in town. Good thing I did, or I might never have gotten your message." He remembered other things about Holly, too—her bright brown eyes and sweetly scented hair and the way her laugh made his pulse race. If she wasn't attached to a pack . . . well, why not ask her to join his?

Tony spoke up. "If she's the same girl I met in Boulder a few months back, she was pretty damned good. A nurse got sliced up pretty bad and Holly healed her nearly as fast as I've seen Betty do. I remember the nurse saying that she'd been doing all their healing for a few months and everybody liked her."

Tatya still sounded dismissive. "Well, she'd still have to be tested, and I doubt she'd pass. I've known Holly her whole life. She's not terribly impressive . . . at *anything*."

"So," Ivan said with more than a hint of disdain in his voice. "When you were taken off probation six months ago, your sole assignment was to find and train new healers so we wouldn't have such a shortage. You were to visit each and every pack and use your magic to search for the ability. Yet, in a world filled with wolves, you had a potential healer in your backyard and simply ignored it? You never even *asked* who was doing the healing in Boulder after you left?" The noise that rumbled from his chest was more than a growl, but less than a snarl.

"The council has lamented the fact that nobody has been presented to the healers' circle for testing—thinking that perhaps the ability has disappeared from our people, but I'm beginning to think something very different." He shook his head and turned toward the door. "You must have very strong shoulders, doctor. I will be waiting in the car. I will drive you to this *scheduled appointment.*"

Eric winced at Ivan's words. Tatya only smelled of confusion. After the door had closed behind him, she turned. "You worked with him, Thompson. What did he mean when he said I have strong shoulders?"

He walked past her toward the door. "It means you've been getting plenty of exercise, doctor—digging your own grave."

Chapter Two

"WELCOME TO COOBER Pedy, Australia, darlin'. Good luck finding your sister. Sorry I wasn't more help." The elderly man tipped his sweat-stained leather hat as Holly grabbed her suitcase and got out of the pitted, rusty Land Cruiser. The sun was just rising past a series of tall hills of sand, which she'd learned were tailing piles from opal mining. They surrounded the town, making it look like a valley, instead of the flat desert it was.

Her smile of thanks was genuine, but the one she got in return was not. There was something about the man that was deeply angry, but the emotion was too far below the surface to even inquire about. He probably couldn't remember a time when he *wasn't* angry. She smelled it behind the dust and sweat like roasting jalapenos at a farmer's market. She smelled his fear too—a tang that tightened the glands at the back of her jaw. Still, she refused to let it change her mood, and refused to give into the wolf that lurked below the surface. "Thanks for the lift, Mr. Bates. It would have been a long walk in this heat." Actually, it would have only been about fifteen minutes, but it *was* hot so she was grateful for the air-conditioned ride. Even at sunrise, the temperature was hovering around a hundred, if the thermometer in the car could be trusted.

He pulled away from the curb just as the lights lining the main street began to flicker off. Holly turned and stared at the attractive rock face of the building housing the Black Opal Lodge. Rose's letters and phone calls had made the town sound like a throwback to the Stone Age. But while not large, the town had paved streets, landscaping, and seemed like any other small mining town she'd ever visited in Colorado. Oh sure, it had the eclectic oddities. The "Big Winch" in the center of town really *was* a big winch, and signs warning of the danger of falling into one of the hundreds of mine shafts that dotted the outskirts of the town were all over the airport. Her nose had registered the distinctive scent of decayed flesh wafting on the breeze—some of it human—so the signs weren't there just to amuse the tourists.

Her favorite bit of memorabilia, though, was a leftover spaceship from a movie she remembered seeing a few years back. It was one of dozens of old movie props lying around randomly, as if there would be another scene shot after dinner. But hey, even a spaceship was nothing compared to some of the strange things towns on the Colorado plains could boast.

She wished she'd been able to reach Rose to tell her she was coming, but her phone was out of service. *I hope Dale didn't already give up on the mining idea and move.* Holly loved her brother-in-law, but wondered how her sister could stand constantly moving from place to place, to the next get-rich-quick scheme on the list. It had been nearly a month since she'd heard from her sister, which was unusual. Either things were going amazingly well and she was too busy to call, or she was too broke to afford minutes, and too proud to ask for help. Both had happened in the past, so there was no way to judge.

Still, since Holly had finished the assignment Lucas had given her nearly a week early, she might as well visit. It seemed silly to change the date of the plane tickets when she could have a little fun. She picked up her bag and walked into the motel, letting the cool air evaporate the sweat that was making her bangs stick to her forehead. The young woman behind the counter was about her age. Even though she was professionally dressed in a tailored white shirt and jacket, she wore multiple earrings and a spiked and highlighted blond mop—the style nearly identical to what Holly saw every day in downtown Denver. She looked up from her computer as Holly walked across the tastefully decorated wood and stone entry.

"G'day, miss. Welcome to Coober Pedy. Can I help you?" She smelled of eucalyptus and spearmint, but with a touch of citrus that said she was happy. But the scents couldn't completely eliminate the obvious— the girl was a snake shifter. She smelled oddly musty, but not with the sharp, pungent tones of a viper. The two women acknowledged each other's identities with a slight tip of the head that no human watching would recognize.

"Sure. I need a room for . . . well, actually I don't know for how long. Tonight for sure, but I'm visiting family, so I might stay with them starting tomorrow. I don't know how big of a house they have. In fact, I don't even know where they live yet. It's sort of a surprise visit." She smiled ruefully at her own rambling, not sure why she was telling the girl all of it. When she was done she paused, hoping she didn't sound as stupid as she felt.

But the woman only flicked out her tongue to lick her lips and then laughed brightly. "Well, you tell me which family and I'll tell you where they are and whether they'll have room for ya. There's not many folks in town I don't know. There's not that many of us, as you could probably tell."

"Dale and Rose Barry. All I know is that they live in one of the underground houses on the edge of town."

The woman tapped one finger on the keyboard and clicked her teeth together. "Barry. Barry . . . They're not locals. Full blooded?"

Holly shook her head to show that they weren't Sazi, but human. "They're new in town, probably six months. From America. He's a miner."

Another light laugh showed off perfect white teeth that would shrink when she shifted to become tiny rows lining her mouth. "Who isn't, darls? Not many cockies in this town . . . *farmers* I think you call them.

No, we're all either diggers, or would like to be, and at least half of us live in dugouts. But I *do* seem to recall some new people over near Roy's place. Tell ya what, miss. You check in and get a quick rinse and I'll make some calls. We'll find 'em for ya."

"That would be *great*. It's been a really long day and I could use a hot shower." She held her hand out across the desk. "I'm Holly, by the way. Holly Sanchez, in case someone wonders who's looking for Rose and Dale. She's my sister."

The blonde took her hand and gave it a firm shake. "I'm Adelaide Matthews. My dad owns the motel. And yes, before you ask, it's spelled like the city. Can't imagine why my mum picked that name, but I've gotten used to it. If we can't find your sis before dinner, Dad's a great cook. He's making his famous chook casserole tonight. Even the locals show up for that, so it might be your sis'll come to you before we can find her."

Holly wasn't quite sure what *chook* was, but the whole point of coming here was to experience new things, and now that she was a werewolf, there weren't many things that could poison her. Even the five-alarm chili her father made didn't bother her anymore.

She passed over her credit card, wincing a little when she noticed the room rates. Her card didn't have a very high limit. It was too new, applied for when she found out about this trip. She'd always operated on cash. *Here's hoping Rose has a room. I doubt Lucas will consider this a Wolven expense.*

Adelaide rang a bell on the counter and a boy of

about fourteen came out of a nearby door. "Take Ms. Sanchez to room eight, Tom, and don't be bothering her for a carry-up fee. Remember what Dad said about that."

The boy let out a deep sigh and Holly nearly smiled. But instead she studiously kept her eyes on the contents of her purse as she put away her card.

THE ROOM WAS spacious and comfortable, a welcome change from the conditions Holly had been living in since she arrived in Australia. As she luxuriated under the hot shower, she couldn't help but smile at the friendly people she'd met thus far. The terrific people in the Melbourne airport who'd helped her find her luggage when it went missing, and Adelaide downstairs who was going to track down Rose. Of course, there was Crocodile Annie too, the rough old woman with the snake bite, and . . . well, she couldn't quite seem to forget Eric Thompson, the reason for her trip to begin with.

She remembered him from long ago, when she was just a teenager and he was the bad boy sent to Boulder to be *tamed* by Lucas. But she'd never found him particularly bad. Mostly, he'd seemed sad . . . and restless. They'd enjoyed a lot of long talks in the restaurant while she was closing up. She'd basked in the attention and the roses he'd bring. She'd even tried to sneak out to see him, except her father refused to let her date. But, of course, Eric was nearly a decade older. It hadn't seemed like a big deal at the time, but now she realized how it must have looked. Even if Dad *had* allowed her to date, he never would have allowed her to date *him*. "That man's trouble. You keep your distance," her father had said every time Eric walked into the restaurant.

By the time she'd gotten up the nerve to stand up to her father, Eric ran off with Vicki Bailey. She'd heard he got sent off shortly thereafter to Wolven Academy, where his "aggressions could be channeled."

They'd apparently been channeled pretty well. She couldn't help but remember every tiny detail of their most recent encounter as she let the shower wash off the dust and soak away the tightness in her muscles.

The sky had been the most amazing blue—a color she couldn't seem to compare to anything she'd ever seen, except perhaps really high-end turquoise. The sunglasses she'd brought barely kept her from squinting, so she'd taken Annie's suggestion and was wearing a straw hat that fit her better than the leather one Annie wore.

Annie was a real kick now that she was feeling better. She'd been mumbling incoherently and screaming at things only she could see when Holly had first arrived. But then, she'd also been nearly dead from a snake bite that had turned her leg black, the tissue so decomposed it was squishy to the touch.

Her old dog had apparently kept predators away from his mistress, based on the scratches and cuts that had torn away chunks of fur and flesh. It was a good thing Holly had Sazi strength, because the old woman probably weighed two hundred pounds. The old, yellow dog never made so much as a growl, which had surprised her. He must have encountered Sazi before, because all he did was sniff at her and then painfully get to his feet and move aside while she carried Annie into the ramshackle hut where she lived.

It had taken Holly two full days to heal the woman's injuries, working only with the instincts that came with her healing gift. It would have been nice to be trained, but nobody had ever made the offer, and nobody would return her phone calls when she asked about it. Of course, there was no money for medical school. Hell, even her savings for community college had once again disappeared at her father's hands. Both Raven and Cat had offered . . . but no, Holly couldn't take their money. She had *some* pride.

Holly had managed to find enough canned food stashed for them to live on, but the water left something to be desired. Still, at least her system could process it better than she could have when she was human. She would have been in the bathroom for the whole time without the healing magic to keep her gut stable.

When Annie had finally come to, she'd thought Holly a doctor. It was probably better to let her believe that. People didn't handle the knowledge of magic too well in today's world.

Holly remembered the trip into Tarcoola to get supplies more strongly than anything because she had felt so incredibly . . . *free*. She'd finally been away long enough to have forgotten her anger at her father for the empty savings account, and had been in Australia long enough that the sights and scents seemed almost normal. Slowing the truck for a family of kangaroos didn't seem any odder than stopping for a herd of deer.

Do I really have to go home? What would happen if I just disappeared?

Of course, that thought had come to a screeching halt when she drove up to Annie's cluttered homestead and saw another vehicle in the yard. *Shit. They've come to tell me never mind. I'll bet Wolven's already found him and I'll be sent straight back to the airport.*

But it hadn't been Wolven. Not precisely, anyway. The old, tan Toyota belonged to the very man she'd come to find—Eric Thompson.

He'd walked toward her Jeep with a confident stride and a sudden wide smile on his tanned face that made her mouth go dry. "Well, as I live and breathe. Little Holly Sanchez."

She couldn't help but grin as she got out from behind the wheel, took off her hat, and leaned against the side of the vehicle. "Not so little anymore."

"So I see." The look that raked her up and down was anything but innocent and she really, *really* enjoyed it. "All grown up and looking lovely, darlin'." She couldn't have planned her outfit better. When he'd last seen her, she was stick thin, her chest board flat, and she'd mostly worn shapeless, utilitarian clothes because they held up better in the rigors of the restaurant business.

But thankfully, that day she'd been all woman.

The sunflowers on her hatband matched the tiny yellow flowers on her sleeveless cotton top. While she still didn't have much of a chest, this was her favorite shirt for making the most of what she did have. She'd tied the tails so it exposed her midriff and her khaki shorts were a lot shorter than what they usually wore down here. But the sun had felt so *good* today. It was hot . . . really hot, but she didn't burn anymore, so she didn't mind exposing her brown skin to the heat. His nostrils flared and he caught her scent, the fur and magic smell that said she was no longer human. "Your curves aren't the only thing that's changed about you. You've taken after your father. Better late than never, eh?"

She shrugged. It did no good to be mad about it anymore. "Not by choice, I'm afraid."

He growled. It was instinctive on his part, and it had a protective edge that made her shiver—in a good way. Annie was in the doorway, letting them have their moment to talk, but they couldn't keep talking in riddles forever. "Who?" The question was a demand, and she knew why. Attacking a human and turning them against their will was a death sentence.

Another shrug. "Corrine. You probably remember her. But it's been handled and I'm dealing. Mostly." It *had* been handled. Corrine had been put down on the spot by her uncle Raphael. Holly didn't actually remember it. She'd been unconscious and near death at the time.

Eric's face grew dark, his eyes flashing and his scent filled with peppery anger. "That damned *bitch*.

I thought I made it crystal clear to her when—" He shook his head at her confusion. "That's a story for another time. For now, let's go in and see Annie." He shook off the anger and offered his arm with a flourish. "Are you ready to examine your patient again, *Doctor* Sanchez?"

"Oh." She stopped cold. She didn't want him to get the impression that . . . "About that. I'm not—"

He smiled and winked. "I know. Maybe not an M.D., but a healer nonetheless. And you never could resist a sick dog. That's what gave you away."

Heat rose to her face at that moment, and the sensation of his hand pulling hers until it was tucked under his arm was hotter than sunshine against her exposed skin. "It's just . . . he was in so much pain."

He pushed a strand of hair back from her cheek in a gentle way that made goose bumps rise, staring at her with those so-blue eyes, nearly the color of the sky. "Don't apologize. You gave an old dingo a new lease on life. *Never* apologize for helping. That's where *I* went wrong."

It was so nice, so sweet. Just like the Eric she remembered. Then she remembered him running off with someone else. And worse, how *smug* Jasmine had been, tormenting Holly about it endlessly once she realized how much it bothered her. She pulled back, her body stiffening, so suddenly that he took a step back. She could tell he was about to say something, but Annie called them both inside.

Things happened too fast after that. She waited until they were alone again, after dinner when Annie went out to check her trotlines in the stream, before she gave him the message Lucas had given her. He left soon after. She wished she knew what they wanted with him, but Lucas would only tell her it wasn't *bad*. So that was something.

Back in her hotel room, the hot water finally gave out, and Holly was left standing in the bathroom of a nice hotel, feeling confused and frustrated. Eric leaving when she was a teenager had probably been for the best. But it had hurt. And she wasn't too young now. Maybe she'd only imagined it, but it sure seemed like the hug he'd given her as he left was a lot longer than it should have been. And she couldn't remember a single hug from a cousin or friend where her neck was nuzzled by nose and lips.

Except he's gone and you didn't do a thing to clear things up between you.

She was just toweling off when the phone rang. She threw on the fluffy white robe that had been neatly folded on the counter, and grabbed the receiver before it reached the third ring.

"Hello?"

"It *is* you! Oh. My. God! I can't believe you're in Australia!" The words were followed by a delighted screech so loud it forced Holly to pull the handset away from her ear.

She couldn't help but laugh. "Well, if I ever wanted to talk to you again, Rose, I sort of had to come. You haven't called in ages! What's the four-one-one, anyway?"

"Where do I start? It has been *amazing* down here,

little sis. I can't wait to tell you all about it. And I can't believe your timing! You need to come right over and—" There was a pause and then Rose's voice sounded even more excited, if that was possible. "No, wait. I've got a *better* idea. Here's what we'll do. Why don't you take a nap for a couple of hours and then come over around eight. It must have been a really tiring trip. Those flights are wicked long." Of course, Holly couldn't tell her that she'd already been in the country for a week. The Wolven part of her life had to remain a secret, otherwise Lucas would never trust her for another assignment. She didn't know if she wanted to be a full Wolven agent, but she didn't want to be deemed "unsuitable" either.

"Well, I *am* tired." There was no denying that. Healing Annie had taken a lot more out of her than she'd planned. The leg had been so black and squishy it was ready to explode. The rattlesnake toxin had infiltrated nearly every part of Annie's system so she'd had to move fast, and it had taken days to get all the tissue in Annie's leg corrected so she didn't lose it. Thankfully, it had only been a regular snake, not a Sazi, so she didn't have to worry about the woman becoming one of them.

"Of course you are. So you rest and have a good dinner and then come over. I'm hosting my first FMU meeting down here and you'll finally get to meet everyone! Lots of us from the Internet boards have moved Down Under. *Char186* is down here, and so is *Nobodystoady*. You know both of them and I know they're going to love to see you. Oh, you've *got* to come!"

FMU—Family Members United. She hadn't thought of the group since . . . well, since she was attacked and turned into a werewolf. "Are you sure they're going to *want* to see me, Rose? I'm not one of you anymore. That's why I dropped off the boards."

Rose's voice turned deadly serious. "What happened to you is the *reason* I keep active in FMU, Holly. Nobody should have to go through what you did. We have to fight to keep the animals under control. The only way to prevent more attacks is to remain vigilant."

Did she consider the term "animals" offensive now? She hadn't before. It had slipped off her tongue pretty damned often. But now she felt a twinge when she heard the word out loud. She wasn't an animal. Neither was Cat, her best friend in the world and another attack victim—of a jaguar serial killer.

It occurred to her she'd never told Cat about FMU. Was it embarrassment at being a member, or simply honoring her pledge to keep the strict code of silence the group demanded? Without even realizing she did it, Holly reached up to touch the tattoo on the back of her neck, covered by her hair. Five teardrops of rich red, in the shape of a wolf print, spoke of her family lineage. All of the "insiders" of FMU had a similar mark. She'd gotten hers at sixteen, when being constantly tormented by her sisters, as well as being the pack's on-call babysitter and fry cook, demanded she find some outlet so she didn't go insane. That year, she'd wanted nothing more than to drive her sisters Jasmine and Iris—as well as her father and the other pack members, from the face of the earth.

But what did she feel now?

Was this trip even a good idea? She *knew* Rose was still active in the group. Was this her way of dealing with that part of her past so she could move on, or the still rumbling fury inside that her humanity had been stolen from her? Either way . . . "Sure, I'll come to the meeting. I'd love to finally meet Charlene and Matthew."

"Yay! Okay, so I'll make plans for one more mouth to feed. Find a pencil. I'll give you the address. *Don't* come until after eight o'clock. I want to get the meeting started and then have you appear. It's going to be wicked sick, Hol! I can't wait to see the looks on their faces." Rose chuckled and it made Holly shiver. "I have a feeling nobody is *ever* going to forget this meeting."

Chapter Three

"I SAID I won't tell you!" Paolo's strong, masculine face was set in tight lines of anger. It matched the bittersweet taste on Nasil's tongue that made his glands salivate. Paolo's attitude was odd, considering his rather compromising predicament of being tied with silver chains to a concrete bench in the center of a plastic sheet, in front of a variety of knives carefully laid out on a counter. Either he was too fervent, or too foolish to be afraid . . . yet. "There's nothing you can do to make me talk."

Was he really that clueless? A smile turned up one side of Nasil's mouth. The other side remained drooped and impassive, reminding him once more of the price this operation had cost him. It simply added to his determination to end it. He pulled a pair of long plastic gloves from a box and rolled them up his arms. The box was already half-empty from the other *discus-*

sions that had led him to Paolo's location. "I think it may be too early to say there's *nothing* I can do. While it is true my magic isn't as strong as it used to be, my abilities as a snake weren't the reason I was given the title 'the Tormentor of Akede'." He ignored the slight slurring of his words. He'd worked hard to get his mouth to the point it would talk at all. He wouldn't quibble about the niceties.

Paolo let out a low, angry hiss and then clamped his teeth so tightly shut the jaw muscles twitched under his brown skin.

Nasil picked up the first knife, a recent favorite, with a long thin blade that was perfect for flaying, and a rubberized patterned grip that wouldn't slip in his hand when wet. But then he paused and stared for a long moment at the man who had betrayed him, who had betrayed all of their kind, and ruined nearly every single thing he'd worked on for decades. Paolo had known Sargon, former king of one of the largest empires to ever exist, and a massive king cobra so powerful he could kill with a single touch. He'd watched Sargon for years while they'd lived and schemed in the jungles of South America. Although he hadn't known him for the millennia Nasil had, he'd seen the brutal and creative torture Sargon was capable of. So no doubt the rattlesnake shifter had some inkling where this conversation was going.

And he believed he could withstand it.

Interesting.

Likely he'd be concentrating so hard on surviving, to prove his strength, that asking questions might well be useless. But if not torture, then what? What was important to the man? Nasil tapped the knife on the counter while he thought, and while Paolo stared with glittering black eyes, roiling with hatred and anger. Pride. That was what drove Paolo. Pride in his strength—both magical and physical—and in his intelligence. Pride in his *machismo*. Tough, capable, and insufferably egotistical. Those were things not easily stripped away by knives. And mere physical wounds would be easily healed by his Sazi magic.

Of course, Nasil had already stripped a slice of his pride away. He'd captured him. Paolo had not even seen the attack coming, and when he'd woken from the tranquilizer, he'd struggled mightily against the chains, until he realized he couldn't break them. So that was one blow.

Then what are my other options? Paolo was easily as cruel as Sargon himself, just without the finesse. He considered rape the only truly satisfying liaison, and believed those beneath him to be expendable, no matter the situation. He'd always been shortsighted and petty. Nasil had been forced to clean up after his frequent explosions of anger, and the insatiable, perverted lust that often ended with the broken, ruined bodies of young women snatched from surrounding villages. Yet Nasil had no desire to rape him in return. He doubted he could get hard, much less climax with the man.

No, there wasn't an ounce of charity in Paolo, nor sympathy, so he wouldn't be expecting any. The taste of cold metal determination on the air said as much.

While torturing him just ~~on principle could be en~~tertaining, it wouldn't solve the immediate problem. Nasil had to break Paolo to get the information. Give him something to fear that he couldn't put a name to—something that would make him crawl into bed each night wondering when the next attack might come. Nasil put down the knife and reached out to grab the lone chair in the empty room, formerly an underground bunker of some sort, reinforced with steel and dug deep into the earth. He spun it and sat down, straddling it so he could prop his nearly useless right arm on the back. It annoyed him when it flopped about like a dead eel. "Perhaps I should start this conversation by telling you what I know first. You may not mind telling me what I need to know."

"Pah. You just know you can't break me, amigo. You're afraid to even try, because you know you'll fail and when I track you down later, I'll teach you what *real* torture is." The English was flavored with a thick Honduran accent. Nasil could speak most of the Spanish dialects Paolo used, but he favored American English simply because there were more words in the language. So much easier to express oneself.

Again with the ego. It was barely worth a reply. And he was truly sick of being called *amigo* by a man who didn't even know the meaning of the word. "Hardly." He smiled and could taste the truth of his own words. "No, I know *exactly* how to make you talk . . . and we'll get to that soon enough." Another pause, and Nasil could almost see another chink in Paolo's armor appear. Sargon had offered scant praise for anyone in his circle, but he *did* praise Nasil often for his ability to know just the right method to extract information. It was impossible for Paolo not to wonder what lay in store.

"No, I just want you to know how futile it is to withhold anything from me. There's very little I don't know already. Mostly I captured you because I *could* and because you annoyed me. You got cocky, deciding just because Sargon was dead, that somehow *you* were in charge of the priests of the order and the mission to raise Marduc." He paused for effect. "You were *wrong*. You aren't bright enough to complete the plan."

Nasil allowed disdain to creep into his scent, which wasn't hard to do.

Paolo opened his mouth at the goading. He couldn't help himself, and that would be his undoing. "I was bright enough to realize that Sargon was not coming back, despite your assurances. I was bright enough to find another location for the Goddess to be born, which *you* couldn't find without help from Lord Sargon's worthless child. And, I was *bright enough* to ensure that, even now, you can't find the Goddess's resting place. So, you'll not be there for her birth so that She can imprint on you. No, she will imprint on *me*, and I will be the one to sit at Her right hand, as Sargon would have done if you hadn't betrayed him."

Nasil felt his mouth nearly open in disbelief and only just managed to keep it shut. Instead, he shook his head wearily.

"You're a fool, Paolo. I already know where she is,

right down to the quiet, cool cliff cave. I know she's about to be born, and I know where you've been getting the meat you plan to feed her as her first meal. The *only* thing I need you alive for is to tell me the name of the healer you're using, to make sure you've placed her in the right location. I need to talk to him or her to make sure all the details are accounted for. I don't really care who Marduc imprints on. I just want to be sure she isn't born feral."

It was a bluff, of course. While he did need the name of the healer, he also hadn't been able to find the egg. All he'd been able to get from the priests he'd captured was a general impression of the area, but not how to get there, nor the name of the nearest town. Unfortunately, Paolo had a certain right to his cockiness. He'd managed to hide it well enough that all of Nasil's best efforts couldn't find the egg. But Paolo couldn't know that.

"Someone broke their vow of silence? Who? I demand to know their name."

Nasil gave a little laugh and leaned forward against the chair rungs until they squeaked in protest. "There's little left of them to punish, I'm afraid. I only need the name of the healer and I'll be on my way back to the Old West."

Technically speaking, America *was* west of Australia as the planes flew. He'd been able to pinpoint the location that much, along with the fact that there was a cave. He studied Paolo's reaction closely.

Surprise, followed by studious blankness. *So the egg is in the American West. I thought as much. Excellent.*

Unfortunately, there were a lot of caves in the western states. Many of the indigenous tribes had used them as homes, just as they did on this continent. "Somehow you must have found a healer that's not known to the Sazi council. I've been keeping track of the movements of the others, and nobody has traveled in that direction."

The blankness continued and now Nasil was starting to wonder whether it was intentional, or whether he just didn't understand what was being asked. "You *are* using a healer for the birth, aren't you? You know that part is an absolute necessity—whether it is Sargon, me, or you who is attending the hatching?" Ye gods, *surely* he didn't believe he could remove the healers from the process? It would be like removing egg whites from a soufflé, leaving a gooey egg custard behind. Except that egg custards don't fill the night sky with terror, wreak havoc with the world's weather, and kill every living thing in sight.

Paolo's eyes flicked away for the briefest second and then they were back again, glaring defiance. "Sargon was not concerned about it, so I am not."

Sargon was not concerned about it? Not *concerned*? Rage poured through Nasil. He might consider the winged snake of legend that his lord had been fixated on to be a foolish and dangerous endeavor, but at least Sargon *recognized* that danger and had tried to minimize it. It was clear Paolo did not. And now, instead of a sentient being of immense power that merely needed guidance to become queen of the Sazi—to lead the snakes to their rightful place as leaders of the other shapeshifters, there was the potential for the complete destruction of the Earth. "You *fool*! Sargon and I spent the better part of a *thousand years* searching for just the right healer to hatch the egg. Not *concerned*? We plotted and planned and even tried to *breed* them to fit the requirements of the ritual. And now you're going to leave it to be born *alone* in the wild? There will be no guidance to make sure it comes into power with a *mind*?"

Nasil couldn't remember a time when he was this angry, and the rage added speed to his muscles. Even with his new disabilities he was still more than a match for any Sazi. When he stood and landed a vicious punch to Paolo's face, it was in the blink of an eye. Paolo's head whipped with the force, the chains raking along newly exposed skin, and it was only the fact that the concrete bench had been bolted to the floor that prevented the entire apparatus from sailing across the room into a wall. Blood appeared on Paolo's face, trickling from his nose in a slow line, accompanied by the taste of burned flesh on the air.

At last there was the tiniest glimmer of fear in the man's eyes and the sweet, spicy taste of panic began to bleed through his pores to surround him like a cloud. He hadn't seen the blow coming, probably couldn't even imagine that Nasil was still capable of such speed and force.

Honestly, I wasn't sure of it myself.

But the black mamba genes in his mother's blood still served him well, and even though it tingled from the strain, his left arm finally felt nearly normal for the first time in months.

"Now," Nasil said with the cold darkness of old

filling his voice, a sound he hadn't heard since he was Ea-Nasil, the new enforcer of a new king, before there was an old world and a new world, but only *one* world. "You *are* going to tell me what I want to know. And while I'm quite certain I'll enjoy the process, I'm also quite certain you will *not*."

He reached toward the counter, noting that Paolo's eyes were following his every movement. Instead of reaching for a knife or other weapon, he grabbed a simple sports bottle filled with water. Well, *mostly* with water, anyway. He raised it slowly to his lips as though considering his options. The relaxed, casual movement was meant to distract, so when the attack came it was a surprise. The nozzle was between Paolo's lips before the breeze from the movement even rustled his hair. Nasil pushed forward in the same motion, causing Paolo's head to tip back almost violently. One hard squeeze was enough to empty the majority of the contents directly down his throat.

Paolo lurched forward coughing and spewing, realizing almost immediately what had just happened from the lingering taste of the drug. He tried to spit out the fluid still remaining in his mouth. He coughed and spit frantically, to no avail. The drug was in his system now.

"Congratulations. You're the very first test subject of the final batch of the compliance drug you used on so many. I believe you were in the meeting with Syed when he unveiled Batch 32." Nasil felt a smile twist his mouth, because Paolo had indeed been in the meeting . . . and heard the rather interesting *details* of the new version of the drug.

Now his eyes were wild, nearly crazed with fear, and Nasil knew he had him. Paolo's greatest pride was in his *control*. He had to control others, and he had to have absolute control of himself.

That had just ended.

"That batch wasn't stable!" Paolo nearly screamed the words, and again tried to make his body reject the fluid. "Bastard! *Puta!* I will kill you!"

"No, I don't think so. What you'll do is be oh, so compliant, *amigo*. And after all, wasn't that most important? Isn't that what you told Syed when he asked whether he should destroy the batch and try a new formula?" Of course it was what he'd said. After all, mere human lives, or more precisely, human minds, didn't matter. Even lesser Sazi lives didn't matter. "In a few short minutes, you'll tell me every-thing I want to know. You'll *do* anything I ask. You'd suck my dick if I had any desire to have your filthy lips touch me, and you'd *enjoy* swallowing every bit you sucked out. You'd scramble and beg for more and weep if I refused. Hmm . . . maybe I'll instruct you to *remember* that part, but not remember you were forced. Will you lust for me forevermore . . . maybe even fall in love, and have no idea why?" There was a certain torment to unrequited love that made the potential delicious. Nasil couldn't help but let out a little chuckle.

Paolo knew full well that one of Nasil's unique gifts was the ability to make people forget periods of time and details of events. It was invaluable for com-ing and going with ease in places where he shouldn't be able to gain access.

Paolo had no love of men, and a shudder overtook him without warning. How many times had he lashed out at those under him for even making a *joke* about being gay? How many times had he made rude comments or gestures toward Nasil because he had a male lover? Yes, even the *thought* that he might voluntarily offer himself to a man cut another chink in his armor. Things were about to happen to him that he would have no control over and now he was truly beginning to feel the fear that he'd so often instilled in others. Paolo tried his last strategy then, one that should have worked. A wave of power poured out of him, and Nasil watched as his body tried to shift to snake form.

And failed.

Another wave of power, and another failure. Nasil waited until the third attempt was met with nothing more than a slight ozone scent that mingled nicely with fear. "Didn't I mention the *other* drug I gave you?" He reached forward to roll up Paolo's sleeve to reveal the tiny red mark on one vein. "It's something very exciting I heard about down here and had to come see for myself. The inventor called it RSA17. The problem is it's unpredictable. You might wind up with more power, or less. But for the time being, you're stuck in human form. No slithering into the bushes to escape, *amigo*. It's just you and me . . . until I tire of toying with you."

"You're bluffing. There is no such drug. You're just using your magic in a way I haven't seen before. But eventually, you'll grow weary and then I will escape and kill you. I will *kill* you."

Nasil wiped the spray of spittle from his face. He knew that Paolo would do just that if he escaped, so it would be best to gather what information he could—just in case the shifting-receptor inhibitor drug the man named Roy had called "the cure" didn't work as promised.

He turned to the counter to survey his tools, listening to the jingling of the chains as Paolo struggled and fought, scorching his skin with every movement. The smell of burned flesh wasn't particularly enticing, but the fear that accompanied it was an old favorite. It reminded Nasil that the full moon was near and he'd have to go hunt soon. But that was for later. For now—

"I want to make sure there are a few things you'll remember—things that will make you wake up screaming in the night. So, we'll skip all the mundane tools of torture, and move you right up to the head of the class." He reached for another glove at the very edge of the counter, made of leather and heavy with plates of solid lead sewed into the fingers. It was the only thing he could find that would allow him to safely handle the weapon he was about to use.

He opened the lead box he'd had created and removed a very old, and elaborately crafted obsidian knife. The glass blade, chipped to resemble snake scales, was mounted in a bone handle resplendent with gold and gems. It wasn't just the sharpness of the blade that made it useful, but the hideous magic it housed inside.

"What is that and why do you hold it so cautiously?"

Apparently, Nasil had allowed Paolo to see the fear the blade instilled in him. *This* was what made *him* wake up screaming at night, after two millennia of existence with a madman who couldn't ever manage to do the same, no matter how hard he tried.

Nasil spoke with his back to the man, continuing to stare at the seeming innocence of the antiquity, turning it slowly with carefully protected fingers. It was a risk to even touch it with his good side. But the information was that important to gain. "This is the blade the human mate of the wolf stuck in me during the fiasco in Atlantic City last year. It has been enchanted somehow as a weapon specifically against our kind. It not only sucks our Sazi magic into it, it poisons the body as well."

He turned suddenly, letting Paolo be very aware of the stumbling gait, the flopping arm, and his mask of a face. "It's responsible for what you see before you. Half of my body is paralyzed . . . from one single, amazingly painful wound in my side. My human lover is being slowly poisoned to death merely from tending my wound and continuing to lay with me at night." He raised his shirt then, to show Paolo the still-open wound surrounded by gray, dead skin that had to be periodically cut away by his lover Bruce. "You see that it never quite healed. It's not as bad as it once was, but it will hound me . . . *remind* me until the day I die." Nasil tapped the blade against the counter, and watched a wild look fill Paolo's eyes. His gaze flicked between the arm that Nasil was intentionally keeping flopping and the light catching on the glass. Each ting of sound made him flinch. "What part of your body should we start with, Paolo? I am fortunate in that *certain* parts of me still respond to stimuli. Shall we ensure you're no longer able to breed? Will the women laugh at you when you can no longer perform? Is that what will make you wake up screaming at night?" He flicked his tongue out repeatedly, catching the tumble of emotions riding the air.

A look of disgust filled Paolo's face, but his scent still tasted of a panic and dread. "I will tell you what you wish to know. Just put away that . . . *thing.*"

What Paolo didn't realize was that it wasn't fear of the knife changing his opinion. According to his smell, the knife had merely allowed time for the drug to kick in. "Oh, you'll tell me what I want to know anyway. This part is just for *fun*. For all the pain I saw in Bruce's eyes from your taunting and petty injuries. A trip here, a shove there. Yet he bore the insults and the wounds for me, so that he could remain by my side. But it was your mistakes that allowed the human woman to gain access to the casino so that I was attacked. It was *your* failures that allowed the blade to go missing in the first place. Your cocky arrogance that made you believe you were the only smart person in the world . . . that every *other being was stupid and less.*"

Without another word, Nasil lunged forward and made a slicing motion that came within inches of Paolo's face. He intentionally didn't move too fast to be seen. He *wanted* Paolo to register the movement and react instinctively to avoid the blade.

He wanted Paolo to understand the nature of the weapon. The man's initial surprise was followed shortly by the scent of pain. The scream that was ripped from his throat was fierce and penetrating. That was both the beauty and the horror of the blade. The damage could be done with no actual contact.

The knife began to throb under the thick leather and metal. It absorbed Paolo's power like paper absorbing water. "Now it has a taste for you. You see how it seeks you out?" He laid open his palm, the knife flat on the rawhide-covered lead. As they both watched, the blade twitched and moved of its own accord. Nasil moved his hand closer to Paolo's face and another scream followed. Paolo thrashed his head to the side so hard it knocked the blade from Nasil's hand. It fell and landed on Paolo's thigh, where it caused a minor cut through his pants. The welling of blood was nothing, really—barely more than what dripped from his nose. But it was enough for the infernal poison to enter him, as he'd soon find out. And the tip of the knife was pointed directly toward his crotch.

Paolo jumped like a hot poker had been stabbed into him and the knife fell slowly toward the floor— much slower than any ordinary object should. Nasil knew it was the magic being pulled into it that helped ease the fall.

Nasil leaned forward and put his lips right next to the man's ear and whispered. "Where is the egg, Paolo? I'll put the knife away for the *exact* location. You know you *want* to tell me. You want to do anything I ask, don't you?"

He moved back, picked up the knife, and tapped it on the counter. He looked into coal black eyes glazed over with both drugs and pain. "Tell me, *mi amigo*. Tell me and I'll give you pleasure instead. Won't that be better?"

The slackened face nodded, but his eyes followed the movements of the knife with a fear that bled from his pores. His words were slurred and slightly sing-song, but Nasil has no doubt they were the truth. "*Sí*. The egg is in Colorado, near the green table. There is no healer, but there is a guard, the high priest of the Order of Marduc protects it."

"Is there a password so he will know you sent me and I may be trusted?"

Paolo shivered again, his brain obviously realizing the information shouldn't be revealed. But when Nasil moved the blade in an ever-so-slow arc toward him again, his lips loosened. "The passcode is *serpent moon*. That is when the Goddess is to be born. So says the prophecy."

Very fitting. "Thank you, Paolo. That's just what I need to know. And now I will take away the blade." But he didn't remove the glove, because Paolo really couldn't be allowed to leave that easily. Yes, he would eventually die from the poison that, even now, was beginning to chew away at his magic. But after causing so much pain to so many, he really deserved a little payback from those who could no longer speak.

The cell phone in his pocket began to cheep and Nasil checked his watch. Right on time.

He pressed the button to answer the call and began

to speak without waiting for the other person to talk. "You will stop for gas at the station nearest the Coober Pedy airport tomorrow night at precisely seven o'clock. You will open the passenger door when you go inside to pay. When you come out, you will have a passenger, whom you will not notice and will not engage. The passenger will be me. I will ask you questions while we drive and you will answer them completely and honestly. You will take me to the meeting you're attending and speak freely about the drug RSA17 when asked. Do you understand?"

"I understand." The words sounded mechanical, which meant the compliance drug the caller had been given the previous day—the batch that actually worked correctly—was activated.

Nasil turned off the phone without another word. "Well, apparently I have a meeting to attend tomorrow night, to find the location of the rest of the RSA17. When I return, we'll talk again. That is—" He moved toward the door and placed the knife, point toward Paolo, on the floor. "If you're still alive when I return. Oh, and you don't want to scream or call for help, do you?"

Paolo shook his head, and his lips closed. But his eyes were wide, watching Nasil's movements.

Even as he stepped back and took off the glove, the knife was vibrating, sensing the Sazi energy that surrounded Paolo. It lurched forward once, so slowly it was hardly noticeable. The glass blade made an odd scraping sound against the concrete. Paolo's eyes were locked on it.

Once the knife had sought him out the same way, but it seemed to be very selective. Once he'd used the knife to slowly kill one of the priests, it lost a taste for his magic. But Nasil still wasn't willing to risk it discovering a new appetite for him. "You'll survive without food or water for a day, but I wonder, will the blade reach you before I return?"

Nasil closed the steel door behind him and walked into the sultry Australian night. He wondered whether there would be anything left of the great and feared Paolo Montez, mentally or physically, when he returned a day from now.

And he realized he didn't really care.

Chapter Four

"SO? TELL ME about these enemies of the Sazi. Who would dare attack us and how big a threat are they really?"

Eric and Ivan were parked in the empty lot of a rural clinic in the small town of Cortez. Tatya was inside the high-tech semi-trailer getting everything set up. Eric had wanted some time alone with Ivan to talk about things, and it just seemed easier to jump right into the middle of his questions.

Ivan shook his big, bald head. "I can't tell you that, my friend. And *you* should know better than to ask."

Eric unbuckled his seat belt and turned so he could watch the other man's face. He sort of had to, since Ivan was wearing the special Wolven cologne now. Apparently he'd sprayed it on just after he'd walked out of the building. So now he was a blank slate to Eric's nose, and to Tatya's as well. While the special chemical that Bobby Mbutu had created was terrific in the field, making agents all but invisible to even the best Sazi nose, it was frustrating to them too, because it was completely indiscriminate. *All* emotions disappeared, so they had to rely on plain old body language and intonation to guess intent. It made keeping secrets much easier. "I'm a pack leader. I have the right to know about anything that could endanger my wolves."

Ivan smiled, but didn't turn to look at him. He kept watching out the window, staring at the trailer. "You're not a pack leader *yet*, young wolf. That will only happen if the council approves you. If we do, then of course you will be privy to information that will help you protect your pack."

Eric felt a frustrated sound escape his mouth. "That's a mere technicality, and you know it. The council wouldn't be going to all this trouble unless they planned to install me. Besides, do you really think Lucas is just going to let me wander back to Australia now that he's got his clutches in me? I'll be conscripted into Wolven if I don't make the cut for pack leader."

Ivan dipped his head once, not denying the logic. "True. And when that happens—"

"Oh, for God's sake, Ivan! If you'd just—"

The telephone in Ivan's pocket started playing "God Save the Queen," a tribute to his adopted home, no doubt. The little BlackBerry looked tiny in his wide hand as he pressed the button to connect the call. "What is the problem, Tony?"

Ivan didn't leave the car, meaning the call wasn't sensitive enough to worry about.

"Thompson left his cell phone here," came the light baritone over the speaker, and it caused Eric to frantically pat his pockets. Damned if he hadn't left it in the rush. "I went ahead and answered it when it rang. It was his mother calling. Said it was an emergency, so I figured I'd pass along the message."

Mom? There was only one thing that would make her track him down, rather than wait for the weekly call he always made. *Shit. It's Derek again. It must be.* He sighed, shook his head, and pounded his fist on the door's armrest. It must have spoken volumes to Ivan, because he gave a slow shake of his head. "He heard, Tony. I'll have him call. Tell Lucas we're at the site. Tatya's inside now, working out the details. I'll let him know what I've decided after we get back."

What *he* decided? That was interesting. Eric was starting to wonder just how much power Ivan had on the council, and what it meant that he was down here.

Ivan clicked off the phone and handed it his way. "I presume you'd like to call her?"

The laugh that escaped Eric was more bitter than warm. "*Like* to? Hardly. But I probably should." He reached for the phone almost reluctantly and dialed the international number from memory.

He heard Ivan mutter under his breath. "Wolves. With wolves it is always something."

"Hello?" Eric's mother answered on the first ring,

but cautiously, her voice telegraphing the fact that she didn't recognize the number on the display.

"Hey, Mom. I got your message. I'm calling on someone else's phone, so let's keep it short. What's up?"

"Eric!" Now her voice changed to not only happiness, but real excitement. "Oh, sweetie! We're all just so excited for you. Your own pack! I always knew you'd be a leader someday. And you'll be closer to home so you can visit."

Eric felt his heart fall into the pit of his stomach. The glowering look on Ivan's face didn't help any. He raised one hand in protest and mouthed the words, *I didn't say anything. I swear!* To further cement his innocence, he spoke his outraged confusion into the phone, hoping maybe a lie would throw her off track. "Mom, why would you think that? I'm just in the country doing some testing. I don't know anything about a pack."

"Oh, you're always being so modest. But there's no reason to hide it. We heard it from a reliable source, someone you don't even know. So you can't possibly get in trouble for it."

That raised Ivan's brows and he motioned for the phone. Eric reluctantly handed it over and winced at what was going to come next. His mother might be Alpha Female of the Canadian pack, but there shouldn't be any way for her to find that information out.

Ivan opened his door while speaking. "Mrs. Thompson, this is Councilman Ivan Kruskenik. I'm with your son, and I'd be *very* interested to learn where you found out this information—especially since it hasn't been

approved or discussed outside the council chambers."
He shut the door before Eric could hear the response
and even though he rolled down his window, the
traffic on the highway nearby made it impossible to
make out her voice once Ivan had moved a dozen feet
away.

He could see lips moving rapidly, but really, he
didn't want to know. He rolled up the window again.
This just *had* to have something to do with his older
brother, the Alpha Male of his former pack. He just
didn't know what yet.

After a few moments, Ivan finally walked back
toward the car and opened the driver's door. "Delilah
has a question to ask you. I'll allow you to answer
it . . . under the circumstances."

God. Weren't there always *circumstances* when
it came to his family? This time he got out as Ivan
climbed back in. The air had chilled to near freezing
and this close to the full moon, it felt good. The air
smelled of piñon and ice. He almost wished he could
disconnect the call, pretend none of this was happening, and go out and run in the trees. "Okay, Mom.
What's up?"

"I didn't mean to get you in trouble." That much
was clear. She sounded contrite and afraid, meaning
that Ivan had done his job. Eric couldn't argue with
that. He was pretty ticked off too that someone had
blabbed. "But you *have to* accept Derek into your
pack, sweetie. They're going to put him down unless
you do."

Whoa, whoa, whoa! "What the hell, Mom? When

did we move from 'Congratulations, sweetie' to 'you have to'? Who's going to put Derek down? He's the pack leader there, for heaven's sake. Who *could* put him down?"

There was a pause where all he could hear was his own breathing. But he knew she was still there. She did this every time she needed something important. "Wolven, Eric. Wolven is going to put Derek down unless someone agrees to accept responsibility for him."

Eric let out a breath he hadn't realized he was holding. Damn it. Not again. "What did he do this time?" So Wolven had finally caught up with Derek. No. It was *reality* that had finally caught up with him, now that Eric wasn't there to blame everything on. And they had. He'd been considered the pack fuck-up for as long as he could remember. Except he *wasn't*. It had been Derek. Unfortunately, the older Thompson brother was the handsome one, the powerful one, and the charming one.

And Eric wasn't.

Of course, nobody believed Derek was also the sneaky one, the conniving one, and the violent one until Eric finally went so far away that there was no possible way to blame him for things.

"It's a long story," his mother finally said. She sounded beaten, tired, and so very frightened. That was going to make it even harder to say no. Which he fully intended to do. "The short version is that a human girl is injured . . . seriously. She may or may not be pregnant with Derek's child."

Eric could fill in the gaps by himself, even though he didn't want to. He stared into the night sky and tried not to think about the poor girl's future. She might become one of them, or her body might not handle the change and rip itself apart. If she survived, the baby might not.

Either way, it was a death sentence for Derek.

There'd been rumors of things like this before, when Eric was there. But he couldn't get anyone to investigate and the girl had simply . . . disappeared. "Even if I were going to get a pack, Mom, why in the world would I want to take him in? How long did I try to convince you that he was dangerous? Maybe he *needs* to be put down—for everyone's good."

"*Eric Matthew Thompson!*" The shock and outrage in her voice said he'd overstepped but frankly, at this moment, he didn't really care. "He is your *brother*! He just needs some help . . . some time away from everything."

"What help is there in the middle of nowhere, Mom? Even if I get this pack, there aren't any treatment facilities nearby. We might not even get a *healer*. What help could he possibly find down here?" Eric opened his mouth to say more, but there weren't any arguments that would change his mother's mind. Derek was still the golden boy in her eyes, and this was all just a *big mistake*. Better to delay and hope it became a moot point.

She started to speak, but Eric cut her off. "You know what? Let me think about it, Mom. There isn't even a pack at this point and the council might not make their decision until the next quarterly meeting." He'd reached the car again and could see the staff of the mobile MRI unit descending the steps with coats on. "I've got to go. They're about to start the next round of tests on me. We'll talk soon, when I've got my phone back, okay?"

"But . . . but what do I tell her, Eric? She's set the sentencing for tomorrow."

"Tell *who*?" His hand paused on the door handle.

"The Wolven agent who's here. The tiger named Raina. She said her investigation warranted a death sentence and she's carrying it out tomorrow. Derek's been confined to his house with a magic barrier. I can't even get in to talk to him. To find out if what she says is true. *Please!* I have to be able to tell her you'll take him in. He'll die. My boy will *die*." She started to cry, the sobs sounding like hiccuping static over the speaker.

Shit. Now what? Eric pulled open the door and ducked his head in, letting the warm air from the heater chase some of the chill from his skin. "Did you know about this, Ivan? What the hell am I supposed to tell her? Can you order Raina to give some sort of stay of execution until I even know if I *have* a pack?"

Ivan looked at him with confusion and crossed his arms over his chest. They barely fit between the steering wheel and his chest. "I believe your intentions were very clear when it came to your brother. Didn't you tell me when you left for Australia that you wanted to let him rise or fall of his own accord?

Now he has. Wouldn't a stay of execution merely delay the inevitable? If he's part of your pack, it will be *you* who will have to bloody your hands to enforce a death sentence. This way you have no responsibility."

Even though the phone was still outside the car, Eric couldn't help but hear the word *please* being repeated over and over, between sobs. "I know. But—" He thought about it for what seemed like an hour, but was probably only a few seconds. "Being a pack leader is all *about* responsibility. I guess there's no difference whether I take on a dozen unknown problems, versus one *known* one. It'll just help make the decision I've been struggling with anyway—whether to bind the pack or let them have autonomy. If I bind him, he can't get into any trouble that I won't know about in advance."

Ivan's face was skeptical. "He's strong, Eric. And unpredictable. We'd planned to give you a first pack that was all lesser wolves, to build you into the position slowly . . . before we introduced any alphas who might challenge you. And he *will* challenge you. You have to know that."

Eric nodded, even though he hadn't planned to agree. "I know. But I've gotten tougher over the years. I'm not the same person I was when I left home." He took a deep breath and stared at Ivan, willing him to tell the truth. "But it's not just me or him. There will be innocent wolves who have nothing to do with this. Men, women, and children who I wouldn't want to be terrorized if he goes off the deep end—either here or in Canada. So be honest. Who would win if it came to a battle between us? You've known us both for years."

Ivan uncrossed his arms and rested his hands on the steering wheel, his fingers tapping the padded leather cover. "Truthfully? I don't know. You're nearly equal in strength and fighting ability. But you play by the rules, and I don't know that he would. He might not *allow* the fight to be just between you two. He'll take any advantage." He let out a sigh. "But I believe I would put my money on you in the end. So, if you feel strongly about it, I will call Raina and have her guard him until the council decides. That is the best I can do. If you are granted a pack, he will be spared and delivered into your custody. Will that do?"

It was the best he could hope for. He moved the phone back to his ear. "You catch all that, Mom?"

"Oh, thank you, my darling. *Thank you*. And thank the councilman too. I'll go tell the agent to expect his call." She ended the call and Eric handed back the phone just as Tatya stepped down the stairs and motioned with her hand for them to come forward.

Ivan was still shaking his head as he began to dial a number. "I hope you know what you're doing, old friend. I fear this isn't over. And I fear you will regret this choice."

Eric clapped him on the shoulder with a wry smile, which was a lot like slapping a rock. It made his hand sting. "Regret is the price we all pay for charity, Ivan. Charity doesn't save the world, and often doesn't save a single life. But it's a chance. Then it's up to the people being helped to move forward. It'll be up to Derek whether this second chance means anything."

The only reply was a rumbling growl.

Eric got out of the car to allow Ivan to make the

call in private. Frankly, he didn't want to know the details of the arrangement. He was coming to grips with the fact that he was probably going to have to make some sort of peace with his brother. If Derek didn't die, he was going to be losing his pack, he was going to be exiled from the place where he grew up—the only place he'd ever lived, and moved from a major city to the wilderness. After the initial gratitude wore off, and the shock to his system from the binding had faded, there would only be . . . desperate, angry loneliness.

Gee, won't that be fun?

Eric had reached Tatya, who was carrying a clear plastic clipboard with what looked like a questionnaire tucked under the clip. The standard white lab coat over her outfit was a little big for her small frame. But with her hair rolled into a coil at the back of her neck, she looked every inch a doctor. It seemed a shame that she was going through the very same thing Derek was about to. The Boulder pack was no more, she was moving to Paris, and was in trouble with the council. And from what Eric had been able to see, she had that same alphic egotism that Derek possessed—which Eric seemed to have been spared. *Thank God.*

"We're ready to start."

"We?" Was one or more of the humans still inside?

She rolled her eyes and let out a sigh that said as clearly as her scent that she was still annoyed and frustrated. "Okay . . . *I'm* ready to start. The machinery can be handled by one, but I'll need some help from Ivan at the start and finish. There won't be any danger to you. I promise."

The British anthem began to play in the distance. Eric didn't bother to turn his head. No doubt Ivan's life had gotten much more complicated with his move up the political ladder. Eric shrugged and glanced toward the machinery. "I didn't think there would be. I've had an MRI before. My ankle got screwed up when I was a kid, and it took forever to heal." No need to mention it was Derek who screwed it up. Just one more reason why he'd need to start the new relationship on *his* terms. Not his brother's.

"Good. That will help speed this up. The machinery's been improved since then, but the experience will be the same on your end. Of course, we're going to be taking images of your chest and throat, so you'll need to be completely inside. You're not claustrophobic, are you?"

"No. I—"

Ivan strode up behind them. his power moving air ahead of him so hard it was like a semi passing on the freeway. "We must go. Eric, get in the car. Tatya, destroy any record of us having been here. You have two minutes."

Tatya was obviously taken aback by the clipped words. She furrowed her brow with an annoyance that matched her scent. "Ivan, what in the world?"

He flicked his eyes her way and then abruptly slammed a wall of power against her so hard she stumbled back and dropped her clipboard. "I will not tolerate arguments from you anymore, doctor. Not as a council member, and not when I speak for Charles, as I do now. When he says we evacuate, we do so. You now have one minute if you value the machinery inside, or I will simply destroy the trailer."

There were some things in Sazi life that nobody questioned, and one of them was that Charles Wingate ruled absolutely. He was not only the Chief Justice of the council and de facto king of their kind, but a powerful seer. Unfortunately, his gift of seeing the future was unpredictable. He might see an event only moments before it happened. But it *would* happen. So, if he said *move,* you moved and quickly. Her eyes widened and she sprinted up the stairs so fast she was a blur. Eric followed Ivan back to the car and jumped into the driver's seat. The big man didn't argue. While he was a perfectly adequate driver, he was a better shot—if it came to that. It bothered Eric that he didn't have a weapon. Magic was great for avoiding humans and for fighting hand to hand, but it didn't stop a bullet. But after the show of power outside, he decided it was better to be cautious, former partner or not. "Any idea what we're up against, or was that just a message to Dr. Santiago to start treating you with more respect?"

Ivan shook his head and a harsh breath vibrated his lips. "I've allowed too much familiarity in my role as Charles's bodyguard, Eric. It's not just the doctor who doesn't show proper respect to my new office."

Ouch. But he didn't reply, and add to any possible punishment.

Ivan sighed and started to open his mouth when

movement across the parking lot caught his eye. Tatya had turned off the light in the trailer and was racing down the stairs. She pushed shut the metal door just as Eric heard tires squeal in the distance.

They all looked the same direction and could see a black sedan coming toward the clinic at a fast clip. Plain human sight might not have noticed the three masked figures dressed in black and wearing flak jackets that were visible through the open windows. When he saw automatic weapons poke into the air, Eric turned his head toward Ivan, damn any *familiarity*. "Do we stay to fight or leave?"

Tatya reached the car and climbed in the back, nearly echoing Eric's words. "Fight or flee?"

"We leave." The words were barely out of Ivan's mouth before Eric had the car in gear and they were burning rubber across the asphalt as he turned to get back on the road. The scent of hot rubber, along with the variety of emotions filling the car, nearly made him sneeze. He coughed and snuffled to fight past the urge. He couldn't afford to be blinded while driving. He was glad now that they'd filled the tank on the way to the appointment. Tatya had complained, of course, but he'd always found it best to take advantage of slow times to prepare. And as they raced into the night, he noted with satisfaction that the station they'd visited was closed for the night.

"Wouldn't it be easier to just call nine-one-one?" Not only were the authorities better equipped to deal with masked gunmen, the three of them weren't doing a thing wrong that they could be stopped for.

At least Ivan's reply sounded more like *him* than this new persona. "Nyet. It would only mean more bloodshed and long delays. I asked Charles the same question. His instructions were to lose them so we don't lead them back to the site of the new pack."

"*Lose* them?" That was a lot easier when the driver knew their way around the area. He didn't. "That might be easier said than done." He raised a hand to take in the darkened, deserted landscape. "Any idea how to manage it? Maybe I should switch places with the doctor. These are her stomping grounds."

"Uh, no," said an amused voice behind him. "Cortez isn't my stomping grounds. Boulder was. I'm as lost down here as you two."

"Should we ditch the car and shift forms? I *can* lose them in the dark among the trees. But it's tough to take a car into canyons and through streams."

"I vote for stopping and fighting," Tatya said from the backseat, her words edged with a snarl that spoke of the moon's influence. He felt it too, sultry and tingling on his skin. He could resist it, but he didn't really *want* to. "I've defended myself against guns before. We're all alphas and I'm a healer. They don't have enough bullets to take us down before we can take *them* down."

That sounded good to him too, but Ivan shook his head. "Those aren't our instructions. Charles was very clear. Lose the car and then make our way with all haste back to the new headquarters." He peered through the windshield. "Is there enough starlight to drive as we did in Kiev?"

"With the lights out?" Eric mulled. He'd done it before, but not recently. Still, it could provide an advantage, unless—"Are we dealing with humans here, or other Sazi?" If their pursuers could *also* see in the dark, it didn't make any sense to risk it.

Ivan shrugged. "I do not know. Charles could not see that part. He only saw it was imperative that we lose their car and make it back safely."

One corner of Eric's mouth turned up as he glanced in the rearview mirror to see the sedan gaining on them. "I sort of consider that imperative too. Okay, we'll give it a shot."

Speaking of shots, there was a series of pops in the distance with resulting tings as the bullets entered the trunk. He pressed down on the accelerator and watched the landscape come at them faster. Yes, they could shoot back, but it was better to let the others waste their ammo and save what they had for when it was critical.

Eric took a deep breath. The tricky part was immediately after the lights went out. He'd have to get his eyes to adjust quickly. He focused on the long stretch of straight roadway and then closed his eyes. He felt a moment of panic, as he always did, driving completely blind. But he kept the wheel frozen in place, so there was no way to go off the road unless he did something stupid. He let the breath ease out of him and flicked off the lights.

Tension sang through the car, and Tayta made a small noise that wasn't quite panic. Eric totally understood the feeling. It was one thing to see in the dark while standing still or running. Wolves did that every hunt. But to be speeding into the darkness with so little time to react was a different thing entirely. Eric opened his eyes and was pleased that they had adjusted in the small amount of time. He could just make out the edges of the roadway—the landscape dimly lit by the headlights behind them and the starlight above. Two more blinks and he felt confident he could get them there safely. Of course, they couldn't avoid any deer they might encounter, but . . . "Could one of you extend your magic in front of the car to chase off any game that might get in our way? I would, but I have to concentrate on driving. And some illusion would be nice too. I won't have to work so hard to lose them if they think we're already gone."

"Very clever," said Ivan with approval in his voice. "I can remove the sight and sound of us easily enough if the doctor would push away any animals."

Eric could see Tatya's bemused expression in the shadows of the rearview mirror. "First time I've ever chased away prey, but I can definitely put the fear of God into anything in the area. I'll try for a wedge shape off the front bumpers—I can probably give you a couple of car lengths. Much past that and it'll lose potency."

"No arguments from me," Eric said with a shrug as he added a little pressure to the pedal and watched the needle climb past ninety. "I'll take anything at this point."

He shuddered as magic began to fill the car, slowly at first and then with ever-increasing strength. Ivan's magic was as powerful as he remembered, and there was no denying that the former Alpha Female of the Boulder pack was a power to be reckoned with. Even his own skin began to crawl with an unnamed fear that had nothing to do with hurtling through the darkness at ever-increasing speeds. His fingers twitched involuntarily on the steering wheel and he could sense the movements of bodies in the darkness as they fled from the roadway.

The vehicle behind them began to fall back. Likely they were confused now. Their headlights *should* reveal the rear bumper and reflectors of the car Eric was driving, but with the illusion magic Ivan was providing, it would appear only as inky blackness.

But they weren't easily fooled, because they suddenly stepped on the gas and began to inch closer. Eric could see the concentration on Ivan's face as he stared into the passenger mirror intently. In the next instant, flickers of light caught Eric's attention in the driver's mirror and he heard a popping noise. Tatya let out a little scream and everybody ducked as the rear window exploded into fragments of glass. But their concentration didn't waver. The pursuers wouldn't see any sparks as metal hit metal. There would be no sound of glass to the pursuer's ears. As far as the gunmen were concerned, they'd just wasted a clip of ammo on nothing. Eric could only hope that the glass had fallen inward, or they'd spot it glittering on the roadway.

Tatya remained carefully in place on the seat, while wiping glass from her shoulders and legs onto the floor. She shook her head and Eric could hear a rain of glass bounce off the vinyl.

Unfortunately, it seemed the other car had a more

powerful engine than theirs, and unless the magic worked soon to make their adversaries doubt themselves and double back, they were going to catch up. Eric pressed the pedal down harder, but there was nothing left and the needle on the speedometer had topped out at ninety-six.

The magic flowing from the backseat suddenly faltered and Tayta let out an anguished cry. "*Lucas!* No!" Ivan's attention was pulled away from the mirror and Eric also looked into the rearview in alarm.

"Vat is wrong, doctor?" The accent was creeping into his voice, reverting as it always did under stress.

"He's . . . I don't know. Ivan, we have to get there soon. Something's very wrong. We only have a one-way mating, but he's just . . . there was a flash and now—" She shook her head, tiny movements that matched the abrupt scents that told of her fear and worry. There was a frantic look on her face and her blue eyes were wide. "We have to go faster."

Eric's attention returned to the road as he saw a flash of movement and realized they'd just very nearly hit a deer. Obviously, whatever was wrong, her attention was distracted enough that she wasn't putting out the same kind of energy.

"There isn't any *faster*. But I really need you to get your head back in the game if we want to get there *at all*. A deer just got close enough to hit. If I have to push away the deer too, I'm going to tire out too fast to finish the drive."

Her eyes got even wider, if that was possible, and then her jaw set with a hot determination that smelled like burning wire. Her eyes began to glow with a blue-green light that was nearly turquoise and fear once again began to make his heart flutter. "I'll clear the path, but Ivan needs to get rid of that car. Can't you blow their engine or something? I remember Lucas did that once."

Ivan's eyes flicked sideways at the same moment Eric's did. He felt his brows raise. "Is that even *possible*, Ivan?"

"For Lucas? *Da*. But for us? Unlikely."

Still, it got Eric's mind working. A car engine was actually a pretty simple thing. Fuel, spark, and air. That's all it took for a combustion engine. And if you remove *one* of those— "I have an idea."

He eased off the gas and saw the lights behind them begin to grow larger. Ivan growled and glared at him. "Vat are you doing, volf?"

"Trust me, Ivan. I might not be able to blow the engine. But I'm betting I can still disable it. No battery . . . no drivie. You just keep them from seeing us, and I'll do the rest."

That was all the explanation there was time for, because he could sense the car close in on their bumper. It wasn't easy to keep his attention on the road and also feel backward with his magic. One thing he'd always been good at was being able to tell the shape of things with his magic, and batteries had a nice regular shape, no matter the vehicle. His magic flowed across the front of the grille, searching for the solid, rectangular mass. And then he found it.

His fingers began to drum a rhythm on the steering wheel as he stared into the darkness. Another touch of the gas kept the other car just a few feet off their bumper. He could only pray that Ivan was doing his job and they didn't know they were so close. Gunfire from this distance could do some serious damage, and somehow he had the feeling the bullets would be silver. Just right for making sure Sazi didn't get up after being hit.

He tried to move the battery with his magic, but it was bolted down. Luckily, though, there was a tiny bit of give in the wire leads going to the terminals. The next portion of road was going to be tricky. There were a lot of curves and a couple of them were sharp. He gripped the wheel tighter and used his magic as a third hand to pull at the leads. There wasn't any way to know which was positive or negative, so all he could do was shake them both.

"Vatever you're doing, it should be soon. Don't forget about the road construction ahead. I von't be able to hide the dust we raise on the dirt."

Shit. He'd forgotten about that. He was thrown sideways against his belt as he jerked the wheel to take the car around one of the tighter curves and the pursuing car got dangerously close. He hit the gas again to give them a little more distance. The amber lights of the road signs were visible. There was no more time.

He gritted his teeth and threw everything he had backward to push and tug the leads frantically. They were budging, but not quickly enough.

The lights were looming and he could see where the pavement had been rototilled down to the base. It would be a bumpy ride for about a quarter mile afterward and with the vehicle headlights that just rounded the curve ahead, he was going to need his own lights to see through the cloud of dust the other vehicle would raise.

"Now!" The word was shouted as he slammed every ounce of power he had backward. He felt metal give as the grille deformed from the pressure and the hood of the sedan flew up. The horn began to blare and the vehicle braked, with no visibility. The leads finally gave in a flash of movement. The lights went out as the car stalled in the middle of the road.

Eric pulled back his magic just as the tires dropped off the pavement and a teeth-rattling vibration began to shake the car. No doubt they startled the driver of the semi approaching, because it blared an air horn as they passed by in a shower of dust and gravel.

"I'm going to leave the lights off for a bit longer and suggest you keep your magic going too. No reason to give away our location after all this trouble—in case there are any others waiting up ahead. Who knows, we may get lucky about the dust."

Ivan nodded, but there was no response from Tatya in the back. He glanced in the mirror and worried at the strange, vacant expression in her eyes. "You okay, doctor?"

Whatever her expression was, her voice was even odder. She kept looking at her hands and then touching her head. She opened her mouth wide like she was trying to pop her ears after swimming. "I . . . I don't really know. I can't remember the last time I felt like this. It feels like I'm missing a finger or a hand, but that doesn't make any sense because they're right here in front of me." She wiggled her fingers with a frown and tried to pop her ears again.

Eric remembered his mother saying something similar once. Like Lucas, his father had been mated to his mother, but not the other way around. Ivan let out a small, worried growl that made Eric glance at him. Ivan tilted the cell phone his way to reveal the message of *No Signal*. They couldn't even check.

At least he could turn on the headlights. There was no sign of their pursuers, and nobody else had joined the chase. But still he kept his foot pressed hard against the floor, using his own wedge of magic to drive away the wildlife—since Tatya no longer seemed capable.

When the lights of the compound came into view, he let out a sigh of relief. Eric's nerves were frayed to the last thread from the intense concentration he had to pay to the road at this speed, his ever dwindling supply of magic, and the constant tapping of long, painted fingernails against the car seat behind him. It didn't help that with every breath he drew, the scents of worry and fear flooded his nose. Even Ivan was starting to smell worried, so either the cologne had worn off, or his emotions were overpowering the chemical's ability. Eric wasn't surprised at his worry, though, because he was beginning to share it. None of the calls Ivan had tried to place after they had gotten a signal had been picked up.

That wasn't like Lucas at all.

He let his foot ease off the accelerator as they

neared the turnoff to the long graveled driveway. He opened his window a crack to let in some fresh air to help get rid of the soggy fog of worry pressing against him. The wind began to whistle in ever decreasing tones as he braked. But as soon as he made the turn, panic made his stomach drop. He slammed his foot down on the gas pedal once more, making rock spray up behind the car and the back end fishtail.

Carried on the thin, focused breeze were two new scents—acrid gunpowder . . . and *blood*.

Chapter Five

"WELL, DON'T STOP there! Keep going!" The excitement in the voice made Holly smile. Cat was always interested in what was happening to her, and yet it amazed her every time they talked. She should be beneath Cat's notice. Her friend was not only incredibly beautiful, she was disgustingly rich—heiress to a vast computer fortune. Yet Holly had never met a more down-to-earth person. Admittedly, Cat was more of a geek than a social butterfly. Unlike her hardware-creating father, she loved coding, creating software from scratch. In fact, Holly's uncle Raphael was getting used to finding the bed empty in the middle of the night because Cat had gotten an "inspiration" and was plunked in front of the computer, her fingers flying over the keyboard.

Thankfully, Raphael wasn't Holly's uncle by blood—because how messed up would *that* be to have a BFF who was also your *aunt*? She would also feel strange gushing over the couple's newborns as rabidly as she did if they were her cousins. The boy and girl were fraternal twins, mirroring their parents rather than each other. Ray—Ramon Eduardo, named for Raphael's grandfather—was the image of his mother with thick blond hair and piercing blue eyes, while little Maggie—Margaret Janet—had her father's permanently tanned skin and dark curls. Holly smiled at the thought as she decided how to respond to Cat's question.

"Oh, c'mon! You can't leave me hanging. What happened after Annie went down to the river? Did you and Eric work things out? I mean you said you were going to talk to him, find out what really happened."

Holly could imagine Cat's eyebrows wiggling as they always did when she was trying to get her to spill. She felt her face redden and twirled the phone cord around a finger while she paced the short distance to the end of the bed and back. "There wasn't anything to talk about. I told you, we hadn't even made it out the starting gate when he left." But the remembered sensation of his arms around her made her words a lie. She could still feel his fingers skimming through her hair with one hand while the other rubbed lower and lower until— *It was pretty sweet when he tucked that thumb in my back pocket and squeezed.*

Woo! . . . Interesting.

The voice made her blush even harder. One of

Cat's special gifts, inherited from the Sazi who attacked and turned her, was telepathy. There was no thought that could be hidden from Cat if she'd met you, even briefly. Thankfully, she only used the skill to tease or if there was a crisis.

So squeezing your butt isn't reconnecting, huh? Raphael didn't do that until our second date.

"Stop that!" Holly felt herself exclaim, laughing as she said it. "Okay, so maybe we reconnected a little. But we didn't kiss or anything."

"Yet—" Cat spoke in her ear once more, which was good. She wasn't sure if Cat could see memories or worse, *fantasies*, and didn't want to find out.

"From your lips to God's ears, Cat."

"Okay, I'll let you off the hook for now about the handsome Mr. Thompson. What have you been up to since he left for America? Just playing tourist?"

The first comment perked up Holly's ears. "He *is* back then? Is he okay?"

"Yup. I asked Uncle Chuck about him when you called me from Annie's. All Eric's coming back for is some testing by the healers. He promised Wolven had nothing to do with it."

Holly felt a large weight lift from her even though it still totally weirded her out that Cat called the Chief Justice *Uncle Chuck*. But he was Cat's godfather, a friend of her parents from before the attack that made her Sazi, so she had a unique privilege. Holly was thankful for that relationship. It was probably the only reason Holly was alive today.

What Cat said next perked her ears. "Apparently,

he's got one heck of a howl. They think it's some sort of actual *weapon*. Some of the seers said he's going to be important someday." Pride mixed with awe in Holly's mind. The Sazi seers knew their stuff. They guided everybody's daily existence—kept them safe and in balance with humanity.

Then Cat let out a sharp laugh. "But hey, they said that about Raphael and you too, so what do they know?"

Had they? She opened her mouth to ask what Cat had heard when her friend continued, "I could track him down if you want. I know almost all the healers now. One of them must know something."

Holly shook her head so hard she felt her newly cut hair slap against her cheeks. "Are you kidding? I don't want him to know I've been *asking* about him. He'd think I was some sort of creepy stalker-girl."

"Oh. True that. And I'm not really good enough yet to sneak a peek at the big minds. They're probably the only ones who would know anything. Okay, then. Change of subject. I take it you found Rose? Are you getting together for a bitch session later? It's still daytime there, right? I always get messed up on the time changes."

"Yeah. Afternoon here, which means it's yesterday there. Weird. But yeah, I found Rose." Holly had always called her talks with Rose bitch sessions, because that's all they wound up doing—bitching to each other about one thing or another. For a long time, Rose had been her only confidant, the only other person in the family who understood the frustrations of being a mere human in a world of wolves. But Rose had come first, so she was treated like an ordinary kid. By the time the two sets of twins—Jasmine and Iris, and Lily and Pansy—came along, Rose was old enough that she didn't care that they turned.

Holly had never had that luxury, because Rose was already away at college when she was born, and Mom had died having her. There was nobody to defend her or help her when the bullying started. It wasn't until she was sixteen that Holly had really gotten to know Rose and realized how much they had in common.

But did they still have anything in common? "We talked, and we're getting together later tonight."

"Whoa. You sound . . . *odd* all of a sudden. Is everything okay with the two of you? I thought you were really excited you were going to get to visit with her." Holly could hear background noises fade in the distance. Cat must be padding—probably barefoot— through the rambling house in Albuquerque to a place where they could talk more privately. But Raphael was a wolf, and could probably hear their conversation anywhere in the house. Anywhere, that is, except Cat's computer room. When Holly heard the metallic thud of a door shutting, she knew that Cat had gone into the specially reinforced, soundproofed room that had cost a small fortune to install. But it was a haven for her—where a paranoid cat could escape her duties as Alpha Female of a pack of wolves and *know* she was utterly alone and safe. "Okay, now you can dish."

Holly took a deep breath. It was now or never.

"There's some stuff I haven't told you about my past, and I'm afraid it's coming back to haunt me."

There was a pause long enough that she wondered whether the connection had gotten broken. "Are you still there?"

"Mmm-hmm. Just thought I should keep my mouth shut at this point and not ask the obvious."

Holly sat on the bed and threw herself back against the pillows. She stared at the ceiling while blinking back tears. Cat's voice sounded so . . . *careful*. Was she hurt? Offended? Pissed? "Like why haven't I brought this up before when I've talked about my family?"

"You said it, not me. But I thought we agreed—the no-secrets thing was why I told you about all that stuff back in California."

Holly let out a sigh that carried over the line and picked up a small red accent pillow and started to thump it on the bedspread. "I know. I know. Part of it was that I'd honestly forgotten. I'd already sort of gotten out of the group before we met."

"Group?"

"FMU. Family Members United. It's a support group that a bunch of us human kids started. Mostly online in a password-protected forum. The original bitch session, but with more people. Rose is a member and so was I. There's a meeting tonight at her house and she wants me to come." Once again her stomach roiled and bile rose into her throat. It shouldn't be this hard to *think* about the group.

"And this is a bad thing? Jeez, I would have *loved*

to have known about them after I got turned. I needed all the support I could get."

The pillow went sailing across the wall to hit the mirror. She winced as it wobbled, but it stayed attached to the wall. "But that's the thing. It's *human only*. I'm not sure they're going to like having me there tonight."

Cat's voice turned incredulous. "Holly, you were an attack *victim*. It was *so* not your fault. If you were already a member before, I can't imagine they wouldn't still be supportive. I mean, who better to understand?"

Her head shook of its own accord, pulling hard enough on the phone cord that the whole unit nearly fell off the nightstand. She was going to destroy the room if she wasn't careful. "You don't know what they're like, Cat. It's sort of the KKK of the Sazi world. Utterly loyal, but only to *our kind*. More than a few would enjoy cross burnings and lynchings, except it would only piss off the animals, not kill them."

Another long pause and she realized she'd actually said *the animals* out loud. It had felt strange, and yet utterly natural too.

"Um. You're shitting me. Right, Holly? And you were a member, *why*?"

Holly threw up one arm, even though Cat couldn't see it, and brought it down sharply against the nearest feather pillow. "Anger. Hate. All that rebellious teenage crap. It was my life, Cat. The same shit you saw and put a stop to. If I haven't thanked you yet today for helping me get my head on straight, thank you."

"So you were active in this . . . *group* until you turned? Even after you met me?"

"Not so much. They started to get a little too radical for me about the time I turned twenty-one. I joined at sixteen. I dropped out when they started talking about requiring all members to move to states that allowed concealed carry permits. That just seemed . . . creepy, y'know?"

"Yeesh. KKK with a side order of IRA. And Rose is still a member?"

Holly's eyes moved to the clock radio on the table near the window. Just an hour left. She'd slept away most of the morning, not realizing just how tired she'd been, and the smell of baking chicken "chook" casserole from downstairs had made her wander down for an early dinner before she called Cat. "Yep. One of the founders. She swears that everybody is going to be glad to see me, but I'm not so sure."

"Well, you'll certainly get your answer."

Her brow furrowed and she sat up on the bed and leaned back against the headboard. "Answer?"

"If they welcome you with open arms, they're a support group. If not . . . then I'm thinking hate group or cult is a better word for it."

"Yeah, that's sort of where I was going with it." A wave of what felt like panic rushed over her just then, but she couldn't place the source. Still, it reminded her. "And you *can't* say a word to Raphael about this! The FMU has to be kept secret."

"Hello? I say again, cultish."

"I *swore*, Cat. I take that as seriously as I took my promise to you when everybody else thought you were insane for hearing voices in your head."

Fine. I promise . . . so long as they don't endanger

anyone here. But if they threaten my kids or my people, all bets are off.

That Cat had resorted to telepathy said she didn't like it, but she'd do it.

"Hey, if they so much as *look* at those kids, I'll be right alongside you telling Wolven about them. Okay?"

"It won't be Wolven, Holly. It'll be *me*. Sister or not." Cat's voice had taken on the utter ruthlessness that had been instilled in her by witnessing the slaughter of her parents. Holly couldn't help but shudder at what Cat would do to protect her children.

"Just remember to listen tonight, okay? Weigh *support group* against *radical cult* when they talk and make your own choice. For your sake, and theirs, I hope it's just a nice, friendly group."

She couldn't possibly realize how much Holly hoped that too.

THE SUN WAS just setting behind the tailing hills as she reached the far edge of town. She'd taken her time walking, admiring the stunning opals displayed in shop windows—wishing she could afford the ones she liked. There was something about the ones they called *painted ladies* that she loved. Her favorites were the really red ones with blue flashes. Apparently, a painted lady find a few years back had caused a mining rush that was still going on. It was probably what had brought Dale here.

Once she left the paved main roads, the dirt underfoot began to sparkle in the sun's fading rays. She found herself scuffing her feet to watch the glitter swirl in the wind—like standing in the middle of a snow globe. One of the store owners had called the gleaming bits *oelic*, the equivalent of fool's gold. Pretty, but worthless.

The address Rose had given her wasn't what led her to the house. It was the landscaping that screamed of her sister's touch. Rose had always loved xeriscape plants, and the drought-resistant flowers that tumbled from nooks and crannies in the piles of stone spoke of her skill. There was nothing else like it around— a tiny bit of paradise in the sweltering heat. Old, concrete-coated wheelbarrows bloomed with desert paintbrush and purple ice plants, while a discarded bathtub overflowed with delicately scented moss roses. One rather strong odor made her wrinkle her nose. She knew that creosote was a desert plant and had heard it was pretty, but it smelled like old rail-road ties.

She glanced at her watch. It was eight o'clock on the nose and yet she hesitated just at the edge of the property, staring at the cars parked near the staircase that she presumed led down to the front door. A window at ground height had been opened and she could hear voices and laughter drifting into the coming twilight.

A woman's voice that sounded just like *Char186*'s podcasts rose over the others. "I just *love* those purple flowers outside! What did you say they were called?"

Then a man's baritone. "Hey, Tom. You know of anyone that's got an alternator for my ute? It's a 'seventy-three, and the shop can't find one."

A tenor was laughing. "For a *'seventy-three*? You jokin'? I heard the Rex is denying seats to galahs now. I think you might qualify." Everybody laughed. Not evil laughs . . . just warm and friendly ones that spoke of good friends at a party. She shook her head at her own paranoia.

I'm being ridiculous. These people are my friends. Cat was right. Either they would support her, or they wouldn't. She could always leave and go visit another city if she wasn't welcome here. There was nothing to keep her.

She squared her shoulders and walked toward the stairs. The breeze dusted her nose again with creosote and she wound up in a sneezing fit just as she reached the door. The laughing stopped and then the door swung open so fast that she had to turn her head to keep from spraying snot all over her sister.

"Holly! C'mere, you!" Rose reached for her in a rush. Holly barely managed to stop sneezing long enough to give her big sister a hug. After a tight squeeze, Rose pulled back and held her at arm's length. "Gorgeous hair, perfect skin, and still as skinny as ever. God, I hate you." But her scent was pure love and happiness—sugar sweet, like an early morning donut shop.

Holly laughed. "I missed you too."

Rose turned to the group seated in the tastefully decorated room carved into the pale, cool earth and grinned as she put an arm around Holly's shoulders. "Look, guys! The meatspace convention is complete! *LittleSis* is here!"

It's been a long time since I've heard myself called that. LittleSis was her screen name from the FMU forum, and she was amazed at how many faces lit up at the announcement. She was quickly surrounded by people, and overwhelmed by scents and faces. Familiar handles were shouted out so fast she could barely keep track, and she had no hope of matching them to faces. In addition to *Char, Birdofprey, Hissyfit, Nobodystoady,* and *DickODoom* gave a shout-out. In fact, only two people didn't come to greet her. An older, heavyset black woman with silver hair glared at her from her spot on the couch. And a youngish Middle Eastern man sat primly, tucked far into the corner, out of the way and alone. He looked like he'd had a stroke. Half of his face drooped. Holly noticed that nobody was including him in the conversations. They weren't even glancing his way. She figured that she should take that as a hint. Maybe he was sensitive about his condition. She tried to smell what might be wrong with him, but there was no scent of sickness about him.

In fact, he doesn't smell at all. That seemed odd and it made her glance at him again. He didn't notice. He just kept staring ahead blankly, as though in his own world. Yet there was an intelligence to his eyes that told her he was fine mentally. Maybe he couldn't hear or talk. Either way, she'd follow the others' lead and ignore him until he chose to be included.

When everybody had finally calmed down enough to sit back down, and Holly had a glass of wine to sip on, Rose turned to her. "So, tell us all about your trip."

The woman on the couch interrupted with a snarl. "We don't have time for that now, Rose." She rolled her eyes. "Yes, yes. It's *LittleSis*. How exciting. La-dee-dah. But I plan to be home by ten and we have a lot of things to discuss."

There were looks of annoyance around the room, but nobody spoke up. Rose turned her head and mouthed the word *Breakneck*.

Oh! Martha Tamu, known as *Breakneck*, was the forum Super moderator, and was the lone human born to a pride of Kenyan lions. She was a snarly, bitter woman online and apparently she was no better in person. It was nobody's fault that her older brother had once pounced on her in cat form and had fractured her neck. She'd eventually relearned to walk, albeit with a limp, but she'd managed to inflict her festering resentment on everybody she met thereafter. Holly had learned it was best not to antagonize her, so she just nodded pleasantly. "Of course. I don't mean to interrupt your meeting. I could just go and talk to Dale for a bit while you guys do your thing. Is he home?"

Rose laughed. "He never *leaves* home, but he's not really available. He signed on a new patch and caught a flash so he's starting a drive. He'll probably be at it all night."

She must have had a confused look because Char laughed and citrus filled the air as she spoke with a thick Australian accent. "*LittleSis* must not know our lingo, *Rosebud*. I think you gobsmacked her."

Rose joined in the laughter while *Breakneck* continued to glare. "Quick vocab lesson, sis. A *patch* is a new lease from the government for a mine. They're pretty rare lately, so Dale got all excited and started on it last night. Opal mining is done at night with a UV lamp. The raw stones glow like blacklight posters, so when he spotted a flash of color, he decided to go down the hole and start a new hole sideways to see if he could find some more. That's called a *drive*."

"Ah! Got it. Okay, never mind then. I'll just sit here and be quiet."

"That would be nice." *Breakneck*'s words dripped with poison and more than a few people in the room smelled annoyed again. They were scared too, which bugged Holly.

Rose just nodded quietly. Apparently, *Breakneck* was in charge of the meeting, because she started snapping orders. "Toadie, treasurer's report. Char will be next with the old business—"

A cell phone chirped just then and Toadie reached into his pocket, ignoring the sour face and lowered brows. He glanced at the display and his scent turned excited, even though he gave no outward sign. "I've got to take this. It's Miguel. Char can read the report. She helped me write it."

Finally, there was an actual smile from *Breakneck*. "Hopefully it's good news."

Even Rose held up her hand, two fingers twisted together. "Fingers crossed!"

Holly sort of tuned out when Char started talking. She'd been to enough meetings of the Denver group to know how it would go. There was never enough

money. There were never enough people to help, so
nothing got done. They planned useful, important
things about awareness for family members and trying to start a private insurance group to help with the
bruises and nonthreatening cuts that everybody
seemed to get. But again, nothing, because nobody
wanted to fund the pot and nobody wanted to be responsible for the work.

But her ears perked up when she heard, "So, we're
down to only eighty thousand in savings. The loss of
the New Mexico plant really hurt our resources."

Eighty thousand? What the hell? She remembered
dreaming of the day when they'd have *one* thousand
and how much could be done with that amount. But
now they were *down* to eighty? She found herself
starting to listen more intently, and noticed that the
man in the corner was as well. Apparently he wasn't
deaf.

Breakneck sighed, but then shrugged. "It'll have
to do, I suppose. I'm less worried now that everything's coming together. *Hissyfit,* have you heard any
hint that they know of our plans?"

Hissyfit's eyes widened and he nearly choked on
his drink. After a few sputters, he replied, "Are we
going out of order now? My report's in my case in the
kitchen. Should I go get it?"

He got a withering look in response. "A simple yes
or no will do, unless you need a cheat sheet to spit
out a single word."

"Oh." He looked abashed and sunk back into the
cushions in a futile attempt to escape *Breakneck*'s
intense gaze. "Um . . . well, I mean—"

"*Yes* or *no*? Or should I just give someone else the assignment?"

"No." The word was a whisper, his eyes downcast, and he smelled ready to cry. Holly suddenly remembered another reason she'd left the boards. The bullying by one or two of the members was nearly as bad as what she got from her sisters. At first, the forum had seemed liberating. She could chat and post and enjoy herself. But then came the sniping and the snarky responses to even the simplest questions. Near the end, she was feeling more depressed logging out than when she arrived. She remembered *Hissyfit* from the early days of the forum, when it was just a ragtag group who sent IMs back and forth. He'd started out beaten down by his viper-shifter older brothers. Over the course of a year, he'd gotten to where he was relatively confident. But if this was what he'd been reduced to since *Breakneck* took over—

Words started popping out of her mouth and she couldn't seem to stop them. "Would you knock it off with the pressure already? *Hissy* doesn't have to ask *how high* when you say *jump*."

All motion stopped in the room. Only *Breakneck* moved—her head turning slowly in Holly's direction like a creepy doll in a horror movie. "Gained quite the smart mouth when you got your teeth and fur, did you?"

Emotions roiled over the room and assaulted Holly's nose. Disbelief, anger, and betrayal rode on a blanket of fear that permeated her senses and threw her into a fit of sneezing.

Now Rose stood up, her fists clenched and shaking

with outrage. "*Damn it!* I told you that in *confidence*."
Then she turned to face the others while Holly tried to
get a fit of sneezing under control. "Yes, fine. Holly's a
wolf now. She was *attacked* and nearly killed because
of one pack member's petty jealousy. She stood up for
a friend and was nearly put down. I hope we're better
than them, because being turned doesn't mean she's
against us. If anything, she's *more* one of us. After
everything that's happened to her, to come to this—
to become what she loathed . . . well, I don't doubt
she's going to be more than happy to see what we've
planned to end the *animals* once and for all."

Holly fought to snuffle up the thick mucus that had
formed in her nose from the scents as a wet cloud of
sorrow abruptly replaced the anger, except for Rose's
and *Breakneck*'s. More than one person gasped and
Char had a hand to her mouth, her eyes open wide in
shock. All eyes were on Holly and most were now
filled with sympathy. All except the man in the corner,
who was watching her with a furrowed brow. His arm
was bent up and was resting on the other forearm and
his fingers tapped his lips as though he were sizing up
an opponent. Once again she couldn't help but wonder
about him, and why she still couldn't smell him.

Why?

*Plans . . . eighty thousand . . . plant in New Mex-
ico. End them once and for all*. Shit. Could FMU
have evolved so much in the time she'd been gone?
Could they have gotten even more radical—going
beyond simple talking to *action*? Worse, could they
be doing illegal things to fund their revenge?

Crap. The man in the corner must be a Wolven agent who had infiltrated the group. He was wearing that special cologne Lucas did when he was on a case. *And now he's wondering what the hell I'm doing here with them.*

Maybe it would help her case—and she didn't doubt there would be one now—if she got more information he could use. *Once and for all* had a very final ring to it that she didn't like.

She dug into her memory, called up the day she was attacked. The fear and the anger she felt when Corrine and her cronies surrounded her. They'd planned to kill both her and Cat—with the knowledge of the rest of the pack members. She felt her voice harden and anger fueled her. Maybe she wasn't dealing as well as she'd claimed to be to Eric. "Of *course* I'm with you. They wanted me dead just because I was friends with someone they didn't like. I *hate* that damned pack! Everything's changed. My life's a wreck. I used to love to watch deer in the forest and now I can't stop myself from chasing and *eating* them. And talk about irony. I was going to be a *vet*. You remember, Char. The change turned me into a freaking healer. Great! A healer who can't even get near her patients. Small animals are terrified of me now . . . and who wants to hire a vet who terrifies pets?" She felt tears well and realized she hadn't ever let this out, not even with Cat. Her hands were clenched so tight she could feel her nails cut through skin. But the healing magic sealed the wounds as fast as they happened. "I have to live where they tell me, can't go to the schools I want, and will always ... *always* have them looking over my shoulder. God, I *hate* this!"

She let the tears that had been trying to flow for months come out. Char stood up in a rush, tears likewise streaming down her face, and ran the short distance to where Holly sat. She threw her arms around her and hugged tight. "Don't cry, *LittleSis. Please* don't cry. We can make it better. We can give you back your life. I swear." She turned her head to look back, burying Holly's face in her thick dark hair that smelled of fresh apples. "We can make her a special case, can't we? Couldn't she be a spy for us, like Toadie? We still need someone inside to feed us information, right? And when we're sure of the formula, we can make her one of us again. Right? Holly's not just the little sister of the wolves. She's *our LittleSis.* She's one of us."

Apparently, Holly's speech had even affected *Breakneck*, because her eyes were filled with teary outrage, not *at* Holly, but on behalf of her. "We don't need anyone in the wolves right now. We already get all the intel we need. But yes, when all the tests are done, we'll make her human again. Sooner if she's willing to take the risk. We still have some vials of the most recent batch."

Say what? Human again? What the hell were they working on? The man in the corner smiled, but with his face affected, it was more of a leer.

She opened her mouth to ask the obvious question when the front door opened in a rush, and Toadie raced in, pumping his fist in the air in triumph. "Two out of six, baby! Nobody even saw us coming with everything else going on."

Cheers erupted from the room, leaving Holly completely confused. But it seemed the Wolven man in the corner was likewise at a loss from the way his brow furrowed and his eyes narrowed. Toadie swept around the room, slapping outstretched hands like a baseball player rounding the bases after a grand slam.

Holly! Cat's panicked, angry voice slammed into her mind like a brick to her temple. *You have to come back. There's a helicopter heading your way to pick you up at the airport.*

What? What's happening? I'm at Rose's. I'll go back to the hotel and call you—

No! No time. We'll send someone for your things, but we need you back in the States as fast as possible. You might be the only person left who can save them. The pilot will know where to go. Don't even worry about your passport. He'll take you straight to the jet. We've cleared it.

Holly's mind was reeling. There was too much input from too many places. *I don't understand. Save who? What's—*

There's no time. Lucas and Uncle Chuck are down and we're evacuating Albuquerque as soon as I can get out of here. I'm with the kids in the computer room for now. I've already killed five, but there are more of them than I can fight off and still keep the babies safe. I'll have to wait for Raphael and the others to get back. I . . . crap! They're breaching the door! Just get to the airport. I'll let you know where we wind up.

Cat? Cat! But there was only silence. The connection shut off before she could find out anything else. The room started to spin and Holly was having a hard time breathing. *Two down out of six.* Lucas and Uncle Chuck? What in the hell was going on? She stood in a rush, her muscles twitching from the sudden rush of adrenaline. There were few things Cat couldn't handle and if things were bad enough she was panicking—

Shit.

Rose's telephone rang just then, and her sister went to answer it among the cheers and clinking of glasses. "Hello? Yes, this is she." Rose turned to her and then put a hand over the mouthpiece. "Holly? There's a man on the phone who said your flight's arrived. I thought you said you were staying for a week. What's going on?"

Her jaw moved, but nothing came out for at least two tries. She glanced at the Wolven agent and held up her hands in frustration. He'd have to handle whatever was happening alone. The half of his face that worked registered shock at her actions and suspicion soon followed. But she couldn't worry about that right now. "I forgot . . . that is . . . Look, something came up back home. I have to go back right away. It's . . . my apartment, or—" Hell, she couldn't even think enough to come up with a good lie. "—something. Anyway, I have to go. Sorry."

She rushed out the door so fast they wouldn't be able to stop her and started running toward the airport. It was dark enough now that nobody would see her if she ran full out and stayed off the lighted streets. The trick was going to be not falling in the holes that dotted the landscape.

The lights of the town disappeared behind her. It wasn't until she narrowly avoided one mine shaft, sending her skittering sideways and wrenching her hip hard enough to make her cry out, that she realized she was being followed.

The snake was fast, too fast to be anything but a Sazi and there was no way she could outrun it now. Every movement was agony and even though her body was healing rapidly, it was going to catch her before she could reach the airport.

She stopped and turned to face her pursuer. The helicopter would wait for a few minutes. They'd expect that it would take her time to get there. She raised power in a big enough burst that she hoped it would make the snake back off. It did, but it just let out a series of small hisses that she realized was laughter. "Who are you and what do you want? I'm prepared to fight if I have to." And she could. She'd stayed with Cat and Raphael for a time when Cat was heavily pregnant and couldn't exercise. Raphael had needed a sparring partner. He'd showed her a lot of the same moves he'd taught his wife. While Holly wasn't as vicious as either of them, she was flexible and fast and could put the hurt on nearly anyone.

The voice was male, a medium baritone that slurred a little around the edges, like he was drunk. "Who I am doesn't matter, and I have no desire to fight you. If I wanted you dead, you already would be."

Holly threw a sudden punch at him that connected hard enough to make pain sing up her arm. Then she stepped backward to put some distance between

them. But the ground disappeared under her so fast
that she was afraid she'd stepped in a hole.

It was no hole.

The snake had gotten behind her before she could
blink, sometime between the punch and her step
back. She tried to scramble to her feet, but he coiled
around her tight enough to make the air whoosh
from her chest, and raised a net of power so fast that
she couldn't expand her lungs again. Panic filled her
but she couldn't move. Was she going to be kid-
napped? Raped? Killed?

"That was well executed but foolish, child." He
raised his head above her until she could see venom
glistening off fangs that were at least six inches long.
"I merely wanted to talk, but you may have me take
the information by force. Still, I did sneak up on you,
so I'll give you a chance to make amends. Are you
willing to talk quietly, or shall I begin to make you
scream?"

She couldn't smell whether he'd enjoy torturing
her, but she'd known plenty of snakes who did. In
fact, she couldn't smell him at all. Which probably
meant—

He eased the magic surrounding her enough that
she could answer. She made her voice as calm as she
could and tried to make it so her scent didn't telegraph
what she was feeling. He flicked his tongue repeatedly
while he waited for her to reply. "Okay. We can talk.
You're the man who was in the corner of my sister's
house, aren't you?"

The mouth opened wider as he lowered his face

until his flicking tongue tickled her nose. "Very good, but I'm curious as to how you saw me. Nobody else in the room did."

Nobody *saw* him? Was that why nobody had looked his way? "I have no idea. Are healers immune to illusion?"

"It wasn't illusion, which is why I'm curious. I find it very interesting. But that's not why I caught up to you."

He was beginning to ease his grip on her. If she timed it right, she could likely slide out from his coils and race to the airport before he could catch her.

Maybe.

"Why did you then?"

"I find myself in need of a healer . . . one that's not known to the Sazi council. I believe you're just the right person. If you agree to help, I'll let you live."

Something that the council wasn't supposed to know about couldn't be good. She shook her head and readied herself to move. "Sorry. Not interested. I guess you'll have to kill me."

That little hiss came out of him and a drop of venom slowly fell from one fang to land on her exposed shoulder. She let out a sound that wasn't quite a scream as it sizzled and bubbled her flesh. She pulled away hard, intending to slide out. She made it halfway and clutched at the ground to yank herself free. But he merely tightened his coils and his magic until she was frozen in place. All except for her head. Not many alphas could do that. She'd seen Lucas do it before, but nobody else. "Brave *and* clever. A dangerous combination. I *should* kill you. But I won't. No, I'll simply turn you over to someone who's likely quite irrational by now. You're just his type—young and small and alphic. Oh, yes. He likes a good fight. But he's quite brutal and very strong. He'll likely beat you unconscious and then tie you down with silver, naked and ready for fun and games. He likes sinking his fangs—along with other things, into pretty young wolves. And after that? Well, who knows? But you're a healer, so you'll probably last longer than the girls before you." He leaned close enough that she could feel his warm breath on her neck. Chilling words hissed into her ear. "Possibly for *years*. And, I should warn you that he was quite perverted when he was sane. I doubt he is anymore after what I did to him earlier."

A shudder overtook her and he chuckled low at the revulsion that she couldn't keep from her scent. There were some things worse than death, and she knew it. "What do you want?"

He nuzzled her ear with his nose and she felt him blink against her hair. "First, you're going to let me accompany you back to America. Then you can go about your business until I call you. When I call, you'll come. Alone . . . without telling a soul. And you'll help me make sure that a child is born. I could drug you to ensure your compliance, but it might interfere with your healing abilities."

Her brow furrowed. "That's all? Just help with a childbirth?"

The snake leaned back. His mouth split open under eyes that glowed golden red from the power he was expending to keep her still. "That's all." But something in the pit of her stomach told her there was more to it than that. She wanted to run screaming into the darkness. Still, if he really did let her go, she could tell Wolven or one of the council and have him captured.

Something of what she was thinking must have showed on her face. *God, don't let him be telepathic too.* He abruptly shoved his tail between her legs hard and put his full weight on her as he slowly unwound himself. She rocked back and forth on the ground as each coil unlooped and her flesh crawled as his tongue flicked against her neck, then her chest and stomach while her body was still frozen and she couldn't stop him. Once he was uncoiled he lay down over her, smothering her face against his dry, hot scales. She couldn't breathe and tried not to think about what might come next. But then he stopped and she realized he'd been doing it intentionally, feeling her up to give her a taste of what lay in store if she tried to run or hide. "I should mention . . . *Holly Sanchez*, that if you fail to show up, or if I discover you've told anyone about me—" He paused and slammed his mouth down suddenly. She screamed as his fang impaled her wrist and locked it to the ground. Poisoned venom spread into the tissue, burning hot as fire. She would have screamed again, but he froze the sound in her throat. The bite started to heal even with his tooth still inside and he had to jerk to pull it out. He licked the blood off the tooth and smiled again. "It will be your *sister* I take to my friend. I don't think she'll last as long."

Tears sprang to her eyes, both from the pain that was slowly crawling up her arm, and the thought of Rose being held captive by a lecherous, insane snake. She couldn't help it and it made her angry that he'd managed to get under her skin like this.

He leaned close once more, until she could smell the rabbit he'd had for dinner on his breath. "I think we understand each other. Remember, when I call, you'll come." He released her and moved back so she could sit up. She rubbed at the wound on her wrist, now sealed but still spattered with drying blood. It felt like someone had ground out a cigarette on her skin and even now it was bruising and scarring as her body struggled to dispose of the poison. "I'll meet you at the helicopter. You needn't do a thing for now. The pilot won't even know I'm there."

As he slithered off into the darkness, favoring one side so that his tracks weren't a perfect *S* shape, she called out. "I don't even know your name. How will I know it's you when you call?"

She couldn't see his body against the night sky, but his eyes suddenly appeared in the darkness. "Oh, I think you'll know. But *Larry* will do for now." He blinked and then let out that hissing chuckle that was starting to make her shiver each time she heard it. "Don't let the pilot take off until I'm on board. I have to pick up something before we leave. Otherwise, who knows where it'll wander off to."

She didn't get whatever the joke was. But he apparently found it funny enough that Holly could hear him hissing long after he disappeared into the distance.

Another shiver overtook her. What sort of devil's bargain had she just made?

Chapter Six

IT WAS TOO quiet.

The stink of fresh blood hung heavy in the air. Not even a breath of breeze moved it, so it felt like the scent was plastered to Eric's skin. The door to the office was open, hanging off one hinge, and as they approached, the lights went out, throwing the whole compound into inky darkness. Heavy clouds that should have meant rain, but didn't smell of it, blocked the light from the moon and stars.

Tatya immediately shifted to wolf form in the shadow of the sedan and Eric helped her pull the clothing from her fur. With a nod, she slunk into the trees to start checking the perimeter. She was a pack leader, and from everything he'd heard about her, a skilled hunter, so he didn't spend any time worrying about her.

Ivan handed over his gun and moved close to whisper in his ear. "Stay in human form. The gun is loaded with silver. I'll get to higher ground to see how many are left." *Left* was the operative word. There had to be some, because there weren't any bodies, and there was too much blood for just one downed person. He squatted down next to a pool of blood the consistency and color of Hershey's syrup in the dark.

As Ivan stripped off his shirt and pants and carefully put them through the car window onto the seat, Eric dipped a finger in the blood and brought it to his lips. He spat it immediately out. *"Viper."*

Ivan let out a little growl. "Then they could be anywhere. Keep watch in the bushes, and I will hope there are more rattlesnakes than tree-climbers." Eric had figured *higher ground* probably meant climbing a tree, and that would definitely be easier with the eight-inch-long claws Ivan had in bear form. Plus, he had the advantage of thick winter fur. Even a Sazi snake would have a difficult time reaching flesh through the undercoat.

Eric felt air press against him from the distance. His hackles rose and he turned the gun toward the rustle of a bush ahead. The scent of sage and creosote dusted the air as a stray breeze moved. Ivan nudged his shoulder with a wet nose and then lumbered off into the night.

He'd spent many nights in the pitch black Outback and had learned to focus in on the slightest sound. Black on black moved ahead and Eric didn't wait for confirmation. He pulled the trigger and felt the pistol jump in his hand. But his wasn't the only flash to light the area. Twin shots rang out to his left, a hairsbreadth faster than his, and then a hiss and shout of pain filled the air before all went still again.

"Nice shot, Thompson." It was Tony's voice and it came from above. He spun in a circle, looking up and finally spotted the waving arm on the roof. He flicked a cigarette lighter to highlight his face and called out with a hand cupped to his mouth. "All clear, everyone! That was the last of them."

He closed the lighter, slid down the roof feet first, and as soon as he reached the end, flopped onto his stomach, grabbed the gutter with black-gloved hands, and dropped neatly to the ground. "Glad you finally got here. I was starting to get cramps up there. But I couldn't get them to come out of their holes until you got here to lure them."

Tony reached inside the building and flicked on the light switch as the hum of fluorescent lamps buzzed in his ears. The sudden bright light made Eric blink more than once but he ignored it as he went to inspect what they'd shot. It was easy to tell which was his bullet, because it was a small dime-sized hole in the snake's spine, versus the quarter-sized shots from Tony's massive .50 caliber. One shot was right between the eyes and the other high on the back, where the heart would be. He wore the big gun in a shoulder rig and the damned thing stuck out like a sore thumb. "Nice shots. How do you keep that thing concealed, anyway?"

Tony looked down. "Nah, yours was better. I have the advantage, in that I can see the target. You tagged it blind. And this isn't my carry piece, for what it's worth. It's from the armory inside. There's bigger stuff too, but it's hard to move around quick with them. Don't know why Lucas set this place up with this much firepower, but I'm glad he did."

"Where is Lucas?" Tatya's voice was both a command and a cry. They turned at the same time and saw her looking around frantically, sniffing the ground, searching for any sign.

Tony thumbed toward the building. "In the basement. I'd like to say everyone's okay, but I'd be lying. They're in bad shape." Tatya was gone like a shot and before they could reach the rectangle of light, they heard her cry of anguish. But she was a healer. If they could be saved, she'd be the one to do it. It was best not to follow and get in her way.

Ivan appeared then, dressed once more in his brown polo shirt and slacks. He reached out his hand toward Eric and flicked his fingers. Eric returned the gun and watched as he checked the chamber and smelled the barrel. He motioned with his head toward the snake. "Were they all vipers, Tony?"

He shook his head. "No. There were raptors and spiders too. God, I *hate* those damned spiders! I'll be having nightmares for a week."

Ivan's eyes narrowed as he looked around the empty yard. "And where *are* all these attackers? How is it that Lucas is injured, but *you*—a three-day wolf, are not?"

It was a logical question, and one that Eric had been about to ask as well. Tony's eyes narrowed for a moment, and anger sprang into the air. His words were clipped but careful. "The simple answer is, I don't know. I was inside working on the data, and Lucas was outside with David looking at whatever he'd found. I heard a commotion—growls, snarls, and hawk noises and grabbed the first gun handy and went outside. Lucas and David were already down by then, and I shot at whatever got in the way so I could get to them." He let out a frustrated breath and stared into the sky. "The birds were trying to pick them up to take them away. I clipped the wings on one and it dropped Lucas. They did take David's body, which pisses me off."

"Wait." Eric raised his hand to stop the story. "You said *they're* in bad shape downstairs. Who else was here?"

Tony cursed. "Shit! That's right. You were already gone by then. Charles showed up just after you left. He's down there too."

Charles? Charles was so injured he couldn't stand outside to tell his own story? Eric believed this tale less and less. "The head of Wolven and the Chief Justice of the council are so injured they needed help, but *you're* okay? I'm thinking we should cuff you right now, because something smells really foul."

Ivan's voice rumbled, his eyes fixed on the new wolf. "You *do* work for the highest bidder. Lucas made that very clear to the council."

Tony's voice likewise lowered, and a thick Italian accent took over. "Let me make this crystal clear— and be sure your noses are primed and ready. I. Am. *Not*. Involved in this. I didn't set anyone up. I didn't turn my back or close my eyes when it started. I don't know *why* I'm still kicking, other than I'm a damned good shot. I don't know where all the bodies are. I spent my time getting the wounded secured and guarding them. I was inside until you showed up. All I can figure is that they carried away their dead." He paused for a long moment, letting them both take a long smell to see if he was lying, but there was nothing other than anger mingled with honest confusion. "I don't know why they didn't target me, but they didn't. Unless I shot at them, they flat-out ignored me. Take from that what you will. You want to call Aspen to check me out, then call her."

Aspen Monier, now going by Josette Cooper, was the only seer Eric had ever heard of who had hindsight, the ability to see the past in someone's mind. That Tony was willing to subject himself to that spoke of his innocence more than anything, because Aspen would be outraged to hear of a serious injury to either Lucas or Charles, and wouldn't be gentle with whoever might be involved.

A long shadow cut across the compound and they all turned, ready to take on whatever might come. It was Tatya, naked except for a pair of boxer shorts that didn't fit very well, and an oversized T-shirt. There was blood splattered across the white cotton and she looked about ready to collapse.

"They're stable, just barely. But I can't wake them up, and I don't know why. They're in some sort of deep coma and their wounds aren't healing right. It's as though they have no magic of their own to heal. I'm having to do all the work."

Ivan nodded toward the doorway. "You should go lay with Lucas. You're his mate. Just having you nearby will do more good than anything."

She nodded wearily. "I'm just so tired. I could really use some meat. I haven't eaten since breakfast." She looked around into the darkness, frustration plain on her face. "What the hell happened here? Why are all the bodies gone and what could take *both* of them down?"

Tony let out a deep sigh. "There *is* one way to find out."

Tatya narrowed her eyes. "I'm not letting you near Lucas right now. I don't trust you. In fact, I've never trusted you, and have no idea why my husband ever did!"

Tony threw his hands into the air and smelled peppery with anger. "What is this, anyway? Beat on the new guy day? You're giving me a hell of a lot of credit to think *I* could hurt either of those guys. I'm a fucking *three-day*, people! I have second sight and hindsight and I'm a good shot. That's it! Nothing more. I've wondered for the better part of *two years* now why Lucas keeps stepping in for me . . . why Charles keeps telling everyone to leave me alone."

He paused and his face grew startled. "Maybe that's it," he said quietly, almost to himself. "Maybe *this* is why they've been keeping me around." He waved his hands at the looks of disbelief on their faces. "No, no. Stay with me on this. This attack was *coordinated*, like a war. Air force, infantry, and marines, all timed to wear us down. They waited until you left, they took their dead and injured, and they left one person alive to tell the tale. Someone wanted me to live. We just don't know *why*." He nodded and crossed his arms over his solid, muscled chest. "I need to hindsight one of them, and I'm thinking it should be Charles."

A three-day with both second sight and hindsight? That was just plain *weird*. Those gifts were normally reserved for the strongest of alphas, not a wolf who had no control over when he shifted and had to shift on every night of the full moon.

Now Ivan was nodding. "We all wondered why you were so important, but Charles was adamant. If he saw this event as a possible future, you would be the only person able to find out the truth. He would want you to stay close to Lucas."

Tatya shook her head and leaned against one of the iron posts holding up the steel roof over the porch. "No, there's Aspen. I'd rather call her in. I can keep them stable until she arrives."

Ivan shook his head grimly. "She's been missing for nearly a week. Only the council knew. Her husband's frantic. He's been calling in every favor he knows to find her. The last lead he had was that she was somewhere in Arizona, but he couldn't figure out who might have taken her, or if she went there voluntarily. It wouldn't be the first time she disappeared on her own. Sometimes she removes herself from the puzzle, so she *doesn't* interfere."

Eric turned to Tony. "Is your ability a secret? Does anyone other than the council know you have hindsight?"

He shrugged and pursed his lips. "Secret? No, not really. I've been working for Wolven for a year now. The hindsight is what I do to close up old cold files. Pretty much anyone who's anyone knows. Pack leaders, healers, the psychiatrists."

Eric raised one finger and started to pace. It always helped to move while he thought. He often went for a run when he was trying to figure out a case. "Maybe we've got this backward. Maybe they left you alive because of what *they* don't know. Charles was known to be so secretive that it drove everyone insane. Lucas was following some sort of thread about a big, world-ending plot for nearly a decade now, but nobody knew the details. If they got Aspen out of the way—"

"Because she's far too powerful and unpredictable—" supplied Tatya.

"And relied on *me* to get the information—" Tony added with a growl.

Eric found himself nodding. "They could capture you and force you to tell all. They have to know we'd be rabidly curious about this—blood everywhere but no bodies and two of our greatest warriors out cold. That just *screams* mystery."

Ivan let out a short bark of a laugh. "They apparently don't know Tony very well. He doesn't . . . squeal."

Now Tony smelled distinctly disturbed. "No, I don't. But they might not have to torture me. Has Ahmad told the council about our little adventure in Atlantic City? Did he mention the new drug the followers of

Marduc came up with? The one that makes people compliant zombies?"

The bald man nodded grimly, while Eric tried to figure out who or what *Marduc* was. "My very thought. Are you *certain* you didn't get any injuries? Could you already have the drug in you?"

Tony shook his head, but his eyes were nervous. "I've smelled it before, and I haven't here, to my knowledge. But I can't be certain. The sucky part is that if I *had* swallowed it or had it injected, I wouldn't know because the first instruction is not to remember taking it. Goddamn it!" He let out a deep sigh. "I guess that answers it then. I can't do a hindsight. We can't take the risk. But if I don't, we'll never know what happened." His eyes went blank, as though he was seeing something nobody else could. With a strangled sound of pain, he dropped to his knees and pressed his fists to his head.

Tatya moved toward him, her eyes wide. But Ivan held her back. "Someone is contacting him mentally. This happens every time. Don't interrupt him or it'll only be worse."

"Shit. Shitshitshit!" Tony said after a few long moments. He took a few long pulls of air into his lungs and tried to get his eyes to focus. After a few blinks and shakes of his head, he looked up at them. "Not good, people. Really, *really* not good." He pulled a cell phone from his pocket and swore at the lack of bars on the lighted display. "Bet they took out the towers."

He stood up and moved toward the building. "We need to move this conversation inside, and quick."

Eric followed the others down the stairs and finally got his first look at Lucas and Charles. They were laying on the floor, nearly naked and definitely unconscious. Tatya had done her best, but they'd nearly been ripped to shreds. Fang marks mottled their skin with poison, and talon punctures laid open their rib cages. Part of Charles's ear was missing, which should have healed itself by now. It was a small miracle that Tony had been able to keep them from being taken if the tear marks were any indication. They were breathing on their own, but he could see why Tatya had said it was touch and go.

Tony plopped down on a stool and motioned for Ivan to shut the door to the stairwell. "That was Nikoli contacting me through the pack link. Chicago was also attacked, and it seems like it was at nearly the same time as us. From the coordination I saw here, I'm betting it happened everywhere. We need to figure out a way to contact all the packs, prides, and nests, and find out how many people are left. Nikoli reported the same things I saw—snakes and raptors with a few spiders."

Ivan went pale and he stared at Charles's still form. "He foresaw this nearly fifty years ago, and I remember every detail he revealed. He told me a little of what he saw—a new Ravaging, like what happened long ago. But this time, from within."

"Sazi upon Sazi?" Tatya's voice was horrified, and for good reason. There'd never been a true war among their kind.

Tony shook his head and sighed. "I'd like to say

I'm surprised, but I'm not. The whole world's like this right now—everybody right on the edge of something massive. A war to end all wars. I hate it . . . but I also don't know how to stop it." He slammed his fist down on the desk and the monitor shuddered and blinked out for a second. He swore and hit the same spot again and the image on the screen returned. "Damned crappy equipment. I'll fix it later . . . if there *is* a later."

Ivan squatted down next to the Chief Justice. "Charles and Lucas have been making plans for a very long time. But they wouldn't bring anyone in to their confidence, so now we know nothing of what they've set in place to correct this."

A phone rang just then and they looked around frantically, seeking the source of the noise. It was coming from the corner of the room and sounded like it was behind a wall. *No, not a wall. A safe.*

He reached for the handle and twisted. For some reason, it wasn't locked. Inside was a cell phone that was of an odd design. It was larger than one on the shelf, and much heavier. Eric couldn't tell if it was an old phone, or a really new one. He flipped it open and put it to his ear cautiously. "Hello?"

"This is Cat Turner, Alpha Female of the Albu-querque pack. Who is this?" The voice was female and snappish, each syllable beating a staccato rhythm on his frazzled nerves.

"Eric Thompson," he replied. "Alpha of Four Corners. If there's a pack left."

"Is Ivan there? I was told to call him."

Eric passed over the phone. Instead of plastering it to his ear, Ivan held it out so everyone could hear. "Good to hear your voice, Cathy, but I'm afraid I have bad news."

She interrupted him, sounding sad, angry, and frustrated all at once. "At this point, I probably know more than you do. Charles contacted me mentally when he was being attacked, and gave me very explicit instructions. I'm calling at the very second he said to call, when he knew you'd be in the building and able to find the satellite phone he had me order for them."

She let out a little choking sound that nearly ripped out Eric's heart. "Here's all I'm allowed to tell you at this stage, and *please* don't try to get everything out of me until it's time to tell you. I'd probably say the wrong thing and then everything would get screwed up. Anyway, you're to instruct Tony Giodone, if he's still there with you, to do a hindsight on Charles. He said to be really careful, because it'll be hard to tell what is the past and what is a potential future— which will look like the past, but isn't."

"Oh, fuck," muttered Tony. His annoyance mingled with fear and rode through the room on air-conditioned comfort. "Like I need that kind of pressure."

"Uncle Chuck said that both Holly Sanchez and Eric are supposed to attend the hindsight."

"You mean *literally*?" Tony asked the question with astonishment on his face. "I've never taken two people on a ride, and certainly not into a seer's mind."

"It's not negotiable. That part I *was* told to tell you," she said with a finality that made Tony shut up and just shake his head with a frown, eyes glittering with pent-up anger.

"I've arranged for Holly to be there tomorrow at his request, and Charles said that Asri Kho is on her way to you too."

"Any idea what I'm looking for in the big guy's mind?"

"Yes," she said with confidence. "You're looking for a location. He said his conscious mind has been blocking the information so he needed to be *unconscious* for it to reveal itself. He let himself be attacked and apparently refused to fight back." She sighed loud enough it came over the wires. "Seers really confuse me, so I don't know how literal he was being, but I got the impression that it was *him* that kicked Lucas's butt so he'd stay out of the way." She paused. "Tatya? Are you there?"

"I'm here." Her voice was dull with fatigue and probably shock at the news. "What am I supposed to do?"

Another pause, so long that Ivan had to prompt to be sure she was still there. "Cat?"

Her words chilled Eric's blood. "I know you and I have never gotten along, and I didn't want to be the one to tell you this. But Charles insisted. There's a chance . . . just a *chance*, mind you, that Lucas won't make it through this. Charles said if it's a choice between you and Lucas, you have to pick *you*. He said both he and Lucas are expendable."

The healer's voice was flat and cold. "Charles can go to hell." She didn't look down at him when she said it, as though not even acknowledging he was there with them. "I plan to make sure *both* of us make it through whatever this is."

That made Cat laugh. "I'd say the same, so you go, girl! I just hope we both wind up with husbands. Because Raphael never came back from rounding up the pack members and I can't find him in my head. I don't know whether to go look for him or not. Who'll protect the babies?" Her voice cracked just a bit, and Eric felt a pang of sympathy. He'd heard Ivan updating Lucas on the Albuquerque pack when they were driving him here from the airport. Who'd have ever thought a jaguar and a wolf would be double-mated? And with newborn twins . . . he didn't know what he'd decide either.

Tatya stared at the phone for a long moment. Her face moved through a dozen emotions and the conflicting scents made his nostrils twitch. Finally she settled on careful blankness. "He's alive. I'd know if he wasn't. And so would you, if you could think straight right now. And Catherine, you *have* to think straight. For him, for your babies, and for your *pack*. This isn't just about your own family. You're the Alpha, whether or not you want to be. So *be* the alpha. The job's not all rainbows and sunshine."

Cat's voice was cold and dark. "I am aware of that, thank you. I'm not exactly hiding in a closet with the kids, you know. The whole pack is here with me. But Carly's injured and Betty's nearly exhausted from treating snake bites. There's only a dozen of us against more than fifty of them and not a rainbow in sight. I *do*, however, have twenty-plus dead bodies scattered around a quiet cul-de-sac and no way to remove them. I can only pray nobody's called the cops yet, or we're all screwed." She paused and Ivan opened his mouth to speak, but she cut him off. "My nerves are just a bit frazzled. So, if you have something *helpful* to add, Tatya, feel free. Otherwise, zip it."

The doctor glared at the phone and opened her mouth as if to speak. But Ivan gave her a warning look and she shut it again.

"Cat, the pack leader in Chicago mentioned there were raptors and spiders there. Have you seen anything other than snakes?"

"Uh . . . no." Her voice took on a peculiar, concerned tone. "*Should* I be watching for birds and spiders?"

"Couldn't hurt," Eric said with a nod. "You're a cat, so you should be able to smell the birds. I've never smelled a spider, though."

Tony cut in. "Gotta watch out for those spiders. They're nasty bitches. They don't smell strong on their own, but they can emit some sort of knockout gas from their glands. It stinks bad, but it makes you loopy too, sort of drugged. And they may make a sound, this weird trilling noise like crickets on crack. You can't miss it. If you hear the noise, find something to plug your noses with or you'll wind up down for the count." He shrugged. "Been there, done that. Watch out for their webs too. They're strong enough to hold a Sazi and *big*. Oh, and listen for wind chimes. That's what they use as alarms to tell them they caught something."

"Eww." Cat sounded disgusted and Eric couldn't help but agree. Still, maybe it *was* meant to be that Tony was here with them, since he'd encountered a spider before and had lived to tell about it. "That's disgusting."

Tony let out a little snort of derision. "Don't worry about the disgusting part. Just concentrate on the *dangerous* part. They eat Sazi like we eat coconuts. Drill a hole and suck out the juice. Nasty business, spiders. All that works on them, according to Lucas, is cutting off their heads at the same time as taking out their hearts. A sword or several clips of bullets will do the job. If you don't have either, *find them*. They're a bitch to take out. It took both me and Lucas last time, and four clips."

A *sword*? Is that why they'd offered Eric his own pack? "I trained with swords in college. Foils, saber, and dagger. Are there any in the armory?"

Tony nodded. "Several. Take your pick. I brought the ones I used in Atlantic City and Lucas had a few already here." He pointed toward what looked like a walk-in refrigerator at the back of the room. "Right through there. But don't be long. We've got a hindsight to do."

"Is there anything else, Cathy?" Ivan's voice held a weird combination of concern and cold determination.

"No. I—" She cut herself off. "Wait. There is one

other thing that I'm supposed to tell you. Charles said that when Holly arrives, Eric's supposed to take her around the perimeter before you do the hindsight. I don't know why. But it sounded really important that you wait for her to arrive. I think she's supposed to notice something nobody else does, but that's just my own guess." She let out an audible sigh. "Anyway, that's the state of the union. I've got to make other calls now. Keep this phone handy. I'll be checking back with more information later."

She ended the call and they were left staring at each other. Tony finally broke the silence. "Well, I guess if we're supposed to wait for Holly to get here, we might as well get some sleep. It sounds like we're going to need it. Nobody goes outside alone, and we take turns keeping watch—two per shift. We have no idea if or when they'll be back. There's food in the kitchen, and plenty of bottled water."

Tatya glared at nobody in particular. "I can't imagine for the life of me what Holly Sanchez has to do with *anything*."

Ivan just shook his head and put the satellite phone back in the safe, being careful to shut the door but not lock it. "If Charles believes she's necessary, she is. Perhaps she brings *objectivity*, which you seem to be lacking lately."

They stared at each other for a long moment, neither giving an inch. "I was going to start to call the other packs to check on them. But maybe I'm only *objective* enough to make dinner. I'll leave you to do the important work, Councilman." With that parting shot, Tatya flounced up the stairs with Tony following at her heels.

Eric didn't know whether Holly would bring objectivity, but he couldn't deny he was looking forward to her arrival.

Perhaps a little too much for his own good.

Chapter Seven

HOW IN THE hell did she get away? Nasil turned in a full circle, watching every movement on the tarmac at Denver International Airport. But there was no sign of the small dark-haired woman. Holly Sanchez.

The last thing he remembered was exiting the private corporate jet that had been sent to bring her home, and then getting into a limo that was to take them to where another helicopter was waiting.

Then . . . nothing. He'd woken just now, nearly fifteen minutes after they'd left the plane, alone in the back of the plush car. Of course, the driver hadn't seen him, so he hadn't known to wake him. That was both the benefit and downfall of the powder he'd made from the ancient feathers of the original Marduc. It had been Sargon who'd discovered the carefully wrapped pile of feathers in the red pyramid in Honduras—a package that had thickness and weight, but was empty when they opened it.

Invisibility. It was a dream that crossed time, race, and species. The only Sazi known to possess it was the brother of Tahira Kuric, the new leader of the Hayalet Kabile. But his was a magical ability, and couldn't be transferred at will.

The feathers, on the other hand, could be ground into a dust to coat the user.

Except she *could see me*. That spoke of a unique ability, but he didn't know *how* unique. There was no way to put it to the test. Maybe *all* healers could see him. He'd have to be careful around those he knew. Still, for most purposes, the powder did what he required.

His ears detected a noise that wasn't the blast of jet engines, but with all the other sounds it took a moment to place it. Then he spotted it—a helicopter just taking off, and he could just make out the dark-haired female passenger. *Damn her to hell!*

This operation must be costing a fortune. Two helicopters and a private jet for one passenger? The Council didn't throw around money like this for no reason. He would know, after spending more than a decade in the employ of the cat councilman, Antoine Monier—spying for Sargon. Few things had annoyed Antoine more than the constant refusal to reimburse expenses. The girl must be far more important than he'd given her credit for.

And far more clever. That made her dangerous. Yet she could still be useful. He just had to plan carefully. He'd had many centuries to perfect the art of patience and caution. This was no different than any other crisis he'd had to find a way out of.

He reached into his pocket and pulled out his cell phone which had also been carefully coated with dust and glanced at the display. *Finally, a decent signal.* He moved to a quiet spot near the outer edge of the terminal, where there were no people to hear, and dialed a number.

"*¿Sí?* Who is this?"

Nasil made his voice intentionally soft and warm. It had disgusted him to no end to give the command to Paolo when he left Australia, but he was worth more alive than dead. A smitten minion was far better than a bitter enemy or a dead body that someone might eventually discover. He just hoped Bruce would understand the necessity. Paolo hadn't been insane yet and probably wasn't poisoned enough to die anytime soon. The knife had gotten stuck in a crack in the cave floor a few feet away from him. Since he was still under the control of the compliance drug, Nasil had decided to take advantage. "Paolo, it is I. Your paramour."

The voice on the line lilted with pleasure. "Nasil! I have missed you. When will you return? We have much to discuss . . . and much to *do* together."

A shudder of revulsion overtook Nasil and he narrowly avoided vomiting all over the concrete. He had to swallow a few times and take a deep breath before he replied in that same nauseating tone. "Soon. I will return soon. But until I make it back, I hope you can do a small favor for me."

"Of course. What do you require? I will warn you that I seem to be a little forgetful today. I can't for the life of me remember why I came to this horrible little town."

Nasil sidestepped so a luggage tram wouldn't hit him. Paolo wasn't stupid. For a thug, he was annoyingly thoughtful. If Nasil didn't come up with a good reason why he might be in an opal mining town on another continent, he'd worry on it like a bone until he finally remembered. No, it was far better to keep his mind fuzzy and occupied. Still, just in case Paolo had managed to get past the drug and was pumping him for information, he didn't dare reveal what he'd learned about NSA17. "We were there searching for a new seer. Don't you remember? There was supposedly a very powerful snake with foresight down there somewhere. You decided to stay and search, while I came back to check on the Goddess."

Now there was a long pause on Paolo's end. *Did I go too far by mentioning Marduc?* Hiding her from Nasil had been Paolo's primary focus for months. Would Paolo believe he'd changed his mind so drastically and teamed up with Nasil willingly? He needed to add to the lie. "It was one of the last things Sargon asked of us."

"Ah! *Sí, sí* . . . I remember now." That last part was absolutely true, and it solidified the false memory. Sargon *had* wanted to find the seer, and he *had* tasked them with the assignment. But when their lord failed to return from Germany, where he'd planned to capture and enslave the power well Tahira Kuric, all discipline had fallen apart. "You are correct. It makes sense for me to stay. I know people in many of the snake nests here." Another pause, and now his words were more careful, bordering on suspicious.

"You *will* have to give the password to the priest to be admitted to the lair, of course."

Everything hinged on this. If Nasil didn't answer just right, everything would be lost and the illusion would shatter. He flipped through the possible intonations. Angry? Defensive? Confident? What would Paolo be expecting from him? He settled for offhand and casual. "Naturally. And you were brilliant to set it up that way. The first words out of my mouth *must* be 'serpent moon.' Then I greet the head priest and tell him you sent me. Isn't that what you said? Because otherwise one priest will attack me while the other runs with the egg to take it to the secondary location." That part was supposition, but it sounded like something Paolo would plan.

Nasil waited on pins and needles. If he'd guessed wrong, Paolo would likely hang up and immediately start making calls to stop him from arriving at the site—wherever it was.

Paolo's answer sounded relieved but slightly confused. "Precisely. But I must admit that I'm still amazed you came around to my way of thinking on this. I was so certain you were against me fulfilling Sargon's plan."

And now the biggest lie of all. Nasil had to swallow down the bile that threatened to rise in his throat. "Eventually I saw the truth in your vision, my friend. And I can't deny you have a way of convincing a man in less . . . *vocal* ways. I hope your bruises are healing. Mine might take *days*."

Coy and coquettish. How disgusting. But how like

a new sexual conquest. Likely Paolo was touching his face now. Nasil didn't doubt he'd been wondering why he was battered and burned. But he hadn't been lying. Paolo *did* like his foreplay rough. And to tell him that an alpha of Nasil's caliber would take days to heal—well, that was icing on the cake.

Paolo puffed and preened at the supposed compliment. "Yes . . . well, you aren't the first to compliment my . . . *technique*. I hope you heal quickly and are ready for another session. Even now I'm touching myself in anticipation."

Nasil shuddered and tried not to think about silver chain burns being a turn-on to *anyone*. He forced himself to chuckle, and hoped it didn't sound like the gagging it *felt* like. "Unfortunately, I'm in a public place, so I can't play phone games with you now. I'm about to board a plane to take me south. Do you still want to meet at—" He paused to look at the faded receipt he'd pulled from Paolo's wallet before he unchained him. "La Cocina Restaurant in Cortez when we're ready to start the ritual?" It had been the only clue, but it made perfect sense. *Green table* must mean Mesa Verde . . . the Four Corners area. It was one of the original homes of the Sazi—powerfully magical and still nearly as deserted as it had been a thousand years ago.

The last barrier fell at the mention of the familiar name. Paolo's voice relaxed completely. "I would enjoy eating there again. They have very good tortillas—hand thrown on a stone hearth. And they know how to make proper green chile."

Actually, that *did* sound good, and it reminded Nasil that he hadn't eaten for the entire flight. While he hadn't had any reason to believe the food on the plane was tainted, he also wasn't confident enough to try it. "It's a date . . . *amigo.*"

"Now, what is your favor? Will it involve blood and pain?"

Nasil pursed his lips. "Not at this precise moment, but there is a strong chance it *could.*"

Paolo laughed heartily and it made the phone vibrate lightly in Nasil's hand. "Then I am your man. What would you have me do?"

"There is a woman who lives in Coober Pedy named Rose Barry. I need her collected and kept for a time. She's human of Sazi descent—wolf by blood, but she will damage very easily, so no torture. I need her locked up and kept healthy and unharmed. I require her sister's cooperation on another matter, and I fear she might be tempted to go to the Council without some *persuasion.* Yet not so much persuasion . . ."

"That she's tempted to call Wolven instead. Ah! *Sí, sí.* I understand. Yes, of course. That's a simple matter. I will call you when it's done. I will have her kept by one of the local nests. That way she'll recognize the accent, and not have any way to identify why she was taken. I've found with humans if you simply deprive them of sight with a blindfold, they're often completely disoriented and very easy to manage. Is hers a powerful Sazi family?"

Nasil shrugged. "Not especially. But she's well connected—born to the Omega of the Boulder pack."

An odd noise came over the wire and it took Nasil a moment to realize it was Paolo spitting onto the ground. He did that often, as a substitute for a verbal curse. "Pah! Lucas Santiago's nest. I've met him. He's powerful, but has little common sense about the correct hierarchy of a well-run family. It would be worthwhile to keep a low profile when taking even a human under his protection."

He had a point. "Take her with no threats. No sound at all for her to cling to and remember. There's a powerful seer in that pack and he knows a wolf with hindsight."

"A challenge, but a worthy one. I think a quick strike and then full sensory deprivation immediately. Sight, sound, and those plastic nose clips swimmers use. She can breathe from her mouth. And most definitely no torture for that one, so a female snake to guard her."

Nasil was frankly surprised at the thoughtful process. Perhaps Paolo was not so much a simple thug as he'd thought. "Excellent. I will leave it to you then. Now I must find a plane on which to secret myself for the trip south."

"Until we see each other again, *amigo.*"

"Until then." Nasil clicked off the phone, relieved that at least he wouldn't lose his hold over Holly. He could only hope Paolo could handle an assignment that *didn't* involve torture or rape. But Sargon had trusted the man to perform nearly the same level of assignment as Nasil's own, so perhaps there was hope.

But first things first. He needed to sneak into the control tower and find out where a certain helicopter was going. It was better to know where little Holly Sanchez had been spirited away to. So much the easier to capture her later.

Chapter Eight

"So AFTER THIS Larry guy went hissing into the night, what happened?"

Eric's voice held astonishment, fear, and pride—all wrapped in a heady dose of angry outrage. The combination tickled Holly's nose and she had to pause, her hand in the air. The sneeze that threatened was stuck in place. Eric waited impatiently, his fingers tapping the steering wheel while she squinted her eyes, trying to force herself to breathe again.

"Ahhh-choo!" She snorted and then opened the window a bit. "Sorry. I hate it when that happens. Let me get a little fresh air in here. Too many scents in the car."

Eric let out a sigh as the chilly night air swirled through the car. "No, *I'm* sorry. My fault for getting emotional. I forgot you've got a wolf nose now. But I just can't help getting pissed when people do stuff like that . . . and to someone like *you*—it just makes me want to beat his head in."

Holly didn't quite know how to respond to that. Part of her wanted to smile that he was so upset. Part wondered what the hell "someone like you" meant. It was probably better to just get back to the story and not overanalyze every word. "I think I handled it pretty well—all things considered. The second I hit the airport, I called Rose, naturally. She promised to get everybody out of there right away and then take Dale away for a few days. I suggested a big city where they'd be harder to find."

A heavy gust of wind hit the car and tried to force it off the road. The air smelled of ozone and the rain that would follow soon. Storms often popped up when there were multiple powerful Sazi in an area, making council meetings a challenge to plan. *Nothing like a meeting of alphas to end a drought.* Eric's voice had sounded surprised, but now Holly's nose was so plugged from the cold air that she couldn't smell his emotions.

"Why'd you even wait for him? Why not just take off and leave him stranded?"

Holly let out a little laugh. Yeah, that was the obvious choice, but the wrong one. "Because then he'd still *be* there. Rose wouldn't have time to leave. I might not be able to fight him, but I figured I could ditch him somewhere along the route after we were out of the country."

Eric shook his head and let out a frustrated sigh that sounded surprisingly like her father. She felt her hackles rise, and tried not to take it personally. Instead, she pulled a tissue from the box in the console between them and blew her nose.

"That was a big risk. You could have gotten tortured, or thrown out of the plane for all you knew."

Holly looked at him askance. "That doesn't make any sense. Why would he do that? No, he needed me healthy so I could make the trip, so he could tag along and stay invisible. And he was invisible, even if I don't know how he did it. Not a soul noticed him the whole way. That's what kept me healthy. If he'd dumped me out over the ocean, why would the connecting flight in Germany even need to take off?" She shrugged. "And I agreed to let him ride back to the States. My word means a lot to me." Eric's left foot was tapping on the floor, but he was controlling his emotions enough now that she had no idea what he was thinking. "I *did* think this out, you know. I had a plan—with contingencies in case something went wrong. I might add that the plan *worked*, too. I'm here, and he's not." The words were a little sarcastic, but they were born of frustration so she didn't really care. Jeez, if this was the reception everybody was going to give her, this was going to be a really sucky place to be for the few days she planned to stay.

Eric let out a slow breath and then nodded. His scent turned to the dusty smell of embarrassment, combined with enough spice to make her eyes widen and her heart thump. "No, you're right. You *are* here. I'm sorry. I just keep thinking of you as a pretty human girl, and forget one of the reasons I liked you to begin with was that you had a *brain*—unlike a lot of the wolves in your pack. And now you're a wolf, but still have the brain. It's just confusing." He looked at her then, just a glance with a hint of a smile. It was that same smile he'd used in the restaurant all those years ago and even now, it made her blush to her toes.

"So, I'm sorry. Go ahead with the story. How'd you ditch him?"

Eric reached across the car and put his hand over hers and gave it a squeeze. All of a sudden she felt flustered. Her stomach did flip-flops and any hint of annoyance flew out the window. And of course her nose had plugged up again, so whatever he was feeling was hidden. God only knew what *she* smelled like now, but he seemed to be breathing just fine, so he'd know. That was one of the benefits . . . and one of the problems with dating wolves. There was nothing hidden from them. It was all right there for everybody to smell.

I need to change the subject pretty quick, or everybody at the site is going to know I've still got a thing for him. As casually as she could, she pulled her hand out from under his to grab another tissue. He didn't seem offended. He just put his hand back on the steering wheel. She blew her nose again and tried to collect her thoughts. "It wasn't that hard, really. I just put him into a healing trance in the back of the car and slipped out. Once I was on the helicopter, I let it go. Not terribly exciting, huh?"

"A *healing* trance? You healed your attacker?"

She shrugged. "Can't do a trance on someone unless they *do* need healing, and that arm of his really did creep me out. It flopped around like a dead fish." Eric had that annoyed smell again, and now *she* was embarrassed. "Yeah, I know what you're going to say, so don't even start. I made my attacker more dangerous. Brilliant move, Holly. But I figure it's even odds on whether he'll be just a little grateful, and maybe a little more willing to let things slide."

Eric shook his head, even though he wasn't annoyed anymore. Now he was just . . . well, not quite sad, but more disappointed. "That *would* be nice, but it just doesn't happen that way, hon. The bad guys take advantage . . . *whatever* advantage you give them, and just keep being bad. I know you meant well, but—"

He was doing it again—making her sound all naïve and innocent. "No," she interrupted firmly, because this was important and she wanted him to understand. "I didn't *mean well*. I meant to get away. And I did. He's a bigger alpha, and even hurt, he'd already proven I couldn't win in a fair fight. But don't get all confused about me, Eric. More than my body grew up in the past ten years. Yeah, I'm a healer, but I'm fully capable of killing someone to protect myself. I already have several times. But I didn't have any weapons to fight with on this trip. Now, I *did* think about pushing him out of the plane. He fell asleep at one point and I could have popped the emergency door next to him. But he'd probably have survived. I've heard of alphas surviving pretty nasty plane crashes, even ones that involved fire. And if he lived, he'd be *pissed*. This way, he's a little annoyed that I got away, but once he figures out I partially healed him—" She felt her shoulders rise and fall in an unconscious shrug. "Well, I'll hope for the best. At least I'm here."

There was a long silence as she watched the bits of landscape she could see by headlight. She could smell again, but there was no sorting out the jumble of emotions he was bleeding. Finally he spoke and his voice sounded . . . odd. "You've killed a man."

It was a statement, rather than a question, but it deserved an answer. "Three, actually. Head and heart with a gun. They were going to kill my friend Cat, and they'd already killed my sister and broken my hip. I didn't have much of a sense of humor at that point. I thought I did pretty well hitting moving targets while hopping on one leg." She let that sink in so that he could smell she wasn't lying. If he wanted to know about her, he was about to get a crash course. "I've taken martial arts classes and Raphael taught me teeth-and-claw fighting." Her brow furrowed as they rounded the next corner and she pointed toward what she saw through the windshield. "Um . . . what's with all the cars? Is that where we're going?"

It looked like an RV city in the distance. Dozens of travel trailers and land yachts lit the darkness. Eric reached into his pocket, extracted a cell phone, and flipped it open. She could already smell his emotion turn from curious and shocked to alert. "That's the place, but they weren't there when I left to pick you up." He raised his brow and hit the gas a little harder. "I don't know what's up."

He paused to turn onto a recently graveled road. "But I think we're about to find out."

Chapter Nine

THE SCENE HAD every appearance of a refugee camp, and Eric quickly realized that was exactly what it was. There were wolves, cats, raptors, humans, and bears . . . adults and children of all ages. They were battered and bandaged and smelled of pain, anger, and fear. He recognized a few here and there in passing, but there was no getting to them through the throng. There were too many scents and too many voices to make out what was going on. He grabbed Holly's hand once she got out of the car and started to push his way through toward the main building.

A long burst of automatic gunfire abruptly stopped all sound so quickly that he could hear the final empty casing hit the metal roof with a ting. "Thank you for shutting up . . . finally." The words came from a bullhorn, and were distinctly Tony's. "The council members would like to talk now."

Eric moved a few more people aside and pulled Holly with him until they could see the four figures on top of the building. Tony handed the bullhorn to Ivan. The great bear's gravelly voice filled the air. "For those who don't already know me, I am Ivan Kruske-nik, new leader of the bears. Some of you remember me as the bodyguard of the Chief Justice. Beside me . . . with the rifle, is Tony Giambrocco." Tony raised the Uzi and waved it comfortably before insert-ing a new clip with a slap that made several people around Eric flinch. Steam still rose from the barrel into the cold night. "He's a member of Wolven and will be helping to enforce the rules we set down here today." Ivan looked out over the crowd and let out a sigh that carried over the speaker. "I know you're all confused and frightened, and aren't quite sure why you're here. That's why we wanted to tell you all at once, so there weren't any rumors or secrets."

The man to his left, Ahmad al-Narmer, leader of the snakes, reached for the bullhorn and Ivan let him take it. There was murmuring through the crowd, and more than a little anger directed his way. "I am Ah-mad. I doubt anyone here has not heard of me. I lead the snakes . . . in all things *except* what has hap-pened today. For reasons that are still unclear, snakes and raptors all over the world have suddenly attacked packs and prides. Some of you have seen some spider-shifters as well." Now Eric was hanging on his every word. The earlier attack hadn't been the only one? "I pledge, on my honor, that I and those I control had nothing to do with this. Bobby Mbutu is a snake, as well. But you know he has always been, and still remains, a protector of all and a trusted member of Wolven. We know many of your groups lost people. The council feels your pain, as we have lost some of our best as well."

Crap. Had Charles and Lucas . . . Eric felt a buzzing in his head. What in the hell was happening?

Ahmad kept talking. "We would ask that any pack, pride, or nest leader here today find your council member and relate as much as you can about what happened. As for the rest of you—" He handed the bullhorn to Antoine, leader of the cats. He began to speak like the showman he was.

"My good friends . . . it appears my sister, Josette Cooper, contacted many of you and told you to leave your homes and travel here. I have not been able to reach her to know her reasoning. But as one of our most powerful seers, I don't doubt she *had* a reason. It might be that the attack on you would have been far worse without the warning to leave. Often she doesn't know the details, but only feels a crisis at hand. Be that as it may, we are here. But there is no way to stay low-key with this large a group, even as deserted as the area appears. This small plot of land is right next to a national park that is heavily visited by the general public. However, Tatiana Santiago has informed us that she and her husband own a great deal of land, just to the south of Mesa Verde—one of the original Sazi homesteads. Once we are organized and resupplied, we will travel there until we can determine the scope of the danger from the snakes and birds who were not killed in today's battle. I hope you will all stand with me in supporting those snakes who are among us today—who are as frightened and confused as you."

"Why should we?" came a man's voice from the crowd. Eric turned his head to see who spoke, but couldn't find the person. He realized then that Holly was plastered against him by the crowd, holding his hand so tight he could feel her nails dig in. The sensation made him more than a little dizzy and he didn't think it was all from the situation. She was likewise scanning the crowd. But instead of smelling fear from her, the hot metal scent of determination bled from her pores. It occurred to him then, even more strongly, that she was no longer a shy human sibling in a family of wolves. She was an agent of Wolven—sent to a strange country to find him, and now prepared to take on whatever threat the crowd would offer.

Another woman shouted. Eric followed Holly's eyes and a shock of awareness drifted on the breeze. "They tried to kill us! Why should we trust any of them?" It was Iris Sanchez, now Renault, who'd moved from the Boulder pack to Canada. He noticed Holly didn't race toward her sister. In fact, she only rolled her eyes and turned back to face the group on the roof.

A third voice grew bold. "Kick 'em out before they slaughter our children!"

More murmuring started. This could easily turn into a riot. But Tony just fired off another short burst and dropped the automatic rifle across his arm when the talking stopped. He yelled to the crowd without checking with the others for permission. "Maybe you didn't *hear* the nice councilmen. They said *drop it*. I'll clear up any confusion you might still have. If any of you draw blood on anyone else here, *I'll* draw blood. My shooting is one of the obstacles on the Wolven course . . . and I use *silver* rounds. We have one healer on site, people. It might take a while to get to you if anything untoward happens."

Ivan stepped around Ahmad and took the bull-horn from Antoine. "If Eric Thompson and Holly Sanchez have returned, please report to the main building. We're waiting for them to begin. And we would ask that any group leaders also report to the main building."

Eric glanced behind him and Holly nodded. They started to push their way to the front of the crowd. He noticed that a few others were also moving through the sea of bodies. He recognized the Second of the Minnesota pack, Adam Mueller. Had he finally taken over as leader of that group? He certainly had the ability. Adam was supporting a small Latina that Eric didn't recognize. The woman was obviously pregnant, and was limping enough that the Sazi around her were reacting to the scent of her pain. But her face was set with determination and she didn't acknowledge the touches or helping hands offered.

Ivan continued to speak as they made their way up. "Finally, a few announcements: We have supplies on the way, but for those who stocked up before you started your trip, please share with others until food and water arrive. We'll keep everybody updated with information as we hear it. Until then, please just relax as best you can. If you have injuries, Dr. Santiago has set up a triage site at the white RV with the sunset mural. Snake bites, open wounds, broken bones, and children first, please. We have two portable bathrooms right now, with more on the way, so do the best you can to keep them clean. There are three power hookups for those who need to charge batteries, but there's no working cell towers nearby, so no signals. If anyone brought a portable generator or has outdoor-rated extension cords, please see Antoine."

Ivan was still talking as they reached the building and were let inside by Bobby Mbutu. He grasped Eric's hand in a solid shake but there was worry etched on his dark features. "Glad you both made it back safe. We were getting worried." Bobby closed the door behind him and gestured for them to follow him.

"When did all *this* start?" Eric waved his hand to encompass the whole area. "I've only been gone for a couple of hours. Has your wife made it here yet?"

"Not yet. But I never worry when Asri's late. She drives even slower than I do, and I've yet to see a situation she can't handle—even pregnant, she's scary. As for all these other people, it's freaking weird. People started arriving just after you left. The first group was from Canada. They'd been told two days ago to pull up stakes and come here—without telling a soul."

"Yeah," Eric agreed. "I just talked to my mom earlier and she didn't say a *word* about this." Reality settled over him with mind-numbing suddenness. "Has anyone heard from her? Are they okay?"

Bobby shook his head. "The Quebec pack got hit hard and fast. We only have rumors at this point. We think your mother and brother survived, but a lot of the pack is just . . . gone. I'm really sorry, Thompson. I know it's hard."

Eric couldn't quite wrap his head around that. He'd spoken to her just a few hours ago! How could so many be dead?

Now Holly's voice was shaking a little. "I saw Iris outside. Has anyone heard from Pansy . . . or from my dad?"

Bobby just shook his head and she nodded grimly. Eric could smell Holly's worry, but she shook it off after a moment, apparently determined to not think about it. They passed through the kitchen on their way to the stairs. Several Sazi cats he'd met before from the California pride were stirring massive pots of what smelled like beef stew. Holly dipped in her finger as she passed by. "Needs garlic," she said to the tall blond woman. "And put in a few whole peeled potatoes to soak up some of that oil and salt. We don't need people drinking extra water when we're already low. And hello? Why isn't there bread baking? It's cheap and fills people up so they don't need as much meat."

Eric looked at Bobby and shrugged. "Holly *did* run the pack restaurant in Boulder. She's a hell of a cook." Actually, he was starting to realize she was a hell of a *woman*.

Bobby nodded his head at the questioning cat with

the spoon. "Well? You heard the lady. There are plenty of spices in the pantry and another bag of potatoes in the bin in the corner. The flour's brand new and I know there's at least a few cakes of yeast. C'mon, everybody! We're going to have people beating down the door pretty soon. We need to be ready for them."

With Bobby barking the orders, the others scrambled to obey. Holly shook her head and kept walking while muttering under her breath. "Figures they'd put people who'd never cooked for a crowd in charge of the kitchen."

Bobby let out an exasperated noise and spun Holly around to face him. "Back off, Sanchez. We're doing the best we can. It all happened pretty damned fast. We're trying to take it one crisis at a time. It's not like we've ever had to plan for this sort of thing before."

And therein lies the problem. But Eric didn't dare say it out loud. Instead, he just bit his tongue and tried to keep his emotions blank. He heard a metallic bang behind them and turned to see the four men from the roof coming in the back door.

Tony followed in the wake of the others, but seemed perfectly at home with them, as though a three-day wolf was equal to council members. Oddly, none of the others disputed his position. "About time you made it back." Tony dipped his head to Holly. "Good to see you again, Ms. Sanchez. What strange and wondrous things did you find on your walk around the perimeter?"

"Shit!" Eric slapped his forehead with his palm.

"With all the confusion, I completely forgot to take her around. But surely there can't be anything left at this point, could there? I mean, all the people tramping around would have ruined any evidence. Shouldn't we just go ahead with the hindsight?"

Ahmad flicked his eyes in Tony's direction. "Didn't you say that was a direct order from Charles—through his goddaughter?"

"Yeah, but she didn't mention anything about all these people, either. I tend to agree with Thompson. But still . . . you guys are in charge now. You make the call."

After a long pause, where the council members shrugged and pursed their lips, Ivan finally spoke up. "Go. Catherine was clear, and Charles undoubtedly knew there would be people. Do the best you can."

"What am I looking for? And why *me*?" Holly sounded justifiably confused, in his opinion. Eric didn't understand what the goal was either.

"That part is not so clear," Ivan admitted with a rueful smile. "Apparently, it's something you will see that others can't."

Eric looked at her, startled. Holly realized what it could be at the same time. "Like I saw Larry!"

"Larry?" Antoine and Ahmad said the word simultaneously, and both sounded worried.

Holly nodded. "A black snake who attacked me in Australia. Well, not so much *attacked* as . . . accosted, I guess. He forced me to take him along on the trip back to the States, but I ditched him at the airport. He doesn't know where I am."

Ivan let out a growl, and Tony asked the same question that was on Eric's lips. "Larry? Not a very tough name. Should we be worried?"

"Larry is *Nasil*, Tony." Ahmad spit the word, and Eric winced as some of the venom from the great snake landed on his arm. "We should be *very* worried. The snake attacks are growing more clear. Nasil is very powerful in his own right, and if the lesser snakes consider him to be the successor of my father—"

"*Dammit!*" Tony's voice was worried now too, and more than a little pissed. "I thought we killed him in Atlantic City."

"Nasil is very . . . *sturdy*, it appears."

"He's . . . damaged, if that helps any." Eric noticed Holly was careful to not mention that he wasn't as *damaged* now as he had been when she met him. "Half of his body doesn't work right. But he was still alpha enough to freeze me and . . ." She paused, and Eric wondered if she was going to tell them about her sister. She took a deep breath while the others watched her intently. "He threatened my sister if I didn't cooperate. But I called her before he got to the airport and told her to leave town."

Ahmad sighed in frustration. "She might as well have remained. There is no hiding from Nasil. He is as clever and dangerous as any man I've ever met." A woman walked into the room just then—a stunning beauty of Middle Eastern descent who lowered her brows at the look on Ahmad's face. He glanced at her and let out a hiss. "Nasil still lives, Tuli. This young wolf encountered him just today."

"Merciful Anu!" she hissed. "No *wonder* the snakes of the world have gone insane. It's a very good thing Tony's wife is still safe, but we'll need to put extra guards on her. She was the one who nearly killed him. He'll want revenge." Tuli shook her head in frustration. "He must have managed to get the compliance drug distributed more widely. The snakes probably won't even remember attacking. But *why*? Why now?"

"Bet the egg's still alive then too." Tony was tapping the butt of the automatic on the floor, making an odd, ominous echo through the room. "It's no wonder the attacks were simultaneous. It must be time for that . . . *thing* to be born! We need to get all these people out of here. We'll be nothing but a smorgasbord for that thing when it hatches."

Eric wished he could figure out what was going on. He was getting hints and pieces of something large and frightening, in a nameless, faceless, monster-under-the-bed way. "But where would we send them? They were sent *here* for a reason."

Ahmad raised his eyebrows and looked at Antoine, who shook his head. "There isn't the slightest possibility Josette would have anything to do with helping Marduc be born. She's fought snakes her whole life." He glanced at Ahmad meaningfully. "As *you* well know."

The snake representative merely shrugged fluidly. "I know that our raptor representative, Angelique, is quite insane from that drug. Who's to know for sure? Your own twin, Fiona, betrayed us after ingesting the drug. Why not another sister as well? She hasn't checked in, after all."

"But," Ivan amended. "We have only a few testimonies that it was actually your sister calling. It could easily have been an associate of Nasil's *posing* as her—what easier way to get a large number of Sazi in one place for the creature's first meal?"

Antoine nodded. "I'll make some calls." He motioned toward Eric and Holly. "You two should go walk the perimeter. Look for anything unusual."

Ahmad removed a small walkie-talkie from his pocket and held it out for Eric to take. "If the creature has already been born, do your best to warn us before you're eaten. I don't expect you to survive. I don't expect most of us to survive. Nobody except Lucas and Charles have ever encountered a quetzalcoatl in the flesh. Marduc is the bringer of storms—a Sazi so powerful she's the equal of the whole of the council. And we don't have the whole of the council to fight with." He grimaced. "Apparently, Nasil has seen to that."

A quetzalcoatl? A half-snake half-bird creature like the one worshipped by ancient peoples? It was a *Sazi*? He stared at the others, where shock and fear mingled on the faces of the best of their kind. "Or," Eric felt himself say, more musing to himself than addressing the group, "maybe we were all sent here because we *might* stand a chance. The group seems to have been pretty selective. Even pack leaders didn't know which people were being culled."

"As good a hope as any to cling to," Ivan said with a nod. "Go and do your walk, and then we'll see what Charles has on his mind. He's in stable condition. He can wait until you return. Take your time and find what there is to find."

"I DON'T THINK they meant for us to go this far." Holly looked back at the encampment, just a bright light in the distance. "It's pitch black out here."

Eric flicked on a flashlight and handed a second one to her. "We have no idea where the fight started. Even Tony said he heard fighting in the distance before the screams and snarls started. We'll circle the camp in a spiral and move closer with each pass."

They walked in silence as the minutes ticked by, moving their lights among the cactus and sagebrush. Eric was looking for scattered sand—signs of a struggle that might lead to clues. He didn't know what Holly was looking for, and likely would never spot it anyway.

"Worried about your mother?" Holly said after a time.

"Yep. And you're probably worried about your dad."

"Yep. But there's nothing I can do about it. I couldn't find Iris again in the crowd. But at least I know she's safe." Comfortable silence fell over them. The crowd in the distance became white noise in his ears as they picked their way through the brush. He glanced up in a never-ending check for silent raptors riding the night winds, or the glint of the spiderwebs that Tony had warned about. "The sky looks a lot like Australia here. Big and wide and open."

"I liked Australia." He could hear the smile in

Holly's voice and turned to look at her for a second. He didn't dare look at her too long. There was something about those deep brown eyes, the color of dark caramel, that kept sucking him in. Apparently he telegraphed his thoughts because she asked abruptly, "Did you ever want to kiss me? I mean, back when we were kids?"

Why not be honest? Nobody could hear them. "Pretty much every day I saw you. Still do." The last two words popped out before he could stop them. She stopped cold and turned her flashlight on him. He didn't look at her. *Couldn't* look at her, but the smell of shock and sudden desire flooded his nose.

No. There was too much going on right now to risk getting close to anyone—much less Holly. But once again the image of her lying naked and ready for him, writhing in anticipation, sprang to his mind for the tenth time since he'd left Crocodile Annie's house, and for the thousandth time since he left Boulder. He'd wanted her even then. Lord, how he'd wanted her. There was just something about Holly he couldn't seem to get out of his head. But her father, rightfully, had threatened him with harm if he'd acted on his feelings. She'd been a minor, and he an adult who should know better.

But she isn't a minor now.

She'd also been human then. So when Lucas insisted he join Wolven to get him out of town, he'd gone without argument. And he'd never come back.

His hands twitched with a need so strong he had to shake them to stop it. He nearly dropped the flashlight in the process, and walked even faster.

Fur against fur, flesh against flesh.

He pushed away the thought. He didn't dare risk being with Holly. There was too much danger. Even the council considered him a *weapon*.

Were her nipples peaking right now in the cold breeze? Would she taste like honey and spice?

Pain erupted in his face. The jagged points of a massive yucca ripped through the cloth of his shirt and sleeve and nearly took out his eye. The scent of coppery blood filled the air and dozens of cuts stung like fire from the mild poison in the razor-sharp spines. "Damn it!" He hissed the words as quietly as he could and wiped at the blood running down his face. There seemed to be a lot of it.

"Oh!" Holly raced forward and shined her light on his face. "Ouch! That must sting."

"Yeah, but I'll heal. Let's get back to work. They're waiting for us."

She clucked her tongue at him. "Oh, for heaven's sake. Just stand still a minute. I *am* a healer, after all. And we need you in top shape in case we run into something."

Holly touched his face before he could stop her. Warm, soothing healing magic coated him, filled him. It was a softer sensation than Dr. Santiago's. He felt her magic seal the wounds, making his skin tingle as cuts turned to scabs and then to tiny scars in the wink of an eye.

Her hand slid down his face to his neck and then to his shoulder. Had she been standing that close a second ago? He could smell the sweet wildflowers and berries that made up her true scent. He remembered it well. She had been a bright spot in a building filled with fur and grease and meat. But now she smelled of fur too, along with emotions that she shouldn't be feeling. *Surely she can't feel the same about me as—*

Eric didn't know exactly the moment his eyes locked with hers, but when they did, he couldn't seem to think. He saw himself reaching for her, and couldn't stop himself.

Her mouth was so incredibly warm—superheated compared to his cold lips. She *did* taste like honey, and her nipples pressed against him through the thin sweater she wore. His tongue invaded her mouth, tangled with hers, and then his arms pulled her close enough to make her gasp. The little moan that followed made him abruptly hard. Once again he let his hands roam over her back, as he'd done during their parting hug in Australia. Then it had been a guilty pleasure to feel the outline of her bra, the toned muscles of her back. He both pulled her against his erection to let her know what she'd done to him and put a hand on her breast to fondle that sweet nipple at last. He couldn't wait until he was gliding his tongue across it. She ground her mouth against him, writhing and wiggling enough to make him frantic. All he wanted to do was strip off her clothes and throw her to the ground, and that was exactly what he planned to do.

At last.

Whoosh. The unmistakable noise of feathers sailing through the air at breakneck speed. Adrenaline of a totally different kind broke them apart so fast they both stumbled. Holly picked up the flashlight she'd dropped and played it across the starlit sky.

Whatever had been there was gone. Yet a scent lingered—something he'd never smelled before. Something big . . . and venomous. The thick, pungent scent of poison hung in the air, nearly strong enough to harm on its own.

"C'mon!" Holly shouted before racing into the darkness. "I can see it!" He moved in her wake as quickly as the discomfort in his pants would allow. Apparently women didn't have the same problem of running while aroused that guys did. But the longer they ran, the easier it got, so that by the time he finally caught up to her, he was nearly normal again.

"What was it? What did you see?"

She was squatting down next to a piñon tree. "Not much, really. Just a flash of something shiny in the air. But—" She reached down and seemed to lift something off the ground, her thumb and forefinger pinched together. "I did find *this*."

"Find what?" It wasn't until he reached forward to touch her hand that he realized there was something sticking up from her fingers. Something long and sharp, and yet smooth. "What *is* that?"

She regarded him with open amazement. "You really can't see it? It's a feather. A really *cool* feather." She moved her fingers around while playing the flashlight over them. "It's like a holograph—different colors depending on how you turn it. It's really a shame you can't see it."

He nodded and then looked back toward the lights

of the camp. It was time to head back. Hopefully by the time they got there, the night wind would have blown away the scent of their kiss. "I think you found what you were meant to. Let's head back and see whether I'm just blind, or if you're the only one who can see this."

Chapter Ten

"I THINK WE should have followed it." Holly watched as the others examined the feather that only she could see. They poked and twisted it, which only had the effect of cutting gashes in their fingers. "Maybe I could have gotten a better visual on it or even found where it's nesting."

"And maybe it swooped over us because it knew we were there. We might have only been saved from being dinner by that hillside filled with yucca. It could simply have been a tough angle to grab, and following it would have made it turn around." While what Eric said made sense, she didn't have to like it.

"So, thus far it's impervious to flame, to magic, and to blades." Ahmad frowned and stinging magic filled the small room. "What about silver?"

"We can check that right now," Tony said and jacked a round from the chamber of the rifle he was holding. Ahmad put the feather on the table and lined it up with the fingers on both hands so Tony could find it. He pressed the bullet down on the feather and then looked at Holly. "Anything? I don't smell smoke."

She shook her head. "Not a mark on it. If that thing is covered with these, we're in deep shit."

Tatya appeared in the doorway just then, looking harried and exhausted. "What's so important that you had to send a runner over, Ahmad? I've got people lined up outside the triage trailer." The woman didn't even glance her way. No surprise there.

Ahmad picked up the feather and held it out toward her. "What am I holding?"

She looked at him oddly, impatience and confusion mingled in her scent. "You're not holding anything. Is this some sort of joke? Because it's not very funny. I have patients to diagnose and treat."

Ahmad's voice lowered to a dangerous rumble. "I *never* joke." He shot an angry glance at Tony when he let out a small, amused snort. Tony zipped his fingers across his lips and looked away innocently. Ahmad walked forward until he was towering over the tiny pack leader. "Diagnose *this.*" He put the feather on her palm and closed her fingers around it until the doctor winced and cried out. When she opened her hand, there was blood staining the palm. The wounds healed almost immediately, but the color remained. "*That* is the 'nothing' I am holding. We were testing to see if all healers could see it, or only Ms. Sanchez."

Tatya felt the edges of the feather and then turned to Holly with an odd look. "You can see this?"

Holly nodded and shrugged. "Don't know why, but yes. It's silvery and sort of iridescent."

Tatya got a wily, snide look on her face. Holly had seen it before and it never boded well. "Then I suppose you can find it if I do *this*." She threw it across the room with force. It was the wrong move. Ahmad hit her with a blast of power strong enough to make her grunt and drop to her knees.

Now his voice was razor-sharp and dangerous. "That was beyond foolish, doctor. If we didn't need a healer at this point, I would put you down—Lucas's wife or not."

Holly's eyes followed the feather's path. While most feathers floated on a breeze and landed gently, this one fell with weight and purpose. It spun by Eric's head so close it probably trimmed his hair, and landed under the desk in the corner. She intentionally didn't react to Tatya's pissy games, or to the punishment she earned from Ahmad. She just walked over to the desk, reached down to pick the feather up, and then brought it back to the table where she put it back in the mason jar Eric had found to store it in. It landed in the bottle with an audible tink, making her think there must be some sort of metal in the feather. She screwed on the lid and then shook it a few times so everybody would know it was inside. The tone was musical, like a crystal wind chime. "We probably need to keep this somewhere it doesn't get lost. Maybe with a label."

Antoine shook his head. The big cat was very obviously worried. He was leaning against the wall, musk glands going overtime. It made him smell like a wet cat box to her nose. "*Non.* It is best if only those in this room know of its existence." His French accent was getting thicker. Holly noted that all the council members reverted to their primary language when stressed. "It will be difficult enough to tell the people outside that their worst nightmare is one they can't see. They don't need proof. It will panic them. Already there are children who start crying when branches move in the wind. We don't need them running screaming into the night to alert the humans."

"Speaking of which," Tatya said in a much more humble voice. "That park ranger stopped by again. I used a little persuasion on him and convinced him there weren't nearly as many people here as his eyes told him. I *also* told him we would be going to the new site come daybreak. I hope that's true."

Tony tapped his rifle on the toe of his shoes. The leather of his gloves and his shoe squeaked in different pitches. He tipped his head. "That all depends on what hints the big guy can give us. I think it's time to do that hindsight. I'd like to do Lucas too, just to see if there's anything he saw that could help us. Number of fighters, maybe, or how many they killed."

"Agreed," Ahmad said with a nod. "There are few secrets to be kept at this point and I believe you're capable of keeping any . . . *confidences* you might find."

Tony shrugged. "Have so far. Nothing in this head that anyone would *believe*, even if I told them. Best I could hope for is to write a novel someday."

"Which you won't do, of course." Antoine's voice held both humor and a command.

Tony smiled, but it was a dark smile, rather than a friendly one. "Of course. Doc, would you make sure they're both in good enough physical condition for a hindsight? I need to take a leak upstairs and then we'll be ready." He motioned toward Holly and Eric. "You might want to do the same. No telling how long this will take."

It couldn't hurt. Holly shrugged and followed him up the stairs. But she'd barely taken two steps toward the kitchen—which thankfully now smelled of baking bread—when Tatya screamed from downstairs. Tony flew by her, rifle barrel leading the way. She and Eric weren't far behind.

"*Mon Dieu!*" Antoine's voice sounded both horrified and fascinated. Holly pushed her way into the room to see everybody gathered around Lucas's bed. Or *was* it Lucas? The man she'd known her whole life seemed to be . . . *melting*. No, it was more like bits of him seemed to be blending and then reforming and turning into something completely different.

"For what it's worth, this is *very* cool to watch with second sight. I don't think this is going to be fatal . . . per se." Tony sounded very sure of himself, and Holly couldn't figure out why. Tatya tried to get to Lucas, but Ivan was holding her firmly in a bear hug. She wept and wailed as her husband of many years basically became another man before their eyes.

It was over in moments and the medium-built Latino with the familiar salt-and-pepper hair was now a slender, muscled Native American with waist-length, shining black locks.

Tatya sniffed the air and then panicked all over again. "Who is that man? That's not Lucas. *Where is my husband?* Is this some sort of sick joke?"

Tony stepped forward first, once the new body was fully in place. "No, actually I think this *is* the real Lucas. Remember that girl back in Boulder? What was her name . . . Liz? The badger. Anyway, she could see through illusions. This guy here—" He picked up Lucas's hand and checked for a pulse. "This is *exactly* how she described him when we were at her house. She saw through the illusion he'd put around me too. I think this is who he used to be, when he was Inteque. I've seen his aura shift when he changes personas, like putting on a new suit. He changes everything—visual, scent, and aura. I watched him change from his Lucas persona to one that I've seen before . . . just once. But, we've got a bigger problem than just that thing out there."

At the questioning looks from the council members, Tony met each of their eyes in turn. "Guys, Lucas isn't Sazi anymore. His aura's flat *gone.* He's full-blood human."

AFTER EACH OF them had sniffed Lucas and tested him for magic by pressing him with theirs and waiting for an answering ping, Holly watched as each of them tried to come to grips with what was possibly the first Sazi to ever lose his magic. That he was one of their greatest was apparently totally freaking everyone out, so that they were now trying to gather themselves in various rooms, deciding what to do next. Tatya was inconsolable, and couldn't even bring herself to touch this strange man until she heard his voice and could see the man she knew as *Lucas* in his eyes. She poured healing magic into him until her skin was gray and gaunt. But there didn't seem to be anything to heal. Holly had only touched him briefly, but he was in perfect health . . . physically.

Except that his eyes were still closed, and nobody seemed to be able to wake him up.

"So, what do you think?" she asked Eric in hushed tones as the council closed themselves in a room to confer and Tatya parked herself at her husband's side. Holly had managed to fill two bowls with the fragrant beef stew before the cooks opened the doors to the rest of the refugees. She blew on a spoonful. "Do you think it has something to do with the snake attack?" She chewed with gusto while Eric stirred the contents of his bowl. They'd added the right amount of garlic and the salt level had gone down significantly.

He took a bite and let out an appreciative *Mmm*. "Glad you had them suck out some of the salt. It's nearly too salty now."

She nodded. "That's why it's the last thing you normally add to a stew. It builds up fast and is a pain to get back out."

They ate for a time, cross-legged on the floor. You'd have thought that *furniture* would have been top on the list of things to buy for new pack headquarters— before they brought down people, at least.

Eric finally responded as she dipped a chunk of

bread in the sauce. "What do I think? Frankly, I'm stumped. I can't think of a single snake bite that could cause this kind of reaction. And one of the pack leaders of the Minnesota pack, Myrna Mueller, was a Sazi historian. She visited our place a lot when I was growing up. I heard nearly every story about the early days of the wolves, and I *never* heard a hint of this."

Holly shook her head and raised her brows. "I've heard of her. She never made it to Boulder, but I heard she had some *great* stories. Nothing about a big snake bird, huh?"

"No, I didn't mean that. She had *plenty* of stories about Marduc. Once I heard the name I realized what we were up against. It's not good, for the record. But it's not *this*." He pointed toward the stairwell.

He paused long enough that Holly had to prompt him. "So? Four-one-one me." He opened his mouth to reply when she heard a chirping sound, like birds in the woods. It made her heart race. She reached for the small pink object and held it up with a flourish. "My cell phone! We've got a signal back. Maybe it's one of the family." That made Eric sit up straighter. She opened it and saw a weird series of numbers. Was it Australia? "Hello?"

"Holly? Oh thank God I finally reached you!" She had to struggle to recognize the voice and then realized it was Dale. He sounded really . . . odd.

"The cell towers went down. It's been a zoo here. I don't even know where to start. I'm just glad you and Rose are safe."

There was a pause and then his voice went flat. "Then you haven't heard. I'm so sorry, Holly. But Rose is dead. They're *all* dead."

Rose? "No, that's not true. Maybe she just went without you. But I told her to go before Larry came. But he couldn't have come because he was with me. Dale, *no*!"

Now the voice sounded tired, as though he'd been crying but there weren't any more tears. "I don't know what you told her, Holly. But she never came to tell me. I was working the drive and found a few decent stones. I realized it was nearly daybreak when I got topside. When I went in the house . . . there they were. Scattered in every room. Most were snakebit, but a few had been stabbed." Dale came from snake lineage, so he'd know what it looked like.

Eric touched her shoulder, sympathy plain on his face. But there was nothing to be said. Her sister was gone. That was two of the Sanchez sisters who were dead now—both taken too young and for stupid, evil reasons.

"God, Dale. I don't know what to say."

"I warned her. I swear I warned her this was going to happen. One of these days, I told her. One of these days they'll find out and stop you. Kill you." Now he was crying again, and his sobs tore at her heart. "And now . . . they did. But—" He paused and snuffled a few times. "I *can* make sure it doesn't happen to anyone else. You know people in Wolven now. Rose said you worked for them. She was real excited for you, except she missed you being like her. She was going to change you back, like they changed the others back."

Whoa. Eric's face registered the same shock. He took the phone away from her. "Dale? You don't know me, but I'm Eric Thompson. I'm a Wolven agent and I'm here with Holly. Repeat what you just said. "Who are *they* and what sort of *change* were they planning?"

"Hello, Agent Thompson. I'm glad Holly's got someone there with her. I was worried that they'd gotten her too. Rose would be . . . *heartbroken* to have something happen to her baby sister. She . . . that is—" He snuffled again and seemed to mumble to himself for a time.

Eric spoke forcefully. "Stay with me, Dale. I know you've had a shock. But stay with me, okay? You there?"

"Yeah. I'm here." The cold, dead voice was back. God, Holly wished she could reach through the phone lines and hug him. He had nobody, was in a strange town, and his wife and everybody he knew was . . . gone. "Ask your questions. I'll tell you what I can."

"Who are *they*?"

Another snuffle and then a fairly firm voice. "FMU—Family Members United." He paused and then said with a small chuckle, "You know, they'd originally wanted to call it Family United, just so they could call themselves FU. But Rose was the one who suggested *Members*, just so nobody would really notice them out there. Wanted everything low-key. You can ask Holly about that. She was there at the beginning too."

She felt her face grow hot as Eric turned steely eyes on her. He'd have questions after he was done with Dale. Dear God. Could she have stopped all this?

"Go on." Eric's voice was firm and sure, but his scent was just short of furious. The question was *with who*. "What change had they planned?"

"They developed a drug. The actual name was RSA17, but everybody in FMU called it *the cure*. It sounds like just what it was. A drug that could change a Sazi back to human. It could have been a great thing—a way to heal attack victims like Holly, help those who are near-turns get rid of the side effects. But the thing was, they didn't want to give people a *choice*. They decided to go on the offensive . . . change anyone they felt like. And they *felt* like starting at the top. All the big dogs of the council."

"Like Lucas."

Dale agreed. "Him for sure. He was on Rose's short list for not protecting Holly back when she was human. And their dad was another one. Rose thought he deserved to know what it was like to be *just* human. He'd always looked down on Holly and Rose. And his wife too, if Rose wasn't bullshitting me about that. But the thing was, they couldn't ever get the drug completely stable. It had some weird side effects. Made people crazy, like Lucas's son. The youngest one."

Holly's hand flew to her mouth. "Michael." She whispered the word. Everybody had wondered what happened, why he'd turned so hostile and strange. They'd blamed it on the mating with Cat, but was it? Had he been *drugged* and they had no idea?

"Could they have been working with a bunch of snakes and raptors? Maybe like in a coordinated attack?" It was a logical question and Holly wouldn't have thought of asking it. Would the FMU work with snakes intent on killing? The whole point *originally* was to end the brutality of the animals, not encourage it. Or were her sisters and the others victims of that compliance drug Ahmad had mentioned?

"Not *with* them. But yes, they knew about it. Matthew—he used the screen name *Nobodystoady*—had ties to a snake group that was planning attacks on the council. He didn't know details about what they were doing, but he'd gotten times and a couple of places. A couple of FMU members followed behind the snakes and shot darts with the drug at whatever council members they recognized were being attacked. They just didn't care anymore if anyone died, or got hurt. I tried to get Rose to see how many lives would be ruined, but she just kept going and going. And. . . . well, I love her. *Loved* her, I mean." He paused and then broke down completely. "She's really gone. My . . . my *Rosebud*. My beautiful—" The last was a whisper and the line abruptly clicked off.

Eric frantically pushed buttons, trying to call him back, while Holly felt the feeling seep out of her lips and fingers. Her bowl of stew landed, hot and wet, on her lap—and she didn't care. Didn't move out of the way or even react.

"Holly? Sweetheart, are you okay?" She felt Eric's hand on her shoulder, but couldn't move to acknowledge it. When he tipped her chin up to look into her eyes, he seemed out of focus. He smelled so concerned, so worried, but she couldn't do anything to end his pain. Then he moved away and she was alone again. Had someone put her in a rocking chair? She seemed to be moving, but wasn't sure why.

After what seemed like a lifetime, but was also no time at all, she heard a new voice. "Holly? Holly, it's Iris. Look at me, little sis." She looked up and realized the reason things were out of focus was because she was looking through a salty film of tears. Iris's eyes were likewise red and swollen. "I just heard," she sobbed. "She didn't deserve that, Hollyberry. Rose was better than that."

Holly felt her head nodding at the familiar nickname she'd grown up with. When Iris held out her arms, she fell into them, her body racked with sobs. "I didn't know, Iris. I swear I didn't know."

"How could you have? Sweetie, how could any of us?" Her sister's scent was filled with such compassion, such warmth, that she seemed a completely different person than the snide, petty teenager from years ago who'd left home to marry a hot, rich guy in Canada. At least Iris hadn't tormented her like the others. She'd mainly been aloof and distant.

But now they held onto each other for the longest time, until the worst of the tears passed. But the ache remained like dull metal in Holly's stomach. Iris pushed her back and held her at arm's length, wetness still shining in her eyes. "Okay, look, kiddo—I've got to get back outside to my family, and it sounds like you have important stuff to do in here. But we'll keep in touch." Iris turned her head and looked up at Eric. Holly hadn't even realized he was still there. "Thank you so much for coming to find me, Agent Thompson. I always knew Dad was wrong about you." She patted Holly on the head and ruffled her hair. "You take care of my baby sis, huh? There aren't many of us left." Iris flicked her eyes back to her, still petting her hair. "You heard about Pansy, right?"

Holly shook her head. It hurt to open her eyes that wide. They were too swollen. "No. What—"

Now Iris sighed sadly. "Dominance battle last fall. She finally picked a fight she couldn't win. I'm not surprised Dad didn't tell you. I think he was embarrassed. He always tried to convince himself that the toughest fighters were the best kids. Rose might have been human, but she was probably the most aggressive of any of us. Weird that the three quiet ones are the ones who survived. It's just you, me, and Lily left now."

Three out of six gone. "Have you heard from Dad?"

Iris shook her head. "Nothing yet. But I heard from someone outside that Raven Ramirez took over when the attack happened. He was at the airport when the first call came in. It sounds like he fought off most of the snakes and then evacuated Boulder to the summer hunting lands in Wyoming. Fingers crossed, huh?"

"Yeah." There was a dull feeling in the pit of her stomach.

Eric spoke up. "I'll be right back, Holly. Just hang in there, okay?"

She nodded as Eric walked out. Iris watched him leave with anxious eyes. She was holding her body rigid, her fingers clenched tight around Holly's hand. Once he was gone, she began to whisper hurriedly.

"Holly, I couldn't say this with him in the room, but you need to keep your distance from Eric Thompson." The panic on her face and in her scent were real, but Holly couldn't figure out why.

"What do you mean? What's wrong with him?"

Iris shook her head, tiny little movements, and constantly flicked her eyes around the room, watching. She spoke at a frantic pace, as though trying to make sure she got everything in while there was time. "It's the whole family, Holly. The whole Canada pack is terrified of them. Derek is insane, and he's a total racist. His mother too. They treat anyone who's not pureblood Canadian like *animals* up there, but we're too afraid to leave. And the rumors I've heard about *Eric*!" She gripped both of her hands and stared at her with wide eyes. "They didn't send him away because he was the *nice* one. Oh, sweetie, *please* don't get involved with him. Dad was totally right about them and I should have believed him. I know I said Pansy died in a dominance battle, but I don't know for sure. That's what *Derek* said. But I'm afraid he . . . he *did* something to her. And Doug too. They were outspoken against him. He's been arrested a ton of times—*arrested* and held in jail for assault and attempted rape—but his mother keeps buying his way out of trouble. I don't know how she does it, but nobody on the council would believe Pansy when she complained."

Iris started abruptly as footsteps sounded on the stairs. She scrambled to her feet, nearly tripping in her effort to leave. "Just think about it, okay? Be really careful."

Eric walked in the room and stared at Iris like she'd grown a second head. Holly didn't doubt he could smell the fear, bordering on panic, that rose from her. Iris didn't say a word to him. She just lowered her eyes and bolted out the door. Eric shrugged and looked down at Holly with a sad smile. "I found you some clean pants and some more tissues." He held out a pair of blue jeans that seemed her size. She looked down and saw that the stew had dried into a thick crust on the fabric of her pants. All of a sudden her skin started to itch underneath. Or had it been itching for a while and she only just noticed? "I've been holding off the council for as long as I can, Holly, but—"

Shit. The hindsight. She'd completely forgotten. Iris *couldn't* be right about him. She had to have made some sort of mistake.

But she's lived under the family's rule for five years. Why would she lie?

Holly faked a little snuffle and nodded. "It's okay. I'm sure I'm not the only person who lost family today." She managed to get to her feet with a little effort. She stumbled once because one foot had gone to sleep, and Eric caught her. There was no hate in his eyes when he looked at her. No scent of condescension when he touched her. In fact, he'd been near her for a whole summer and she wasn't stupid. She *knew* when people looked down on her. She'd always been able to sense that sort of thing. No, Iris had to be wrong. This time, Holly wrapped her arms around him and gently kissed his cheek. "Thank you."

"For what?" He squeezed her tightly and planted a kiss on her forehead. "You had quite a shock . . . on a couple of fronts." He paused, and then lowered his voice. "I haven't told them yet, by the way. Figured you'd rather do it, in case . . . well, just in case."

In case she didn't want to admit her involvement? That was sweet of him, but also not fair. "No. I'll 'fess up. I left the group before any of this shit happened, but I still should have told someone they existed. I left *because* they were getting radical, and it scared me. Maybe I deserve to be punished for keeping this secret."

He suddenly smelled nearly frantic, from what little air she could pull in through her nose. "I can't judge that. But don't *suggest* it, huh? Right now, I don't know what some of them might do. At least wait until you see how they react to you knowing about the group at all." He paused and then draped the pants over her shoulder, looking extremely uncomfortable all of a sudden. "I just don't want to lose you, okay? I think I might still . . . that is . . . I . . . oh *hell*!"

He released her abruptly and walked away. He hesitated for a moment when he reached the stairs, then nearly ran down them. The scents he left behind made her mouth dry and her heart race. Lots of confusion and the wet scent of sorrow. But was that cinnamon and sugar that drifted to her nose, or just the cooks starting dessert in the kitchen? *Might still . . . what?*

She started to follow him when she heard footsteps behind her and recognized Tony's scent. He touched her on the shoulder on his way past. She could smell fur and oiled leather as he got close. "Sorry about your sister, kid, and sorry we can't give you time to deal with it. But we need to get this over with, and you're supposed to be part of the party. But hey—" he said with a nod and a surprising amount of compassion in his scent. "Once this is all over, I know some people you can talk to. They're pretty good."

Holly nodded and he winked before trotting lightly down the stairs. She started to follow him, but the pants were totally stuck to her legs now. They pulled on her skin and held like glue.

She waddle-walked to the bathroom to change and finally got a look at herself in the mirror. *God, I look like I'm the last one alive in a horror movie!* It was no wonder Eric had kissed her forehead. It was the only part of her face not spattered with dried stew. It looked like she had thrown up on herself. It had even splashed into her hair. She glanced around the room. At least there was soap and a real towel, rather than just the cheap paper towels she expected.

It wasn't a perfect solution, but she was able to scrub the grime off her face and body by wetting down half the towel and giving herself a sponge bath—after she'd peeled off the ruined jeans and sweater. And the soap actually smelled pretty good, although she wouldn't have thought to blend pears with cucumbers as a fragrance. When she saw there was a brand new package of combs in the drawer, she decided to give her hair a quick rinse too.

Fortunately, the pants Eric had found for her mostly fit, although they were a little tight, and the T-shirt she had on under the sweater was still in decent shape.

Just the act of cleaning up made her feel a little more like herself. Yeah, her hair was damp and her eyes were still red, but nobody would comment on that part. And the tube of cherry lip balm she'd bought at the truck stop on the way down hadn't totally melted. She slid it across her lips and then surveyed herself in the mirror

Not perfect, but presentable. At least my freckles don't stand out so much with a little color.

Eric was waiting for her when she emerged, leaning on the wall at the top of the stairs. He smiled nervously as he looked her up and down. "You look like you feel better."

She nodded. "A little. Just trying not to think about it for now. I don't want to screw up whatever I'm supposed to be doing in this hindsight because my head's flaming out."

"You and me both. Sorry for . . . well, just sorry. I'll meet you downstairs." He bolted again, leaving her shaking her head. What was he *sorry* for? Sorry for caring? Sorry for treating her like a person? Or, could he have overheard Iris . . . no. That just didn't fit.

But if his goal was to keep her confused, he was doing a fine job.

Chapter Eleven

WHY IN THE hell does she have to look so good? He'd just managed to get to where he could face Holly again, and then she came out of the bathroom looking totally hot and smelling like cherry pie. They really needed to get this hindsight over with so he could go find something to do outside. Because the more time he was spending with her, the worse it was fighting to keep his hands *off* her.

And could there possibly be a worse time for this? Not only was there a major crisis, she'd just lost one sister, and the other one . . . well, he wasn't sure what was wrong with her, but she didn't seem quite *right*. Whatever she was scared of, she wasn't faking, but he wasn't sure snakes were the problem.

Eric crowded into the small armory where Charles's bed had been moved. "Okay, so let's go over this," Tony said when Holly appeared. "We're going to skip doing a hindsight on Lucas. I just don't trust myself enough to try this on a human, and we have no idea what shape his brain's in right now. Charles seems to be in good shape, except that he's in some sort of coma." He shrugged. "It might be self-induced for all we know. But since he instructed it to be done, we're going ahead." He held out his hand and flicked his fingers. "Here's where we start the touchy-feely part that I hate. Thompson and I get to hold hands like kiddies on the playground, and since I've never tried to take two people along for the ride, you and Holly will need to *both* hold my hand. I think it'll have to be the same hand, but you might try holding your other hands too. Complete the circuit, as it were. No promises on whether this is going to work. I might wind up taking along one or the other of you. But once we've started, *neither* of you let go. Okay?"

The onlookers moved to the side so Holly could get close. Tony had brought in chairs for them to sit on and when he sat down on the one closest to Charles, it left Holly sitting next to Eric, so close that their legs touched from thigh to knee.

He tried to concentrate on what Tony was saying, but it was harder than he imagined. Holly's leg was soft and slender and thrummed with power, and her scent—

"You get that, Thompson?" Tony snapped his fingers inches from his face. Once again, he'd gotten distracted. That was getting annoying—and dangerous.

"Neither of us let go. Got it."

"And neither of you comment when I'm watching the memories. We're just there to take in images, and some of them are rough. Most people fixate on the last important thing they did. In this case, it'll probably be bloody. He was pretty ripped up when he came in. But we have to live through it, and nothing there can hurt you. Got it?"

They both nodded and Tony took off his black gloves and wiggled his fingers. "Sorry if they're sweaty, but it's the only way to avoid visions. Holly, you first and then Eric. You'll have to scrunch together. I'll try not to make this too long so you don't cramp up."

Holly reached out her hand and Tony took it. Then Eric placed his hand over Holly's. She slid her fingers through his and there was suddenly tension in the air. Tony looked at each of them in turn and then at their joined hands. He got an odd look on his face. At Eric's questioning look, he just shook his head. "Never mind. You'll figure it out. Let's get started. Everybody keep their lips zipped. We're going in."

Tony shut his eyes and touched Charles's face. Darkness descended on the room so abruptly that Eric wondered who turned out the lights. But it wasn't just the lights. He couldn't sense any other people nearby except Tony.

"You guys both with me?" Tony's voice echoed in the darkness.

"I'm here." And then she was. Holly glowed green-gold in the darkness, seeming to be across a vast room. Apparently she could see the colored band around herself too. She held up her hand to her face in wonder. "What's wrong with me?"

"Nothing," Tony said after a moment. "You're just seeing what *I* see every day. You're in *my* head right now and I have second sight. But if you want to see something interesting, touch each other."

His voice sounded amused. Eric held out his hand, noticing the rich blue band around each finger. When he touched Holly's hand, the colors merged and turned the rich turquoise of a peacock feather.

"Pretty!" Holly's voice sounded delighted. She held out her hand toward Tony, whose aura was a pale, gunmetal gray. "What color do you think it'll make if I touch you?"

Tony gave that same secretive smile. "There won't be one. That's the interesting part." He touched her hand to prove his point. There was no merging of colors. Just green touching gray. "But we have things to do. I'll let you two mull that over on your own time."

"But I don't—" There wasn't time for Eric to finish his sentence, because light suddenly flooded his vision, so bright it hurt his eyes.

Tony had said to expect a battle, so Eric prepared himself for the worst. But there were no biting snakes or swooping raptors. Instead, there was a quiet study and Charles writing at his desk.

"Well, this is a surprise. But memories are screwy things." Tony held up his hand and the vision stopped. He pulled backward and the picture zoomed in."Let's see what he's writing."

As they got closer, they could hear the scratch of an old fountain pen moving across the paper. Tony manipulated the image until they could see the writing as it appeared. About half of the page was already written. Holly started reading out loud, even though everybody could see it.

" 'I've discovered that writing is an exercise which improves the memory. The mere act of putting words on a page sharpens them, focuses the mind, and reminds one of things long forgotten. The issue today is forgotten memories and a stolen future. But first, let me welcome you, Tony.' "

Tony's eyebrows shot up and he crossed his arms over his chest. "Very interesting. He knows he can't talk to me directly, so he's writing what he wants me to know. Never had this happen before. But then, he's a seer, and they're just weird."

Charles moved his pen down to the next line and Holly gasped as she read, " 'And welcome Eric and Holly. It is no accident I asked you to attend today.' "

Charles tapped the pen on his chin for a moment and then dipped the golden nib into the ink once more. The scratching of the pen was soothing, but he had a sure hand that let them read along quickly. " 'If you have not encountered Marduc yet, you soon will. She is not to be trifled with. Already she's stolen my ability to foresee where and when she will appear, as she did last time when Lucas, Jack, and I encountered her. It's important that you know that while she is newly born, she is by no means a child. Nor is she simply a reincarnation of the earlier being we fought around the time of the Mayan empire. She is one and the same, and has existed since the dawn of time.' "

"Whoa. We apparently have some new issues, guys." Eric realized Tony wasn't talking to them. He must be able to speak to the others in the room while he was in a hindsight trance. "Charles is narrating the hindsight. Seems this Marduc is the *same* Marduc they fought in the Mayan period."

" 'She learns as she sleeps,' " Charles continued to write. " 'She has all the knowledge of the world as it passes her by, and with each day she grows, she becomes more powerful. All we were able to do last time was destroy her vessel, and that's all we will be able to do this time as well, I fear. We found no way to destroy her completely.' "

"This is crazy," Eric said to nobody in particular. "Why tell us we're doomed? Why waste the time?"

"No commentary, please." Tony turned to him with eyes that were narrowed in annoyance. "I have a hard enough time concentrating on what's going on. I don't care if Holly reads, because that actually helps me focus. I'm watching all sorts of things here, recording everything, in case people want to know whether he was smoking or the sun was shining."

Eric shut up, and Holly picked up the narrative again. " 'Just last week, I had Lucas in my office to talk about this.' " Charles paused and tapped the pen on the paper, and suddenly the image changed. Charles was in a different part of the room, magically transported to a chair in front of the fire, and Lucas—wearing a flannel shirt and jeans—was in the chair across from him.

Tony laughed. "Oh, *very* cool. He's bookmarked his own memories by writing them down. Man, I wish more people would do this—except I generally get stuck doing a hindsight on people who don't *want* to remember."

"Do you remember the last time we fought Marduc?" Charles tapped the pipe he was holding to empty the bowl into a waiting ashtray. The fragrant scent of cherry tobacco filled the room, strong enough to make Eric dizzy.

"How could I forget? We barely survived. We won't be so lucky this time, I'm afraid. We fought her when you, Jack, and I were at our most powerful. And, while you've changed little, I'm not so fast anymore, and Jack is dead," Lucas said.

"Oh, I've changed. I merely hide it well. But we weren't Charles, Lucas, and Jack back then, were we?" Charles smiled and it took years off his face.

Lucas laughed. "No indeed. We were the bloodswords—Inteque, youngest son of the Great White Wolf, Colecos the jaguar god, and Sasha the bear who ruled the North. From gods to mere men in only a lifetime or two."

Charles laughed as he tamped more moist, heavy tobacco into the pipe. "Or three or four. And only Jack could see the beast, which we considered good sport back then."

"Lots of things that were 'sport' back then would make people pale today. I wish we had someone with *third sight* who could see Marduc this time around."

Charles held a match to the bowl until it caught. "Actually, we do."

Lucas leaned forward in his chair, his scent both excited and curious. "We do? Who? We need to prepare him."

Charles shook his head. "Not him, *her*. And I fear I can't tell you yet. You know her and you'll try to protect her from the task."

Of course, now everyone knew that person was Holly, and Charles was probably right that people were going to try to protect her. Eric knew *he* would certainly try.

Lucas stood abruptly and walked the few steps to the fireplace. His scent bordered on anger, with a healthy dose of frustration. "You know, I get really tired of you hiding everything from everyone. Why can't you just let things play out as they will?" He poked at the fire viciously, taking out his annoyance on the chunks of glowing wood.

Charles's responding chuckle was maddening to Eric. It was secretive and amused and patronizing. "Josette said the same thing to me just last week. She's grown tired of letting me rule, I'm afraid. Thinks I've saved the lives of too many, and have ruined any chance we have as a species."

Lucas turned, poker in hand. "Who does she think should have died?"

"Who *doesn't* she? She thinks Raphael should have been allowed to confront Jack. Of course, Jack would have killed him and we'd never have known about his . . . carnal tastes. She believes I was wrong for saving my goddaughter. And," he admitted with a sigh, "she might have been right about that. If Catherine hadn't been turned, she wouldn't have mated with Raphael, and Michael wouldn't have gone insane."

"That's not true," Holly said.

Tony shook his head. "He can't hear you, kid. Just listen quietly. He's still talking and we're missing it."

"—and the others wouldn't have attacked Holly Sanchez . . . another person, I'll add, that Aspen thinks should have been left to die."

Eric felt a growl rise in his chest, and it widened Holly's eyes. She moved a step away from him and turned back to the image. Now, why would it bother her that he'd growled? Unless . . . surely she didn't *want* to die? She had said she was dealing with it. Had she lied to him?

"She was quite upset," Charles continued. "Josette said if I got to play God with people's lives, then she could too. I fear she'll do something rash." Charles shook his head and took another puff of the pipe. "But she's saved enough lives of her own, and she knows the risks—possibly better than I. There are times I envy her ability to see all threads of time. It's a wonder she's not mad as a hatter, though. But I'm still in charge and I'll keep watch over her. For now."

Lucas smirked as he sat back down. He picked up a glass half-filled with a rich amber liquid and took a sip. "It's a lifelong appointment. That was the deal when you signed on. You can't hand it over to someone else."

Charles met his eyes for a long moment. "Precisely. I'll serve for the rest of my life." He paused, and then closed his eyes and sank back into the chair.

"She's awake, Lucas. Marduc has been invading my thoughts for nearly a month now. She's blocking my sight as well. I fear if I'm not removed from the equation, by force if necessary, she'll be able to use me as a weapon."

The glass slipped from Lucas's suddenly limp grasp and bounced on the thick Persian rug, spilling its contents across the colored patterns. "Who have you told?"

He sighed. "Just you, just now. I hope to think of a way to get the proper information to those who need it in a way that won't alert *her*. And, it might be that I have to die to manage it."

"What do you see in *my* future? Is my time also about to end?"

Charles shook his head and offered a warm smile. "You'll live out a happy lifetime and grow old with your family."

It was a skillful lie—or rather, a masterful avoidance of the events to come. Eric was impressed, but then Charles had lived for millennia, more than long enough to learn how to manipulate words without lying. As a human, Lucas *would* grow old with his family. He'd die in the span of a normal lifetime unless they could find a way to bring him back to his old power.

"Enough of this talk of a nebulous future. Indulge me for a moment, old friend," Charles said with another smile. "Walk with me again in the past, when we defeated a great monster and saved the world, so that I might remember the details to pass along."

"Not a bad idea," Lucas agreed with a nod. "Maybe together we'll remember something that can help. If she can block *you*, she's probably blocking all of the seers."

"She's very subtle. It was only when I heard a whisper in my mind making an oh-so reasonable suggestion to leave a door open that I caught on to her. But now I don't trust myself to do anything but listen to old stories about a different time." He leaned back and put the pipe between his lips. "Tell me a story of swords and dragons."

Lucas laughed, but there was a tightness around his eyes now. "There once was a fierce dragon who brought the rains and amused herself by eating the citizens—"

Holly screamed as the ground under them suddenly dropped away. Tony quickly spoke to those in the room. "It's okay, people. Just a scene shift. We're all fine. I should have warned you that this sort of thing can happen."

They were in a dark jungle. A massive white wolf padded among the sea of green ahead of them. A flash of color off to his left caught Eric's eye and he looked over to see a spotted cat, nearly double the size of any regular jungle cat, leaping lightly from branch to branch. The cat looked down on the wolf with glowing gold eyes and shook his massive yellow head.

"You glow like torches in the dark. If we have any hope of sneaking up on the creature who eats the souls of my people, we must arrive in secrecy. Cover that white fur with mud, or at least turn human so you'll blend in and not betray our location to her eight-legged warriors." The language wasn't English to Eric's ears, but for some reason it was translating into words his mind could understand.

Tony's voice interrupted the scene, making Eric blink to bring his mind back to the present. "Hey, looks like we get a front-row seat for the actual battle. Shame we're not in the cat's mind, though. Then we could see what this thing looks like."

The wolf shook his head, and his voice was Lucas's. "You worry too much, Colecos. I think your bright pelt would make a better target for warriors who live in trees than mine. The spiders don't see in the dark the same way cats do."

The cat looked taken aback. He sniffed the air a few times and then nodded. He leapt to the ground and shimmered briefly before turning into a short man with a bowl-shaped haircut and nut-colored skin. "No reason to risk you being right . . . for once."

Lucas—or more precisely, Inteque—laughed lightly and also changed form. Taking the appearance of the man on the cot in the next room. "Speak nonsense to the ears of the gods if you like. They already know the truth. Now, let us unload our beast of burden and continue."

Tony spoke again to those out in the room. "Yep, that's Lucas all right. He's Inteque, the white wolf."

"*Beast of burden?*" The words were as thickly accented as Ivan on his best day. Apparently, they weren't going to get to see the massive polar bear. The only way Eric even knew they were in Charles's head was the angle of the image. They were looking far down at Lucas, as though standing on a roof. "If you are not very careful, young wolf, the she-devil will be the least of your worries. It will be *Sasha* you will see in your nightmares."

All three men chuckled quietly as hands helped relieve him of a leather pouch the size of a suitcase. When he changed forms, he was taller than either of the others. He reached for a stack of clothing, brightly patterned with red and green dye. His hands were *massive*. Charles must hide his appearance even now, the way Lucas had until he turned human. The amount of power it would take to hold an illusion at all times—sleeping, making love, even while injured and unconscious. It was almost too much for Eric to wrap his head around.

"Yeah, yeah," Tony said after a moment. "Bonding moment, bonding moment. Now tough guy wrestling. Don't care." He moved his hand forward and the image blurred. Eric realized it was fast-forwarding as easily as a movie. Tony paused the image to see them still walking through the dark. "Don't care." Another flip of his hand, and another pause. "Still don't care." Another blur and another stop. Now they were eating dinner. "C'mon, you guys. Get to the action. This is as bad as a porno movie with a *plot*." Holly snorted but kept any comments to herself, and Tony smiled as he stared at the images.

"How do you *do* that?" Eric couldn't help but ask. Hindsight must be a really strange gift to have.

"No talking, please. Seer concentration zone. I don't know how I do it. Seems to come with the package."

Holly leaned in close. "Healing's like that too. You just *do* things, without a clue as to why or how they work."

A diagonal flash of red cut across the image and the scream that followed made them all jump. Holly grabbed for Eric's hand without thinking. He didn't mind.

"Whoops. Time to back up. I think we're here." Tony spun the image backward more slowly. People who died reanimated, blood sailed through the air to tuck back into bodies, and spiders shot up into the trees like yo-yos. "This looks a lot like an ambush. I think it's about to get ugly."

It had been Charles screaming, as something unseen cut at him from above. He could apparently hear it and feel it, but there was nothing but air and trees to see. Then came the spiders, dropping down and shooting webs to surround them. But the men had their swords now. Charles swatted away a spider without raising a hand—using the sheer power of his magic. He used his sword to cut through the cocoon the spider had spun around Lucas. But even with the weight of his muscles behind it, it was like hacking through a tree with a pocketknife.

Tony spoke quietly, so they didn't miss anything that might be said in the image. "I can testify to the strength of those webs. I remember Lucas telling me that they didn't have any silver back then. Remind me to hit up a coin shop and pick up some old silver dollars to melt down into blades. Burns through that silk like butter." Now *that* was useful knowledge. Maybe this hindsight wasn't such a waste of time after all.

With Jack and Lucas working together, it didn't take long to dispatch the spiders. They were as good with a blade as anyone Eric had ever known. He'd never seen a sword like the one Colecos carried. It looked like a canoe paddle with a short handle. The edges were lined with flakes of obsidian. And boy, was it effective. Spider legs were severed with barely any fuss and when humans attacked, the blade made short work of limbs and heads. From looking at the hilts, he was pretty sure those exact weapons were here in the armory.

Sasha alone was fighting Marduc, because the others were busy. He changed to bear form to fight and Eric realized why. He had nearly foot-long claws to rake along the creature's sides when she passed by to attack. But it was like watching a fight filmed in front of a green screen. There was just nothing to see.

But then Colecos did something interesting. He changed forms, leapt onto the creature's back and dug in with all four feet. The creature screamed and tried to unseat him, but he held on. He bounced in the air like a marionette on strings and Eric could see the intense concentration in his glowing eyes. "The head is about two feet in front of me. If you cut off my nose or hands, I'll eat the hearts of your children." Then an unearthly noise filled the air. It was a sound that chilled Eric to the bone. He wondered how many of their "best" warriors would be able to stand up to it.

"Crap. I won't be able to do that." Holly's voice grew very quiet and worried. "I'm not a cat like him. How am I going to be able to hold on and tell you guys where to cut?"

Eric let out a noise that didn't quite convey his disbelief. "Don't worry. You're not getting anywhere near that thing."

She stared at him quizzically. "Of *course* I am. Why do you think I'm here watching this? You heard Charles. He kept me alive just for this moment."

Eric shook his head. He wasn't going to argue with her now, but there was no way in hell he was letting Holly get any closer.

He watched Charles grab the tail of the beast to keep it from flying away. Inteque cut at it again and again with one heavily muscled arm, while the other stabbed at where the heart should be. Without even realizing it, Tony had started to creep the image forward faster. They clawed and sliced ever faster, with Charles kicking away any spiders that came too near.

"There aren't any snakes. Did you notice that?"

Tony paused the image, with Jack hanging upside down in midair and Lucas burying one of the blades into Marduc's body. "What?"

Eric gestured toward the frozen image. "No snakes. No raptors. Just spiders to defend her back then. She's upped the ante."

"How did she manage that?" Holly asked with interest.

"I don't think it's Nasil controlling the snakes. You heard Charles say Marduc's been trying to control even him. There aren't many spiders left, but there are tons of snakes in the world. What if she's some sort of supreme pack leader? I know my brother can *make* the wolves in our pack attack on his command, why couldn't she?"

"And who are huddling outside at this very moment?" Holly added thoughtfully. "Cats, wolves, and bears. Might as well attack the families of those that defeated you last time. No raptor families. Hardly any snakes—only those who are really tough alphas that she probably couldn't control. I think you're onto something here, Eric."

"But why include *me* in this group? I'm okay with a sword, but nothing like these guys. It's pretty clear they did this on a daily basis. I haven't picked up a sword since college."

"Actually," Tony said with a smile. "I think I know the answer to that. Let's make sure there's nothing else to see here and we'll get back to real life." He spun the image forward to see the eventual death of Marduc and the destruction of . . . a batch of eggs. Very interesting. Tony froze the image and stared at the pile of white orbs. "Yep. Looks just like the one we saw in Atlantic City. Leathery with those strange pinkish spots. And I remember Ahmad saying Marduc was born pregnant. So we'll need to destroy the eggs, or we'll have to go through this again. Provided, of course," he said wryly, "that we survive *this* time."

They wound up back in the study, with Charles

finishing the memo they'd just experienced firsthand. "'I hope you saw information that will be useful to you,'" Holly read. "'For obvious reasons, I couldn't tell you this in person. She might cause me to give false information in an attempt to keep her movements secret until it's too late. But she can't hide my memories, so I will have to find a way to become so injured I can put myself into a healing trance. Amber taught me how years ago, for times when she wasn't close by. Unfortunately, she always *planned* to be nearby, so I don't know if I can wake up by myself. If I cannot and if no healers survive the battle, please select a leader who is calm in temperament, and strong enough to best even the most obstinate council member in battle. I will destroy this letter as soon as I finish writing it, so none but you will know its contents. Good luck, my friends. I wish you strength, and hope we meet at the end of the journey. Sincerely, Charles Wingate, formerly Sasha, ruler of the Great White North.'"

"Okay, gang," Tony said after Holly finished the final word, "Let's wrap this up. We have plenty to do and—"

You great white FOOL! Did you think there was an area of your mind I could not control?

The voice was female, but so deep it was nearly male. It echoed through the darkness, searing along Eric's skin like red-hot coals.

"Guys, this software officially has a virus. We're leaving *now!*"

Eric once again felt the world fall out from under him as Tony tried to pull them away from Charles's mind. But the voice in the dark wouldn't let go so easily.

I think not, young seer. You know far too much to be allowed to leave. Silvery eyes appeared in the blackness, each one as wide across as a big screen television. You will remain here until I can either break your minds or kill you.

Pain seared across Eric's body and mind with white-hot intensity. Holly screamed and dropped into a fetal position on the floor. Tony grunted and fell to his knees. Blood appeared from a dozen cuts in his skin and Eric wondered if the same was happening to his body.

"This isn't a drill, people. Marduc's inside Charles's mind. Get us out of here!" Tony yelled the words just before his throat was slashed by unseen claws. He grabbed at the wound and his eyes went wide. Eric threw power at the silvery eyes, aiming for the very center. He kept pushing as fast as he could, hoping to take the pressure off the other two. Holly managed to get to her knees and stumble to her feet, even though he wished she'd stay down.

She went immediately to Tony's side. Green power bloomed in a wide arc around the wounded seer, until Eric couldn't see them through the light. Her power was diminished by at least half before Tony started breathing, coughing up thick clots of blood as he struggled to get air. She threw another burst of power into him and he collapsed onto the ground, either out cold or dead.

Eric was running out of power fast. Why weren't

the council members helping? Had they already been killed by Marduc? Was this a *real* attack, rather than just a psychic one?

Eric was concentrating so much on blinding the snake with power that he didn't see Holly come up beside him. "I'm sorry, Eric," she said softly as she touched his face. "But at least one of us has to survive. Please stay safe, and know that I wanted to."

He felt a shock of pain and then he was falling. Green energy pressed in on him and turned into a soothing cocoon that he couldn't seem to escape from. He smelled berries and cinnamon, but the scents were tainted with fear and intense pain. He heard a woman scream and then the green light faded. Everything went black.

Chapter Twelve

"ALL THAT EFFORT. Ruined!" Nasil looked around the tiny cave set high in the cliff with anger and frustration. The priests were dead—had been for days, they'd either been eaten by their Goddess or by scavengers. The eggshell was also broken, from the inside out.

He turned and stared out onto the wide open plains. She was somewhere out there, and he had no idea whether she was sane, or even if she was still alive. Nor would he probably ever find out, since she was invisible. What was he supposed to do, call her like a puppy to come back home?

Nasil reached up to scratch his nose and realized once again that he'd done so unconsciously. Ever since he'd woken in the car, he'd discovered that he had limited use of his hand. It was still clumsy, but it *worked*. Obviously the girl had something to do with it, and he wasn't complaining. He planned to use every bit of the newfound ability to find the Goddess.

Hmm. I wonder . . . He went to the nest in the corner and flicked his tongue around the broken eggshell. The taste was immediately unpleasant, not so much from the venom she obviously secreted from her fangs, but from something that made her uniquely Marduc. He would definitely recognize the taste if he encountered it again.

He felt around the nest, hoping to find a few errant feathers. He was nearly out of the invisibility powder. It would be good to restock. He winced as one sliced open his hand. But there were only two. Barely enough for one more trip.

"But that's all right. I only need one more trip to find you, I think," he said quietly.

Unless I find you first—

The voice seemed to come from everywhere. It pressed in on him, and flowed out through his own mouth. What the hell?

"Where are you?" he demanded of the air, turning in a circle, but feeling no presence. "Show yourself."

I remember you, said the voice, now a hissing contralto in his mind. You assisted the snake who wished to be my mate. You found my resting place . . . with my help, of course.

Nasil felt his blood chill. Marduc was fully sentient and able to remember their search? From before they'd even opened the tomb?

Of course I remember. I have always been and always will be. Did you expect a child to be born from the mind of a queen?

And she could read minds? Terrific. He threw out a burst of power in the hope he would be able to think faster than she could read. Then he'd have to find a way to block his thoughts. "What would you have of me, my queen?"

I'm not ready for you yet. You're not like the others. But you will serve me . . . soon. I've tasted you now and can find you at will. I will come back for you when I'm ready to have alphas worship me. But first I need more food.

The abrupt absence of the mind dropped him to his knees. He tried to think, analyze what she'd said. *Not like the others*. What others?

He needed to go to the gathering of Sazi he saw in the valley. The odor of various species had drifted upon the breeze. He couldn't imagine why that many wolves and cats would be living in such tight quarters. Mammals didn't like to live in snake piles, where there were a thousand others around you to keep you warm. Something important was going on to make them pack together so tight. As soon as Bruce arrived, he'd make him comfortable and then journey down into the valley.

And even as he watched, a lone car turned off the main road and headed in his direction. He couldn't wait to see his lover again. To touch his hair and his skin. But first he'd need to clean out one of the caves, make it habitable for a time. Then he would find the girl. He had no doubt she was somewhere within the gathering of Sazi. This was where he'd traced the helicopter.

And with Marduc already born, there was nothing to stop Nasil from using her healing magic to make him and Bruce whole again. Even if it took every bit of magic she had.

After all, if Marduc was alive, she would be searching for the healer too. And it would be far better for Holly Sanchez if Nasil found her first.

Chapter Thirteen

"WHAT IN THE hell were you *thinking*?!" Eric looked absolutely livid. He paced the length of the RV, making the floor squeak and the whole vehicle rock. He ran his fingers through his hair repeatedly with an expression that would send most people running. But underneath the angry scent was thick, wet worry and enough fear to make her tense. "Do you have any idea how reckless that was?"

Holly had seen him like this before, back in Boulder, after she'd gotten back from the hospital and refused to file a complaint with the pack. She tried to remember what it had been that time. Oh yeah, Jasmine had tried to pull her arm from the socket for daring to borrow her comb. Hardly a unique occurrence, and telling the pack leaders at that point probably would have gotten her sister a slap on the wrist. Of course, *that* would have succeeded in making Holly's life hell for a month after.

She had to struggle not to smile at the memory of Eric's frustrated outrage on her behalf. He'd been so protective then, at a time when she had nobody.

But she didn't need protection anymore. "I already told you. I was thinking exactly what I said before you went into the trance—one of us had to survive. I picked you. How was I supposed to know it would be as simple as putting Tony in a trance to break the hindsight connection?"

He turned and glared at her, fists clenched so tight the knuckles were white. "You *picked* me? So you were just going to sacrifice yourself without even bothering to check with anyone?"

Okay, that was over the line. Holly tried to sit up on the bed holding the sheet to her chest. It was a slow process, because any movement made her head pound. She'd used up so much power healing Tony and putting him and Eric in a trance that it had taken Tatya to bring her back from the brink. "Excuse me? Who exactly was I supposed to 'check' with? The guy bleeding to death on the floor? The council that I couldn't see? *You?* It's not like there was a lot of time to wait for people to *think* about it. Besides, did it ever occur to you that maybe that's why I was *supposed* to be there—because I could make that decision?"

And speaking of being there, she still couldn't figure out why he was here. Who'd elected him her nursemaid? She was wobbling, which was annoying. It didn't really portray the image she needed to pull off the tough words. Sitting wasn't working, so she let herself ease back down to rest on the wonderfully soft pillow. Whoever's trailer this was, they had good taste in bedding. "Look, if you're only going to yell at me, why don't you just leave? I've got a headache and there are enough people here to yell at me that I don't need another one."

Eric sat down on the couch, leaned back, and closed his eyes. "Nobody's going to yell at you." He sounded tired when he said it, as exhausted as she felt.

She turned her head to stare at him incredulously. "Uh, news flash. *You're* yelling at me. And I haven't even met with the council yet about the other stuff."

His eyes didn't open as he spoke. "I already told them about it."

Her mouth opened as she gasped in sudden outrage. "*What?* Damn it, Eric! You said I could tell them in my own way."

Now he turned his head to look at her. "Yeah, that was before you were unconscious for this long. Have you checked the windows, Holly? That's not sunrise outside. It's *sunset*. You've been out for a day."

She looked out the windshield. It was hard to orient herself inside the trailer. She had presumed it was sunrise, because it had been dark when they'd begun the hindsight. A *day*?

"You nearly died, Holly." Eric's voice was softer now. "That's why I'm here in the trailer with you. I thought they needed to know in case someone knew of a way to reverse 'the cure' on Lucas. They had Tony do a hindsight on you while you were out, just in case you didn't make it. You've been cleared of any wrongdoing with the FMU."

They'd done a hindsight on her? "Wouldn't I remember having a hindsight done?"

Eric shook his head. "Apparently that's standard procedure. Tony usually wipes all memory of it. He said he was going to ease your memory of Rose, too. Did he manage that?"

While she realized it had just been a few hours since Rose died, it *did* feel like it had been longer. She nodded absently, still confused.

"Good," he said, rising slowly to his feet. "Then you're probably right that I should leave. Lots to do, and all that." He stood up and the scent of frustration, mingled with something that she couldn't quite place, made her brain even more befuddled. "I made you a sandwich—roast beef with horseradish. You should probably eat. You didn't get much stew in you yesterday before you ended up wearing it. Let me know when you're ready to talk, and we'll . . . well, we'll see where it goes."

He walked the few steps to the door and opened it. He paused with one foot on the ground outside, like he wanted to say something. But he just shook his head and closed the door behind him.

She stared at the closed door for several minutes, her mind completely blank. She finally turned to stare at the photo someone had taped to the paneling above her head. It was a peaceful scene, with a long stretch of white beach and palm trees. A woman stretched out on a lounge chair, while a pair of redheaded children played in the surf—their smiles frozen in time. Was it a family portrait, or a long-dreamed-of vacation? It should have reminded her of California or Cozumel. But instead, it made her think of Australia and a little mining town. Maybe it was the way the sand sparkled.

It made her think of Rose . . . and Eric. Why had it been so easy to talk to him when she was fifteen, but now they struggled to even speak a sentence to each other?

Holly? You'd better be there, girlfriend. If you're dead, I swear I'll kill you . . . Holly?

Even though it made her head throb with each word, Cat's voice made her smile. She let out a breath that she didn't know she was holding. There was still hope if Cat was alive. Not dead yet, and glad you're not either.

Not for lack of trying—apparently for both of us this time. Cat's voice sounded stern in her head, but Holly knew that Cat would understand her reasoning.

Eh. Throw a couple of people into a trance and temporarily defeat the big-bad, and people call a person reckless. She paused. Not that you'd know anything about getting scolded for surviving.

In fact, for most of Cat's existence as a Sazi she'd been on the wrong side of the council for being, as Cat called it, *proactive toward her own survival.*

Moi? No, not me. I'm the very picture of discretion and temperate behavior.

Holly laughed out loud. This was just what she needed. She reached into her pocket and pulled out her cell phone. She still had service and a nearly full battery. Do me a favor, huh? Call me. I've got a blinding headache and could use a friendly voice in my ear.

Cat didn't reply, but a moment later the phone started chirping. "Knew you'd find a hideout with a phone," she answered without even checking the display. "Everybody okay there?"

"Not everyone," Cat said sadly. "We lost Betty. She was never quite the same after her last childbirth. It got ugly and she just wasn't fast enough. Even I barely managed to get away. But the babies are fine and Raphael managed to get the rest of the pack away. Betty died a hero. She planted herself in the doorway and wouldn't let a single snake through until . . . well, by then she was gone. We owe her a lot."

Holly had never really thought of the former psychologist of the Boulder pack as particularly heroic. Mostly, she'd been . . . solid. A comforting presence. "Does anyone here know? And do you know what's been happening out here?"

"Yeah," Cat said sadly. "I know the basics . . . Lucas and Uncle Chuck and the whole snake-bitch thing. Lucky you—you get to *see* the maw of death coming."

Holly fluffed her pillow and threw back the covers to get some air. It must be ninety degrees in the trailer. Except . . . crap. She was nearly naked, wearing just her panties and bra. And the drapes were open. She tossed the covers back over her and started to look around the room for her clothes. But after a few seconds of trying to spot them, her head started to pound again. She plopped back down on the pillow.

Screw it. I can just bake. "Yeah, lucky me. You probably heard about Rose too."

Cat gasped and Holly could almost see those green eyes widen in her mind. "No! What happened? Surely not the snakes? Why would they attack *humans*?"

Holly told her everything she knew. By the time she'd finished her story with Eric leaving the trailer the landscape outside was bathed in darkness. "So, that's the story. I mean, I can't even wrap my head around the whole Marduc thing. A creature that scares the *Chief Justice*? That's just freaky. Hell, I can't even figure out what's up with a guy I used to totally crush on."

Cat laughed, and there was a sharp quality to it that made Holly wince. "You're joking, right? The woman who harassed me for not memorizing every word of the official Sazi manual hasn't figured out the obvious? *Too* funny!"

"Okay, apparently I'm missing something right in front of my nose. Clue me in."

"Hmm . . . let's see." Cat's voice was teasing again. Holly could put up with it from Cat, because at least she'd get some answers from her. "Handsome bad boy sent to Boulder ten years ago to channel aggressions, but instead of spending time with *other* aggressive wolves—as is totally normal for wolves—he spends all his time with a human girl who's jailbait. Fast-forward a decade and within a few days of seeing you, said bad boy has his tongue stuck down your throat and he's assigned to stay at your side in a lonely trailer to keep you alive." She paused. "Getting any flashes of inspiration yet?"

Holly bit her lower lip before replying. "Um . . . he likes me?"

"Um . . . no. He 'likes' you in that same subtle, unassuming way that my husband likes *me*."

A laugh escaped Holly's mouth. "Well, that's a whole different thing. You and Raphael are mate—" The word caught in her throat as the realization finally struck home.

That's why I'm here in the trailer with you.

Mated couples shared energy when one of them was hurt. Healers nearly always insisted upon bare skin between both parties. *I've insisted on it more than once.* He'd been dressed when she woke, but for how long? "*Crap!*" She couldn't help the panicked tone in her voice.

Cat clapped her hands slowly and sarcastically at the other end of the line. "At last. Give the dog a squeaky toy! You're my BFF, Holly, but sometimes you can be really dense."

"I'm *mated* to Eric?" Heat flowed into her face. She tentatively sniffed at her shoulder. It was awash with the scent of Eric's skin. They'd snuggled in bed for a whole day . . . *naked*? Her heart was beating like a trip-hammer. Wasn't that what she'd dreamed of as a teenager? Having a powerful alpha male enthralled from the moment they met, a slave to his passion—desperate to woo and win her?

And haven't I wanted that alpha male to be Eric?

"Maybe. Maybe not. At the very least *he's* mated

to *you*. That's how it works, if you remember. If he's mated to you, you can pull energy from him when you're hurt. Since his boots haven't quite parked under your bed yet, it's hard to say whether it's mutual."

She flushed at the thought of Eric's boots on the floor, his clothing strewn across the room. But this was *Eric* they were discussing and she was just . . . Holly shook her head. "No wonder he's pissed at me, then. He's stuck with *me* when he could have some alpha babe."

Cat's voice turned incredulous. "Uh, hello? You *are* an alpha babe, Holly. No, he's probably pissed for the same reason Raphael was pissed at first. It's scarier than hell to be attracted to someone so strongly when it's not your actual *choice*. You know the drill. One-sided matings don't always work. Even with a double mating like mine, it's not a guarantee. Raphael and I have to work as hard as any other couple to make it through the day. Plus, you're in crisis mode down there. When there's chaos all around, it's really hard to convince yourself it's okay to give in to those animal impulses."

Holly made a strangled sound but nodded, nearly causing the phone to slide down her neck. Her hands seemed to be completely numb on her stomach. Concentrate on Cat. "I remember. You guys really had some ups and downs."

"My advice?" Cat's voice softened and it was almost as though Holly could feel the touch of her soft hands. "*Don't* do what we did and beat yourselves up for wanting each other. When the time is right, just give in. It only makes you nuts otherwise, and you've got a lot of other things to think about—a lot of innocent people to protect. If you're constantly avoiding each other, running scared, you'll never learn to work together when you really need to. Trust me. If Eric was in that trailer, you can bet it was at someone's instruction. Which means they likely all know, and they'll understand what happens next—what *has* to happen next. Everyone will give you space."

Great. Now everybody was going to be watching them, *knowing* they were going to be wandering off together. "I'm sorry, Cat, but I think you're wrong. You *have* to be wrong. I mean, he's gorgeous and yeah, I enjoyed kissing him. But *mated*? I don't know if I feel that way about him."

"Maybe *you* don't. That's the thing. Quick test. Where is he right this second? Think about him really hard. What's he doing? Don't analyze it. Just let it pop out."

Holly concentrated for a second and saw him in her mind's eye. "Sitting on the roof of the building. He's on guard duty." She paused, suddenly sick at how easy that was. "But I could be guessing. It makes sense that all the alphas would be watching for Marduc, or more snakes."

"Duh," Cat replied. "So go check. I presume there are windows if you're in an RV."

"Hello? I don't have any clothes on."

"Hello? Turn off the lights or wear a sheet," Cat said in the same lilting tone. "Holly." Her voice was firm. "You *need* to know this. Yeah, a mating compulsion is terrifying to think about, but *living* with it isn't so bad. Just go look."

Holly sighed, turned off the light over the bed, and rolled until her feet hit the floor. With the phone tucked against her shoulder, she wrapped the sheet around her and tiptoed toward the nearest window. "Oh! Here are my clothes." They were neatly folded on the bench seat behind the table. "Hang on a sec while I put them on."

Cat only sighed. They both knew she was stalling. But Holly really would feel better if she was dressed.

It only took a few seconds to slide into the clothes. They were *her* clothes, too—from the suitcase that was tucked under the table. The clothes she'd been wearing had disappeared, the pants likely returned to their owner. On impulse, she walked the three steps to the kitchen and opened the fridge. Her stomach rumbled at the sight of the waiting sandwich—fat slices of pink meat on homemade bread. And hadn't Eric mentioned horseradish?

"You're *stalling*," came Cat's voice from the phone.

"I know. I know." She took a deep breath, put the sandwich on the table and leaned down to look out the window. The building was at least a football field's length away, but she could pick out Eric instantly from among all the others on the roof. "He's there." She said it more to herself than to Cat, but she didn't doubt her friend had heard. He turned just then, rifle barrel resting loosely on his shoulder as he stared intently at the trailer.

Did he know she was watching?

* * *

"YOU'RE GOING TO drive yourself nuts if you keep staring like that."

Eric started at the sound of Tony's voice and turned his head. Tony hadn't moved from his perch on the other side of the building.

"I can *feel* her, moving around inside the trailer."

"Yep," the other man said, never taking his eyes off the distant landscape. "You get used to it."

Eric sighed and moved the automatic rifle so it hung from the sling over his shoulder. "I don't know. Maybe I should have just told her."

"She's a bright kid," Tony replied, his eyes constantly moving from side to side, sweeping the darkness for any sign of movement. "She'll figure it out on her own."

"She's not a *kid*." Not anymore.

The other man shrugged. "She's younger than me. She's a kid. If you're younger than me, *you're* a kid."

"I'm thirty-six."

Tony flicked his eyes toward him, showing a flash of blue-white light. "Month?"

"June." His eyes moved back to the trailer. She was eating now, and enjoying it. It made him smile. But it quickly faded when the creepiness of it settled over him once more.

"Okay, so you're *not* a kid. You've got a month on me."

They were silent for a time and Eric let the cold wind fill his nose with scents. There were animals out there, but they weren't shifters. All the predators in the area were making the rabbits and deer give the whole area a wide berth. He shook his head. "This sucks, y'know?"

"The Marduc thing, or the mating thing?"

"Both."

Tony finally turned and walked across the roof. He pointed to his old spot. "You. Over there. Use that sniffer of yours, and I'll watch for little slithering lights."

"Why?"

Tony leaned in close enough that Eric could smell his scent, which was an odd combination of gun oil and wildflowers. Tony lowered his voice to such a soft whisper that Eric had to really listen to hear him. "Because if you're spending all your time watching your mate, you're *not* watching the trees. Since I don't give a shit about your mate, I'll take this watch."

A growl tried to bubble up but Tony just pointed to the end of the roof. He didn't back away or smell afraid. "You'd win a fight against me, but I'm not the one who put me in charge of this gig. Talk to the man over there if you have a problem with your job." The tall blond man on the far corner of the building turned his head. Antoine would likely have no sense of humor if he decked the wolf.

"Fine," he said, his voice hissing with frustration. "Just watch *closely*."

Tony's ready smile, empty of meaning or emotion, flashed in the dark. "Always do." As he walked over the crest of the roof peak, Tony continued to talk.

"See, this is how it works. It's all about *adjustments*. All you gotta do to make it through a mating is make adjustments."

"What kind of adjustments?" Eric couldn't believe he was talking about this, much less asking for advice. But Tony was recently mated too. Maybe there was something to be learned from him. Eric sat down on the roof edge and turned his body so he could see both the vista and Tony in his peripheral.

"Like what just happened here. I told you to walk over there because you didn't volunteer to do it. When you fully come to grips with the mating, you'll be the one to suggest it—you'll know that your judgment can't be trusted when your mate is at issue. My mate's not here, or you'd see a totally different side of me. She's in my head twenty-four/seven, and I know she's fine. If she wasn't . . . well. Same with cat-boy and the snake king over there." He thumbed his finger to the other end of the roof,

"If Ahmad is the snake *king*, I am *not* 'cat-boy.'" Antoine's quiet, dry voice drifted on the breeze. "However, as far as the mating is concerned, Tony's correct. I find myself more . . . *focused* when Tahira is elsewhere."

Ahmad let out a small noise that wasn't quite a growl or a hiss. "Tuli has informed me that the moment I find myself less than my best, I should locate her. She will be happy to, as she so coyly phrases it, 'kick the shit out of me' to get my mind back on task."

Eric couldn't help the sudden burst of laughter.

The others were making the same noises, so hopefully Ahmad wouldn't knock him off the building with a burst of power.

"She could do it too," Tony said as an aside. "That's the trouble with mating with an alpha female. My wife's turning into one all of a sudden, and it's killing me. Male wolves get all these protective instincts after mating and the women want to kick our asses for it."

"Indeed," Ahmad added in an unusual display of comradery, while inspecting the edge of the broadsword in his hand. "Wolves aren't the only species to feel the urge to protect. But there is one truth from the animal kingdom that is equally true for our kind. The female is more dangerous than the male."

Antoine's dry French-accented voice found Eric's ears as the scent of frustration and embarrassment rode the wind. "My worst mistake to date was to tell Tahira to stop putting herself in danger. It is apparently a supreme insult—or so my sisters have informed me. She immediately joined Wolven, just to prove she was fully capable of defending herself." He shook his head in frustration.

"And she got *my* wife to join up too, I might add." Tony's voice was sarcastic. "Thank you *so much* for that little bit of reverse psychology."

Eric's laugh choked off as his own words to Holly started to pulse through his brain. "Crap. I just did that." At Tony's raised eyebrows, he explained. "I just yelled at Holly for nearly killing herself to get us out of that hindsight."

"Speaking as the person she saved by being *reckless*, you're screwed, Thompson."

Eric turned his head to the other two men, but they just shrugged.

Great. Just perfect.

The door to the fire stairs at the end of the roof opened and Ivan stepped out. "Antoine?" He kept his voice so low that Eric had to struggle to hear over the wind whistling. "Phone call, from Josette. I will take your place here."

Antoine's mood abruptly shifted, turned serious as death. He swore under his breath. Nobody had heard from the other seers since this all started. Antoine strode toward Ivan, surrendering his rifle and bolting down the stairs.

Ivan walked to the corner opposite Ahmad and began to stare out into the distance, his stance alert, and his scent worried. A call from Aspen usually spoke of bad things to come.

Eric wasn't sure he wanted to know the details of that call.

It must have lasted only a few minutes, because it didn't seem like any time at all before Antoine was back. The scent that preceded him didn't speak of a warm and happy conversation. "Ivan? Ahmad? She would speak with you both now. Bobby will be there as well. Please hurry. The connection isn't very good."

Antoine turned to Eric and Tony. "You will be alone up here for a few moments, so be alert. I must go collect Holly." As he passed them the weapons he'd taken from Ivan and Ahmad he raised his brows and said,

"And no, I don't know why my sister wants to talk to her, so don't ask."

HOLLY SLIPPED OUT the back door of the RV, into the cool night. She adjusted the makeshift backpack, made from some grocery bags and twine she'd found in the cabinet and started hiking away from the camp at a brisk clip.

She just needed to *move* for a few minutes, to think and to plan. There was no doing either one while stuck inside that trailer. Everything was happening so damned fast and nothing made sense.

Was sneaking out reckless? Yeah, probably. And she had to admit she'd like to have her phone with her. But the call from Cat had eaten more than minutes. The battery was drained, so it was on the charger.

Lightning flashed in the distance, the beginnings of the storm that had been brewing over California a few days before. Already she could taste rain on the cold wind.

A flash of movement caught her eye and she paused to look. *What the hell?* A dark-skinned woman, completely naked and sporting white hair to her knees, was striding purposefully into the darkness. She was holding the hand of a young blond girl, dragging her along. The child's face was utterly blank, as though she was sleepwalking. Holly recognized the girl from the camp, and the woman with her was *not* the girl's mother.

"Hey!" she called out forcefully, causing the woman to turn her head. "Where do you think you're going with her?" There was a shock of surprise on the woman's face, but it quickly disappeared and her broad features turned dark and angry. The woman picked up the child and tossed her over her shoulder like she was a sack of flour as she began to sprint away.

"Come back here!" Holly sprinted after her, putting on a burst of speed in an effort to catch up. But the woman was no slouch when it came to running. Even barefoot, with cactus ripping at her naked legs, she was putting distance between them. Holly sniffed the air to catch the woman's scent. It was strongly musky, unpleasantly so. She realized she'd smelled it before—on the hillside while kissing Eric. *Could that be Marduc's human form?* Shit!

But then another scent came from behind her— masculine, powerful, and very angry.

Holly skidded to a stop as something leapt over her, but still nearly ran into the biggest cougar she'd ever seen in her life. His eyes were level with her neck, so he barely had to look up to see her face.

"You had no authorization to leave the camp." She recognized the voice, despite the slight growl from his animal throat. Antoine Monier wasn't someone to trifle with, but even so—

She pointed to the rapidly disappearing form. "That woman! She has one of the children from camp. We have to get her!"

Antoine turned and stared into the distance. "I see nothing. I've been following you for several minutes and you've been running alone."

"No, I haven't!" She felt her temper rising, even

though he could probably strike her down with a single blow. "She's *there,* Councilman Monier. Use your nose and ears if your sight isn't working. I can see her just as clearly as I could see that feather."

That widened the golden eyes of the cat and he raised his nose in the direction Holly was pointing. "*Merde!* It is faint, but I can detect it. Still, my sister Josette would speak with you back at camp. Go back and take the call, and be quick about it. I will track this thing."

Holly looked at him dubiously, but he seemed to be able to follow the scent as he raced off into the night, altering his path in the direction Holly could still see the hint of movement from. She didn't like it, but to refuse a member of the council was a death sentence. She wouldn't be much good to anyone if she was dead. And, he was one of the most powerful and vicious on the council.

She turned and ran, full out. Her heart was racing from more than exertion when she reached camp. "I think Councilman Monier's in trouble," she said to Ivan who was waiting impatiently for her. "I saw Marduc—at least I think it was her—and he took off after her. She's got a girl from camp, and I think something bad is going to happen."

Ivan looked toward the roof. "Tony, Eric, come with me. We might need someone who can shoot on the run."

Tony nodded once and handed his rifle to Eric. Then he slid down the roof's edge before grabbing the gutter with gloved hands. He dropped to the ground and then held up one hand. Eric tossed down the weapons before taking the same path down.

"Which way?" Eric asked, his scent both worried and determined as he pulled out the clip to verify the ammo in his gun.

There was something about the way he was standing that made her want to throw her arms around him and hold him tight. It made her heart flutter with an odd sort of panic when he stared into her eyes. After a long moment where her mouth was so dry she couldn't speak, Holly pointed to where she had come from.

Finally, she could get words out. "That direction, probably about a half-mile away. But I don't know how much farther they've gone since."

Tony adjusted so that the rifle was dangling down his back, the barrel pointed at the ground. He pulled a walkie-talkie from his pocket and turned it on. Eric did the same. "We shouldn't have any problem finding them. Let's hit it."

Eric turned to her as she was walking in the door. "We'll be on—" he paused and looked at the red display on the handset. "Channel eight. We'll go down to three if the storm kicks up. Let the others know where we've gone—so they know where to send the body bags."

Nobody was laughing. She crossed her arms over her chest and stared out into the darkness. The look on her face made Eric pause and let out a slow breath. He reached for her hand and squeezed it tightly for a brief second before leaning in for a sudden kiss. It was so soft and tender that her stomach clenched. "Don't worry. We'll be fine. Go talk to the seer."

She walked in the building as they took off at a run. Bobby Mbutu and Councilman al-Narmer walked past her, their dark faces ashen—abject fear in their scent. She wanted to ask what was happening, but they quickly got into a waiting brown sedan and drove off, tires spitting up a cloud of dust.

Iris was waiting just inside, her face nervous. "They're waiting for you downstairs." She grabbed Holly's hand and whispered. "Something really bad is happening. Everybody's really worked up. *Please* be careful. I don't want to lose you."

Holly walked down the stairs, trying to keep up her courage. Seers usually didn't call to talk about *good* news. A couple was waiting at the bottom of the stairs. They were both wolves, but she didn't recognize them. They had that certain aura that screamed *pack leader.* She lowered her eyes automatically, giving proper respect. "Someone called for me? I'm Holly Sanchez."

"Adam and Cara Mueller," the tall man said. "Alphas of the Texas pack. The phone's in the next room. We're here to make sure the call stays private."

As Holly nodded her eyes happened to drop to the bandage on the pregnant woman's leg. It smelled . . . bad, like something was decaying. "Are you okay?"

The woman shrugged, but her face was filled with pain. "Snakebite. I'll heal."

Holly shook her head in disagreement. "It's *not* healing. I can smell it." She knelt down and ran her fingers over the bandage, her face right next to the tightly stretched belly. The heat from the wound made her hand sting like needles were being poked in it. "Did you have Tatya look at this?"

The alpha shook her head. "Dr. Santiago is sleeping. She exhausted herself before she got through with the most serious cases."

Tatya had *exhausted* herself? Holly had known the woman her entire life, and she'd *never* been tired enough to stop healing—even when Holly had nearly died. She'd passed out briefly, but had been able to continue to heal her the next day. And that was with near-death injuries. These were just standard wounds. Very strange.

Adam tapped her shoulder. "You'd better hurry. The seers are waiting." His voice was firm, but Holly didn't stand up.

"The seers can keep waiting," she said firmly. "Your baby can't afford to battle this snakebite. It could cause an early birth or miscarriage."

The couple looked at each other in shock and the woman's hand went to her stomach. "The baby *has* been kicking a lot tonight, Adam."

Holly nodded. She could see the movements just under the skin. It worried her. Adam Mueller's frown deepened, and he helped Holly guide Cara to a chair before she knelt down again by her leg. She closed her eyes and let power rise. It flowed into the leg. There was no need to unwrap it. She could see in her mind the pair of puckered wounds, the skin black around the entry points. It was very much like Annie's wound, except the venom reacted to her magic by becoming even more toxic. Cara gasped and the scent of pain filled the air. Holly felt Adam's hand brush her as he reached for his mate's hand. She'd heard about Sazi snake bites, but had never actually encountered one.

She pushed more energy into the wound and felt a sudden jolt of power that made the hair on the back of her neck tingle. *What the hell?* She saw Eric in a flash. He'd stumbled mid-run and couldn't catch himself before he tumbled to the ground. Ivan grabbed his upper arm and hauled him back to his feet. Eric shook his head like he was dazed and the image faded.

What did it mean? Obviously, Cat had been right. Their connection was at least a one-sided mating. Would she always pull on his power . . . ? Now it made sense. Lucas had been mated to Tatya, and was arguably the most powerful wolf in the world. If she'd been drawing on his power all these years . . . no wonder she'd been the most powerful healer. But maybe she wasn't anymore.

With the added energy, Holly was able to burn the toxin away from the wound and heal it with hardly any effort. She felt farther into the woman's body to check for anything else that could be wrong, and felt a smile come to her face. The tiny life inside the alpha moved contentedly and then settled down, no longer trying to avoid the poison. "The baby's fine. She didn't get infected with any venom." And Holly didn't even feel mildly tired. She noted that when she didn't need the extra power anymore, it dispersed into the background.

I bet Eric's going to want to talk about this.

"A little girl?" Cara rubbed her stomach, smiling, and then elbowed Adam with a wink. "Told you it wasn't a boy. Better hit that baby book again."

Adam dipped his head with closed eyes and his mate did the same. "Thank you, Healer Sanchez. Cara and I are eternally grateful."

Healer Sanchez. It was the first time anyone had called her that. Yeah, she'd been doing it for a while now, but for a pack alpha to *bestow* the title on her . . . That made it official. Word would spread through the packs.

Her head buzzed. "Um . . . you're welcome. I . . . I should probably go take that call now." As she stood up, she noticed Cara flexing her foot with a delighted expression. That was the nice thing about healing. People were so happy afterward—even when everything else around them sucked.

She walked into the room. Other than the phone on the table, there was no furniture. "Hello?"

"We've been *waiting* for you for some time, Holly." Holly recognized the disapproving voice immediately. It was Nana, the seer from the Boulder pack.

"Nana! You're okay!" She raced to the phone and picked it up, staring at it as though she could see the old Indian woman if she just looked hard enough.

The excitement in her voice made the old woman chuckle. "Yes, I'm okay. As is your father. I know you've been worried."

Another weight lifted from her chest. "Does Iris know? Can I tell her?"

"Of course."

A second woman's voice cut in. "We don't have time for this, Nana."

Then a third woman chimed in, her voice deeper, with a Russian accent. "We must *make* time for the social niceties, Josette. It keeps our family strong. Let the girl settle a bit. She's had a difficult few days."

Holly recognized Josette Monier's voice. She'd heard it when the woman had visited Uncle Raphael. It had been the first time she'd met a cat. Josette had made several cat noises for her, which had made her giggle. This time, she wasn't laughing.

"May I remind you both of the seriousness of the situation? She needs to get her hands on that knife and get it to those who can use it."

"Knife?" Holly felt her brow furrow. "What knife?"

Nana sighed. "My associate shows the impatience of her animal today. Not surprising considering the matter at hand. But she is correct that we have a special task for you, Holly. There is a knife we've found mention of in old texts. The Duchess has seen *you* obtaining it, in a cave somewhere near your present location. We must ask that you bring this vision to fruition. It could save all of our lives."

"The Duchess" must be the third woman she'd heard, with the Russian accent. It was no use asking "why me?" She'd watched Lucas and the other pack members swear and roll their eyes at the strange demands of the seers. But they'd kept them safe and undiscovered by humanity for millennia, so they knew what they were doing. "What does it look like?"

The Duchess spoke. "I saw a black blade, made of ancient volcanic glass, decorated with rubies and turquoise on the—"

"Bone handle." Holly's blood had officially run cold. She'd seen that knife. *Nasil* had been fascinated by it on the plane ride. He'd remove it from a heavy metal box and moved it toward his hand, and then away again with a wince—as though simply getting *near* the thing hurt.

"You have it already?" Josette's voice was excited.

Holly shook her head and felt a dull weight in her stomach. "No. But I know who does. Ahmad referred to him as *Nasil*."

"Shit, shit, *shit*!" Josette's voice was livid and Holly had to step away from the phone when she let out a screech so loud it would probably be heard upstairs. "Ea-Nasil still lives? Ahmad *swore* he'd been eliminated."

Holly shrugged. "No, he's alive. He rode with me on the plane from Australia." She hastened to explain, so they wouldn't get the wrong idea. "I was his prisoner. He threatened my sister, and had me frozen about half the time." She hadn't mentioned that part to Eric. It was sort of embarrassing to be unable to move. "I got away at the airport, and I don't know where he is now."

"Apparently he's nearby, or Leyla wouldn't have seen you with the knife," Nana said after Josette's tantrum was done. "You must still obtain it. And I'm very sorry, Holly, but you must do this alone. I've watched you grow into a confident, intelligent woman, so I have no doubt you know how dangerous this will be. Yet we must ask it of you—to save us all."

The room spun, just a little, and Holly's mouth felt dry. She knew she wasn't the first to be asked to do something that could kill her, but it didn't make it any easier to hear. Not only did she have to go out and find Nasil, she somehow had to get the knife away from him and get it back to someone here. Words aimed toward Josette spilled from her lips without even meaning to. "Are you sure you didn't just pick me because you think I shouldn't have survived?"

There was a long pause, and then Josette spoke. "I said that to Charles in *confidence*. I'm surprised he told you. Ahh. He must have had you involved in his hindsight. I'd apologize, but I stand by it. Much would have been different if you'd died. We might not be at this place now."

"Not true," the Duchess said while Holly's head buzzed with the implications. "My vision occurred *years* ago. The girl hadn't even been born yet. It was only when you showed me the photographs of the packs that I recognized her. While it was only one possible future, her survival wasn't a mistake. Nor do I believe she needs to do this completely alone. The impression I had was that there were two people in the cave where the knife is. The other was a male, and might well have been Ea-Nasil himself. But it also might have been someone else."

"One moment, Holly." Nana's voice broke in. "Let us confer."

The voices faded until she could just barely hear snatches of conversation. *"I don't see why not,"* and *"No, too many complications,"* then *"There'll be no stopping him anyway."*

There was the sound of shuffling feet and then brief static as someone picked up the phone. "Very well. There is one who, if he is at your location, may accompany you. The alpha wolf, Eric Thompson, can travel with you. He will not alter the future. Is he available?"

She started to answer when a low, mournful sound abruptly filled the room. It pressed against her skin, pulled at the wolf inside her so strongly that she couldn't resist it. She couldn't even get out words. "That howl," Nana said with an odd lilt to her voice. "It calls to me. Even over the phone. It sounds like Inteque's father, the Great White Wolf."

Holly started to move toward the door without a word. She couldn't resist that call. It boiled in her blood, yanked at her stomach, and dazed her mind. The outer room was already empty, meaning Adam and Cara had already responded. She shifted as she raced up the stairs and then she was outside, following the other pack members as they all tracked the sound.

The closer she got, the more aggressive she felt. Something was making her incredibly angry. Her lips pulled back from her teeth and she put on extra speed, passing by lesser wolves. Faster and faster she raced into the darkness, the howl leading her. Lightning flashed all around her, striking the ground with enough force to make her fur stand on end. The incessant boom of thunder made her ears hurt.

When she passed through a stand of piñons she saw it looming large over the bear and two wolves. A snake with wings, it seemed to be twenty feet long from the wide, fanged mouth to the slender, feathered tail. A thick band of feathers fluffed around its neck, so that it looked like it was wearing a clown collar. But this was no clown. It held in one taloned claw an unconscious, bleeding cougar. The other was wrapped around a small child who looked to be either asleep . . . or dead.

The animals on the ground were looking around, trying to locate what their noses could smell. But she could see it. This must be Marduc. She raced forward past the others and leapt with all her might into the air. She sank her teeth into the leg, just above the talons. Bitter, toxic blood filled her mouth. She wanted to spit it out, but it ran down her throat as the creature screamed, the sound like a speeding race car hitting a barrier. But her attack had the intended effect. The talon opened and the big cat dropped to the ground. Holly let loose her jaws and tried to drop to the ground, but Marduc was fast. Holly screamed as her leg was impaled with a foot-long fang and all she could think to do was latch onto the other talon and worry on it until it too opened. The child dropped the equivalent of two stories and lay still on the ground.

Eric howled again and more wolves leapt into the air, like Holly had. She felt the howl like a blow to her head. Her mind spun and she nearly choked as blood began to flow from her nose and mouth. It wasn't just her either. Marduc pulled loose her fangs and shook her head. She dropped hard and fast, but managed to recover and spread her wings before she struck the ground. Holly took the opportunity to drop the rest of the way to the ground. Her wounded back leg collapsed upon impact. She rolled two or three times, and wound up on top of a patch of prickly pear cactus, too exhausted to roll off them again.

Holly looked up to see Marduc assessing the number of wolves, cats, and bears who were leaping and snapping just short of her talons. Apparently she decided the odds weren't as good as mere moments before. As the sky flashed she let out another screech that was lost in the immediate clap of thunder, and then the fierce quetzalcoatl flew off into the sky.

Holly blinked dazedly and then Eric was beside her in wolf form. She hadn't ever hunted with the pack when he was in Boulder, so she'd never seen his wolf. He was a pale yellow, identical to his hair color, with a broad chest and powerful legs. As he looked down at her, his eyes began to glow a brilliant, deep blue. His panic at the sight of her bloody, battered body was apparent. When he changed forms and reached down to pick her up, it was with thickly muscled bare arms, and magic-filled turquoise eyes.

If she hadn't been in so much pain she might have smiled.

Chapter Fourteen

I'm ready for you. You shall serve me now, my alpha.

Nasil woke with a start, sweat pouring down his face. He sat up on the air mattress so quickly that Bruce nearly rolled on top of him.

He carefully slid out from under the thick comforter and stood. He ran a hand through his hair, and then shook his head again, trying to wake up. He remembered Bruce arriving and eating the dinner of fried chicken that had accompanied him. They'd made love and it had been good, but not as good as it once had been—before Bruce became so ill.

Then he'd dreamed of a dark woman with long, silver hair who called to him, raked his skin with poisoned teeth to taste his blood, and made his mind putty. He looked down to see that the dream had aroused his body too. When was the last time the thought of a *woman* had aroused him? Yes, he'd had women in the past, but that was before he'd met Bruce. The innocent human had stolen his heart and made him betray his old master.

I can do more for you than a human, my alpha. I have chosen you. You will be my mate and will implant your seed in a goddess.

The voice in his mind made him stumble and crack his head against the wall of the cave. *Marduc!* Fear filled him so completely he nearly vomited. And yet, his body was hard again. *What the hell is happening to me?*

The low, feminine chuckle in his mind made his skin both twitch and ache. *I have happened to you. You are my chosen. Kill your lover and come to me, Ea-Nasil. We shall be one and we shall rule together.* A low hiss followed her words. It filled his mind until nothing but the sound remained in the dark room. He *had* to obey her. Had to *have* her.

He felt himself walk to the farthest corner of the wide room and open the lead box. The black knife should have been invisible in the darkness. But instead, it glowed from within, as though begging to be used for the purpose it was created. He felt apart from himself as he picked it up and walked back to the mattress. He looked down at the man snuggled under the covers, his arm spread across the empty space where Nasil's body had lay. Bruce's formerly smooth cheek was pockmarked with sores now, earned from spending too much time with Nasil's poisoned body.

The knife was raised high over his head, though he didn't remember doing it. Part of his brain realized what was happening and rebelled. He *would not* kill Bruce just to please her.

Obey in all things, my mate, and we will lay together as only snakes can. At last you will be the god you were destined to be.

It had been a thousand years since he'd had sex with a female of his species. Sargon had instructed him not to breed. Now he could be what his *lord* had dreamed of being—but hadn't been strong enough to become.

But you're strong enough. I feel it. I would have you inside me.

No. Not at the cost of Bruce.

You must. I command it.

His muscles twitched. He was fighting, but as the knife inched downward, he knew he would lose. Bruce rolled over just then to lie flat on his back. It would be so easy. And he was dying anyway.

He dropped to his knees from the sheer force of the presence in his mind. He couldn't seem to open his mouth to warn his lover. He closed his eyes because his lips were locked tight, his arm out of his control. He was mute and helpless as the knife made an arc through the air. Again he fought, but he felt the weapon plunge into something soft that spilled warmth over his hand. The scream that followed made bile rise. He couldn't look, couldn't think. All he could do was race out into the night. His legs moved of their own accord and even the frigid night air hitting his skin didn't relieve the heat that was boiling his blood.

Yes, now is our time. Come to me, my love.

Chapter Fifteen

NO MATTER HOW she tried to move, there was no relief from the thousands of hair-fine cactus barbs that continued to make her back and butt sting. They'd gotten out all they could with tweezers, but the smallest ones couldn't even be felt when she passed her hand over her skin.

But they sure made themselves known every time she took a step forward.

"You're jumping like you have ants in your pants. Would you stop it, please? I'm already edgy enough." Eric's voice sounded as frustrated as she felt. It didn't seem like he was enjoying the thought of going on this mission with her.

"Sorry," she whispered as they passed the last ring of light in the camp and were swallowed by darkness. She wished they could have waited until morning, but *no*. Aspen had insisted that going tonight was critical to their success. "I can't help it. They *hurt*. I know they'll work themselves out on their own, but right now it's driving me nuts."

"Next time, fall a little to the left. You could have landed on a nice, soft sagebrush." There was finally a bit of humor in his voice.

"Thanks," she replied dryly. "I'll keep that in mind." She stopped and stared out into the darkness. "Any idea where we're going?"

"Yeah. Reach into my backpack and grab that map Lucas gave me." He turned so she could unzip the main compartment. She handed him a folded square of paper that smelled like Lucas—not the Lucas she remembered, but the new one. The *human* one.

That had been a total surprise. After Marduc flew off, Holly had worked on healing the girl, who she learned was named Devon, and Councilman Monier. Not exactly a piece of cake since her body kept trying to heal itself. Eric had flinched when she pulled on his energy, but he hadn't raised a fuss.

He hadn't mentioned it either, so she wasn't sure if he was pissed about it or not. It wasn't like she could *help* it. It just seemed to happen.

She passed him the map and turned on her flashlight. "Pretty amazing about Lucas, huh?"

Eric let out an odd chuckle as he opened the map. "Not sure what to think about it. I suppose it's good that my howl woke him up, but . . . *should* it have? I mean, he's human now, isn't he?"

The topo map mostly showed contour lines, but there was a distinct black line leading from one bold

X to another on the page. It looked like they'd mostly be traveling over flat ground, which suited her. She wasn't sure how climbing would make her leg feel. Thankfully, the bite had happened so fast and had gone through so quickly that there was hardly any poison in the wound. Just a simple flesh wound that was healing, albeit slowly. "Apparently so. I can't feel any magic in him at all, and Tony said he can't see an aura. I guess we'll find out for sure when Raphael gets here."

Eric got his bearings and handed the map back to her. She tucked it in the knapsack again. His voice sounded confused. "Explain why's he coming here again?"

"Three reasons, as I understand it. First off, he also has second sight. So, in case Tony's wrong about Lucas, he'll know. Second, Tatya's mated to Raphael. She can't draw on Lucas's magic to heal and she gave up enough of her own energy that she's in pretty bad shape. I'm pretty much toast too and the seers insisted I do this instead. So, Lucas suggested Raphael as a temporary replacement. The third reason has something to do with Councilman al-Narmer and Agent Mbutu. I didn't get that part."

"That must bite the big one," Eric said with a shake of his head. "To have to call your former rival for your wife to snuggle up naked in bed with her."

"To save her life," Holly reminded him. But poor Cat must really be taking it hard. She wouldn't even answer her phone when Holly tried to call. She knew Cat would put up with it, because there was a life at stake, but she wouldn't *like* having her new husband share a bed with a woman she could barely stand to be in the same room with. The worst part was that everyone knew Tatya had chosen Lucas because he was more powerful than Raphael. What would she do now?

And speaking of what to do now . . . Holly took a deep breath. Time to let the genie out of the bottle. "Thank you, by the way."

Eric stopped so fast he seemed frozen in place. Holly nearly ran into him. "For?"

"For the same thing—snuggling up naked to save my life. And . . . for the other thing too. That had to have sucked."

"Sharing power?" he asked quietly. "It sort of hammered home that last nail, didn't it? No more question about whether we were imagining the mating." He started walking forward again and she followed, not sure what else to say. "It didn't, though. Not really."

"Didn't?" She turned her head to him for a second, but then had to look forward again to avoid a rabbit hole.

"Didn't suck." He smiled, but didn't look her way. She only knew because the light flashed off his teeth. "I probably shouldn't tell you this, but it's actually incredibly erotic when you do that. Gives me chills all over . . . and I do mean *all* over."

The blush came to her face hard and fast, a flame to ward off the chilled air. It was all she could do not to run screaming into the dark. "Oh," was all she managed to squeak out. "That's . . . I mean . . . Um—"

"Yeah," he said with a low chuckle that made her skin feel tight and heated. "Please feel free to heal people anytime you like."

"*Eric!*" She swatted at his arm and he sidestepped, laughing. It made her feel a little better to know he wasn't mad, but it was still damned embarrassing. *So now I'm going to have to think about him getting hot and bothered every time I have to heal someone? Someone shoot me now.*

They walked on in silence, listening to every tiny noise for at least an hour, until her leg was burning like fire and it was all she could do to lift it one more step. It would be nice to have some sort of landmark to go by, but there was just flat nothingness as far as her flashlight beam could reach.

Eric looked at her for the umpteenth time in the past twenty minutes and finally shook his head. "That's it. No more. I can't stand to hear those little noises." He pointed toward a thick stand of piñons. "We'll camp over there, and the seers can just live with it."

She listened intently for a long moment. "What little noises?"

He pointed at her leg before turning to walk toward the piñons. "The ones you're making every time you step. You're obviously in pain and good for you, I suppose, for continuing to push yourself to do your duty. But *I* can't stand it. Okay?"

She was making noises? What *kind* of noises? She took a few tentative steps, but heard nothing. *Of course not, I'm conscious of it now.* She gave up and started to follow him into the trees. He'd already pulled the two-man tent from the big backpack and was busily putting together the long carbon-fiber rods that would hold it up. She started to take off her pack and a sharp pain made small sparkles dance behind her eyes. At last she heard the noise. Every time her foot rolled on a rock underfoot, that pain would shoot up her leg, and a small high-pitched grunt snuck out. She could understand how it would be annoying to listen to.

"Not annoying," he said as he unfolded the tent. "*Painful* to listen to."

Her mouth went dry and she stammered a little. "Eric, I . . . I didn't say that out loud."

He turned and stared before he let out a nervous chuckle. "You must have. How else could I have heard you?"

Holly just shook her head.

Eric nodded and continued to put together the tent. But the scents that drifted from him probably matched her own—confused, terrified, but with just a touch of curiosity.

I'M HEARING HOLLY'S thoughts now? Could she hear his in return? Eric glanced over at her, and noticed again how totally sexy she looked in the tight hip-huggers that did indeed *hug* her narrow hips. *Damn, but you look hot in those pants, woman.* He glanced over at her to see if she looked up. Nope. Must still be one-sided.

He'd heard of telepathy in mating, but it was really weird to experience it. Of course, there *was* one advantage. He'd finally learn exactly what a woman was thinking. Every man's dream.

The laugh shot out of him without warning and Holly turned to look at him. "Sorry. Just a random thought."

Sure. Rub it in.

He heard the voice, but her lips hadn't moved. Should he respond or not? Might as well. It's not like she didn't know. He let out a sigh. "Sorry. I was just trying to find out if it was two-sided."

"Apparently it's not." She sounded more sad than angry, but neither her scent nor her thoughts revealed anything more than what she said.

After what felt like an eternity, but was probably only a minute, he had to break the silence. "Hungry? I brought along a couple more sandwiches and some fruit. Nobody said how long it would take to get the knife, but we should keep up our strength."

She shook her head. "I had that big sandwich before all of this started. I'm good for the night. They should be fine in the pack. It's cold enough that they won't spoil before morning. We should probably just . . . get some sleep."

He stretched the red down sleeping bag just outside the mouth of the tent, which was already growing warm from the lantern blazing inside. "Tent's yours. I'll sleep out here and keep watch."

She lowered her chin and blinked. "You're going to stand watch for something only *I* can see? Yeah, that makes sense."

Fine. He shrugged. "No problem. Then *you* can

stand watch and *I'll* get some sleep. Does that make
more sense?" When she tried to think her way out of
that, he let out a sigh. "Look, Holly. I'm trying to be a
gentleman here. I know it must seem sort of creepy for
you to find out I was in your bed while you were out
cold. It wasn't my choice, but I'll be honest, I didn't
mind a bit, and I'm not positive I really trust myself to
do it again this soon." He let her digest that for a second. "I don't think either of us is as ready as everybody seems to think we should be to take that next
step. I actually like a little romancing before I do the
happy dance with someone."

She snorted at his wording but then her face softened and her scent turned warm and sugary. "I think
we did part of the *romancing* a while back. It might
have been ten years ago, but that was an amazing
summer . . . at least for me." Her lips curled into a sly
smile. "Dad never did figure out where those flowers
came from."

The memory made him grin. There was no doubt
about it—he'd been smitten. When he found out she
loved pink roses, he managed to find a way to sneak
one to her every day for two weeks—all while under
her father's watchful eye. "I think it's what made him
suspicious though. He started watching me like a
hawk."

"My sisters were *green* with envy that I had a secret
admirer—and they couldn't sniff out who it was." She
smiled again and he suddenly saw her as he had
then—a pretty, quiet teenager with hopes and dreams
that were far bigger than she could ever achieve in the

pack she was stuck in. "I don't know how you managed it."

"Strong cologne and lots of illusion magic," he finally admitted. "I'd make them see two books when I was actually carrying one along with a rose, or see a hat on my head, when the flower was behind my ear. Lots of different stuff. It got to be fun after a few days. There wasn't much else to do to entertain myself."

"Entertainment? That's all I was?" He watched her face. It was carefully controlled, but her scent told a different story.

"At first," he said with a nod. "But not so much at the end."

"So you don't care that my family is Mexican, or that I used to be human?"

He shook his head in confusion. "Why would I care? I've always thought your heritage is part of what made you so pretty."

She paused and he could see her nose flare. Was she checking to see if he was lying? Why would she do that? More to the point, why would he lie? "I never really cared what your background was, Holly, and I knew full well you were human when I asked you on a date. In fact, I think my emotions getting the better of me when I asked you out was what finally gave me away. Right after that your dad stormed into my apartment."

"He *what*?" she asked, her mouth agape.

"Oh yeah." He still remembered the bruises and cracked ribs. "Threw me up against the wall so hard a full sheet of drywall broke clean in half. I lost my security deposit from that little visit. He told me to get out of town or he'd file charges with Wolven. So I did."

"*What?* You're kidding." Anger poured from her. "That son of a—"

Eric raised a placating hand. He didn't begrudge Jake Sanchez anymore. He'd gotten over that a long time ago. "He's your *father*, Holly. I won't deny I was doing *exactly* what he claimed—I was flirting with a fifteen-year-old. *Man*, was I flirting. I've spent a decade being completely mortified about that, and grateful I didn't wind up in jail . . . or worse. It's why I kept fighting the urge to call or just show up on your doorstep. Who knows? Maybe he could smell the mating on me even back then."

"But I was *human* then. It doesn't work that way." She paused and blinked. "Does it?"

Another shrug. "Tony's mated to a full human without any Sazi background at all. You at least had wolf blood. Not that it matters anymore." He smiled and reached for the backpack, then stuck his hand into the bottom until he felt the sharp point of a thorn prick his thumb. He presented the single, slightly wilted pink rose to her with a flourish. "But I can still pull a few rabbits out of the hat, even a decade later."

Holly gasped and took a long deep breath, her nose buried in the pale petals. "It's *gorgeous*! But I can't imagine where you found a rose out here."

He chuckled. "Actually, when Ivan went to Cortez for supplies, I asked him to bring one back. Been waiting for a spare second to give it to you, but there really hasn't been one until now."

Her smile started out shy, but then grew into something different. She leaned her whole body forward until her hands were on his chest and the rose tickled his chin. When her mouth found his, he let her take the lead and tried not to do anything drastic.

She broke the slow, gentle kiss to say, "I'm not a teenager anymore, Eric."

"No, you most certainly are not." His voice was husky and he really hoped this was leading where he wanted it to go. A decade of waiting, of wanting to call, of asking casually about her to see who she was dating, whether she was married, or had kids.

She didn't object when he pulled her closer. In fact, she crawled into his lap and curled up between his crossed legs. He kissed her again, this time not so slow or gentle. He claimed her mouth and kissed her breathless. Her nails dug into his neck so hard it made him crazy. So did the way her tight little bottom wiggled against his growing erection. It was probably just the cactus spines, but he could live with that. He growled low in his chest and felt her pulse race under his fingertips. The scent of her desire matched the heat in her eyes when he pulled back. "Your choice. Time to go to sleep?"

Holly shook her head. "Time to go to *bed*."

Chapter Sixteen

WAS THIS REALLY happening? Was she really spreading out sleeping bags and zipping them together in a tent with the same man she'd been dreaming about for years?

She must be. Who else would be yanking her shoes off so impatiently? "Just a second," she said as he tugged at the sneaker again. "The fabric's caught in the zipper. If you yank any harder it's going to get jammed and break." Eric let out a deep sigh and waited, his fingers tapping a staccato on her shoe sole.

After a few more seconds of wiggling, it came unstuck and the zipper moved smoothly. Eric flipped her on her back so suddenly the whole tent moved. He reached up with one hand to stop the lantern's swaying and ran his fingers through her hair with the other. His eyes were glowing so bright she couldn't even see the pupils. "Tell me what you want, Holly.

Where should I start?" He wiggled his eyebrows playfully.

Her blush caught her unaware. What *did* she want? She'd fantasized about this moment for years. She smiled. "I'd sort of like to pick up where we left off earlier. I've always wondered what it would be like to wake up next to you without my clothes on."

He gave her a sly grin. "All right. You get undressed over here and I'll go over there and we'll meet in the middle."

Her hands felt clumsy and rushed as she took off her shoes and pants under the cover of the sleeping bag. She couldn't help but look as Eric pulled his shirt over his head. She bit at her bottom lip, drooling over the muscles rippling under his skin. Had he always had that tattoo of a wolf head on his shoulder? She couldn't remember ever seeing him without a shirt on before. Well, there had been that one time, when he was helping clean out the basement at pack headquarters. She'd gotten a glimpse of his bare chest when he'd put his clothes into the wash. Yeah, that was a day she'd dreamed about for quite a while.

Finally stripped down to her bra and panties, she snuggled under the cool, down-filled cover and closed her eyes. The shushing sound of his own slide under the covers made her jump. So did the touch of his hand as it snaked across her stomach.

He nuzzled close, hitting all the same areas where she'd smelled him earlier. The scent of him was amazing—clean skin, warm fur, and musky emotions that soaked into her and made her wet. He blew softly into her ear and rubbed his nose against her temple. Her small gasp of pleasure echoed through the tent.

"Wake up, Sleeping Beauty." The words were a husky whisper.

She smiled but didn't open her eyes. "You didn't say that earlier."

"Actually, I did." The words were soft and warm, and she couldn't help but open her eyes. His nose was nearly touching hers, and the blue fire in his eyes sucked her in. "And then I did this." His lips touched hers, just the barest brush of skin. He feathered kisses along the edge of her mouth and chin, finally ending up next to her ear—all while drawing a slow line down her arm with his fingernail. A whimper escaped her. "But you didn't wake up." The words were both disappointed and anticipatory.

"Yes, I did," she whispered in return, and slid her hand up his cheek before pulling his mouth to hers.

The kiss started slow and lazy, with just the gentle brush of tongues. But once he started skimming his hand down her waist, it was all she could do not to pull him on top of her. But she knew this wasn't just about *her* fantasies. He'd wanted to call her for a whole decade?

"Uh-huh," he said next to her ear, reminding her again that he could read her thoughts. "Not just *call* you, though. I *wanted* you. You've been the subject of many a dream of mine. So you just lay back and relax, princess. I'm about to make all your fantasies come true."

He nipped and sucked and kissed his way down

her shoulder. She let her fingers finally play with his hair. It had always looked so very soft, and even though he wore it a little shorter than he had back then, it was as silken as she'd imagined.

His hand slipped under her and she jumped just a bit as her bra strap popped open. He pulled it away from her with his teeth while she watched and began to suckle on her nipple until she moaned and writhed. Fantasy number two fulfilled. His other hand was busy too, teasing the edges of her panties. She'd changed into the lacy ones she'd bought for the trip to Australia—on the weird chance he might actually still remember her.

He raised his face from her breast for a second and smiled. "You nearly got jumped right there in the driveway. Why do you think my thumbs were in my front pockets? They were holding on to keep from tossing you across the hood of the car."

"Okay, it's just weird that you're commenting on my thoughts."

"Yeah? Well then, maybe we just need to make sure you don't have time to think." His hand burrowed inside her panties and a finger slid inside her so suddenly that every nerve came alive. Her back arched and she cried out, clutching at his shoulders. When exactly the underpants came off she couldn't remember, but she *did* remember the moment he started to lick and suckle and probe her with hands, lips, and tongue.

She was helpless, weightless, and couldn't do anything but make noises that weren't words. His tongue was thrusting inside her when the growing pressure finally burst. "Eric!" she heard herself cry as she grabbed onto his shoulders for support, "Yes. Oh God, *yes!*"

The climax rode her so hard she couldn't breathe. It was still claiming her when he rose to his knees, taking her legs even higher. She cried out again as he entered her. The look on his face was intense, nearly panicked, as he grabbed her hips and began to pump into her. She lowered her legs and tucked them between his arms until they were around his waist. All she wanted was the feeling of him inside her, so thick it made her already sensitive nerves ache.

He buried his face in her hair and growled loud enough that it raised the hairs on her neck. "God, I've wanted you for so long."

Mine. Finally mine. She heard the words clearly, but he was suckling on her neck so he couldn't have spoken aloud.

He was slamming into her so hard that her head was pressed against the tent walls, but she wanted every second of it. A second orgasm was growing inside her and she hoped he wouldn't finish before it happened.

"No problem," he said, with a low, possessive chuckle. He slowed down, and changed their position until her legs were tight around his plunging cock. Every motion raked him against her swollen clitoris until she was ready to leap out of her skin. "Come with me, Holly. Let's go over together," he whispered before kissing her again. His tongue began to pump her mouth in counterpoint to his hips and he began to flick his thumbs against her nipples until she couldn't even breathe.

She was trapped beneath him, his arms tight against her shoulders and his hips keeping her immobile while he tormented her—his every movement taking her higher than anyone ever had before.

This hadn't been in any of her fantasies, but it would be from now on, because when her second climax hit, it nearly stopped her heart. Holly screamed into his mouth while her fingers clutched frantically at the ground underneath her. Her entire body clenched so hard Eric had to struggle to move inside her.

Apparently, it was all he could take. His answering moan was so powerful it rattled inside her chest and then he slammed inside her once more before going still.

Power began to fill the small tent. It swirled so fast it made its own wind. The lantern flickered as Eric hurriedly shifted her legs so he could continue to pump into her, his hands holding tight to her hips until sweat poured down his face and his eyes were like twin turquoise stars that dwarfed the light of the lamp.

You too, babe. Your eyes are like supernovas.

Moisture flowed down her face and she didn't know if it was sweat or tears. But God, it felt so good. The climax continued to intensify and Holly began to feel a second heartbeat pounding in her chest.

The magic rode them both until they were so sweat-soaked their hands kept slipping off each other.

Pleasure became pain and then pleasure again until Eric finally collapsed on her and the light inside the tent dimmed, leaving only the lantern's glow.

Eric reached down between them and pulled himself out of her. That's when she realized he had been wearing a condom. "Hadn't even thought about that," she managed to wheeze out. "Pretty stupid on my part."

"Almost didn't bring them," he panted as he rolled off her and collapsed onto his back. "Ivan bought them when he got the rose. Thank God for friends . . . with their minds in the gutter." He tucked his hand under her neck and pulled her toward him. "C'mere, you. I can't tell you how long I've wanted to fall asleep with you wrapped around me."

She rolled over until she was snuggled against him, her head on his smooth chest and her arm wrapped around his waist.

That was fucking incredible.

"It was, wasn't it?" Holly gasped.

Eric pulled his head back and the scent of his shock filled the air. Holly didn't raise her head, but just nodded. "Yep. The mating goes both ways now. Guess you're stuck with me."

He kissed her hair and let out a small laugh while the happy scent of cinnamon and sugar filled her nose. "I can live with that."

A MAN'S HIGH-PITCHED scream woke Eric from a deep sleep. It was far in the distance, but in the direction they had been headed. Adrenaline filled him as he reached for his clothes. Instead of doing the same, Holly shifted forms in a blast of power and left the tent at a dead run.

Quicker this way, came her voice in his head. He couldn't really argue with that, and followed suit. He chased her across the rocky ground, the nearly full moon lighting their path, as they followed the scent of blood and pain on the wind.

Eric saw a flash of movement and realized that a naked man was running away from tall cliff walls. He veered off to make chase. You follow the blood. I'll follow this guy. Holly nodded and turned away. He watched as she lowered her head and streaked across the desert with teeth bared and eyes glowing. *Damn, she looks good as a wolf.*

As he got closer, he realized the man he was chasing was Sazi, and a snake. More precisely, a viper. Could this be the man Holly had mentioned? He did run oddly, with one leg dragging slightly.

The man was fast enough that it was everything Eric could do to keep up. But he'd practiced running in the Outback, pushing himself to go faster every day. It had been something to do to pass the time. But now it was coming in handy. The snake didn't seem to notice he was being followed . . . or he just didn't care. That could be dangerous, and it made Eric reduce his speed. Running full tilt into a trap wouldn't be much fun. He stayed back far enough that he could just barely see the nude man running and tried to watch the landscape for some clues as to his location.

Finally the man slowed and approached a massive

boulder. It was split nearly in half. The wide gap blazed with light from inside. He wished he'd brought his binoculars. He heard movement in the darkness ahead and stopped cold. Something was out there, and the scent of whatever it was made his hackles rise in alarm. While he wanted to get closer to see what was inside, it would be far better to wait until light. A lot of snakes were night hunters. It was possible they could be taken by surprise.

He backtracked carefully, being careful to listen around him. He felt a familiar tingle as Holly pulled on his power. Are you okay? He waited for an answer. But there was no response. Had this been a trick to separate them? Damn it! He should have stuck with her.

He started to run again in the direction she'd gone, his heart pumping a mile a minute, imagining a thousand things that could have gone wrong. The scent of blood hung heavy in the air as he approached a tall cliff, but there were other smells—wet sorrow and thick fur.

Would you relax? I was talking. I can't talk and think at the same time. I'm fine. But you really need to hear this, so hurry.

Relax . . . but hurry. Yeah, that helps. He shook his head and increased his speed just a bit more. Still, his heart stopped pounding quite so hard.

He could see Holly's shadow—in human form, as he approached the old cave. It had obviously been carved by hand, and matched similar openings in the cliff wall to the sides and above. He felt a sense of awe. Here he was at last, entering the ancestral home of the Sazi. The place where the great meeting of the first shifters happened. Had they met in one of these very rooms to talk about the continuing expansion of humans? Did they sing songs and light fires to mourn those who had been brutally slain by the native tribes during the Ravaging?

"We're in here, Eric." Holly's quiet voice carried intense excitement. He loped the last few feet and looked inside the cavern. A human male of about thirty sat in the middle of a blue square of plastic. It had once been an air mattress, but there was a wide gash in the surface that was charred like it had been burned. He was wrapped with two blankets, and Holly had a third. Eric decided to stay in wolf form rather than be naked.

He looked Holly over carefully. You're okay?

She nodded and gave him a small, embarrassed smile. "Sorry I pulled from you. But he was so very sick. I had to do something to help. It's okay. He knows about Sazi. He used to work for Antoine's cat show."

Eric turned his head and flicked his ears forward as he looked him over again. He'd worked with Antoine for a summer and *should* remember him. Could it be—? But he was so very thin and pale. He barely resembled the handler he'd played cards with. "Bruce?"

Bruce's face lit up and he cocked his head. He wouldn't recognize the fur, since the human staff always left the estate during the full moon.

Eric sat down and wagged his tail a couple times.

"Eric Thompson. I stayed with Antoine one summer a few years back."

"Oh! Eric Thompson. From Canada, right?" When he nodded, Bruce held a hand up to his chest and breathed a sigh of relief. "At last a friendly face! This has been a horrifying experience. I suppose I always knew I wasn't completely safe. But I'd always hoped Larry wouldn't turn on me. God, but I loved that man." He lowered his eyes. "Guess I was just fooling myself."

"So what happened here?" He looked around. It was obvious someone had planned to stay for quite a while. There was a massive ice chest and plenty of canned supplies next to a camp stove.

Holly pointed to the floor and that's when Eric noticed the black glass knife on the floor. It vibrated as though it were alive, and seemed to nearly *glow*. "There's what we came for, so I guess the seers were right. That's the knife Larry—or I guess we should call him *Nasil*—was playing with on the plane. I'd know it anywhere. He stabbed Bruce with it and then took off running."

Bruce pulled down the blanket to show a rapidly healing wound in his bicep. "Another few inches to the left and I'd be dead." He shook his head as Eric turned to look behind him. "Don't beat yourself up for not catching him. Nobody can. He's one of the fastest Sazi alive."

"Oh, I didn't lose him," he said before turning to face the entrance. He could have sworn he heard a noise outside, a scrabbling sound like a dozen tiny feet sliding on the dirt. "I followed him to another cave on the other side of this valley. But I kept hearing sounds in the dark, so I stopped. Just like the sounds I'm hearing now." He started backing up. "Holly, you need to change back to wolf form. Bruce, get on my back and hang on tight. We have to get out of here right now. Something's about to happen and I don't want to be trapped inside this cave when it does."

Holly hurriedly picked up the knife and put it inside a metal box nearby. She changed forms and picked up the box in her teeth. Bruce did as instructed and Eric was glad he at least had on briefs. "Back to the tent. Can you find it again, Holly?"

She couldn't talk, so she blinked and spoke into his mind. I'll be fine. You just keep Bruce safe. I just barely healed him, and I don't want him bruised up again. Her words nearly made him laugh. She sounded like a wife giving a warning after cleaning the kitchen floor.

Eric took off out of the cave at a run. Something large and hairy brushed his head as he exited but he didn't turn back to see what it was. But then Holly yelped. Crap! It's got me! Eric!

He turned in a skid to see that a spider as wide as a car had spit silk from spinnerettes on its abdomen and had caught Holly's hind foot. He started back, but Bruce leapt off his back. "No! Don't go any closer. I've seen these things before. They *eat* Sazi. Leave this to me."

Before Eric could get his wits about him, Bruce raced over to where Holly was being dragged backward while she scrambled for purchase and threw out bursts of power. He grabbed the metal box from Holly and pulled out the knife.

With one swipe of the blade, the gooey thread severed. The spider just threw out another thread. But Bruce caught this one intentionally and laid the knife flat on the silk. The spider screamed, a vibrating trill that hurt Eric's ears. Holly didn't waste any time. She raced to Eric's side. Bruce cut the thread just as another five of the creatures started to descend from the cliff openings like some kind of horror movie. Bruce grabbed the metal box and raced back to Eric. He jumped back on his back and they took off, leaving the spiders in the dust.

But as they raced back through the piñons, Eric knew they couldn't stop at the tent. We've got to get back to the base, Holly. We've got to tell the council about this.

She nodded beside him and increased her speed.

"You might want to wrap an arm around my neck, Bruce. We're going to put on enough speed to get back to the others." Bruce obeyed without question. He put the heavy box between Eric's shoulders and lay on it so it would stay steady. "Why don't you just take that out of the box? It's no big deal if I get cut."

"No!" Bruce exclaimed over the sound of the wind. "This blade would *kill* you. It's what was killing Larry and me. It's poison to Sazi. It steals your power and makes you decay. It has to stay in the box until it can be destroyed."

So what did the seers want it for then? Could this be the weapon that could kill Marduc? He didn't know, but it was definitely time to get it back to the people who would know what to do with it.

Yet as fast as they were running, he had the feeling the spiders were still following. Were they leading them straight back to the others?

Chapter Seventeen

"YES . . . OH, YES. That's just right. Deeper, my lover."

Nasil felt his body respond to the being riding him. He couldn't see her, but he could feel hands caressing his skin, and the soft touch of hair on his face. But this act was no better than rape. The chains that bound his wrists and ankles didn't speak of a lover. He was a tool. Nothing more. And yet, he couldn't make his body stop reacting to her. His hips betrayed him, impatiently thrusting upward into the warm, pulsing flesh.

His fists clenched and his teeth gritted together as her movements finally had the expected result. A climax overtook him and when flesh pressed to his mouth, he opened, expecting a mouth on his, but finding a breast instead. He suckled as the orgasm rode him and tasted fluid. It leaked out from her nipple and made him immediately dizzy, yet lazily content.

Damn it! She's drugging me. He managed to hold the fluid in his mouth and not swallow. It made his tongue numb, but as soon as she raised up, he turned his head to the side and let the fluid dribble out.

A small hand patted him on the cheek like a dog as her weight lifted from his hips. "That was quite nice, Nasil. Perhaps I'll keep you around for a little while longer."

He couldn't imagine why. He wasn't the only male bound upon a thick straw bed. There weren't only snakes either. Some of the captives were birds. One man in particular—a tall, thickly muscled Navajo— looked as disgusted with the process as Nasil. She'd had them all in the short time he'd been here, some- times taking more than one at a time. He didn't even *want* to know how.

He was abruptly tired and his arms felt like lead. It might be the drug she'd secreted, but he didn't think so. He felt drained. Could she feed on energy? He looked around and the others seemed equally tired. But they were smiling and their glazed eyes said they probably didn't care.

There was so little information about Marduc, even though he and Sargon had studied the old texts be- fore deciding on this plan. And speaking of *plans*— "What now, lovely Marduc? This romp has been won- derful fun, but we should make plans to conquer the other Sazi."

An image of her was in his mind, but he kept his eyes open, trying to get some hint as to whether the woman he saw in his mind had any bearing on real- ity. "Why so many questions, my lover?" Her voice was soft and sultry and he felt a slow hand caress his chest and tease a nipple. "Isn't it enough to lay with me, to know I'm yours to pleasure as you will?"

He raised every mental shield he had until the image of her in his mind faded. While there was something supremely amusing in the thought that this might have been Sargon's fate, he knew his old master never would have allowed it. He hadn't been ruled by his body. He'd *ruled* it. Perhaps it was time to learn that lesson. It might take everything he had to pull off this plan, but he had to see what his chances were to become a true partner to Marduc. Because it was only as a partner that he could betray . . . and destroy her.

"Hardly." His voice sounded dry and imperious even to his own ears. He grabbed the chain with his good hand and pulled sharply with every ounce of his weight. Thankfully, because the chain was high in silver content, the links weren't terribly strong. He bore the pain as the silver bubbled his skin. Fortunately, he'd endured far worse at his master's hands, so he could set aside the pain into a small box that didn't affect his thoughts. The first chain parted from the ring set in the wall like a hot knife through butter. The other three soon followed. He kept his voice cold and sure. "It was entertaining, to be sure. But I'm here for far more than *pleasure*, Marduc. You said I would rule by your side. That's what I intend to do."

He snapped both arms forward simultaneously. The chains whipped in the air and connected around a blurry object. She screamed and tried to back away. That was it! It wasn't that she was completely invisible. She was more like the ghost cats. If he looked closely, he could see a shimmering area where her body blended with objects beyond. He yanked the chains and caught her weight when she fell on top of him. He'd expected it, so he rolled, and she was suddenly under him. He smiled coldly and rejoiced in the scent of her confusion. "Don't underestimate me, my Goddess," he hissed and then chuckled. "I think we can teach each other much as we conquer the world." He shifted forms on top of her and wrapped himself around her with blinding speed, until he could feel the heat of her warming his skin. The chains dropped away when the limbs they controlled dissolved into his slender form. "Now," he said quietly, flicking his tongue to find her lips. He felt his arousal grow, and this time it was his doing. "Let us do as you promised. We shall have each other as only *snakes* can. And then," he whispered, so the others couldn't hear, "you'll tell me what plans you've made to destroy the Sazi in the valley below."

"You surprise me, Ea-Nasil," Marduc said. He felt her fangs break the skin of his neck and her sweet venom made his heart beat faster. "I'd thought you like the others. But you show *promise*. Yessss . . . let us see if you're snake enough to bed a Goddessss." She shifted forms and Nasil felt his coils unwind because of the sheer size of her. Feathers tickled and cut his skin as she grew and lengthened. She was easily twenty feet long and he felt the brush of wings move on her back. "If you can hold on and mate me as my kind must, we will plan together."

He was abruptly airborne, held aloft by a creature he could barely see. He tightened his grip as she flapped skyward, until the rising sun made the shimmering energy of her sparkle and gleam. Below them, at least fifty stories down, was the unforgiving earth, strewn with boulders and cactus. It would be better not to look down. "You want to be taken *here*?"

"As I must be. I'd thought it would be one of the birds to manage it, but I'm willing to give you a chance." She flapped once, making them rise on the warming air currents and then drop again a dozen feet. She barrel-rolled while Nasil tightened his grip. "And look down below. There's a powerful wolf running across the ground. He'll be a perfect after-sex snack."

Nasil didn't recognize the wolf, but she was right that he was powerful. He could taste the magic on the wind, and while he wasn't interested in *eating* the wolf, it would be useful to question him before Marduc finished him off.

"And if you can't hang on to mate, there will be two meals for me." She laughed, a dark rich sound that made Nasil shudder. Yet, there was something highly erotic at the thought of making love like this—with impending doom hanging over his every move. He felt around with his tail until he found her warm, soft opening. Yes, it could be done with some skillful maneuvering. Holding on with one coil, he drove his fangs into her soft underbelly. She screamed, the sharp sound of metal scraping against concrete. But her scent wasn't angry, it was aroused. He was bleeding from a thousand tiny cuts from her feathers, but the energy from her so bewitched him that he hardly noticed the pain. He managed to lock inside her, his erection swelling until there was no hope of separation until he completed. He moved with her as she floated, dipping and rolling in the sky. He finally got the rhythm of her motions so that he could thrust when she coiled. With each spin, he found another toothhold as one ripped away.

"Nobody hasss made my body react this way in a *very* long time, Nasssil," she gasped. Her body began to tremble and squirm under him. He drove his fangs in deeper, knowing the venom would only heighten her pleasure. He hadn't even *hoped* to bring her to orgasm, but it certainly didn't hurt. "Yessss . . . *you*. You will be the one to share in my plansss. You have courage and power. So much . . . delicious . . . *power*. I sense intelligence, as well—the weight of your experience presses on my mind. And you are capable of a viciousness that rivals my own. Already I can feel your seed from our earlier mating killing the challengers, forcing their way to my eggs. It burns inside me with power. So near, so close to my eggs now. You will father my army of winged serpents, Nasil. I can sense it. And you will lead them into battle against the mammals. We will be a nesting pair the world has never seen."

She flexed around him, pulling his thrusting member in deeper and it made him groan. His own nest of snakes, strong enough to make the world bow at his feet? While he knew it was wrong to even consider fertilizing the eggs of a monster, the sensations were delicious. He was so very close to climax.

His heart was pounding so fast it was making him dizzy. *So very . . . close. Want . . . need . . . this.*

There was no focusing past the hunger of his body for this snake . . . this *woman,* who he couldn't even see. And what was there to go back to? Bruce was dead, by his own hand—the only male he'd ever been interested in. Why *not* rule the world as a god with a goddess at his side?

He thrust one last time and couldn't breathe as the climax took him. He nearly lost his grip from the sheer force of it. She moaned and tumbled as an orgasm claimed her. A series of wing flaps righted them and then she spun toward the ground, and he knew it was so his fluid would travel deep enough to reach her eggs. The complete abandon and exhilaration of watching the ground race toward him while his body shook and tingled in climax made him forget nearly everything he was and everyone he'd ever known. No union would ever be as good, no feeling so *right.*

She squirmed in the air for long moments, up and down in the sky while he hung on with every ounce of his strength. Finally, she laughed harshly. "*Yes!* You have done what nobody else has ever managed! You have fertilized one of my eggs, Nasil. I am finally with child after four lifetimes of failure. With more matings, I know you can fertilize the rest. Then the world will know our *wrath*!" Her triumphant voice dripped with evil intent.

A part of Nasil knew he should shudder to realize what he'd just done. But he didn't. Instead, he felt a smile come to his mouth, buried deep in her sharp feathers.. He would do it again willingly. He *wanted* this, and though he was surprised at the speed of it, he could feel another erection forming, pressing against her belly, even as she laughed and teased him to greater stiffness. He released his fangs and they hissed as one before he took another bite and entered her again. This time his thrusts were hungry, desperate, and she responded in kind.

We'll mate again and again in the skies until you're spent, my lover—until every one of my eggs is a living snake.

He demanded no less. With those children to follow him, the world would finally be his. All would tremble . . . or *die. At last.*

Finally I will step out of that idiot Sargon's shadow to become the ruler I was always meant to be! All I have to do is continue to seduce Marduc, and then Ea-Nasil will no longer be just the tormentor of Akede, but of all the Earth!

But he couldn't seem to shake that tiny voice in the back of his mind. *When did you start to want this, Nasil? Just who is seducing whom?*

Chapter Eighteen

"SO," ANTOINE GLARED at Bruce from across the table. The great cat's arm was still in a sling from the wounds inflicted by Marduc. Holly had healed him as best she could, but he'd been very damaged from the talons and the fall. She was pretty proud of herself that he wound up with only a single sling. "I'd thought you a captive and worried myself sick over your fate. But instead, you were *helping* Larry plan the attack that killed other Sazi. I should strike you down where you sit!" He growled, showing sharp white teeth, and Bruce backed his chair away so quickly it nearly fell over. The scent of fear was too strong this close to the moon. Holly had to shake her head to come to her senses.

She wasn't sure why she and Eric were even in the room, except to verify what Bruce had just told the council members and seers.

"Antoine, put away your claws. We have more important things to do." Lucas might not have power to back it up anymore, but his tone brooked no argument. Josette spoke over the speaker. "Lucas is right, little brother. Love makes us *all* do foolish, dangerous things. Save your energy for the battle ahead. We're fortunate Bruce was with Holly and Eric. The spiders could easily have eaten them both."

"And what exactly are we to *do* about these spiders, who are likely on their way as we waste time talking?"

Antoine apparently hadn't been listening when Lucas was barking orders earlier. That surprised her. Lucas might not be a council member anymore, but people should still listen to him. Holly decided to update them on what had been happening, before she was asked to come in to the meeting. "Everybody's getting ready to head to Texas. Adam and Cara Mueller said there are some caves near their pack headquarters where people can set up house for as long as need be. There's running water and electricity already strung to the site, and it's not uncommon for families to have reunions there."

"And I'll be leading them," Lucas added. "I might not be a shifter anymore, but I haven't lost my memories and I can still plan defense with the best of them. Tony will be with me, and Adam said he's got a good armory down there. They've been planning all along to be Marduc's primary attack point. How that changed, we'll probably never know."

"Likely it was someone Charles *saved*." Josette's

voice was dry. Nobody commented, since most everyone in the room had been saved by Charles at one point. "Has Raphael arrived? Are Ahmad and Bobby secured?"

Antoine nodded. "They weren't happy about it, but yes. Tuli's still wondering why the order included Ahmad, but not her, and Asri is *livid*. She's nearly ready to give birth, and she's waiting for Bobby. Apparently, he's her *coach*. I hope there's a very good reason to lock them in an underground kiva for a week with Raphael draining their power down to nearly nothing."

Holly's mouth dropped open. She knew one of Raphael's gifts was the death touch, but she'd never heard he could remove just *part* of someone's power. And to do that to a councilman? Could they get their powers back later if they were drained like that?

Lucas answered. "There's a *very* good reason. Marduc generally only has control over male snakes, but her control is *strong*. She likely was able to reach Charles's mind because she'd bitten him before, in our last encounter. She'll be seeking out alpha snakes to try to find a mate. She's born pregnant, but must have the eggs fertilized. Sex and food are her primary motivations at this stage. If she sent the snakes to attack, it was either because she was trying to remove a potential threat to her young, or she was just getting the hang of controlling the lesser shifters. Once she masters the three-days and regular snakes, she'll go after the alphas. We *don't* want Ahmad and Bobby controlled by her . . . or worse—called to her bed. Letting her find an alpha powerful enough to fertilize those eggs would be a disaster. The children would destroy us all. Dampening their power will hopefully let them go unnoticed until we're ready to attack."

"I don't mean to interrupt," Holly finally said, "but what about Nasil? Isn't *he* powerful enough? He sure held me without any trouble. Couldn't he already be on her side?"

Once more Lucas picked up the knife and examined it. It had been passed around the room several times, only to be dropped by each person with a hiss of pain. She'd done it too, because how can you know the sensation unless you experienced it?

Gawd. Men and dangerous toys. They just can't stand not toughing it out in front of the others.

Only Lucas seemed to be able to handle it easily, which confirmed that he had no magical power left to slice away. The others watched him spin it on the table. The scent of envy floated to her nose. She shook her head at the same time as Lucas, but for entirely different reasons. "The way Bruce described the effects of the knife, I doubt he's got enough power to interest her. That knife has been chewing at him for some time, poisoning his system. She'd probably consider him damaged goods."

Holly opened her mouth, but then closed it again. Surely she hadn't healed him *that* much. Probably not enough to matter. She noticed Eric didn't bring it up either.

"He wouldn't be interested anyway," Bruce said

quietly. "Larry obeyed Sargon because he had no choice, but he didn't really want the world to fall. It's why he keeps helping you guys. He's been searching for Marduc ever since Sargon died. But not to join her cause. He wanted to kill her before she hatched, so everybody would stay safe. Larry's not evil. I'd know if he was, and I'd never have stayed with him."

Antoine growled, but didn't move. Still, Holly agreed. Bruce probably *would* know better than anyone. But that still didn't explain why she was here. "Then is there a reason you called *us* in, Nana? Do Eric and I really need to be hearing all this?"

Lucas turned to her and looked suddenly . . . *sad*. Nana spoke over the line. "Yes, you do. I dreamed of you last night, Holly. The image I saw was of the black-bladed knife flying to your hand in a battle with Marduc. As Bruce explained it to us, that might happen if it was bonded to you. The magic that created the knife intended to make it a substitute power well. It gathers magical energy and then distributes it at the will of the wielder, one whose magic it has tasted and favors enough to seek out. I believe that wielder is *you*, Holly." Nana paused and took a deep breath. "I believe you are destined to slay Marduc."

As Holly sat there blinking, trying to decide what to say, she realized the implications were too enormous to even wrap her mind around. Eric let out a low growl. "No. Just no. There's got to be someone else. Someone who's not—" He clamped his jaw shut abruptly and the dry, dusty scent of embarrassment rose before he could speak the last word. He wouldn't meet her eyes.

Holly felt a flash of anger prickle the hairs on her neck. He damned well better not be saying she wasn't capable. "I hope you aren't about to say someone who's not . . . *female*, Eric."

Lucas smiled sadly and shook his head. "No, I think he's about to say someone who's not *mine*. He can't help it, Holly. You're his mate. He *has* to protect you. It's in his blood now and there's no changing it."

Eric didn't say anything, but she could feel Lucas's words resonate in his head. There weren't clear thoughts, as such, that she could hear. There was just muddled confusion along with the word *No*.

"It'll take time for him to get over it," Lucas added. "Months, or even years before he doesn't leap in front of every speeding bullet for you." He raised his brows and shook his head. "Ladies, I don't know if it's such a good idea for Eric to be here. The stronger Marduc gets, the more males she'll be able to gather. Not just snakes and birds, but cats and wolves too. I'm thinking maybe he needs to go with us to Texas."

"I agree. He'll have to go," Josette said firmly. "Holly can't be distracted in this, and the future's unclear on his role. It might be the only way Marduc dies is if she's alone."

The future's *unclear*? What the hell? Were the seers just *guessing*? "Excuse me? No way. Did you ever think that the only way I survive to kill Marduc might be if he *stays*?" Now that she knew he hadn't deserted her, and *couldn't* desert her, she didn't want him to leave. She didn't want to be the dragon slayer. But if she had to . . . if she was the only one who could do this, she wanted Eric nearby. She intertwined her fingers with his and took a deep breath. "If I stay, he stays. It's not just a single-sided mating anymore. Not since . . . well, since last night." Nana started to swear. Holly shrugged. "Hey, you're the ones who insisted that we *had* to go last night to find the knife. Well, we did and this is the result. Live with it."

Lucas dropped his head until his lower face was hidden by a hand. Was he *snickering*? That's sure what it smelled like.

"We'll have to confer," Nana said after a long pause. "You should both get some sleep. Tomorrow will be a long day, regardless of what we decide for you."

They hung up the phone without another word. Holly looked around the room. Ivan let out a sigh and rolled his eyes. "Seers. With seers it is always something."

Antoine pushed back his chair and hissed when his splinted arm cracked against the tabletop. "Ivan, I think we should meet to discuss things. Lucas," he said, his voice cooling to near disdain, "I presume you believe you should attend as well."

Lucas bared teeth in something that bore no semblance of a smile. Yet his scent had no particular emotion, unless *tired* counted. "You'd presume correctly. But start without me. I need to have a few words with Holly." He met Eric's eyes and there was command in them. "Eric, please escort Bruce to the holding cell on the main floor and guard him until his trial." When Bruce gasped, Lucas turned to the man and continued without any sympathy in his scent or voice. "No matter what the crisis, Bruce, we can't simply ignore the fact that you did help Nasil with his plans. You could have gotten to a phone, or found a way to get a message to us *months* ago. But you didn't, even knowing full well that people were going to die if the plan went forward. Surely you must know the penalty for that."

Bruce looked around the room, panic etching lines in his face. Ivan and Antoine met his gaze. "Surely you don't expect *my* help," Antoine said with disbelief. "You betrayed me. Betrayed us *all*."

When Bruce looked to her, Holly couldn't meet his gaze. He *had* to have known there would be a price. He'd worked with Antoine for how long? Nearly a decade? "Holly?" he asked hopefully.

She couldn't help but remember Dale sobbing on the phone. "My sister is *dead*, Bruce. Killed by the snakes you allowed to roam free." She shook her head. "It won't bring her back if they kill you. But it won't bring her back if I *save* you, either."

Bruce crumbled then, realizing there was no hope to be had. His jaw trembled as he stood and nodded. Eric took his arm and led him out of the room.

Lucas remained seated until everyone had left the room and it was just the two of them. She stared at his hands, so unfamiliar, even though his nervous habit of tapping one finger as though sending a message in Morse code was the same. "Holly?"

"Yes, Alpha?" His fingernails had been recently trimmed. She knew he went to a nail salon fairly frequently. How could someone trimming his nails not notice the difference between what they saw and what they felt?

There was humor in his voice. "You're more alpha than me now, Holly, and I'm not your pack leader anymore. You can look me in the eye."

She started abruptly. It had been so long since she'd actually looked at his face—she'd always been careful to keep the proper respect for his office, and for the wolf. "Oh. I guess I figured—I'm sorry, this is all so confusing."

He nodded, and she realized his eyes were still the same. Eyes that could hold humor or anger in equal measure. "I know. It's confusing for *everyone*. That's why I wanted to talk to you."

"Do you want me to try to heal you again?" She wanted him to be *him* again. While he was young and attractive . . . sexy, in fact . . . this just didn't feel like *Lucas*.

He smiled and shook his head. "There's nothing to heal. I'm perfectly healthy, except for being human."

Holly felt her face heat, even though it wasn't really her fault. "I know. And I can't tell you how sorry I am about that. I never would have believed it was possible for them to—"

Lucas's face darkened. "For who to do *what*?"

Now she was really confused. She leaned forward in her chair and couldn't understand the surprise and confusion coming from him. "The FMU. You know . . . the *cure*?"

He leaned back in his chair for a long moment, regarding her curiously. "No, I *don't* know. You have to understand, Holly. Those on the council who aren't treating me like a leper are treating me like a second-class citizen. I have been told absolutely *nothing* about what happened and without my magic, I have no way to force anyone to offer the information against their will. The council is no less secretive than they've ever been. Even Ivan seems to have developed laryngitis and short-term memory loss."

She was completely taken aback. "What? That's not right! You deserve to know what did this to you. You're no less an attack victim than *I* am." The glaring truth of her own words was both stunning and terrifying. "Dear God, you *are* an attack victim. We turned into something as bad as them." She said the words under her breath, but he heard them.

"You need to talk to me, Holly. This could be vitally important. What is the FMU? If there are more than just snakes at work here, I really need to know." Lucas's face was worried, but more than that, he smelled afraid. It was an intense dread that was making his muscles twitch, ready to do *something*.

She nodded. Maybe the council would be angry with her, but she only had Eric's word they'd even done the hindsight on her. While she couldn't figure out any reason why he'd lie, she'd feel better if someone she trusted actually heard the story from her.

Lucas sat in silence while she told him about FMU. She even showed him the tattoo under her hair. He began to frown, but let her continue without interrupting. No, she didn't want to shine too harsh a light on Rose and her other dead friends, but she needed to work out in her own head what might have happened to make them go this far. "I don't know if you can truly imagine what it was like, growing up like that. And you'd have to, in order to understand what would make them do this to you, Alpha."

"I'm not—" he protested again, but she held up her hand.

"You're the only pack leader I've ever known. I can't think of you as anything *but*. I'll try to call you Lucas, if I can." He let out a deep sigh, followed by a small chuckle. Holly tried to think of what might make him understand. There were so many tiny things; like the individual snowflakes that make up a blizzard. She wasn't sure why the next words came out, other than it was nearly March and once again— "Do you know that I've only celebrated six birthdays *on* my birthday, in my whole life?"

He shook his head, obviously confused. "No. Why?"

"Because I was born near the full moon." She paused as he shook his head. "The pack never really understood the upheaval in our house the nights of the moon. Dad was the omega, so he got *all* the shit work leading up to the hunt." She chuckled bitterly. "No, actually *I* got all the shit work." Lucas narrowed his eyes and opened his mouth, but Holly held up her hand to stop him. "I'm *serious,* Alpha. On the three nights of every single full moon for my entire life, I have been worked like a *slave* from before dawn until after dark. It only got worse as my sisters left home. And then I'd be left *alone*. Rose left home when I was little, and Mom was dead. Everybody else in the family turned, so it was a party for them. But before I was old enough to watch the other kids—which, I should mention, was required of me once I turned fifteen— there was nobody to watch *me*."

Lucas shook his head and let out an exasperated noise. "That is simply not true, Holly. There were always people around to watch the children. Tatya insisted on that and I know it happened. And being babysat once a month isn't a reason to go join a radical hate group."

Holly was feeling braver by the second, but she couldn't really figure out why. Maybe it was because while Lucas might backhand her, he couldn't throw her against the wall or cut off her air until she passed out anymore. "Reality check, Lucas. This isn't about birthdays or babysitters. The Boulder pack was all about castes and cliques. Nobody included the human daughter of the *omega* in plans. Are you *kidding*? Nobody wanted me around, or Bob Salazar, or even Candy Streeter. We weren't rich, we weren't cool, and most importantly—we weren't *wolves*. You're right. This is about hate groups . . . and there were plenty on *both* sides."

Lucas's mouth opened in shock and she nodded when he couldn't get out any sound. Bringing Candy's name up had been intentional. "You remember Candy, right? Yeah, she was a member of FMU. We all were. Of course, she was only a member until she was *murdered* when her best friend Karol scratched her. Did anyone ever mention that Karol was put up to it? Candy was on the verge of being *cool* and Corrine urged Karol to do it, *for her own good*. Just that last tiny step to be part of the club."

The heat of anger was beginning to rise and she wanted Lucas to suffer through this the way she had. "We'd been taught our whole lives that the only way to be cool was to get lucky in the gene pool. You were dirt if you were human in that school. Candy dreamed of it, wished for it—just like I did, until we both realized we wouldn't turn. That's when we joined FMU, because we realized it wasn't about being a wolf. And then she was killed, because she forgot to put on a silver bracelet that day."

It was only last year that she found out what had happened to Candy—that she hadn't survived her first turn. The kids had been told her family had "moved." Yeah, her parents moved all right. Ran away to escape the pain.

The entire pack had watched the tape of the failed change. About half of the human kids she knew vomited. She nearly had too. It had been a stark look at what was about to happen to *her* because it was just after Corrine had tried to rip out her throat. The same thing nearly *did* happen to her. Her body would have ripped itself apart if Raphael hadn't insisted on having a bunch of healers present on that first moon.

Now Lucas looked sick. "Holly, I . . . I already explained I didn't *know* the teachers at the pack school were telling people that being a wolf was somehow *better* than being human. Tatya was punished for it, and several of the teachers were dismissed and moved to other packs. I fully admit it was terrible that you weren't told about Candy in school, but—"

She shook her head tiredly. "You think this is just about what happened in *school*? Look, this isn't about Candy. You asked why *I* joined FMU. You said there was no reason to join a radical hate group. You're wrong. Once I got to be ten or eleven the car stopped coming by . . . and it's not like Dad had any standing to raise a fuss." Frustration began to edge her voice. She just couldn't help it. "Of course, there wasn't money to send me to a movie or *hire* a sitter every month." She snorted, remembering all the battles for new clothes or shoes. Being *entertained* on every moon would have been out of the question. "Hell, Dad struggled every month just to put food on the table—even though the restaurant's walk-in was packed with meat. That was really hard to understand when we were kids. That the food was the *pack's*, not the property of the Sanchez family. That was made abundantly clear by Tatya, and by *you*. Do you remember that memo? You signed it. It basically told Dad, *Cook, but don't touch*. Know how that read in our house? Feed *us*, but don't eat. And who do you think got meat in our house when there was some? The *human*? Do you think I wasn't reminded every day of my life why *my* plate was empty?" The laugh came out bitter and angry. He wouldn't need a supernatural nose to sense her emotions today.

"Why do you think he robbed my bank account, again and again? To buy a new stove, to buy a new freezer . . . to feed *you*. Pack members had to be granted credit, and were never required to clear their accounts. We couldn't raise our prices because it would be *unfair* to the pack. We *had* to pay our monthly tithe, even though we never saw a single benefit. Never mind that the little human girl wouldn't have new school clothes, or decent meals, or someday go to college. What would *that* matter?"

Lucas was totally stunned, looking almost silly as he blinked with an open mouth. "It's funny, you know, that even *after* you found out he'd stolen every dime I ever made, and *after* I was attacked and turned, everybody conveniently forgot to replace the money. Yeah, there's something to make a girl feel welcome in the pack."

He tried to speak, but no words came out. His scent was horrified, sad, and angry, all at once.

Holly felt tears burning her eyes. It was hard to remember it all without getting angry all over again. She snuffled, and let the salty wetness fall down her face. It was time he saw this . . . heard this from someone. Maybe he was finally in a place in his life that he could understand. "I wasn't an isolated story, Lucas. Every human family member who saved their allowance, or dug through dumpsters for soda cans, or sold birthday gifts, or even *stole* money from someone, just so they could sneak out of the house and escape for a bit could tell you the same. Is it any wonder we banded together—all the left-behinds who weren't quite good enough to be pack, or pride, or nest? We formed Family Members United as a place where we could have *some* acceptance; a sense of belonging. The forum opened on the first night of every full moon and we'd yell and cry and scream to each other. It was online therapy. Well, we'd talk until the *mighty hunters* came back home to make our lives hell again, that is. Trust me, you don't want to hear about the bruises and concussions and cracked bones we put up with. So long as nobody broke skin, nobody cared. It was a wave of the hand and 'oh, you'll heal.'"

"Holly," Lucas finally said, his voice filled with something close to outrage, "Why didn't you ever *tell* anyone? How in the hell were we supposed to know any of this?"

She leaned close enough to him that he would feel the pressure of air on his face. Her hands were clenched into fists and she realized she was shaking, not from fear, but from years of pent-up rage. She slammed her fist on the table, not even realizing she did it until she felt the sting of pain. The words spilled out so fast she couldn't stop them. Didn't *want* to stop them. "Why should I *have* to? Why didn't you *notice*? We were kids. What were we supposed to do? Who were we supposed to tell?"

She stood in a rush and threw the chair against the wall. It felt good to see him flinch from the noise and motion. "We . . . weren't . . . *pack*! Don't you get it? Only the animals got to be pack and live the privileged life of a Sazi with healers and therapists and pack leaders to talk to. The rest of us just got to keep the secrets and clean up the blood and make up the lies so the rest of you could be the exalted rulers.

I would have been tossed out of your office on my ear if I'd asked for an appointment, and probably would have been grounded by Dad for a month for having the gall to *bother you*. No, the only support network we had was *each other*, because nobody else wanted to hear what we had to say. Do you know what that feels like, Lucas? To know that nobody really wants you around? You've been a second-class citizen for a fucking *day*. Try it for a lifetime. At least people are being nice to you after you turned human. Try having everybody *hate* you because the fact you lived caused someone they actually *liked* to die? All the wolves loved Corrine. She was vicious and nasty and spiteful. That's how she got to be third female. I was the friend of a *cat* who stole our land and stole our Second male. I was human scum who was a wannabe wolf . . . and I had no right to live. I wasn't *supposed* to live. Even Josette says so."

Holly had wanted to be a wolf so desperately she could taste it, and all the *real* wolves had always snickered that she would dare to dream it. Now it sickened her every time she thought about the fact that she was an *alpha*, one of the elite. And it had made her an entirely different person—one she didn't like so much.

She hadn't intended to say *any* of this, but now it all seemed to be flowing out of her in a stream she couldn't stop. "Do you know that we dreamed . . . we *prayed* in the FMU for the day someone would come along and wave a magic wand to either turn us into Sazi or turn *you* into humans? But when *I* was turned, I became one of the animals to them. I lost my humanity with the wolf, and lost the wolf to my humanity. I'm the worst of both, a wolf who hates being one. A healer who terrifies the animals she'd hoped to heal, and doesn't want to heal the animals like her." The reality of her situation hit her like a blow to her chest. "And now the FMU actually created the wand to make it all better, and they picked the wrong Sazi. How whacked is that? You're human . . . when it's *me* who wanted to be." She shook her head. "And as much as that tiny part of me still wants to laugh and point and tell you, *ha, ha, serves you right* . . . it's not fair. To either of us. It should be a *choice,* not a cowardly attack. I'm sorry for that, Lucas. More than you can ever know."

She was tired. So very tired of all of this. What she wouldn't give to still be in Boulder, going to vet school and not having the end of the world hanging over her head.

But then you wouldn't have Eric. She felt a dull lump in her stomach, and knew it was probably true. Without magic, she probably wouldn't be mated. She didn't even know if he'd still like her. She'd just been a kid when they'd gotten to know each other. Was she even that person anymore?

Lucas looked lost. He shook his head, trying to process everything. "I honestly don't know what to say to you, Holly. Here I've been struggling to protect the Sazi from outside enemies, only to discover that we've been *creating* an enemy in our own home who hates us even worse." He lowered his forehead into his hands and suddenly smelled as tired as she felt. "Our own family wants us dead?" he whispered.

She shook her head and touched his hand. "Not dead, Lucas. Just . . . human. It's not a death sentence."

He looked up then and raised his brows over pained eyes. "I was born in the year 264 A.D., Holly. Tell me how dying sixty or seventy years from now *isn't* a death sentence."

She had no answer for that, and couldn't quite wrap her head around that long of a life. All she could do was pull back her hand and shrug helplessly. Mostly she wanted to leave. There was too much pain, confusion, and anger roiling through the room. No, it wasn't precisely her fault this happened. But it was a sin of *omission*, rather than commission.

"Y'know," Lucas said after a long pause, "this wasn't at all what I wanted to talk to you about. But now that I know all this, there's really no need to even ask."

"You might as well," she responded with a shrug as she sat back down. "It can't hurt anything at this point. I'm sure you already hate me, so what's the difference?"

Lucas sighed and leaned back in his chair. "I don't hate you, Holly. I'm not really sure *what* I feel about you. I thought I'd gotten to know you pretty well over the years, and now it turns out I didn't know you at all. But if you don't want to heal 'animals,' it really doesn't do much good to ask this."

"I already told you. I'll do whatever I can to help you. You're no less of an attack victim than me. It turned you into something you didn't want by force. I'll fix that if I can."

A sad chuckle left his lips. "I suppose I'm grateful for that, but I'm not asking for me. I was hoping you could heal Tatya."

Holly reared back in her seat at the request. The most powerful healer of them all needed *healing*? "What's wrong with Tatya that she can't heal herself?"

"Me." The word was simple, but the implications were enormous. "I never realized just how much she relied on me—for power, for purpose, and even for a sense of self-worth. I have no illusions about my wife, Holly. She's cunning and vicious and a social climber, but she truly believed she was doing right for the pack. Unfortunately, after your revelations, I'm even more afraid for her mental state. If she really *is* as much of a classist as you claim, then having lost me—my standing and power—might be more than she can bear." Lucas might not be Sazi anymore, but the intensity in his eyes sure made them *look* like they were glowing. "I was going to ask if you could heal her *heart*. Can that be done? Can a—I hate to even say the word—but can a *prejudice* that deep be healed with magic? Is there any way for my wife to stop hating *humans*?" He paused and looked like he was going to be sick. "I wouldn't have believed it of her, but now that you've said it, I have to think back on all the small signs I've seen and ignored over the years. I'm beginning to think that she could do something monumentally foolish and wind up getting put down. And yes, I would be able to lose her now. The mating bond is *gone* with the loss of the magic, but I'm not positive she could lose *me*. Not the me that's human, but the me that was the all-powerful Lucas, or Inteque, or whoever the hell I've been." He cocked his head. "Got a cure for that?"

Holly was stunned. "What are you afraid she's going to do?"

Lucas sighed and started tapping his finger on the knife again. "She's already asked if I want her to turn me."

"Turn . . . as in *attack*?"

He nodded and closed his eyes for a long moment before opening them again. "At first I thought it was a joke. But she's asked three times in less than a day. If she is prejudiced against humans, I don't know if she's going to keep *asking*."

The thought horrified Holly. "But that's a *death* sentence. And there's no guarantee that you'd wind up an alpha wolf again or even survive."

Lucas locked eyes with her. While his voice was steady and calm, his scent was pungent with fear and worry. Holly was pretty sure the fear was for Tatya, rather than just himself. "I'm afraid she's not thinking logically enough to care."

Holly shook her head sadly, her heart thumping at the possibility that Tatya might be tempted to murder her husband just because he was human. "I don't think there's any healing magic out there that can change an honest belief—however wrong we think it is. Do you even think she *is* wrong? How do you feel about this *being human* stuff?"

He pushed back his chair and stood up, offering a blank face. But he couldn't hide his scent. He was scared and angry. "I don't think that's any of your concern. I feel fine. It'll just take some time to adjust."

Apparently the meeting was finished. She hadn't really been done talking, but there were an awful lot of things to do before she could get some sleep. And frankly, she wasn't sure she wanted to get any further inside Lucas's head. He never had said whether he thought Tatya was wrong for how she thought of humans. And if he did believe the same, she didn't want to know. She opened her mouth, then closed it again. She nearly offered to talk to Tatya if he thought it would help. But she really didn't think it would . . . and she really didn't *want* to.

Lucas held the door for her, just like he always had at the restaurant. She felt another pang of pity for him, but there wasn't anything she could do about it.

They parted ways without a glance.

Maybe that was best.

Holly passed by Eric on her way outside. She needed to breathe air that wasn't scented with negative emotions. If there wasn't so much danger, she'd love to go for a run. But as it was, maybe she could just find a quiet place where there weren't terrified, worried, angry people to push their emotions up her nose and make her sad.

Do you really feel that way, Holly? She heard Eric's tentative voice in her mind. Do you want to be human again that badly? Enough to risk everything you've gained?

He heard it all? Crap. She hadn't meant to inflict all that baggage on him. "Yes. No. I don't know." She whispered the words under her breath as she stepped out the door. She wasn't lying. There were parts she liked, and parts she didn't. "Can I be alone for a little while? Is that even possible with our connection?" She looked up at the nearly full moon, pale and round in the night sky. It pressed against her skin like a too-tight sweater and made her itchy. There'd be no relief from it until it began to wane.

Tony taught me a couple of things earlier. They might work. But I would like to talk to you about this. Soon. Especially since our relationship is hanging in the balance.

Something happened inside her brain. It was like a screen door banged shut and her mind felt a thousand times clearer. *There's your problem, right there.* She didn't want to care about Eric, but she always had. What if both of them were human? Would there be any attraction at all?

God, if there was just someone to talk to who would understand. But everybody here was all on one side of the argument. *What I need is perspective.*

"What I *need,*" she said with determination, as she spied a small tower rising from one of the land yachts, bearing a familiar gray dish, "is the Internet."

THERE WAS NOTHING to do except think. An hour had passed, then two, as Eric guarded the door to a room not much bigger than a walk-in closet. Bruce had cried and then mumbled for a long time, but now was still. He could hear him turning over, trying to get comfortable. But there was no comfort to be had. There wasn't even a chair in the room, and nobody was around to relieve Eric so he could go get one.

He couldn't understand how Holly could hate the wolf she'd become. He couldn't imagine not being a wolf, to not be able to run and hunt, to hear and smell things that others couldn't imagine. But then, he didn't remember being human. He'd known he was Sazi before he turned ten. All he could remember was the freedom that came with fur. He could climb higher, jump farther, and rarely got hurt. And too, he'd been one of the elite, the son of a pack leader. School was a whirlwind of privilege, good times, and great friends—a place to escape from Derek's constant torment and devious tricks to get him in trouble. Eric had seen the seeds of his brother's dark side even as a child. Except his parents wouldn't believe it of their golden son.

What would it have been like to suffer his brother's torture and have everybody look down on him, simultaneously? Would he have joined a group like FMU?

He shook his head without realizing it. *No, I can't imagine doing that. Their goals are just wrong. They only encourage anger.* Thank goodness Holly had gotten out of the group before they fell off the deep end. He'd like to throttle more than a few people in that organization. To turn someone like *Lucas* into a mere human—

The sound of approaching footsteps brought him fully alert. But when his nose told him it was Lucas and Tony he relaxed a bit.

They both dipped their heads in greeting and he returned the gesture. "Eric, Tony is going to take watch for a while. We need to talk." Eric glanced at Tony. It appeared that he was alert, despite the fact it was nearly dawn.

Apparently he telegraphed his thoughts on his face, because Tony let out a little chuckle. "I just woke up from a nap. I'm a lot better off than you right now. Plus, I've *met* Nasil. If anyone's going to try to spring the prisoner, that's who it'll be."

Eric waved his hand toward the empty chair. "Be my guest. Hope you brought a book."

Tony tapped his temple with his hand. "I've got a wife to keep me company. You'll be surprised how handy that is when you're bored, once you both get the hang of it."

Except she doesn't want *me in her head.* But Eric didn't say that out loud. It was nobody's business.

Lucas was waiting at the door of the conference room where the speakerphone was located. But when Eric followed him inside, he didn't reach for the satellite phone. He instead sat down and motioned to an empty chair. "Have a seat."

"Is there a problem?" Eric asked. He knew Lucas didn't really have a say over him anymore, but he did merit some respect.

"We've been trying to reach out to pack leaders all over the world, in order to update them on the situation at hand. So far, the only group we *haven't* been able to reach is Quebec. Have you heard from anyone?"

He shook his head and let out a sigh. "Other than Holly's sister, Iris Renault, nobody has shown up down here. And she left the pack days ago, before any of this happened."

"When Josette called her. I know." Lucas nodded. "Your mother was the Alpha Female, and your brother the Alpha Male of that pack. Since we're unsure of their status, the council is considering you the de facto pack leader of Canada. Do you accept that appointment?"

"No." Eric was surprised at how calmly the word came out. No laughing hysterically or spouting a string of swear words. "If I'd wanted the Canada pack, I would have challenged my brother for it. I don't. If the council gives me Four Corners, I'll accept it." He shook his head. "But not Canada."

"Is there a particular reason you're refusing?" Lucas was holding his emotions in check so well that Eric couldn't figure out where this was leading. But hadn't Lucas been a prosecuting attorney for a number of years? No doubt he was pretty good at keeping his cards close to his vest.

Eric could play that game if he had to. "I don't think there's any requirement that I give a reason. Or has that changed?"

Lucas shook his head and sighed. "No, that hasn't changed. But I'm *asking* you to tell me. It could help me figure something out."

Eric felt his brow furrow. "Does the council even know you're here talking to me?"

A small smile curled one side of the man's mouth.

"You catch on quick. That's a good thing in a pack leader. This isn't a council matter. It's a Wolven one. You're free to leave the room if you want. Of course, I could simply reactivate your commission in Wolven. Then you'd *have* to answer me, as your boss."

Eric blinked several times, processing that. "But you're human. Can you still *be* the head of Wolven?"

Lucas's smile faded. But there was a hint of amusement in his eyes. "The position is *appointed*, not filled by election. And as I reminded Antoine and Ivan, only Charles can remove me. They're not happy about it, but there's nothing they can do without the full council to override it."

"So you weren't going to *tell* me I was free to go unless I asked. Is that it?"

The only response from Lucas was a small shrug. "Will you answer the question or do I bring in Ivan and Antoine?"

He should just walk out. Without a full council, Lucas probably couldn't get a warrant and Eric wasn't sure they could actually reactivate him. He really hoped not, because the *last* thing he wanted was to be an agent again. It was frustrating, stressful work that demanded constant diligence every waking hour and a cold brutality that he'd tried long and hard to forget. Still, his curiosity was tickled. What could Lucas be up to? "Let's just say Derek and I had a difference of opinion on how the pack should be led."

"Did you feel he was too lenient with the pack members?" Again, with no particular emotion.

There was no helping the bitter laugh that jumped

out of his mouth. "I can honestly answer that question with a firm *no*. I woke up pretty much every day completely amazed that nobody had killed Derek in his sleep."

"So you felt he was likely to be killed by another pack member?"

Ah, now he saw where this was going. He held up his hand. "Before we go any further, Lucas, it's only fair to tell you that I'm double-mated to Holly. Your conversation with her wasn't entirely . . . *private*." He tipped his head in embarrassment. "Actually, *none* of it was private. I got treated to the same rant you did. Trust me—after that, I started taking a crash course in shielding. But if you're asking whether the same situation she experienced in Boulder also existed in Canada, the answer is yes. Quite possibly, it was— *is*—worse. And it's worse in the snake nest I visited in Australia a few years back, if that matters any."

Lucas took a deep breath and held it for a long moment while he tapped one finger on the table. Eric didn't take his eyes off the man. When Lucas finally spoke, he changed the subject. "Ivan mentioned to me that your brother was about to be put down for attacking a human."

Eric didn't feel the need to discuss the details, so he just nodded once. "That's what I was told."

"Were you aware he had significant gambling debts owed to a casino in Atlantic City?"

Eric's brows lowered. "No, that can't be right. Derek didn't gamble. That's the one thing he *didn't* do. And he hardly ever left Quebec."

Lucas shook his head. "No, unfortunately, that is right. I didn't send Raina up there because of a pregnant human. That was just something she uncovered by accident when she was looking for the other evidence."

Eric had no clue where this was going. Raina was *sent* there by Lucas. Lately, he'd been giving all the assignments personally, from what Eric had heard from others. But *why*? "Even if you're right, gambling debts aren't really the sort of crime that's worth putting someone down for."

Lucas's voice was bland when he replied, but his scent spoke of a growing anger. "It is if he was in so deep to a certain group of people . . . or more precisely, a group of Central American *snakes*, that he was willing to sell secrets to them."

Eric wanted to tell Lucas that there was no possibility of that happening, but hadn't Mom mentioned the "foreign dignitaries" Derek had been entertaining from South America? It wouldn't take much for his mother to get confused about the location. She considered anything south of Niagara Falls to be "South America."

Eric's mouth went dry. "What *sort* of 'secrets'?"

"The locations of all pack headquarters. The names and addresses of alphas. The meeting places of the hunts. Information he'd have access to as a pack leader, and all of it useful to an enemy planning a coordinated attack. Raina found all the evidence we need to put it before the council. The question is, what do *you* know about it? You were his Second for years."

Eric couldn't answer. His mouth wouldn't work. In fact, none of his body parts would work. He felt completely numb, and more horrified than he'd ever felt in his life. *Derek, what have you done?* "I . . . I don't know *anything* about it. In the first place, I wasn't his Second—not in truth. I was just his little brother. And I've been in Australia for two years—ever since I retired from Wolven. He never took a trip outside the country when I was in the pack, and we never had snakes visit Quebec."

Lucas nodded. "But you just told me that you visited a snake nest in Australia."

Eric pushed back his chair and stood up. "I have *nothing* to do with any of this. Whatever *this* is." He held up a finger and heard his own voice increase in volume. "I knew one person in Australia when I arrived. *One.* Carl Davros, who I met at a band camp in secondary school, and who happens to be a snake. I slept on his floor for a couple of weeks until I found a place to live. He's never met my brother, and I didn't introduce them."

Lucas's brown eyes might not hold magic anymore, but they had a weight that made Eric step back a pace. "I believe you. Maybe I can't smell emotions anymore, but I can still read body language."

Eric let out a breath he didn't know he was holding. "So is that all you wanted? To ambush me and see if you could surprise a confession out of me?"

"Never hurts to try."

The chuckle that emerged was bitter and filled with the annoyance Eric felt. "Yeah it does. It scared me out of a year's growth." He motioned to the door. "Can I go now? I'd like to get some food and then collapse."

Lucas nodded. "Fine. But you are to report to me *immediately* if your brother tries to contact you. We're not certain yet if your mother is involved, but we want to talk to Derek as soon as we reach the pack up there."

Eric nodded as Lucas stood. He turned to the door as though to leave, but then paused with his hand on the knob. Lucas smiled, but there was no humor behind the flash of teeth. "In fact, let me make your duty clear. You're officially reactivated. Welcome back to Wolven, Agent Thompson."

Chapter Nineteen

THE SILVER-AND-BLACK WOLF had backed against the cliff so tightly he was hunched over on himself. He was baring his teeth, and his hackles were raised, but the stink of fear that painted the air told Nasil the wolf *knew* he was no match for the snakes and spiders who surrounded him.

They waited impatiently for Nasil to make the slightest twitch of his hand that would tell them to attack. Even Marduc, flapping overhead hard enough to raise a wind, was growing frustrated. "Why do you hesitate, Nasil? Destroy the wolf so my people can be fed."

"No." He felt her slap of power as she punished him for refusing, but it bounced off. Ever since they'd had sex, he'd been feeling his power grow. He felt like himself again for the first time in a year, and far more clear-headed. "I would talk to him first. Alone."

"You overstep yourself, my mate." Marduc's words were a hiss that should have terrified him. But it didn't. "I am hungry and he has power. The eggs must have his magic, and game is growing scarce nearby."

He looked at the blurry form above him and spoke into her mind. *This is the wolf who was selling secrets to Sargon about the positions of the packs. I believe he can be of use. We can use him to find out what alphas are in the camp below. If we take them out, one at a time, then—*

Then the rest of the lives there would be mine to terrify and feed on. Her voice sounded pleased. *But the alphas are strong and much of my power is going to feed the eggs until the serpent moon comes. I have little energy to battle them. It's why I plan to send the spiders and snakes before me—to wear them down.*

The Serpent Moon? But that was when Marduc was supposed to be born. What exactly was this Serpent Moon?

She heard his thoughts and laughed, the sharp sound of glass slivers crunching underfoot. *You would call it a "meteor shower" in today's language. They are strange and awful meteors that first arrived when I was born, and the world was new. They return every thousand years. Four times I have missed the call since I was of a maturity to bear young. I will not miss this time.*

Nasil nodded. A tiny voice screamed in the back of his head, but the thrum of power was too strong. He turned to face the snarling wolf. "Derek Thompson. We've met before. Do you remember me?"

"Yes." The word was guttural as the wolf lowered

his front haunches while flicking his eyes from the hissing snakes to multieyed spiders. "You were Sargon's lackey."

Nasil folded his arms over his chest and smiled darkly. "Hardly a *lackey*. His confidante, his right hand, but never a lackey. And now *I* lead, and you will follow *my* commands. Or," he said calmly, sweeping his hand to take in the enthralled Sazi around him, "I will snap my fingers and you'll die a slow and *very* painful death."

The wolf's eyes flickered as he stared skeptically at him. "I've battled worse odds . . . and won."

A laugh rolled out of Nasil's chest. He could taste the lie on the air. "You're bluffing. But even if you weren't, you haven't yet learned the meaning of *fear*. Marduc?"

She landed hard on the ground, causing a tremor that made rocks tumble from above. The wolf's ears flattened against his head. One of the lesser snakes, probably not more than a hundred and fifty pounds, was caught under Marduc's weight and hissed in abject fear before she closed her talons and sliced him into bloody ribbons. Derek watched the slaughter, though he couldn't see the cause, until the snake's head dropped one last time and the mouth opened in death. Then her power dropped him to his belly.

"Crawl before me, wolf, or I will invade your mind and drive you mad before I feast on you." Marduc's voice was low and sultry and sweet. Derek turned his eyes up to find the source of the sound instinctively. She took the opportunity to lean her head close to him. Nasil could feel her feathers nick his face as she passed and knew that even thick wolf fur wouldn't save Derek's skin from cuts.

But Marduc did more than scrape him. A flash of red sprayed into the air and the wolf yelped. It took Nasil a moment to realize she'd taken a nip from his ear. The tip was gone as though it had never been there and the scent of his panic filled the air. "What do you want from me?" Derek's voice quavered, just as it had when Sargon went to visit him. He was weak and no fit leader. But that worked well for their purposes.

"There is a knife in a cave near here. I want you to bring it back to us."

Derek tilted his head, but didn't move from where he was pressed against the ground, tail between his legs. "That's all?"

Nasil shook his head. "Not quite. There have been wolves here recently. I found their scent on the brush. If they've taken the knife, you'll follow them and take it away. If you find the knife, you'll still follow them. Make sure you find and kill the female wolf you smell after you have the knife. Her name is Holly Sanchez."

The female healer had to die. She could see him, so she most likely could see Marduc. That could ruin their plans. Nasil doubted the girl would be any match for Thompson.

"What does the knife look like?" Derek let out a hiss that would make a snake proud as another small piece of his ear disappeared. Marduc apparently had a foot on him, because he didn't move away from the pain.

"It's double-edged and made of obsidian, with a bone handle studded with turquoise."

A huff of air left the wolf as the invisible weight lifted from him. Nasil felt the stab of Marduc's feathers against his arm and the flick of her tongue across his chin.

"You have seen the Blade of Tolkrit? It's nearby?" she hissed.

He nodded. "It's what I used to—" An odd sensation twisted his stomach. He didn't like it, whatever it was. He shook his head. "Kill the human before I came to you." Hadn't the human had a name? Another shake of his head caused tiny cuts across his face.

Yes. Send the wolf. It's better if we don't touch it until the last moment. If it drains him, so much the better. I can feed from the knife when the time comes. That was why it was created—so I will have energy to sustain the young after I bury myself in my nest.

It made sense . . . like stocking a larder for the cold winter months.

"Remember, wolf," she said with a swing of her head. "Fail me in this and I will let my spiders feast. They prefer to eat you alive."

The wolf's eyes flicked to the snapping mandibles of the spiders. He nodded hastily. "I'll get your knife and remove the woman. And then my debt will be paid, right? I'll be free?"

Nasil stopped just short of laughing. Once they had the knife, the attacks on the Sazi could begin in truth. "You have twenty-four hours. If you bring back the knife, along with proof you've killed the girl, you'll owe no further debt to the snakes."

But would he be *free*? Nasil let the memories of old battles fill his mind. He reveled again in the screams of the dying that had sped his heart, and could still nearly taste the blood and terror of the conquered, who shrank and groveled when he passed. How long had it been since he'd been drunk on the taste of fear?

I think not. Nobody will ever be free again.

Chapter Twenty

HOLLY WOKE WITH a start when a door slammed nearby and the shouts of children filled the air. Bright sunlight glinting off glass made her squint and when she turned to get out of the glare, her funny bone hit the bottom of the table hard enough to make her see stars. That's when it occurred to her that she was lying sideways in the booth of the RV, her legs planted firmly on the floor. *Have I been here all night?* She remembered coming back to the trailer to see if her cell phone was charged and ducking under the table to disconnect it from the converter. As consciousness filtered into her brain, Holly realized she ached all over.

Maybe if I move really slow. Inch by inch she pushed away from the thin plastic cushion. One arm was nearly asleep and pins and needles flickered in her muscles until the healing magic began to kick

in. So far, so good. It wasn't until she had one arm
under her and started to turn to face the window
that her back muscles realized what she was trying
to do. Shooting pain flooded her brain and her arm
nearly gave out. She sucked in a sharp breath and
only let out a small yelp before slamming her good
arm on the top of the table to haul herself up the
rest of the way.

There was a rustling sound to her left and she
turned to see Eric, naked from the waist up under the
snow-white sheet, watching her with supreme amusement. God, he looked good enough to eat. His sun-
bleached golden hair was mussed, his eyes still sleepy.
All those muscles that she'd gotten to play with the
previous day rippled and flexed as he stretched slowly
with a wide yawn.

"You'd have been more comfortable in the bed,
but you fought me every time I tried to move you. So
I figured I'd better let you be."

She didn't remember that at all. But she did remember dreaming of being safe in a hole and having
bad things try to pull her out to eat her. "I didn't realize I was so tired. Guess I passed out as soon as I sat
down."

He shrugged one shoulder, and his scent drifted to
her nose. He smelled good—musky, but clean, like
he'd taken a shower before bed. "You've had a rough
few days. We *all* have." He slid his legs to the floor
and heat rushed to her face. The memory of those legs
wrapped around hers while he— *I need to get out of
here.*

Eric hadn't yet mentioned her rant to Lucas and Holly wanted to keep it that way. "Think I'll grab a shower real quick."

But her brain was ready before her body was, and when she slid out of the booth and stood up in a rush of motion, her legs collapsed under her.

Thickly muscled arms kept her from falling. "Easy there. Not so fast." The words were a whisper in her ear that made every inch of her body acutely aware of him. Holly felt frozen. One hand was tight around her waist and the other was flat on her thigh. Her leg was totally asleep and so far her magic hadn't healed it.

Eric began to rub his hand briskly up and down her jean-clad leg and lowered himself until he was sitting on the floor with her sprawled across his lap. Thankfully, when he'd leapt for her, the covers had gone with him. She didn't know if he was naked under the covers, and while part of her was curious, the other part—the *sane* part, said it would be a bad idea to find out.

Holly was staring hard at his neck. *Don't look in those blue eyes. Don't notice the way his tongue flicks over his lips when he's nervous or the way he smiles when he sees you. Everything will be fine if you just don't look.*

But apparently, looking had nothing to do with anything, because Eric lowered his head even while she stared dutifully at his neck and locked his lips over hers. Her entire body sprang to attention and her mouth opened without any conscious thought.

His tongue flicked in and out of her mouth and then swirled and wrapped around hers until she couldn't even think. Her breath was coming in short gasps when he finally pulled back from the kiss and she found she'd put her arms around him at some point, so tight it was hard for him to sit up. "Pity there isn't room in the shower for two," he said with enough heat to make her shiver. "I'd love to scrub your back . . . among other things."

She couldn't think of what to say, so she just nodded. Her heart was pounding so hard it felt like it was in her throat. And when he skimmed his hand over her, it felt like there were a thousand tiny feathers tickling her. She had to grit her teeth to keep from groaning, but even so, a tiny sound slipped out.

Eric chuckled possessively and her pulse raced even faster. "Now be honest." He whispered the words, right next to her ear. "Isn't this better than anything you had before you were a wolf? Why would you want to be human again?"

And there went her warm and fuzzy mood. Holly let out an annoyed sound and moved her arms away from his neck, pushing free of him. "Damn it, Eric. Why'd you have to ruin it? What does that have to do with anything?" She grabbed onto the table to pull herself up and turned her back on him, expecting him to get situated back on the bed.

Except he didn't go back to the bed. He sat down in the booth, totally buck-ass naked, his erection slowly wilting while he stared at her in confusion. "It has *everything* to do with this. Holly, when we used to talk at the restaurant, you wanted nothing more in life than to turn. *Nothing.* It was what you ate, drank, and slept. What's changed? You wanted to be a wolf, and you are. Terrific. Let's enjoy the perks that come with it."

What's changed? Had he really just asked her that? "Were you even *listening* when I was talking to Lucas?"

He nodded, frowning. "Yeah, I was. You said that you were abused because you were human. Now you're not. I'm not getting what the issue is."

She let out a chuckle and crossed her arms over her chest. "Eric, at the restaurant you talked to an abused, depressed, mixed-up teenager without a shred of self-esteem. I thought that being a wolf would fix everything. All the wolves were confident, strong, and smart." She tipped her head. "Okay, *most* of them were smart." She sat down across the table from him. "I *outgrew* that. It took me a few years, but I realized I didn't need fur to be me. I could just be *Holly,* and that was okay. By the time I was turned, I'd realized just how messed up the wolves were—both individually and as a pack. I wanted no part of them. But I didn't get a choice." She turned her eyes to stare out the window at the kids playing. "The kids out there don't know what they want any more than I did at their age." She shook her head. "I'd take it all back if I could. Corrine would still be third. I'd be human and would go merrily along with my life. I wasn't lying to Lucas, Eric. This isn't what I want."

He looked thoroughly confused. He was listening,

but it just wasn't sinking in. She could see it in his eyes. "But you're an alpha. And a healer. You became something more than most wolves. And you want to throw it *away*? Does that include me too?" He pointed at the floor where the sheet was still splayed sloppily. "You don't *want* what we just shared? The magic that flew around the tent when we made love? That wasn't a *bad* thing, Holly. If you think it was . . . well, I find that pretty damned offensive."

She shook her head and replied quietly. "No, sex with you wasn't bad. It was really, really good. But that's only one tiny part of all of this. Wouldn't sex be just as good if one of us was human? You wanted me when I *was* human. So are you saying that wouldn't have been as good?"

A small, angry chuckle erupted from him. "You say *sex* when I say *make love*. Was that all this was to you? Sex with an animal?"

She really didn't know what it was. Apparently she took too long to answer, because Eric stood up in a rush and reached for his clothes. He didn't bother to put them on. But before he stormed out the door, he turned back to her. "You need to figure out what you want in life, Holly. I thought we wanted each other, but if that's not what you want, tell me now while I can still walk away and find someone who has a little self-esteem. Apparently you still don't have any, because if you did, you'd be able to be *Holly*—with or without fur."

She opened her mouth to reply, but the slam of the door stopped her. Nobody seemed to notice the naked man walking across the crowded parking area. She watched until he opened the door of the main building. Lucas tried to stop him, but Eric just brushed right by, leaving Lucas to stare after him with his head cocked.

Her cell phone was still on the table, showing a full charge. She fingered it, wondering whether she should call Cat again. She'd never really had someone in her life that she needed to talk about. She'd always been the listener in conversations about relationship angst.

Did they even *have* a relationship?

There was just something about the word that made her stomach feel strange. *Dear God, I'm in a relationship with someone.*

"And it's not going very well," she said sadly to the empty room while staring at the main building.

Maybe it was better not to think about it for a little while. Her fingers flew over the touch screen of her phone as she tried to get to her e-mail account. There was something wrong with the page and after hopping to a few links on the main page, she discovered the Web mail server was offline for upgrades. *Great.*

She opened her Favorites list and scanned it. There it was—*Free Merchandise Unlimited*—the somewhat tongue-in-cheek title they'd given the FMU forum, thinking that most people would skip over a site that screamed "I'm going to scam you" that hard. She took a deep breath and tapped the link.

When she clicked on the General Discussion page, the very top thread made her catch her breath.

RIP. We'll miss you.

She hadn't yet logged in, but she opened the thread. The posts were all snippets, probably posted from cell phones while on the run. There was a screen name, a location, and either MIA or RIP with *Rumored* or *Confirmed* next to it. A dozen posts with sad-faced, shocked, or angry emoticons followed every name. She realized that the first post wasn't recent. It was from nearly a year ago, so apparently the thread documented deaths over a wider time. She double clicked on the "search this thread" link and entered the name *CandySweet* into the box. Post 92 listed her as *Confirmed* and Holly felt sad for her loss all over again. She started back at the top and scrolled down the posts. She knew of most of the early deaths—sometimes the result of something as simple as a car crash or heart attack. Then she saw a name that made her stop dead.

LittleSis. Boulder, CO, RIP. Confirmed.

It was dated the night she survived her first change and became a wolf. The poster wasn't one she recognized, and hers was the only post the person had made. Someone had signed on with a new user name to leave the information, so nobody would know where the post came from.

She hesitated before clicking on the log-in screen. Would she still even *have* an account? *It doesn't matter. If I don't, I'll make a new one.* They deserved to know about the others, even if they didn't want her around. After a deep breath, she tried to sign in, and found she still could. She immediately went to start a post on the thread. Just typing the letters was somehow cathartic. She snuffled and moved the phone a little farther away when her tears began to fall. She didn't want to get the screen wet.

Rosebud, Coober Pedy, South Australia, RIP. Confirmed.

Char186, Coober Pedy, South Australia, RIP. Confirmed

She kept typing names in a list, until *Nobodystoady, Hissyfit, DickODoom*, and the others were immortalized in print. Then she dropped a line and typed:

LittleSis, Rumors of RIP premature. Turned. Confirmed.

Finally, she dropped down two lines and added: *Breakneck, RIP. Confirmed. Admins and Super-Mods, please take note.*

Another deep breath and then she pressed the Post Reply button. Her avatar, a fuzzy wolf puppy with little sparkles around the brown eyes, looked out at her for the first time in a very long while. She stared at the list for what must have been several minutes and then hit the Refresh button. A flurry of posts followed hers. Most were the same sad faces as on previous posts, but there were some actual comments and they made more tears well in her eyes.

OMG, LittleSis! I'm soooo sorry! Rosebud was the best. Hang in there.

Welcome back LittleSis. Sorry for you—for both reasons.

Love and kisses, LittleSis. 411? What's the sitch?

Of course, there were a few snotty replies, but there always were. Yet the majority of people were glad she was there, and nobody commented too harshly on her confirmed turn.

But the one at the end made her pause.

Confirm again Nobodystoady. Are you certain? :(I've been worried sick.

She looked at the screen name. It was Matthew's own profile. Someone he knew well was logging on to find out information. Was this a parent, or his sister? She'd never met Beth, but he'd spoken of her often.

She hit the Post Reply again. *Can't confirm visual. But have it on good authority. Dalebud survived the attack and relayed. Private Message me and I'll give you more details.*

Another flurry of reponses followed, and each bore only one word: *Attack?*

They didn't know? How could they *not* know about the snake attacks, or "the cure," with all the packs scattered and people dead?

She sat up straight and thought for a moment. What if it *wasn't* the FMU who did that to Lucas? She'd presumed, because Dale had said so. But now she was wondering. She'd blamed it on being out of the group so long, but maybe it was just a splinter group of the FMU who went radical, and nobody else had a clue.

What would Lucas say about her making this stuff public? Was this a situation where it would be better to ask permission or forgiveness? She shook her head. *They'd never grant permission.* But the Sazi needed eyes and ears out there if there was any chance they could be relied on. *Would they help if the cause was serious enough?*

Blood was often thicker than water. She knew well that when it came down to life or death, old hurts flew out the window—forgotten in family unity. In the end even her sister Jasmine had tried to defend her from the bad guys, at the cost of her life. Not everybody came on the forum because they *hated* their family. Most just came for companionship. Sure, it was fun to bitch and have people validate your complaints, but not everybody meant what they posted in anger.

She clicked on the button that said New Thread, and typed a one-word title.

Attacks.

She paused. It would be quicker and easier to use text-speak to type this, but she knew a lot of the older family members who posted here weren't that up on the abbreviations. Anything more than LOL or BTW totally confused them.

It took a long time to type out every letter and space on the tiny keys. When she was finished, her hands were aching and she had to stand and stretch. She stared out the window at the playing children for a long moment, enjoying the laughter and activity. Then she sat down to read the entry again before she posted it.

A lot of you have questioned my post in the RIP thread, and I admit to being surprised so few of you seem to know what's been going on. All over the world, packs, prides, and nests have been forced to scatter after coming under violent attacks by bespelled and enthralled snake and raptor shifters. They're under the control of a big bad named Marduc and . . . well, we're not sure how to stop her. It wasn't just in Coober Pedy where there are multiple deaths. It's everywhere. If you haven't checked in with the shifters in your family, you need to. Now. I fear many of you won't be able to reach them. I can't tell you where they are, even though I may know in a lot of cases. Wolven is involved in this and while they're trying hard to get details, a lot of their agents took the brunt of the attacks.

Yes, I'm Wolven now. I know. Shocking, considering. But I'm not here to hunt any of you. I'm just trying to be fair by telling you what's going on. I'll probably lose a strip of hide for my trouble.

The other reason I want to post is because it's not just Marduc who's attacking and destroying lives. It's you—us—the FMU. For those of you who knew, I can't begin to tell you how angry I am that you did this. You're no better than the worst of "the animals." You didn't ask whether they wanted your "help." How is it any different to force your will on others, than what you've endured? You've taken away some of our best and brightest—and, damn it, we need them to battle this threat. There are attack victims, like me, who would have given their eyeteeth for "the cure," and you've wasted it on those who never did anything to you except try to keep the world safe. You've destroyed matings. Matings. Couldn't you have at least picked people who were single? You wanted them to hurt. Fine. They are. Happy now? But I've had to watch what happens after, and y'know what? They hurt. They feel. Just like we do.

So, now we're all stuck with what a few of you have done. We've got an enemy that nearly kicked the collective asses of Charles, Lucas, and Jack back when they were in their prime. You all know who they are and what they're capable of, so we have a big problem. What I wouldn't give for a little of that "cure" to toss on the enemy who's going to burn down the world shortly.

I wish you all well. I suppose I'll end this by saying you should run if you can, and hide if you must. Marduc's coming, and there's probably no place she won't find you. You should know she's invisible to everyone (so far) but me, so you won't see her coming. Trust me when I say she's the ultimate enemy—a flying snake with metal feathers who tossed around a councilman like he was a ball of yarn. I'll be standing by those I love to put up a fight. Will probably be back in the RIP post soon. But I can't make you join me there. I'll give you a choice, what some of you took away from others, and what so many of us took for granted.

LittleSis signing off. Hopefully not for good.

She copied the post, just in case she'd timed out, and then hit the Post Thread button. Now all she could do was wait to see what people thought. No doubt there'd be responses. There were *always* responses to controversial shit.

There was a lot of activity around the main building now and Holly wondered what was up. Nobody had come to get her yet, but she might as well go face the music. But before she went, her teeth felt sticky and she ached. There wasn't much in the way of hot water, but even a quick rinse would help.

She used the same toothbrush she had yesterday. It had been new, still sealed, so she figured it was fair game. Eric had been right—there wasn't room for two in the shower. She couldn't imagine how there had been room for *him*.

What the hell was she going to do about him? Was he right? Had she never gotten over her low self-esteem and just been blaming it on the fur? She hated the thought, but she never really had given in and let the wolf control her. She hunted alone, healed when forced to, and mostly tried to pretend it didn't exist. What would it be like to revel in the experience like Eric did? To look *forward* to the moon rise?

The RV was starting to feel too small. She needed

to go outside into the sunshine. She took the cell phone with her. There wasn't any reason she couldn't read posts in the sun.

Soon she was sitting on a lawn chair she borrowed from the neighboring trailer, breathing in the cool, crisp air, and chomping on a bacon sandwich offered by the same neighbor. Meat was probably a good thing this close to the moon.

She tucked her feet under her on the flimsy chair and rested the cell phone on her knees so she could eat with one hand. As soon as she logged on at FMU, a new screen popped up, showing there were three private messages in her mailbox. The first was from the owner of the site, *Rattlegurl*, thanking her for telling them about *Breakneck*. She promised Holly they'd keep the flame wars on her thread to a minimum since they felt it was an important "other side" to the discussions that normally appeared.

The second message was from *Nobodystoady*. She opened it after taking a deep breath.

Hi, Holly. I'm Beth.

Matt talked about you a lot. Thought I'd update you on what I've found out. We called the Coober Pedy police after we saw your message and they confirmed there was a "massacre" at Rose and Dale's house. A body was found with Matt's wallet. Mom's flying over to identify. We're trying to hold onto hope, but I fear you're right. Dale was taken in for questioning, but has been released and is no longer a suspect. They

have a man in custody that they think is respon-
sible. A Honduran national named Paolo Mon-
tez. They weren't supposed to release his name,
but it slipped. If you're right about the bespelled
snakes, then Wolven's going to have to do some-
thing, because they denied bail. The full moon's
tomorrow. Thank you for posting what hap-
pened. I knew Matt was getting into something
big, but could never figure out what. He was
spending a lot of time around some shady char-
acters, and we were afraid something bad might
happen. We didn't even know he was in Austra-
lia. Last we heard was he was in Central Amer-
ica. I'm afraid I don't know anything about
this "cure" but I hope you find what you're
looking for.
   Blessings and peace, Beth

She replied with a simple, *Thank you, I'm sorry.*
There wasn't really anything more to be said.

The final message was from a new user, called
Bluetomcat. He had a total of one post, probably put
up just so he could send the message. Her breath
stilled as she read and she abruptly looked around.
The poster was *here*, in the camp.

Hey, LittleSis.
   I know you and Dr. Santiago have been work-
ing really hard to put us all back together. I
would have lost my youngest to a snakebite if not
for you guys using your magic. Maybe I've been

*taking my own issues out on the wrong people.
All I know is that everybody here has been trying to keep us safe and comfortable. I didn't expect help from the animals, but before now I
didn't know any other than my family. Those
Wolven guys are amazing. They stand watch for
hours, slam down some coffee, and go back to it
again. It's like the National Guard after a flood,
y'know? You don't really appreciate what they
do until you see it firsthand. Anyway, the reason
I'm writing is that I think I can help. I was one of
the people given a vial of "the cure." I was supposed to help in the attacks, but nobody ever
told me I had to, and I just couldn't convince
myself it was necessary. After reading your
post . . . well, I want out. Maybe since you can
see the enemy, you can do something. I don't
know, but I'm really worried, because when
Wolven and the council are running scared, I
figure the situation's bad. I'm probably a chick-
enshit for not just handing it to you in person,
but I don't have life insurance to take care of the
girls, and I can't imagine Wolven would have
much sympathy for me after what I've done. I
can't fix Lucas, but maybe I can keep him alive
to be with his family after this, like I'm with
mine. I'll put the package in the wheel well of the
trailer you're staying in. Good luck.*

She looked over at the trailer. There was no sign of
any sort of package yet, but no doubt the vial was

small. She hit the Reply button and typed a simple, *Thank you. Will do what I can.*

"What the hell do you think you're doing, Sanchez?" Holly started so hard the chair rocked and nearly fell over. Her finger automatically hit the Log Out button, just like she used to do when Dad would catch her online.

She looked up to see Tony standing over her, rifle still slung over his shoulder. "Um, just surfing the Net to kill time."

He reached for the phone so fast she nearly couldn't end the Internet session, but she saw it blink off just before he raised it to look at. He pressed the Call button and swore when the dial tone buzzed. "I cannot *believe* this!" He shook his head and started to walk away.

"Hey!" she shouted and leapt from the chair so quickly her foot got tangled for a second. "Come back here with my phone!"

But he had too much of a head start. He reached the main building in seconds and even though she was hot on his heels, she couldn't get the phone away from him. He blocked her effort to grab it and growled. "Knock it off, kid."

"Tony? What the hell are you doing? We're supposed to be helping these people, not threatening them." Lucas glared at the pair of them, but his jaw dropped when Tony tossed the phone his way. He caught it on the fly and stared in utter disbelief at the screen.

"Our new healer has been playing on the Internet. The phone works too."

Lucas turned shocked eyes her way. "How long have you had a phone signal, Holly?"

She shrugged. "Couple of days. Why?"

"Oh, for God's sake! Why in the hell didn't you *tell* us? We could have been contacting other packs for two days."

What was all the fuss about? She pointed toward the stairs. "You have a phone inside. What's the big deal?"

Tony let out a burst of laughter. "That's a special, secure satellite link-up, kid. You have to know the GPS location or another set's ID to reach anyone. You can't just call a phone number and have it ring." He pointed at the phone. "Not a single person here has a working phone. The raptors and snakes took out the local cell towers when they attacked. Even the land lines in Cortez are down, waiting for repairs. We've been blind and deaf, and you've been *surfing the Net*. See why we're a little ticked?"

Okay, that was embarrassing. She felt her face heat as they both looked at her with heads shaking. She mumbled under her breath, "Well, you could have used Raphael's too."

Lucas scowled. "Excuse me? Raphael has a phone that works too?"

She shrugged. "Probably. Cat gave me this one for Christmas, and I know she gave Raphael an even better one." She pointed at the screen. "His number's in the phone book. You can call him to see if he has it with him."

Lucas punched the buttons so hard she was afraid he was going to put his finger right through the screen. A second later, she heard ringing on the line, and then Raphael's voice. "Hello?"

"Jesus Christ, Ramirez!" Lucas yelled. "You had a goddamn working *phone* and you couldn't mention it when you got here?"

There was a long pause and then a sheepish reply. "You said the towers were out. I didn't even . . . um, think to look." Another pause. "Oops."

"Oops? *Oops?*" Lucas thundered. "Get your ass back here with that phone. We've got calls to make."

"But *you're* calling *me*. That means the phones are back, right?"

Tony was shaking his head, his fingers rubbing the bridge of his nose, a grin that was as much frustration as humor on his face. Lucas sighed. "No, it means we have *Holly's* phone. Apparently, your phones don't require cell towers."

She could almost see Raphael blush. "Oh. Probably not. Cat designed them. She's been thinking of marketing a new phone. Come to think of it, these two were probably the prototypes. Didn't even think about it until now. Sorry, Lucas. Really, I am. You want to send someone for it?"

Lucas's deep sigh sort of said it all. "No. Just start calling anyone you know from there. We need reports from anyone you have a number for. I presume the number for this phone is in your list, so have them call here." He pressed the button to end the call and started to scan down her phone directory while speaking. "Sorry, Holly, but I'm confiscating this until we try to reach everyone. Go get your charger and bring it back here." He passed it to Tony. "You first. Get hold of Nikoli or anyone else you can, or contact Sue and give her this number so they can call us."

Holly nodded, happy the phone might help. Plus, if she went back to the trailer for the charger, she could also get the vial of the cure. She didn't want to mention it yet, in case *Bluetomcat* changed his mind. "The number's printed on the back. Oh, and keep an eye on the minutes. This is a prepaid unit, so when they're gone, they're gone, and long distance takes two or three at a time. I can buy them online, but I need at least ten minutes left to do it."

Lucas pointed. "Go. Get the charger. I'll take care of getting more minutes." He turned and stalked toward the stairs with Tony on his heels. "Hold off on those calls, I guess. We need to load up the minutes first."

Holly saw Eric coming up the stairs just as Lucas was going down. He looked her way and immediately smiled. But then the smile turned to a frown. Rather than face him, she turned and left, letting the door shut behind her. She raced across the large lot, heading for the trailer. It didn't look any different than before, but she decided to stop to retie her sneaker next to the first wheel well. A quick glance didn't show anything, so after looking around to see if anyone was watching her, she felt up and around the inside of the metal.

Nothing.

She repeated the exercise at the next set of wheels before she stopped, chagrined. Of course he wouldn't put it in the wheel wells that faced the public. *Duh. It has to be in one of the back ones—if he hasn't chickened out.*

But first, the charger. She opened the trailer door and stepped inside. It was where she'd left it, under the table. She probably wouldn't need the twelve-volt converter, but she took it along anyway. After a quick trip to the bathroom she tried to figure out how she could check those other two wheels without being obvious. She glanced out the windows again. *There are just too many people.*

The thought made her blink.

Why did it matter if anyone saw? Did it need to be a secret? Why was she making it one? *Part of me wants it for myself.* It was the truth, but was so totally wrong on every level. It could possibly save them all from Marduc. *Or maybe it will have no effect and I'll have wasted it.* She shook her head, realizing she needed to think about this more. Maybe she *was* still too messed up to have anyone in her life.

WHAT IN THE heck was Holly doing around the trailer wheels? The tires didn't look flat. But no, she was examining them—like she was looking for something. A key? Was she locked out?

No, that wasn't it. Eric watched as she opened the trailer door and stepped inside. What the hell? He crept up to the trailer and listened. When he heard her slide open the bathroom door, he went around the back of the trailer. There was a small cardboard box tucked up on the axle behind the second wheel well.

Holly's name was scrawled on the box in pencil. He opened the tape and found two metal vials about the size and shape of a toothpick case, wrapped in tissue. One had a chain attached, like it was a necklace, but the other didn't. Each bore a white label with the identification, RSA17, in black marker. Eric felt his blood run cold as he remembered his conversation with Dale. Someone was giving Holly the cure. She must have *asked* for it. How could she hate this life so much?

He stared at the vials for what seemed like a lifetime, but when he heard the toilet flush, he realized he needed to do something quick. Closer examination revealed that the vial without the chain had a second label, also handwritten in pencil. *Sorry, I lied. I had two. Yours if you decide to go back.*

If you decide to go back. Then what was the first one for? What was she planning?

Eric took the second vial and slipped it into his pocket. She was only expecting one, and that's what she'd find. He put the box back where he found it, and hoped she wouldn't sniff around too hard to notice he'd been there. He was willing to give her the benefit of the doubt, but he also eased open the mental connection. If she revealed anything that could endanger her . . . or *him*, he'd step in. He wasn't sure what would happen if Holly turned human again. Tatya wasn't doing so well, and that was only a one-sided mating.

Tony held open the door for him when he made it back to the building. He had his brows raised in interest. Apparently, he'd been watching as Eric skirted around the trailers so Holly wouldn't see he'd been there. "Anything you'd like to tell me?" he asked as Eric walked past.

He shook his head, but couldn't meet the other man's cold blue eyes. "Woman trouble. It'll pass."

That apparently satisfied Tony, because he just nodded. "Lucas is waiting for you to make your calls. Better head down."

Lucas had found a way to hook up the cell phone to the speaker so everybody could hear. Eric had heard Amber Wingate's voice once or twice when she'd visited with Charles. She sounded exasperated. "Why would the seers tell you to do that? It makes no sense. Ahmad and Bobby are both double-mated. They wouldn't be *able* to have sex with Marduc. As the Wolven physician, I can assure you they physically *can't* get excited by another woman. No matter the physical stimuli, they wouldn't be able to ejaculate. Double-mates can't cheat. Tell Raphael to bring them back in. They'll be fine—if he didn't already damage them too much by the death touch. Good God, people! Use your *brains*."

Eric entered the room to find Lucas, Antoine, and Ivan looking somewhat abashed. Lucas cleared his throat and nodded Eric toward a chair. "Um, the Four Corners pack leader just arrived, Amber. I'll have to ring off so we can see if we can reach Canada. Is there anything you want us to do about Charles? Or should we just keep him comfortable and let him come out of the trance by himself?"

So Eric *was* officially the Four Corners pack leader? That was news.

"No," Amber said, frustration still in her voice. "He doesn't know *how* to come out of a trance. I couldn't get him to sit still long enough to learn. That man drives me crazy sometimes! But I can't come there. We're locked in Antoine's estate with snakes slithering all over the place. We've got wounded here that are pretty bad. I can't risk them, and I know Charles wouldn't want me to. Oh, and Antoine? I'm afraid we got into the pantry, and the wine cellar. I managed to hide away one bottle of that special cognac, but the rest is gone. It's the only painkiller I have for the humans." Antoine swore under his breath, but then sighed. She sounded apologetic when she continued. "Sorry, but I'm just too tired to put every person here in a healing trance. We really need to outfit your estate with a good-quality medical kit. As for Charles, maybe—" she paused. "I know what we can do. Once Raphael gets back there, call me." She chuckled ruefully. "I'm sure Charles is going to love this as much as you will, Lucas, but since I'm also mated to Raphael, I can mind link to him. Poor guy—I know he can't really help that all the women seem to mate to him, but it has to be rough on Catherine." There was a smile in her voice when she continued. "Tell our resident stud that he'll need to get Tatya and then touch Charles. I'll mind link to him and walk him through the process."

Ivan spoke up. "Not Tatya. She's not entirely stable right now. Lucas's condition has hit her pretty hard.

I don't trust her to enter Charles's mind. Could Holly Sanchez do it?"

Amber's voice perked up. "Holly's there? Sure. She's done healing trances before and has some excellent instincts. Pity she hasn't been trained properly, but she should be able to handle this."

Should Eric mention that Holly might *also* not be entirely stable? He glanced at Lucas and raised his brows in inquiry.

Lucas tapped one finger on the table, then nodded. "That should work. But if Holly's not available for any reason, could Raphael do it alone?"

Amber let out a small sigh. "Well, I'd *rather* not do that, if possible. He has some healing talent, but nowhere near enough to get my fluffy teddy bear out of a jam if it comes down to it."

My fluffy teddy bear. Eric nearly choked in an attempt not to laugh, and he wasn't the only one. Lips all over the room were being bitten and apparently Amber heard some of the chortles. "Yeah, yeah. So now you know what I call the Chief Justice. Like you don't have pet names for your mates."

Did he? Eric furrowed his brow. What was it he used to call Holly back in Boulder? He struggled to remember, but it just wasn't coming to mind. What about the old standbys—baby, sweetheart, or even darling? No, they didn't fit.

It had something to do with her scent. Flowers or strawberries—wait, that was it! Her sisters called her *Hollyberry* when they were in a good mood or when they wanted a favor. He'd called her *Berrybelle* and it had always made her smile.

He used to be concerned with making her smile as a human. He tucked his thumb into the watch pocket of his jeans, touching the cool metal vial. Would it be so terrible if she went back? Eric didn't understand it, but maybe he was making too big of a deal over it.

"It could be dangerous." The others had continued to talk while he'd been musing, but Amber's words grabbed Eric's attention. "I understand the need to get Marduc out of his head, but I can't guarantee that she won't be able to grab on to *all* of us if I try to seal his mind. Frankly, I'd rather just kill her and be done with it."

"Would her death hurt his mind if she's still connected?" Lucas's question was a good one and it made Amber swear.

"Shit! Okay, fine. Call me back as soon as Raphael gets there, and don't mention a *word* about this anywhere near Charles. Unless he's already kicked her out, Marduc's listening to all of you through him."

Antoine nodded. "That's why we put him in a sealed room. We put headphones on him, as well, with a CD playing on auto-repeat. I hope he likes Mozart. It was either that or country-western."

Amber burst out laughing. "I'm trying to imagine Charles waking up humming Patsy Cline. If this weren't so serious . . . but no. Mozart is fine. Call me back soon. I have to get back to my patients."

Lucas was chuckling as he ended the call. He looked at Eric and motioned toward the phone. "Your turn, Thompson. Call every number you know up north. I'd love to give you privacy, but there's no time for that. We're listening to every call so we can bring

Ahmad up to date when he gets back. Hang on for a sec."

He stood and walked out of the room. "Tony?" he called and then started speaking again after he got a response. "Go get Holly Sanchez, would you? We need to see her."

Then he returned to his seat and dialed a number. It was answered on the first ring.

"Raphael, it's Lucas. I'm here with Ivan and Antoine. We just got off the line with Amber, and—"

The Albuquerque pack leader interrupted. "No need to go on. Amber just contacted me mentally—a *trial run*, apparently. I'm on my way back with Ahmad and Bobby. We'll be there in fifteen."

The line went dead and the scent of Lucas's relief filled the room. He leaned back in his chair and motioned for Eric to dial with a wave of his hand.

Eric took a deep breath and dialed his mother's cell number. On the third ring he heard a click and a feminine, "Hello?"

It wasn't his mother. But Lucas recognized the voice. "Raina? Why are you on this line?"

"Lucas?" Her voice sounded surprised, but relieved. "*Finally!* I've been calling and calling, but keep getting busy signals. Where *are* you guys? It's like everyone fell off the map."

Lucas shook his head. "No time for an update. We have to wait for the owner of the phone to get back to tell us how to load more damned minutes on this thing. I promise, you'll get a full update later. Were you attacked up there?"

"Oh, hell yes. Six pack members dead, and the effing pack leader got away. I'm so mad I could spit!"

"This is Eric Thompson. Is my mother okay? Do you have any idea where Derek went?"

"I'm sorry. I can't release that information. It's Wolven business." The reply was automatic, but Lucas spoke up.

"We're all here together, Raina. Eric has just been assigned as pack leader of the new Four Corners pack. There are also two council members in the room. Ivan for the bears, and Antoine for the cats. You can give us a full report. But make it quick."

"Okay." Eric could barely hear the snarl of frustration she released. "Alpha Thompson—that is, *this* Alpha Thompson—oh, hell. Forget it. I'll call him Derek. I did as instructed and entered the pack headquarters after dark and searched the computer system. Lucas, you were right. There were a number of e-mails from the Central American group. But more importantly, there were pictures of Derek and *Sargon al-Akede* hidden in his desk. They were relatively recent ones too. Obviously taken from a distance. I can't imagine Sargon would want any evidence of his existence in a picture in someone's desk drawer, so I doubt he ever saw them."

Lucas looked at Antoine and Ivan. "So, it was going on longer than we thought. Sargon's been dead for a while now." The others nodded grimly. "Go on, Raina. What's the status of the alpha female?"

Raina let out another frustrated sigh. "She's here, but I don't know what to do with her."

"What's wrong?" Eric's adrenaline started to pump. If Derek had dared hurt her—

"She's the one who helped Derek escape. Cracked me over the head with a full bottle of champagne. The lump is just now healing. But she also protected the entire pack, including me, from the snakes. Didn't get a wound on her, and we only lost six against pretty overwhelming odds. That woman's fast and *mean* when she needs to be. Right now, everyone's in the pack gymnasium with the doors barred in case we missed any snakes. I've got Delilah under house arrest for collaboration and accessory to the escape. Mostly, she's seeing to the needs of the pack. Cooking and cleaning wounds and such. There's no healer here, but we've got some medical supplies and are hoping antibiotics will work on Sazi bites. I have to tell you, though, it just feels wrong to punish her for helping her son. Even if her son's a criminal, and an ass." Now her voice took on a tired quality. "You're the council, so you guys tell *me*—what do you want me to do with her?"

Eric sighed. That was so very like his mother. She could be a harpy, or a saint, or both at once. Lucas glanced his way but he could only throw up his hands. "Don't look at me. She's my mom. I'm staying out of this."

The Wolven chief looked at the two councilmen. They both shrugged, but Ivan spoke. "These are extraordinary circumstances we're in. Raina, is there any evidence Delilah was involved with Sargon, or knew anything about this attack?"

Raina's voice was confident. "None. And once I had her under lock and key, I went through *all* the computers here with a fine-tooth comb. When I showed her the evidence I found, including the photos of Derek and Sargon, she was appalled. I think if I'd showed it to her earlier, she might not have helped him escape."

There was a tap on the door and Eric stood to open it. Holly was on the other side and started visibly when she saw him. She couldn't look him in the eye and smelled of dusty shame. She was wearing a new shirt, one with a collar that nearly hid the silver chain she had around her neck. Did she know he'd found the box?

She kept her eyes on Lucas's chest until he waved her into the room.

Lucas shrugged. "Release her?" It was a question to the councilmen.

Ivan nodded, but Antoine looked dubious. "Temporarily. I'm not in favor of a wrist slap for knocking out a Wolven officer. But as you say, these are extraordinary times. We'll confer with Ahmad and, if possible, with Charles when he awakens."

Holly's face lit up when Antoine said that and Eric heard the first brush of her thoughts in his head. He wasn't sure if it was directed to him, or if it was just a stray thought to herself. *Charles is waking up? That will be a relief to so many people!*

He hasn't yet, He replied. *That's why you're here.*

She lifted her head to look at him with wide, panicked eyes. *I can't. I mean, I don't know how—*

Amber will be guiding you, through Raphael. She thinks you can do it . . . and so do I, Berrybelle. I might not be real happy about some things right now, but I do have faith in you. He stared at her, willing her to believe it.

Her eyes went wide when he used the old pet name and she seemed fidgety. But even though her nostrils flared, there was nothing to smell. Nothing for anyone in the room to smell.

Truth and faith didn't have scents.

Chapter Twenty-one

BERRYBELLE. THE WORD made little tingles race over her skin, just like it had a decade ago. *Just for you, Berrybelle,* he used to whisper in her ear as he passed by the counter, and she'd go searching for that one pink rose. It was the name she'd heard in her dreams for years after, even when she was so hurt by his sudden disappearance that she would cry herself to sleep.

But how could Eric be both angry and supportive? That didn't make sense. He could probably smell her confusion as the woman on the phone continued to talk.

"—a lot of work to do here. I'll copy all of the files onto a flash drive and bring them down with me. If you're confident she's not a flight risk, that is."

"No," Lucas said. "I don't want you leaving Quebec. Those people might still need protection. Just go to the train station or airport and rent a locker. Make sure you're not followed, of course. In fact, why don't you make *two* flash drives and mail one to Antoine's estate in France. Amber will keep it safe."

"Will do. Anything else?"

"Yes," Lucas replied with a grim tone. "Be careful. I don't think this is over—not by a long shot."

A series of heavy footfalls came from the next room and the door opened suddenly. Raphael, Bobby Mbutu, and Ahmad filed in. They all looked exhausted, like they'd been awake for a week.

Raphael opened his mouth, but Lucas held up a hand. "That's all for now, Raina. Keep a phone handy and we'll get back to you with more instructions." He ended the call and then looked at the men. "That was quick. I thought you said fifteen minutes."

Raphael shrugged. "That was based on obeying the speed limit. I decided to use my discretion about traffic laws on back roads. The suspension on that sedan holds up surprisingly well on gravel." Holly watched as he turned to her. He winked. "So, I guess it's just the two of us, huh? You up for waking a bear from hibernation, Healer Sanchez?"

She let out a slow breath and nodded.

Lucas furrowed his brow. "It might be a little early to ask that, Raphael. We haven't precisely told her what Amber said yet."

Eric raised a hand. "I did, just a few minutes ago. I didn't think you wanted to interrupt the phone call, so I said it through private channels."

Lucas nodded, as Raphael frowned in confusion.

"You've got a pack link with her already, Thompson? I didn't think you'd been formally assigned as pack leader."

Holly cleared her throat, feeling suddenly uncomfortable. "It's not a *pack* link, Uncle Raphael. It's more of a . . . *mating* one." She smiled and tried to make a joke of it. "Guess who'll be coming to Christmas dinner this year? If he's still speaking to me, that is." She didn't look into Eric's eyes when she said that.

Her uncle looked from one to the other, then shook his head and sighed. "Should have seen this coming, I guess. It took a death threat to get him away from you the first time."

Eric hadn't lied when he told her about Dad, but to hear Raphael say it so casually . . . "You know, you could have at least told me he didn't run off with Vicki. That was just cruel."

Raphael held up his hands. "That was *not* my idea. It was your father's. And it was better than the truth. At least you didn't go chasing after him. Not every solution is perfect, Holly. You needed a few more years under your belt before your judgment could be trusted. By the time you turned eighteen, I'd frankly forgotten."

Lucas slapped his hands down on the table, stopping any reply she might have made. "Daylight's burning, people. Let's get moving. We have a Chief Justice to wake and a Goddess to send back to hell."

ERIC WATCHED HOLLY and Ramirez walk into the next room with anxiety. He didn't like how Amber had said it could be dangerous. It reminded him of when the pack would go hunting and Holly would be at the restaurant all alone, closing up. Someone could have kicked in the door and robbed her, shot her . . . or worse. That was part of the reason why he'd left. He cared too much what happened to her. It was a daily struggle not to protect her from anyone who threatened her. He hadn't won any friends when he'd told Corrine to back off and leave her alone. He'd backed up the demand by gripping that pretty chin and threatening to pull it off her face. It had worked . . . at least while he was there.

Lucas stood, pulling his attention back to the present. "When Charles wakes up, he'll want to go on the offensive. I'm pretty sure he'll forbid me to go, even though I can still handle a sword pretty well. But there need to be at least three people. Ivan, you know swords, don't you?"

Ivan shook his bald head. "I haven't practiced in *years*. I'd be more liability than asset."

"Same with me," Bobby said. "I've practiced more with guns lately. I'm pretty good with a bow, if we have one of those."

"Then I suppose it is you and I again, Antoine," Ahmad said dryly. "Do try to keep up with me this time."

Antoine raised the sling. "I'm afraid this is my sword arm. It was broken in eight places. I'll need at least another day of healing to have enough strength for thrusting through those metal feathers."

"I'm pretty good with a sword," Eric said. "I competed in college."

Ahmad's brows rose. "I'll be the judge of that." The slender, olive-skinned man walked past him, leaking enough power to make Eric's skin sting. He followed Ahmad to the armory, where a variety of blades had been laid out. There were no cutlasses. These were mostly broadswords and were far longer than anything he'd worked with before. But then Eric saw a wooden handle peeking out from the corner. He reached down and pulled out a flat paddle of a weapon with glass embedded in the edge. Jack's war club. He recognized it from the hindsight. He flicked a finger across one of the obsidian flakes, then swung it lightly. It was perfectly balanced and the stone was easily as hard as metal. But could the wood hold up against a sword cut?

"I'll take this one."

Ahmad looked at him curiously. "I don't believe that will last long in battle, but you're welcome to try."

As they stepped out of the room, Lucas gave him an odd look. "Where did you get that?"

Eric shrugged. "It was hidden in the corner. Will it stand up against a metal blade?"

Lucas looked at Ahmad and then back to him. "I think you'll be surprised. Have you ever seen one used?"

He shrugged. "Only in Charles's memories."

Lucas smiled broadly and nudged Antoine. "You'll enjoy this. But sit well out of reach."

The main room was empty of everything except the tables.

"*En garde*," Ahmad said, and immediately swung

the sword as though it were made of paper. Eric side-stepped and held the club like a sword to block the blow. But he quickly realized that position wasn't to the weapon's best advantage. The sword had him on reach, so he needed to make the distance a disadvantage. And the goal wasn't to injure each other. There were plenty of enemies who would do that for them.

When Ahmad lunged again, Eric ducked and stepped inside his reach to deliver a powerful blow to the councilman's chest with the front of the weapon. The thick flat area that he'd seen Jack use as a club. It had broken the jaw of many a snake in the hindsight. Ahmad let out a harsh breath and stumbled back, but recovered quickly and landed a slapping blow against Eric's knee. It could have crippled him with the blade turned to cut—reinforcing that this was practice only.

"Thanks," he said with a dip of his chin. "I like that leg."

"Then you should protect it better," came the cold reply, before Ahmad turned and swung, intending to slice the tip of the sword across his chest. It wouldn't kill him, but the cut would sting for some time. Eric had no choice but to block the blow with the club and hope for the best.

Then something interesting happened. The blade stuck fast in the wood, locked between two of the obsidian flakes. Eric gripped the hilt with both hands and pulled down sharply. The blade bowed and the hilt was pulled from Ahmad's hand. Eric flipped the club over and lunged before Ahmad could react to the loss of the sword. With the extra weight of the attached steel, it took every ounce of Eric's strength to *stop* the blade before it sliced through Ahmad's bicep. As it was, it opened a small gash in the red silk shirt and Ahmad hissed in pain before leaping back.

"Sorry about that," Eric said with a wince as blood began to flow down the arm. "I tried to stop it in time, but the weight threw me."

"Yesss," Ahmad replied with enough power bleeding from him that the wound healed before Eric could even get the sword unstuck from the club. "I'm sssure you are."

Eric heard slow claps and turned his head. "You were right, Lucas," Antoine said, his eyes shining in amusement. "I always enjoy watching my esteemed council brother lose a sword battle. Disarmed *and* cut. Tsk, tsk, Ahmad."

Ahmad simply glared at Antoine and held out his hand for the sword. As Eric made to hand it to him he started to feel . . . odd. A familiar tickling sensation passed over his body. He had a brief moment of panic before he dropped to his knees as he was swept into a dark place.

"Just seal that breach!" He heard a woman's voice and could finally make out a vision in the golden light, as a compact spotted bobcat snarled at the two wolves beside her. He recognized Raphael as the black wolf with a single white paw, mostly because of the blue-white glow that surrounded him. The other wolf was Holly, and she was standing high on her back legs, as though she were straining to reach something. There was a sliver of darkness above her, as though something were trying to break through. Eric threw himself forward, came up under Holly, and raised her until she was standing on his shoulders. He felt his magic pour into her and then into the wall of darkness she was holding up. He didn't even know if she realized he was bracing her, and that was okay.

An image of Charles lying on a bed appeared and the bobcat let out a harsh breath. "I was planning for this to be a little more *relaxed* awakening, but we just don't have time for that. He can put up his own shields to hold her out, but he needs to wake up, uh, *mad.*" Amber stalked toward Charles, ears flat. "I've done this before, but it won't be pretty, people. Be prepared to take cover."

Amber regarded the man on the bed for a moment before nuzzling his nose. She sighed and shook her tawny, furred head. "Next time, teddy bear, sign up for lesson two." She unsheathed her claws as Eric watched, and proceeded to dig them into the big man's thigh. She pulled down sharply, released, and then did it again, almost too fast for his eyes to follow. Holy crap, she was making his leg into a scratching post!

A howl of rage filled the darkness and Eric was abruptly thrown backward. He came to in a flash of pain, in the room where he'd started, now empty. He could still hear a growling bear. Then he realized it was because there *was* a bear growling in the next room.

Eric winced as he stood and realized he must have fallen right onto the war club. Fortunately, it was flat under him, so the only cuts he'd gotten were from the sudden movement he'd made when he woke. Those obsidian flakes were like razor blades. His shirt was covered with tiny cuts that seeped blood when he walked. In a panic, he tucked his fingers into his pants pocket. The vial was safe, unharmed. His heart began to slow down, but then he heard an angry yell.

"I'll *kill* that woman! I swear I'll kill her."

Eric stumbled to the doorway. Lucas moved to one side so he could see. Charles Wingate was hopping around the room in a terribly undignified way, rubbing a leg that looked perfectly healthy. But Eric knew what Amber had done, and guessed there was some phantom pain involved in the process.

"Shields up, Charles," Eric said as a reminder, and the big man turned and blinked.

"What? Oh! Quite right, m'boy!" The power that was flooding the room was suddenly dampened. Charles growled again and tried to put some weight on his leg. He managed it with only a few small stumbles. "Amber did that once before when I was unconscious. Swore she'd never do it again. Damnable cat!"

Holly was on her knees, still looking a little dazed. "She said you had to wake up *mad* to get your shields up strong enough."

"Then she did an admirable job." Charles was calming down and squinting at the bright lights in the room. "Feel like I've been hibernating, and I suppose I have been." He looked around the room slowly, sniffing the air with his large nose. His eyes fell on Lucas and he seemed suddenly older, tired. "I'm sorry, old friend. I'd hoped . . . But you understand why I couldn't tell you."

Lucas nodded, and smelled of both sorrow and resolve. "You didn't lie. I'll live to see old age with my family."

Charles turned to Ahmad. "I presume you've selected your sword? You, Antoine, and I must go on the offensive at once. Now that she's been removed from my mind, she'll panic. We need to take full advantage of her confusion."

Ahmad gave a short nod. "Eric Thompson will accompany us instead of Antoine. I'm . . . *satisfied* with his skill."

Charles smiled. "I wasn't aware Eric was a swordsman, but I'm not surprised. Josette told me there was no reason to save any of you. And yet, it's *you,* those who might not have existed, who are here now and willing to fight. Each seer crafts the future as we see it. But my dear sister-in-law works on the premise that all chaos should be avoided, while I work on the premise that hope can turn chaos to our benefit if properly embraced."

Ahmad raised an eyebrow and smelled of mild annoyance. "Do you plan to wax philosophical for the entire trip?"

The big bear let out a rolling laugh. "I probably will, old friend. I probably will."

Chapter Twenty-two

NASIL WAITED AT the cave entrance while Derek dug through the scattered belongings. "There's no knife here."

He wasn't surprised. The body of the human was gone and even though there was blood evident, it wasn't enough to cause death.

He's alive!

Nasil shook his head. Where did that thought even come from? He strode forward and slapped Derek on the side of the head, knocking him to the floor. "Then use your nose and find out where it's been taken."

"You don't have to follow behind me. I can do a simple job." Derek's voice was sullen, but not angry enough to attack. And his scent was still cowed by the mass of snakes and spiders waiting outside.

"Then *do* it." Nasil turned and hissed to his comrades. They bowed and began to slither off into the distance. "The snakes will give you some time to get the knife. We'll get into position to start the attack as soon as you have it in your possession. But," he added in warning as he turned his back and started out of the cave. "Don't presume we'll save you if they find you. The knife isn't so important to us that losing it will harm anything." It was a lie, but he'd spent most of his life learning to believe lies, so there would be no scent to warn the wolf. Actually, now that Marduc knew of the knife's continued existence, it was her sole focus, so it was *his* sole focus.

You don't have to take her orders.

The voice annoyed him. No, he didn't *have* to. He *wanted* to.

Didn't he?

Find the knife, my mate. I will go now to find a nesting place. But I must have that knife, filled with alphic power, before the moon comes. I can feel the storm approaching. The time to fertilize your young is near. If not today, then tomorrow.

The time to fertilize? Hadn't they already been fertilized? Wasn't that what the endless bouts of exhausting sex had been about?

No, Marduc said sadly. You provided the seed, but only the magic of the serpent moon will make them live. You must protect me until then, keep me safe from harm.

Nasil threw up a small shield while she turned her attention to other things. Why did he keep getting only small bits of information? He'd thought Marduc pregnant with his young, and yet she wasn't. He knew of no meteor storm coming toward Earth. Humans had telescopes and satellites. Such events were known years in advance. Of course, anything was possible, but it seemed highly unlikely.

Perhaps he should make a small trip down into the Sazi village with the last of the feather dust. He hadn't given it to Derek, nor had he mentioned it to Marduc. It might be a good idea to find information about any meteors heading this way. It might be that the great snake's definition of a *day or two* was a hundred years. He knew how easy it was to get confused when you'd been alive for millennia. Why, it seemed only yesterday he'd been plotting with Sargon to infiltrate the council, but that had been more than a decade ago.

That's when I met Bruce.

That was the human's name. Bruce. Why did it trip off his tongue so easily?

Yes, it was worth a trip to infiltrate the Sazi again. There were plenty of things down there worth taking the risk for. Plenty of questions to be answered.

Chapter Twenty-three

CHARLES WAS SETTING a blistering pace. Eric wouldn't have thought the old man had it in him. He was keeping up, but only just, and even Ahmad was having to push himself so as not to fall behind. "You're leading, Eric. Where do we go from here?"

The camp was far behind them, hidden below the horizon of the plateau they hiked. Eric scanned the horizon in the late afternoon sun, looking for something in particular. Finally, he spotted it—a tiny splash of red among the bushes. He pointed toward it. "That's where we camped. It's not far beyond that."

"It would be best to reach her nest before nightfall. It's easier to see her."

Ahmad turned his head sharply and nearly ran into a bush. "But I thought you said Marduc *couldn't* be seen."

Charles smiled and strode ahead. "Oh, she can't.

But it's still easier. You'll understand when we get there."

Suddenly the radio on Eric's hip crackled. "*—rles, come in! Damn it! Are you out there?*"

Eric plucked it from his belt and pressed the call button. "We're here, Lucas. What's wrong?"

"*Attacking . . . from all directions. Screw Marduc. Get your asses back here. Trying . . . to move . . . ple inside to defend.*" They could hear sounds in the background. Screams and hisses and that odd chirping sound he'd heard in the cave before the spiders dropped from the sky.

He looked at Charles. He'd been right that Marduc would attack, but was she actually *with* the snakes? "Do we go back?"

Charles paused, looking back uncertainly. Eric couldn't stand here much longer. He either had to go back or go forward and hope they'd survive. Should he contact Holly? She hadn't watched him leave and was blocking herself off somehow.

"*Damn you, Charles!*" came Lucas's voice again as the static finally cleared. "*You're just standing there, aren't you? Well, Ivan just went down, so you lead the bears again, you bastard! Do I have to give you a blow-by-blow of who's bleeding and dying to get it through that thick skull of yours? Didn't you always tell me to fight the battle at hand, not the one that might come?*"

Eric couldn't take it anymore. Holly? Holly, are you there?

Happened so . . . fast. I can't—

I'm coming. Stay out of the way of those fangs!

He started moving back toward the camp. "Go find Marduc if you have to. But I have to go back. My mate's in danger." And she *was* his mate, regardless of whether she was human or Sazi.

Eric heard sounds behind him and risked a glance backward. Charles and Ahmad had made their decision and were following at a run. But they weren't catching up because Eric couldn't seem to slow himself down.

The scent of blood hit him first. There was so much dust rising in the air, the camp was nearly hidden from view. But as he got closer, he saw slithering forms that moved like lightning. A woman's scream made his pulse race. It wasn't Holly's. *Thank God*.

But the woman needed help. She was racing for the cover of the main building, but her way was blocked by a pair of rattlesnake-shifters. She held a young child tightly against her, her hand pressed against the girl's face so she couldn't see. She screamed again as the snake struck out. She'd never be able to get out of the way in time. Eric threw himself forward and brought the club down sideways, just as the snake's neck was fully extended, fangs bared. The force of the blade hitting flesh slowed Eric down, and he fell to one knee at almost the same moment the severed head of the snake hit the ground. The other rattler's tail started to buzz viciously as he turned to the new threat. He struck quickly, but Eric swung the club and knocked out a fang. The snake shook his head and reared back.

He was ready to take another swing when Ahmad appeared in front of him. "Get her inside. I'll take care of this." Power began to fill the air as Eric grabbed the hand of the terrified woman and started to drag her toward the building. The scent of blood was strong enough to choke on. He saw Holly shooting a rifle with deadly accuracy from the top of one of the trailers. Just as he reached the front of the building and handed the woman over to Tony—who was pushing people inside the building as fast as they arrived—Eric saw movement in the tree next to Holly's head.

Spider to your right! She turned fluidly, a quick roll that looked practiced, and fired into the tree. Bursts of fire erupted from the barrel and a trilling screech of pain shot cold shivers all over Eric's body. Holly stood up and quickly walked the perimeter of the RV, looking for anything that might be climbing up. He felt relieved when she crouched back down and started to fire into the distance.

Where were all these snakes coming from? There were dozens, if not hundreds. There couldn't possible be this many shifters living around here. They must have been called in just for this. That spoke of a long-standing scheme, not just a hurried reaction to losing Charles on Marduc's part.

But there was no time to think about it, because a black snake popped up on Lucas's blind side. Normally Eric wouldn't worry about the Wolven Chief, but Lucas couldn't smell them coming anymore. Eric ran across the parking lot and slammed into it before it could strike Lucas in the back. Lucas turned his head from the fight he was engaged in and let out a harsh breath of relief before returning to slicing at the petite cobra who was rearing and hissing with dogged determination.

Another slice of Eric's club took off the head of the black snake. He felt some regret, because these snakes, these *Sazi,* probably didn't even know why they were fighting.

He looked around, trying to see where he could help most. There were battles being waged by everyone he knew, along with some of the Sazi from the trailers. More than one person was dead and he mourned Ivan's still, bloody form propped on the side of the building before throwing himself at a rearing spider with all the rage he felt inside.

Eric heard Holly's voice in his head as the club chopped into the spider's forehead. Blood sprayed in a wide arc. Hey! Who's that? He looks like you, Eric. And he's got the box with the knife.

He turned to see a familiar back racing into the distance. It was Derek. He watched in horror as Holly leapt down from the RV and raced after him. She shot, and while her finger pulled the trigger, nothing happened. She threw the rifle to the side and pulled a semiautomatic handgun from her waistband and chased after him as he left camp. Holly! Wait for me to get there. Don't catch him. Don't catch up. He'll kill you.

More shots were fired, but he couldn't tell if they were within the camp or outside. He could feel the moment that Holly shifted to wolf form to make it easier to chase Derek. But the closer she got to him, the more Eric started to panic. Holly wasn't a match for his big brother. She just didn't have the level of viciousness needed to kill a man.

Or did she? She'd been firing at the snakes without hesitation. And hadn't she said she'd killed before?

Three actually. I learned tooth-and-claw fighting from Raphael.

So obviously she didn't hate being a wolf so much that she wasn't prepared. Eric just didn't know if *he* was ready to face Derek in battle.

THE BLOND MAN raced ahead of her, his feet barely touching the ground. But she wasn't letting him go. She might be out of bullets, but he was *not* getting away. They needed that knife if the vial around her neck was going to do any good.

The man moved sideways suddenly to avoid a stream. The sun was nearly set and it was going to be impossible to follow him if it got dark. She didn't want to pull power, because if Eric was fighting, he could get hurt. But she needed just a tiny bit more speed. *Just a little. Maybe he won't even notice.*

She pulled on the nebulous power inside her and felt an answering flood. It was so sudden and strong it took her breath away. She leapt forward into the air and felt her teeth connect with the man's arm. The box went flying into the sand and opened, spilling the black knife under a sagebrush.

The man screamed and shook her off, blasting her with enough power that she went flying. Then he was a wolf—massive enough that he towered over her. One eye was circled with black, making it look like he wore a pirate patch. "You'll pay for that, woman." Blood dripped down his forearm, but the scent of it made him growl even deeper.

When the big wolf attacked, she moved instinctively, but he twisted and raked open her flank with sharp claws. She hissed in a breath and tore teeth into his neck, urged on by another flood of power.

Holly, don't. Back off. Let me handle Derek.

She could sense Eric coming, but he was too far away. No, she'd have to finish this. Just get the knife. I'll be okay. But then Derek rose up on his hind legs and threw himself forward. She had to rise up as well or risk him finding the back of her neck. The problem was he was so much taller that it took everything she had just to keep him from doing just that. She ripped at his neck with her teeth, but his power pressed against her so hard that it loosened her grip. No wonder he'd been able to stay pack leader, despite his pack being against him. They simply couldn't beat him in a fight.

Derek grabbed her by the scruff of the neck and tossed her hard. She sailed through the air and landed on a bush. Pain erupted in her shoulder and she realized she'd fallen right onto the knife. It was embedded in her arm and hurt so badly all she could do was scream and howl, over and over.

Holly! An answering howl came from the distance, so piercing that it filled her entire mind. It was the same pack call Eric had used when Marduc was attacking them. But she couldn't answer. She couldn't do anything but scream as the knife carved at her very mind.

"I'll take that." The wolf had turned human again and grabbed the knife and yanked it free. Another howl knocked him back and he looked up to see Eric coming his way. "Wait. Are you his *mate*? Is that why he's so upset?" He laughed darkly. "I've always wanted to deprive him of something important. I think you fit the bill." Before she could move out of the way, Derek slammed the blade into her.

There was no way to describe the sensation as the stone ripped into her heart. Her body began to thrash and she could taste blood in her mouth as the knife chewed at her.

"You *bastard*!" Eric hit his brother with enough force that the knife—still in Derek's hand—was pulled from her to fly into the distance. Holly heard a tiny splash as she struggled to catch her breath. The two wolves began tearing at each other with a frenzy she'd seen only once before. This wasn't a dominance battle. One of them was going to *die*. If she could only get air enough to tell Eric to stop, she would. But every breath made pain flood her. She couldn't get her mind to function long enough to contact him. The moon had taken most of his senses. There was only his animal left, filled with anger and hate, determined to survive.

"Well, well, what have we here?" She recognized the voice over her but could do nothing to stop the slender, olive-skinned man from removing the chain around her neck. "I knew we'd meet again, Holly Sanchez. And while I don't see the knife, I do see something far more interesting." Nasil fingered the silver vial and then tucked it into his pocket. "I was going to kill you, but I see Derek managed to do the job. You won't last long now, healer. The blade doesn't require a head and heart kill. You'll die soon from this wound unless you get treatment." He motioned toward the wolf battle. "But I don't think they'll be finishing in time to save you. And honestly, I'm not sure who's going to win." He grinned sarcastically. "But I'll root for your beau. He looks like the underdog."

"Fuck you." Eric was pulling energy from her now; Holly could feel her magic seep away as he battled for his life. He probably didn't even know he was speeding her toward her own death.

"Really . . . right here? With them watching?" Nasil laughed lightly. "Tempting." He nudged her stomach with a boot playfully. "But no, you're not my type. Not anymore."

"Then go . . . fuck *Bruce* before . . . he's dead. Just . . . leave us alone."

The words had an immediate impact on Nasil. He stared at her for a long moment while the wolves fought inches away. He blinked and shook his head. "Dead? *Bruce*?"

"Snakes probably . . . got him." A deep cough made her whole body heave and shake. It wouldn't be long now.

Nasil left without another word, heading toward the camp. She was having a hard time focusing, but the moon looked really odd tonight. It looked like stars were flashing across the surface, leaving trails of smoke in their wake. Soon there were so many tiny trails that it looked just like a coiled snake if you squinted.

She began to feel . . . strange. Sparkles began to dance in her vision, like little colored fireflies. If this was death, it wasn't so bad. But then her heart, which had begun to stutter to a halt, gave a sharp stabbing sensation and began to beat faster. Her lungs could hold oxygen again and sound flooded her senses.

"Come on! Don't leave me, Holly. Not yet." She looked up to see Eric sitting in the sand, in human form. He was covered with blood and so was she.

"No use," she said when she could finally catch her breath a little. "Lost the knife. Lost the—" She paused, but what the hell. Why not? "Lost the *drug*."

He shook his head. "No, you didn't."

She tried to raise her eyes to look at him, but it was hard to see in the strange golden light coming from the sky. "Nasil took the vial. I was going to tell you, but I was afraid—"

"Afraid I'd turn you in?" Holly nodded. God, she felt like a heel. "I thought about it."

That made her eyes focus. "You *knew*?"

Eric let out a small, embarrassed chuckle. Her nose could nearly make out the scent of his fear over the scent of blood that filled her nose. "There were *two* vials in the box, not one. I took one." He showed it to her. *Bluetomcat* had added a note. *Yours if you decide to go back."*

Holly was actually starting to feel good enough to be angry. That seemed like the wrong emotion to have, but she couldn't help it. "Why would you *do* that? You followed me, spied on me, and then took something meant for me? Can you really not *stand* the thought of me being human again? Is it that disgusting to you?"

Holly only realized she was standing up when her eyes were nearly level with Eric's. He shook his head and smiled as he looked at the vial. "Just the opposite, actually."

The damn sparkles in her vision wouldn't go away. They were making her dizzy. "Would you please lay off the power surge? Thank you for saving me. I hate that I needed saving, but fine."

Eric shook his head, this time with a furrowed brow. "Not me. I didn't have enough juice to even save myself. I don't know where it's coming from."

Where is it? Give me the knife! The voice was everywhere. Holly looked up to see the massive flying snake just over their heads. I know it's nearby. I can feel it. Give it to me and I'll spare you.

Holly started to back up. Eric looked around in confusion, but followed her lead. "No, you won't. You'll take it and kill us."

The laughter that sliced through Holly's brain was like the screech of girders in a collapsing building. She continued to back toward the scent of water.

You're right. But I'll make it less painful if you give it to me. I must have it in my hands before the end of the serpent moon.

"You don't *have* any hands." Another laugh made Holly nearly drop to the ground in pain. She took another step back and felt her foot squish into mud.

Marduc fluttered to the ground almost delicately— except for the tremble of sand underfoot when the massive talons came to rest. Her form shifted until she was the naked, dark-skinned woman with silver hair. Holly hadn't noticed it before, but the hair gleamed in the moonlight like the multihued feathers of her other form. She seemed plumper than before, but not precisely pregnant.

"Guess you didn't find an alpha strong enough to get you knocked up." Holly shifted forms and had to adjust her balance in the mud.

The woman smiled. "Oh, but I did. He just left. It's why he wasn't interested in taking you in front of the wolves. He's already had *me* enough times to fertilize my eggs. All I need is the knife to finish."

Shit. *Nasil* was the father? That was not good. That was *so* not good.

Eric was holding her hand now, but there was nowhere to go, unless they swam away. She felt the press of something into her palm and realized Eric was giving her the vial. But what could she do with it? She'd never even looked to see how it opened. She'd figured there'd be time later.

That's the thing about time, Berrybelle. There's never enough of it. He leapt with no warning toward where Holly was staring. It took Marduc by surprise and they tumbled to the ground. Holly turned quickly and reached into the frigid water, searching for the knife.

But she didn't have to. The moment her fingers touched the stream, the knife came racing through the water. It stabbed her in the hand so hard it nearly came out the other side. The pain was intense, but she couldn't think about that now. She pulled it out of her hand and laid the vial on a rock. With a sharp slam of the blade down, she cut off the top of the vial. Blue liquid sprayed into the air, landing on her hands and covering the knife. She turned and raced toward Eric, but something was happening to her vision. One moment she could see Marduc, and the next not. Back and forth the images switched until she was getting dizzy and Eric was fighting an unseen foe.

No! This can't be happening! She couldn't be turning human. Not this fast. Not *now*!

But there was no time to worry about it. She grabbed the knife handle and crawled over to where Eric was struggling to keep Marduc steady. She had no choice. She blinked over and over, hoping for just one final glance. She was granted her wish. The woman appeared under Eric for a flash and Holly slammed the knife into the woman's chest.

Marduc screamed and Holly sighed in relief. But her blood chilled when the woman began to laugh. "You fools! I could have gotten away at any time." She proved it as Eric went flying through the air to land heavily on the ground a dozen feet away. "This is exactly what was supposed to happen. What *must* happen for my children to be born. Someone had to be tricked into performing a blood sacrifice under the serpent moon. My life energy will flow to my eggs, hidden deep in an undiscovered cave. They'll hatch tomorrow, born with all of my thoughts, all of my memories, and all of my hatred for the shifters called the Sazi. The world will burn as you watch and your precious humans will become nothing more than food to breed more of us."

"Not this time, Marduc." Holly looked up to see Charles walking toward them. The sword he carried didn't look like a sword at all. It looked like a boat paddle with black glass accents.

Marduc must have recognized the weapon he held, because she began to shriek. "You can't have found that! I destroyed them all!"

Charles smiled, and it was a darker smile than she'd ever seen before. "A friend left one with me. You remember Colecos, don't you? The jaguar god you supplanted? He swore revenge and crafted these blades himself in the burning volcanic fires."

But then Charles froze in place and he dropped to his knees, pain etched on his face and rolling from his skin. The weapon dropped from his hand, and Holly prayed it wasn't close enough for Marduc to grab. You thought you closed off that door, didn't you? But I can still get in if I concentrate.

Holly blinked as Marduc the woman appeared. She was writhing on the sand, her hand stretched out to reach the club. She would kill Charles. Holly knew it without a doubt in her mind. "Hold her!" she screamed to Eric and grabbed the blade. He looked around, unable to see where Marduc was. He started to slide his hands around on the sand, but it was too late. *She'd* have to do this. Holly tried to approach, but was thrown backward by a blast of power. Charles shook his head and life came back to his eyes for a brief moment. That was the ticket. She'd have to keep parrying in. Maybe Charles could get his shields up.

She blinked again and Marduc disappeared, just as she was starting to rise to her feet. Damn it! Holly backed up a pace and reached inside her mind, to that tiny thread of power that she'd pulled on before. She used every ounce of her strength to pull. Eric gasped so hard he started coughing.

I'm sorry. I have no other choice. Whether or not she *wanted* to be a wolf, she was one until the drug took it from her. She pulled and he went. She flooded her body with power and felt her strength return in a flash. But Eric was so weak that it might take everything he had.

Her head snapped sideways from a blow that sliced her cheek wide open. Another quick slash hit her in the chest and she dropped to her knees.

A mournful sound came from her right and she turned to see Eric in wolf form, his muzzle raised to the sparkling moon. He howled, the sound totally different than a calling howl. It started low in his chest and expanded outward. Holly's hair began to blow across her face. Eric took another deep breath, lowered his muzzle, and opened his mouth wide. What came out wasn't so much *sound* as *power*. For a brief moment, Holly could see Marduc again. She reached out to slash at Holly with fingernails that looked like claws. But she couldn't get past the press of air that forced her backward, step by step. But eventually Eric had to breathe and the snake goddess shook her head and started forward again.

Open your mind, Holly. I have an idea. Something Tony taught me. She wasn't quite sure *how* to open her mind, but she relaxed, continuing to spin the blade around her to keep Marduc away until he did whatever he was going to. She felt an odd sensation and was suddenly seeing the world from two different locations. It was dizzying. But in both views, she could see Marduc. *Keep the river on your left. I'll keep it on my right, and we'll meet in the middle.*

Holly tried to turn her body to follow Eric's directions, but it was hard. Every time she moved, the perspective changed. She crouched down, watching Marduc as she tried to drag herself to safety. The moon was making the land glow with reddish fire now. They had to move soon. Holly stood perfectly still as she saw Eric's muscles flex. He leapt onto the snake-shifter.

Just as she shifted forms.

Eric screamed as sharp feathers sliced into his skin. But he held on as Holly raced forward. She could feel the club in her hands move of its own accord, as though Eric's hands were on top of hers, guiding the path. Marduc's head was massive, but where the neck joined her shoulders wasn't too thick. Holly slammed the blade home and felt the obsidian edges cut through the feathers like butter. Marduc screamed so loud that it felt like Holly's ears would burst. But she kept sawing, using every ounce of her strength, combined with Eric's.

She didn't remember falling as Marduc dissolved under her. But her head slammed down onto a rock hard enough that she heard the snap of her own neck.

And then red fire dissolved into black and even the glow of turquoise magic couldn't make her feel warm.

Chapter Twenty-four

WAS SHE EVER going to wake up? Eric paced across the small room, back and forth, like he'd been doing for nearly a day now. Holly was finally breathing on her own, after Charles and Raphael and several others had thrown enough power into her still form that she glowed bright enough for even those without second sight to see in the darkness.

"Eric? You need to get some food into you. You won't do her any good if you pass out." Lucas stood in the doorway, the bandage on his arm stark against his skin. The fang wound in his face that had nearly taken his eye was still puffy and oozing. Tatya had helped heal him instantly, but the odds were still even on whether the Great White Wolf would wind up a great black snake.

"You're lucky you didn't lose that eye."

Lucas shrugged. "Maybe. A direct hit on my eye

would have killed me instantly. Now I just get to wonder until the full moon next month."

"Any news on Nasil? Did he really get away?"

Lucas nodded. "He left a note, though, which was odd." He passed over the sheet of paper and Eric moved over to the light to read the carefully printed words.

I've taken Bruce as I have finally managed to fend off Marduc's control. Hopefully that means you've defeated her. I've decided to take no chances on ever again feasting on blood and fear. I've taken the cure, and now that your new healer has fixed Bruce, we'll find somewhere to live where nobody will ever find us again. I gave you the chance to have alpha strength and speed again, Lucas. If your woman is quick with her magic, you might be wolf again. If not, then I look forward to learning who will hold the snake council seat.

My money is on you.

Nasil.

Eric read the note a second time, and then a third. Nasil had attacked Lucas intentionally? As a *favor*? The thought made his stomach hurt and he suddenly realized what Holly had been saying all along. There'd been no choice. "You okay?"

Lucas's chuckle was rueful. "As much as I can be, I suppose. Tough call on whether to be grateful for this. I suppose if I wind up a wolf, it won't be so bad. If not,

I'll probably have a hard time bowing to Ahmad every time he walks in the room. How are *you* doing?"

"It's just so weird that she was fine right after she cracked her head. Walked back to the building and talked to Bobby and even Charles before she suddenly collapsed. I just wish I knew what she said. They're both stonewalling me."

"I'll tell you if you'll just pipe down. My head hurts." Eric turned to see Holly's eyes open and her hand on her forehead, rubbing lightly. He rushed forward to sit down on the bed.

Lucas turned and headed for the door. "I'll get Tatya."

"Hey, Berrybelle."

"Hey, yourself. How long have I been out? I feel like I haven't eaten in a week."

"Just a day."

She sighed and threw an arm over her eyes to block out the light. "How's the cleanup going? Any of the snakes still acting weird?"

He shook his head before he realized she couldn't see it. "No. Ahmad's doing a fine job of snapping those who survived out of it. His form of pack binding involves a lot more ritual than I care for, but he apparently wants to make damned certain he's got better control over them in the future." He paused. "So? You were going to tell me what you talked to Bobby and Charles about."

She stared into Eric's eyes for a long moment. "Some of the drug got in the wound on my hand. I started to turn human."

Eric nodded. "I know. You're in my head and then you're not. It's been driving me nuts."

"Me too. That's what I wanted to ask them about. Bobby's a chemist with both magic and schooling. There was still some of the cure left in the vial. I wanted to see if he could reverse it. He said he'll try, but it'll have to be the old-fashioned way, with hazmat suits and test tubes. He can't risk turning human right now—not with three little dragons and a python to raise." She smiled. "You heard that Asri had the babies and they were born in *animal* form?"

Eric nodded, happy for Bobby. But he felt his stomach drop. He couldn't escape what she'd just said. "So, you really do want to go back? You want to be human again?"

A small smile turned up her lips and her scent was an odd mix of worry and relief. "Actually, no. I realized when I was fighting Derek and Marduc, that I was still *Holly*. I would have fought them even as a human." She paused and curled her hand around his. "But I wouldn't have had *you*. Not like that, and not like now."

He could feel her heart beating, a distant pulse that made his heart race. "I'm sorry I took the vial. It wasn't right. I should have trusted you. You were always the one I trusted. The *only* one I trusted, and . . . well, I didn't."

She shrugged. "I wasn't acting very trustworthy. It's hard to blame you. I swore I'd broken off with FMU, and then went straight to them when I was upset. I *did* ask for the cure, even though it was for a good purpose. But then I didn't tell anyone about it. Hell, *I* would have followed me."

He squeezed her hand. "But I shouldn't have taken away your choice. If that's what you want, then okay. I guess I took the vial because—"

"I know," she said softly. "I saw it in your mind when we connected. You were going to hide it and take it if *I* did. So you'd be human."

He shook his head. "So we'd be *together*. Wolf, human—doesn't really matter to me. I—" He paused but then took a deep breath. "I loved you when you were a messed-up teenager, when neither us really knew what it meant. And I still love you now that you're a different person—stronger, tougher. I was damned proud of you out there. It's not just magic that we have."

"Sure it is," she said with a smile. He felt his heart speed up to match the pulse under his thumb. "It doesn't have to be magic to be *magic*. But it might be that it'll be both again soon."

He frowned, not understanding. "I can't feel you in my head for more than a few seconds at a time. Do you mean that can change?"

She smiled, and he leaned closer until his ear was next to her lips. Her words were meant only for him. The brush of air against his skin made him shiver. "That's what I talked to Charles about. We got Amber on the phone and she seemed pretty confident that there's enough magic between us that a little . . . um . . . *jolt* might kick it back into gear. I apparently still have some healing abilities. I could feel it when

I was starting to wake up. Of course, they could be wrong. But—"

Holly placed a small kiss on Eric's ear and started to trail them down his neck, making him groan. "I think now that I've saved the world, I'm entitled to a little camping trip. Care to join me?"

He chuckled and turned his head so his lips were right next to hers. "I'll bring the roses, Berrybelle."